Rheta
2015

good Book

THE DUST
THAT FALLS
FROM DREAMS

THE DUST
THAT FALLS
FROM DREAMS

Louis de Bernières

PANTHEON BOOKS, NEW YORK

Copyright © 2015 by Louis de Bernières

All rights reserved. Published in the United States by Pantheon Books,
a division of Penguin Random House LLC, New York. Originally published
in hardcover in Great Britain by Harvill Secker, an imprint of
Vintage Publishing, a division of Penguin Random House Ltd.,
London, in 2015.

Pantheon Books and colophon are registered trademarks
of Penguin Random House LLC.

Library of Congress Cataloging-in-Publication Data
de Bernières, Louis.
The dust that falls from dreams : a novel / Louis de Bernières.
pages ;
ISBN 978-1-101-94648-0 (hardcover)
ISBN 978-1-101-94649-7 (eBook).
I. Title.
PR6054.E132D87 2015   823'.914—DC23   2015011829

www.pantheonbooks.com

Jacket design by Oliver Munday

Printed in the United States of America

First United States Edition

2   4   6   8   9   7   5   3   1

Dis Manibus; sit vobis terra levis
In memory of my grandmother's first fiancé,
Pte Howell Ashbridge Godby HAC
Died of wounds received at Kemmel, 19/2/15
If not for his death, I would have had no life.

The Lad Out There

Oh, Powers of Love, if still you lean
Above a world so black with hate,
Where yet – as it has ever been –
The loving heart is desolate,
Look down upon the lad I love,
(My brave lad, tramping through the mire) –
I cannot light his welcoming fire,
Light Thou the stars for him above!
Now nights are dark and mornings dim,
Let him in his long watching know
That I too count the minutes slow
And light the lamp of love for him.
The sight of death, the sleep forlorn,
The old homesickness vast and dumb –
Amid these things, so bravely borne,
Let my long thoughts about him come.
I see him in the weary file;
So young he is, so dear to me,
With ever-ready sympathy
And wistful eyes and cheerful smile.
However far he travels on,
Thought follows, like the willow-wren
That flies the stormy seas again
To lands where her delight is gone.
Whatever he may be or do
While absent far beyond my call,
Bring him, the long day's march being through,
Safe home to me some evenfall!

Mary Webb

Contents

CONTENTS

THE DUST
THAT FALLS
FROM DREAMS

I

The Coronation Party

This was the day that Daniel vaulted the wall.

Not many weeks previously the tiny Queen had begun to lose her appetite. In Marseilles, President Kruger of South Africa, fleeing into exile laden with wealth stolen from his own people, raised the rabble to new frenzies of anti-Britishness, and hotels where British travellers were thought to be staying were besieged.

The Queen grew drowsy. She had never before shown any lapse of energy or attention, but now she nodded off even at crucial moments. She received a letter from a boy bugler in the Devons, telling her how he had been the one to sound the charge at Waggon Hill, and she managed to reply to it.

The Queen travelled from London to Osborne House, on the Isle of Wight. She loved it there, and had long considered it to be her real family home. She had her own little beach with a bathing hut, and there was a miniature house where her children, now scattered across Europe, used to play when Albert was still alive. Across the Solent she could visit the vast military hospital that she had set up at Netley, bringing the scarves that she liked to knit for the wounded soldiers.

The Queen found that she could not speak when the Brazilian ambassador came to present his credentials. She was forgetting how to talk. She failed to recognise Lord Roberts when he returned in triumph from South Africa in order to become the new Commander-in-Chief. He was bewildered and grief-stricken.

The Queen performed her last great imperial act, and proclaimed the establishment of the Commonwealth of Australia. Her visit to the Riviera was cancelled, and the Keeper of the Privy Purse was obliged to pay out £800 in compensation to the Hotel Cimiez.

It had been so long since the death of a sovereign that no one knew what to say, or how to behave. Lord Salisbury refused to talk about the accession ceremonies because it was too upsetting. The well-to-do cancelled their dinner parties and balls, and the frivolous optimism that had accompanied the arrival of a new century evaporated. It was January, and the dark clouds that wept rain onto the land complemented the mood of the people beneath them.

The Queen's relatives and descendants converged on Osborne from all over Europe. In South Africa the war that was supposed to have been won already was carried on by Botha, Smuts and de Wet. Money and young men continued to be expended. The British troops were killed mainly by enteric fever.

The tiny Queen died. The Lord Mayor of London was informed, and then the rest of the world. Whilst the nation lay stunned, the Great argued about what should be done next. Lord Acton announced that King Edward VII could not call himself Edward VII because he was not descended from previous Edwards. Did the Lord Mayor of London count as an ex-officio member of the Privy Council? He decided that he did, and gatecrashed it. Who was in charge of the funeral? Was it the Lord Chamberlain or the Duke of Norfolk, even though he was a Catholic? The Duke insisted on his historic right, and the King conceded. Lady Cadogan received an invitation to the interment that was intended for her husband, in which she was requested to come wearing trousers.

The Queen's coffin was so minute that it might have been that of a child. King Edward and the Kaiser walked behind it as it was drawn through Cowes. It came across the Solent in a battle-ship, flanked by the greatest fleet in the world. In London the route from Victoria Station to Buckingham Palace then Paddington Station was blocked solid with mourners hoping to see the great procession of the gun carriage. Behind it rode King Edward, flanked by the Duke of Connaught and Kaiser Wilhelm, followed by the handsome and slim Crown Prince of Germany, the embodi-ment of hope for his nation, the guarantor of its great future as a beacon of civilisation.

The Queen's body was laid to rest at Windsor. The grandmother of Europe had gone, and everyone knew as if by instinct that a momentous era had suddenly ended. She left behind railways that ran at sixty miles an hour, with carriages that nowadays had roofs on them. Vast liners crossed the Atlantic in two weeks. Bull-baiting had gone, and there was a society for the prevention of cruelty to animals and another for the prevention of cruelty to children. Swearing had become taboo in polite society, and aristocratic men no longer got so drunk at dinner parties that ladies had to make their escape through the windows. There were now aerated bread shops, and Lyons Corner Houses where one was served by 'Nippies' in white frilly aprons. Anybody these days could buy coffee. The River Fleet was no longer an open sewer. Many had electric light, and there was clean water laid on in the working-class districts for half an hour every day, except for Sundays, causing an awful elbowing on Saturdays. Motor cars no longer caught fire when you started them up. They had, however, spoiled the evening drive in hansoms through Hyde Park. The cult of respectability had introduced a blessed order into people's lives, and at the same time opened the door for marvellous hypocrisy.

Much as the people had loved their tiny Queen, there had been something dull about all that respectability, and the grief and stupefaction that had engulfed her subjects was tempered by the anticipation of something that might be more entertaining. The new King was a bon viveur. He loved France rather than Germany. He consorted with actresses. For the last ten years, in any case, the Victorian age had already been slipping away. Fast girls smoked, and wore the most shocking bloomers when they went out on their bicycles. Businesswomen of dubious morality were getting jobs in the City. Saddlers who specialised in side-saddles found their orders drying up. Crowds filled the music halls to hear smutty songs rendered by cheeky chappies and saucy doxies.

The new King, kept strictly in the dark about state matters during his mother's reign, grew impatient with precedent and forged a new path. He upset everyone at court. He gave the right to organise his coronation to the Catholic Duke of Norfolk and not to the Anglican Lord Chamberlain. There was a long and bitter dispute about whether the Lords should be robed, and the decision was changed four times. He sent Lord Carrington, a notorious liberal, as his personal envoy to France, Spain and Portugal. This was the same Lord Carrington who had once, as one of a panel of magistrates that had tried him, scandalously paid the fine of a newly released convict, caught sleeping rough when he had not been able to walk to High Wycombe before darkness fell. The alternative had been several more months in prison, and Carrington had resigned from the bench immediately afterwards, saying that if this was justice he wanted nothing more to do with it.

The King dragged Lord Wolsey from retirement, and sent him abroad, with sashes and medals to present to foreign potentates, even the Shah of Iran, who thereby became the first Muslim to become a member of the Christian Order of the Garter. He cleared out his mother's immense accumulation of bric-a-brac, updated his plumbing, filled his court with men who were interesting rather than important, and with women who were both interesting and beautiful.

In Court Road, Eltham, on 9 August 1902, Mr and Mrs Hamilton McCosh held a coronation party, postponed from June. It was to be a kind of elaborate high tea. They borrowed long trestles from several firms of wallpapers, covered them with beautiful damask cloths, and, at greatly inflated prices, hired enough plain china plates and silver-plated cutlery to see them through the day. The servants set up two long tables in the garden, to accommodate the buffet, and laid out rugs all over the lawn and in the orchard in order to create a grand *déjeuner sur l'herbe*. Chairs were brought out of the house for the elderly or stiff of limb. From the kitchen there appeared plates of ham and tongue, elaborate salads in the French style, Normandy cheeses, and fabulous heaps of fresh Kentish strawberries and Devon cream. For the children there was lemonade, and for the adults jugs of potent fruit cup with sprigs of mint floating on the surface. Chilled champagne would be brought out in time for a toast to the King after Mr McCosh had made his speech.

This was the beginning of the age when riches would finally come to count as much as rank. Court Road consisted of very large detached houses with substantial gardens at the rear. Most had two gateways connected by a small semicircular driveway out in the front so that carriages could arrive and leave without any awkward manoeuvring. The McCosh entrance and exit had impressive brick pillars with THE GRAMPIANS set into them in Portland stone. Between them ran a low wall, just the right height for children to walk along. Mr McCosh had planted a small walnut tree just behind it, because he loved the way the leaves turned yellow in autumn, and was convinced that walnut was the hardwood of the future, without thought to the possibility that long after his death the tree's roots would topple the pillars and wall altogether, so that by the end of the century there would be no memory of the house ever having had a name at all.

Inside were large rooms with high ceilings and small coal fires. On the top floor were crudely furnished rooms with washstands for the servants, but on the floor below that there was a proper bathroom with a real lion-footed cast-iron bath that gave hot water from a boiler house attached to the side of the kitchen. In this boiler house was often to be found the boilerman, dozing in the warmth, or rolling cigarettes, and occasionally getting up to shovel in a new dose of coal. His was a life of bucolic idleness, disrupted only by the occasional breakdown of the whole system, which worked on the thermosyphon principle, without any need of a pump at all.

In general one could gauge the success of the householders of Court Road by the elaborateness of their cornices. Mr McCosh was an intelligent, charming, humane, ambitious, hard-working man with an eye to anything whatsoever that might turn a profit, and The Grampians had by far the most elaborate, extensive and delicate cornices of any house in Court Road. His chief weakness, which he was able to turn to profit even so, was an addiction to golf. He was often to be found playing rounds at the Blackheath when he was supposed to be in his London office.

One disadvantage of his speculations was that he might veer from fabulous riches to abject penury in the blink of an eye. He was accustomed to avoiding paying bills until such time as he recouped his wealth. This he always did, but it remained a sore point to the local tradesmen, who never knew when it was wise to accept his custom or decline it. Their one consolation was that he scrupulously calculated the interest on any debt he owed, and paid it in full.

On 9 August 1902 Mr Hamilton McCosh had plenty of money, it seemed unlikely that it was going to rain, and he was rejoicing in the pleasure of his own largesse.

By his side, frequently departing from it in order to direct the servants, stood his wife. Mrs McCosh had been a great beauty in her youth, and was to retain her comeliness into old age. She was seven years senior to her husband, and had married late owing to a long previous engagement to a milord who subsequently turned out to have had a wife already, locked up in an asylum in New York. It had taken her many years to recover from the mortification of the scandal having become public and being written up in the press, and she had virtually gone into seclusion until the gallant and impervious Hamilton McCosh had hauled her out of it. She had caused much gossip by playing tennis vigorously when pregnant, and was notorious for her outspoken belief that women should vote equally with men. She had become a warrior in what was being called 'the Sex War'. However, her husband would explain that this was because she wanted the right to vote Conservative. She had recently taken up cycling and was still somewhat bruised about the thighs after losing a wheel during a tour of Hayling Island.

Mrs McCosh's great weakness was for the royal family. She followed their doings avidly, and subscribed to *The Times* only to peruse the Court Circular. The coronation party was her idea, even though most of the nation had already feasted a month before, when the King had donated £30,000 to the poor of London, and 456,000 people had eaten and drunk at his expense. The King himself, recovering in bed from an operation, had sent his regrets to each Lord Mayor, and the Prince and Princess of Wales had made up for his absence by visiting twenty of the dinner parties in succession. It had all felt like a wonderful new start.

Mrs McCosh was looking forward to the coronation party, but also wondered if she could bear to see it through, because she was still in deep mourning for the Queen, and had only this very day given up wearing black. She was not at all sure that she approved of the new King, who kept racehorses and had dismissed many of the old Queen's retainers.

'I do hope that His Majesty is fully recovered,' she said to her husband, somewhat insincerely.

'What was it again?' he asked.

'Peritiphylitis.'

'Sounds dreadful. What on earth is it?'

'Darling, I've told you so many times. It's an infection of something that the appendix hangs from. Anyway, they say he's recovered, but won't be carrying the Sword of State to the altar. I do hope he doesn't collapse.'

'Kings of Scotland dinna collapse,' replied Mr McCosh. 'They die heroically in battle or get stabbed in their sleep.'

'My dear, I hope you are not suggesting that our dear present Queen Alexandra may be something of a Lady Macbeth? She is Danish after all.'

'Danish monarchs kill their brothers and nephews, if we are to believe the Bard. And women are strange, unscrupulous creatures. And queens are women. And the Danish Queen married her husband's brother, who killed him. A sorry lot, Danish queens.'

'You must stop being provocative, my dear. It's fortunate that I'm so used to your humour. If that is what one should call it. *Hamlet* is undoubtedly fiction, as you well know. I do wish one could have been there . . . at the coronation, I mean. I should have loved to see Lord Kitchener all done up in plumes, and Sir Alfred Gaselee. And the new Prime Minister, of course.'

'Well, my dear, we are exceedingly lucky with the weather. We couldn't have asked for a nicer day. And we have the Eltham aristocracy to entertain. Talking of which, have we set up the table for the tradesmen and artisans?'

'Of course. They'll be down there at the orchard end.'

'Ah, far below the salt.'

Affecting not to understand his humour, which is how the British love to spoil a joke, Mrs McCosh replied, 'Every table will have its own salt cellar and pepper pot. I'm just going to see that Nurse has got the children ready.'

'Ah, here is Mme Pitt and her little boys,' said Mr McCosh. 'I shall go and greet them, and you can chivvy up the girls, my dear.'

For a reason long forgotten, there was a blue door in the wall that divided the garden of The Grampians from that of its neighbour on the left. The door was old and a little rotten at top and bottom. Its hinges were creaky and rusty, but it still worked, and it was kept unseized because of its frequent use by the children of the two families.

On the other side of the blue door dwelt the Pendennis family, recently arrived from Baltimore, complete with three young sons, Sidney, Albert and Ashbridge, all born a year apart, and each of the younger exactly six inches shorter than his immediate elder, so that they reminded some people of a set of library steps. Every morning these boys shook their father's hand when they came down to breakfast, and addressed him as 'sir'.

The McCosh family had four daughters, blue-eyed Rosie, with her long rich chestnut hair, and fair skin peppered with freckles; then Christabel, an English rose in the making, tall and athletic. Then there was Ottilie, who was clearly going to be of the traditional English pear shape, with a pale round face and lovely dark round eyes set beneath a sweet dark fringe. Lastly there was Sophie, little, thin and ungainly, with uncontrollable frizzy hair, whose humour and manner of speech were already becoming quirky. Her father liked to say that she had a lopsided view of the world, and that it would stand her in good stead. Whilst it would be true to say that these girls deeply loved their difficult mother, it would also be true to say that they adored their easy-going father.

On the opposing garden wall there was no blue door, so the two boys who played in the garden beyond it would arrive simply by climbing over and leaping down. They had worn a hard, flat patch in the rose bed. The wall was seven foot high, and it was already clear that Archie Pitt and his younger brother Daniel were going to grow up into a pair of daredevils and adventurers.

On this day, just as everybody was settling down on their rugs and chairs with their plates of tongue and their cup, Archie, aged fourteen, appeared on the top of the wall in his best clothes, and stood on it, arms akimbo, with all the confidence of a Himalayan goat.

'Archie, what on earth are you doing up there?' demanded Mrs McCosh.

'We have created a spectacle,' announced the boy, 'in honour of the King.'

'In honour of the King?' repeated Mrs McCosh, somewhat placated. 'Well, that's very fine of you, I'm sure.'

'Can we put some of the cushions just down there, the other side of the path?' asked Archie. He had a tone of command unusual in an adolescent, and those immediately below him vacated their rugs and arranged cushions as directed, their indulgent assumption being that Archie wanted a soft spot on which to land.

'Really, one shouldn't tolerate such things in a child,' said Mrs McCosh.

'Aren't you intrigued?' replied her husband. 'I must say, I do admire such confidence in a boy, don't you? And anyway, I know what's going to happen, and I've already given the boys permission. We are going to start off with a feat.'

Archie's parents were as sanguine. They stood below, arm in arm, grinning proudly. Archie's mother, resolutely French, but Protestant nonetheless, like a sort of belated Huguenot, was always known as Mme Pitt, on her own insistence, and was twirling a parasol with her free hand. Captain Pitt, formerly of the Royal Yacht Victoria and Albert, was dressed in naval uniform for the great day, the gold braid glittering in the sunlight against the dark blue. Mme Pitt said, '*Chou-chou*, I hope this is not going to end in tears.'

'*Maman*, we've been practising like billy-o. Daniel's done it heaps of times. And it was your idea.'

'The worst that can happen is a broken neck,' said the Captain.

'*Oh, chéri, tais-toi*. You shouldn't say such things. It tempts the Devil.'

'Let's hope to settle for a sprained ankle, then.'

'*Chéri! Arrêtes!*'

'Is everybody ready?' called Archie. 'Come on, everybody, look!'

Gradually, a hush fell, and even the servants ceased bustling. Mr McCosh stepped forward.

'My friends and, indeed, one or two mortal enemies, welcome to The Grampians. We are here to celebrate the beginning of a new age, perhaps. His Majesty is ... how shall I put it? ...

somewhat older than his dear mother was when she came to the throne . . . but by God's grace he may yet have a long life and remain our monarch for many a good year to come. We have lived well, progressively more well with each passing year under the late Queen, who has given her name to what seems in retrospect an entire age; but now a new term has been coined, and we are already describing ourselves as Edwardians, are we not? When was the nation previously so happy? I would suggest it was at the Restoration. We had in King Charles the Second a merry monarch, and now we have another monarch at least as merry as he was. May he long remain so! And may we be merry too. Our hope, the hope of any race, is in its youth, is it not? We are to begin our celebrations today with a wonderful piece of audacity by our two young neighbours, Archie and Daniel Pitt. They have been practising for days! Pray silence and attention for Archie and Daniel Pitt!'

There was a small burst of applause, Archie atop the wall took a low bow, and his mother grasped the Captain's arm more tightly in her own. 'It'll be wonderful,' he reassured her proudly. 'The boys are completely fearless.'

A silence ensued, and Archie bent his knees in readiness. He raised his left hand, and let it drop, and a few seconds later a small flying boy appeared beside and above him, clutching the top of a vaulting pole. The boy released the pole as he soared above the wall, and at the same moment Archie ducked down and leapt up, circling his shins with his forearms. He somersaulted neatly down to the cushions, landing on his feet as his even more aerial brother landed beside him. Archie put his arm around his little brother's neck and they bowed together, grinning broadly.

There was a collective gasp and then a stunned hush as the partygoers took in the virtuosity and courage of this extraordinary display. In truth, most of them were quite horrified by it. But as Archie and Daniel were so gloriously pleased with themselves, it was impossible not to share in their triumph. The guests converged on them to shake their hands and pat their heads, and the Captain pressed a sovereign into each of their hands, saying, 'Well done, boys! Well done! A train set each, I think! A train set each!'

'Such a pair of acrobats!' said Mrs McCosh to Mme Pitt. 'But I declare I can't imagine how you could have let them do it.'

'I saw them in the garden doing things like this,' replied Mme Pitt. 'It was my idea, the whole thing. And the Captain, he said, "Be it on your head, *chérie*," but now it's all *très bien*, and after all I have nothing on my head but this bonnet. But I think perhaps I won't let them do it again. It is too much for the heart.'

'And how are your other two boys? Are they still in South Africa?'

'Still in South Africa. I have heard nothing for weeks. I pray. I pray, that's all. *Que Dieu les sauve.*'

The children were having their own party in parallel to that of the adults. Daniel and Archie were the heroes of the hour, and so they affected a nonchalant swagger. 'I think that was marvellously brave,' said Ottilie to Archie.

But Archie was hoping that Rosie might have been impressed. He watched her carefully for any sign, but saw forlornly that she was only interested in one of the new American boys from the other side of the blue door. This boy was Ashbridge Pendennis, a year older than Rosie, and already showing signs of the stocky and powerful athlete that he was to become. His hair was very fair, and his eyes were the same shade as the Channel on a winter's day. 'That was mighty fine,' he said to Daniel, who was also hoping for a little admiration from Rosie. 'I couldn't do that, I really don't think.' Ashbridge pronounced the word 'mighdy', and Rosie thought this very charming.

'But you're so strong,' said Rosie. 'You can even lift Bouncer.'

'Where is Bouncer?' asked Daniel. Daniel was slim, with shining black hair and blue eyes that were particularly disconcerting in bright sunlight. It was clear that one day he would be a tall man.

'We shut him in,' said Rosie. 'He makes such a fuss when there's bags of people.'

Rosie hoped that the others would all go away, because she wanted to be left alone with Ashbridge, but Archie and Daniel kept hovering near her, and Ottilie just hovered by Archie.

'Why don't you ask Mama and Papa if you can let him out for bit?' she suggested to Daniel, and shortly found her wish granted. Ashbridge put his hand into the pocket of his shorts and brought something out. 'Here,' he said.

'What is it?'

He pressed it into her hand, saying, 'Don't let anyone see.'

She glanced down. It was small and made of brass. 'A curtain ring!' said Rosie.

Ashbridge blushed. 'I'll get you a proper one when we're older. I've only got half a crown. If you keep it, it means we're engaged.'

'But I'm only twelve,' she said.

'Well, one day you sure won't be. It's gotta be me who gets there first. Will you keep it?'

Rosie looked into his earnest eyes, which seemed to flicker with anxiety and the fear of rejection. She saw that his courage had been very great, and was touched. Ashbridge said, 'Since I came over . . . from the States . . . I didn't like it too much here . . . at first . . . but you made it all fine, Rosie, you really did.'

'I'll keep it,' she said.

'Can I kiss you on the cheek?'

'Not now.'

'Later?'

Rosie nodded gravely. 'Later. Only on the cheek.'

Ashbridge looked at her gratefully, and said, 'Do you want to see me do a cartwheel? I can do five in a row without stopping.'

'I'm engaged,' thought Rosie to herself. 'I'm engaged.' How wonderful to be engaged already, at the age of ten, to Ashbridge. 'I've seen you do lots of cartwheels,' she said, adding, 'But I don't mind if you want to do some more.'

For the adults the party was a great success. Towards seven o'clock, as the food and drink began to run out, it was time for the blessing. To what would such an occasion amount without a blessing from the rector?

Mr McCosh went to release this clergyman from amid the gaggle of spinsters and widows that always surrounded him, and led him up the steps to the door of the conservatory so that he might overlook the lawns. He smiled with all the modesty of a man who feels himself lavishly and rightfully endowed with humility, spiritual grace and local celebrity. He raised his right hand in the classic gesture of blessing and recited:

'O Lord our heavenly Father, high and mighty, King of kings, Lord of lords, the only Ruler of princes, who dost from Thy throne behold all the dwellers upon earth. Most heartily we beseech thee with thy favour to behold our most gracious Sovereign Lord, King Edward, and so replenish him with with all the grace of Thy Holy Spirit, that he may always incline to Thy will, and walk in Thy way. Endue him plenteously with heavenly gifts; grant him in health and wealth long to live; strengthen him that he may vanquish and overcome all his enemies; and finally, after this life, he may attain everlasting joy and felicity; through Jesus Christ our Lord.'

No sooner had the collective 'Amen' been reverently murmured, than havoc broke loose.

Daniel had sneaked indoors and located Bouncer from the whines and barks coming from behind the dining-room door. No sooner had he opened it than the dog had hurtled out and bolted for the party that was going on in the garden.

Bouncer was a large, heavily built brown dog, approximately the size of a Labrador. He was one and a half years old, shiny and muscled, and very aptly named. Out on the lawn he bounced, it seemed, vertically, wagging his backside furiously as he attempted to lick anyone whose face he could reach. In vain did Mr McCosh pursue him and attempt to pin him down. The ladies shrieked as his paws raked their breasts and their delicate white dresses, and the gentlemen vainly headed him off with their canes as he hurtled from one beloved human to another.

Mrs McCosh rolled her parasol and whacked him sharply across the nose, exclaiming, 'Down, boy!' but it had no effect whatsoever. Finally, Captain Pitt managed to seize the dog, and one of the servants was despatched to fetch a lead from the hall. Bouncer was dragged, bouncing and singing tirelessly all the while, back into the house.

It was a good note to end on, and the guests, faces reddened from a glorious afternoon in the sunshine, began to make their farewells. There was much to talk about and to remember. Archie, Daniel and Ash and the dog had made it a memorable day.

In the palace the King put his feet up and smoked a cigar. It had all gone terribly well, apart from the poor old Archbishop having to retire to St Edward's Chapel, and then being unable to get to his feet after pledging allegiance. The King began to think of who the first truly Edwardian Archbishop might be.

He felt downcast. He had lived a charmed life as Prince of Wales, a long round of house parties, shooting expeditions, theatres, horse races, actresses, mistresses. Now it was all over, and the responsibility lowered on him like thunderclouds at the end of August. He had been privately convinced for some time that the monarchy was doomed, but he knew his duty; he would keep his melancholy to himself.

2

Edwardians

Twelve years passed, years that would forever be remembered as golden by those who had taken part in Mr and Mrs McCosh's coronation garden party. One summer succeeded another, each, it seemed, hotter and more glorious than the one before. The roses thrived in the clay of the beds, the apples grew juicy and generous, and wasp traps made of jam and beer were set up in the boughs. In Court Road each summer evening could be heard the thud of tennis balls and the hollow clonking of croquet mallets. Out in the street the ragamuffin children of the poor came up from Mottingham and played games of hide-and-seek, knuckle bones, grandmother's footsteps and kick the can. Sometimes they knocked on the doors of kitchens and asked for drinks of water, soon learning which maids were generous with sherbet and gingerbread men. Gardeners went out armed with buckets, and fetched in the horse droppings for the roses. Gypsy women stopped ladies in the street and offered lucky white heather, with the clear implication that bad luck would ensue from refusal. Almost every day there came by the muffin man, the costermonger, the rag-and-bone man, the milkman, the cats' meat man, the fish carts drawn by enormous rangy dogs. Each tradesman had his own cry. Policemen strolled in pairs on their predictable circuits, armed only with whistles and coshes. In winter the smoke from the fires, the factories and the bonfires of leaves created yellow fog that choked the asthmatic and rolled inexorably down the street like vast waves. Once enveloped, one could see no further than the end of one's hand. People groped their way to the nearest door, knocked, and were given refuge. At eventide and dawn the gaslighter came, and when it snowed the gaslight on the pavements sparkled and danced.

In the great houses of the bourgeoisie and the commercial parvenus, the servants provided the glue that held the social classes together, or bridged the divides. As snobbish and as rule-bound as their employers, they became families within families, with their own intrigues, honours and dishonours, *grands amours*, hatreds and loyalties. Every house had its own rules. In some the servants were treated almost like slaves, but in families such as the one in The Grampians, they were a natural part of its extended society. The one universal truth is that every family was terrified of losing its cook. Ladies lived with the perpetual anxiety of upsetting their cooks or having them poached by unprincipled dinner guests.

There were worms in the buds, however, even in Court Road. Not long after the coronation, in a glade of the New Forest, the handsome Captain Pitt was killed in a duel that was possibly the last to be fought formally on British soil. Nobody was ever to find out the identity of his antagonist. His pistol had been discharged, but there were no powder burns on his forehead where the bullet had entered his head, and in any case the bullet was not from his own gun. That is all that anyone was able to discover. His body had been found by a horseman, lying spread-eagled in a swathe of bluebells, not far from a stream and a pungent bank of ransoms. He was given a military funeral, all the more poignant for the youth of his widow and children, and sailors from the Royal Yacht fired a volley over his grave. His death left behind it the ambiguous sorrow of those who mourn the dead, but are proud that it came about as a matter of honour.

Within a few months his two eldest sons had died in the South African war, Theodore in an ambush and Jean-Pierre of enteric fever. Archie and Daniel would always remember them as jovial giants who used to hurl them across the room into the safety of a sofa piled up with cushions. Mme Pitt, grief-stricken but stubborn, inheritor of three sets of medals, decided not to return to France with her remaining sons, Archie and Daniel. Her circumstances greatly reduced, she moved to a small cottage in Sussex, where she eked out her living by teaching French in local schools and to private tutees. After many years of effort she finally learned to make the 'th' sound in English, only reverting to 'z' when she was in a state of agitation.

Archie had already left Westminster School, and Daniel had to leave early, following his brother directly into Rattray's Sikhs and departing for India. Mme Pitt now lived alone in her little piece of paradise under the South Downs. Back in Court Road, every time they saw that part of the wall, Rosie and her sisters would think of Daniel flying over it on Coronation Day, wonder where Daniel and Archie were, and miss them. On the other side the Pendennis boys remained, and the lives of the children continued to be inextricably entwined, linked by the blue door. Everyone knew that Rosie and Ashbridge would grow up to be married, as certainly as they knew it themselves.

To all appearances the new King had brought with him a relaxed love of the good things in life. People flocked to the races because he was often there, and the whole nation rejoiced when his horse, Minoru, won the Derby in 1909. Witty, popular and shrewd though he was, in private the merry monarch still fell into deep fits of gloom. He was a peacemaker, but saw all about him disintegration and the prospect of chaos. He contemplated abdication and was growing ever more convinced that the monarchy would not survive to see his grandson on the throne. He had personally succeeded in creating the Entente Cordiale with France, repairing the diplomatic damage done by the South African war, but it was impossible to ignore the Nero-esque antics of his nephew in Germany, the 'All Highest' and 'Admiral of the Atlantic'.

Sandwiched between France and Russia, and fearful of them both, the Kaiser had long resolved to knock out France with one titanic blow, and then turn on Russia and crush her too. The easiest way to deal with France was to invade it through two neutral countries, Luxembourg and Belgium. He was convinced that Britain would not honour its treaty obligations to defend Belgium. It was, after all, a mere 'scrap of paper' and his mother was King Edward's favourite sister. Germans in the know began to make toasts to '*Der Tag*'. General von Moltke was later to remark that one's battle plans survive exactly up to that point when one makes contact with the enemy.

King Edward brought his brief and beautiful age to an end on the sixth day of May in 1910. Prostrated by bronchitis but smoking cigars to the very end that they had been hastening, he learned from the Prince of Wales that his horse Witch of the Air had won at Kempton. 'I am very glad,' he said, and his servants put him to bed. 'I shan't give in,' he said, 'I'm going to fight it,' but he fell into a coma and died at the imminence of midnight.

Thus it was left to King George to deal with what his father had foreseen; and to Rosie, Christabel, Ottilie, Sophie, Sidney, Albert, Archie, Daniel and Ashbridge.

3

Rosie Remembers

I loved Ash the moment we first set eyes on each other, and it was entirely mutual, even though we were only little children. When we met he was fresh from America and was very put out by being in England. He told me later that he found it rigid and archaic, but I'm certain that if he had ever gone back to America he would have found it deficient because it was too callow.

Ash was really called Ashbridge, and he was from Baltimore. He had a lovely soft American accent, with that strong 'r' after the vowels. He never lost it and you never would have mistaken him for an Englishman. His family lived on the other side of our house, and he was one of our crowd of children that spent its time larking about, making mud pies, playing sardines and hide-and-seek, and British bulldog, and tag, and kick the can. Our mothers were somewhat genteel, but we children were almost wild when we were outside. We romped and fought in our walled gardens, whilst our respective governesses and nurses gossiped together and had tea in the conservatory. In May, Beeson's men used to come and remove the windows of the conservatory. Thanks to the Luftwaffe and lack of funds, they're off permanently now. When we were older we all played tennis on the lawn, in never-ending combinations of doubles and singles. We played American tournaments, and knockout competitions, and generally you won if Ash was on your side. If Ash and Daniel were both on your side, you would definitely win. Ash was school champion at absolutely everything. I remember a doubles game where you had to run round the net as soon as you'd hit the ball. We called it American Tennis, and it was completely exhausting, but it was such hilarious fun. The problem was that there was never really a winner, because the games were not won by a pair, but by the east end or the west end. Sometimes all nine of us played at once. My mother liked to play croquet, and every year she would aspinal the hoops, making a great ceremony of it, and then causing arguments when she wanted to play croquet and we wanted to play tennis.

Because Ashbridge was American we got into the habit of calling ourselves 'the Pals'. 'Light-heart and glad they seemed to me, and merry comrades'. We were: Daniel and poor Archie, Ash and his brothers Sidney and Albert, and Sophie and Ottilie and Christabel and me; five boys and four girls. We had battle cries of 'Long live the Pals!' and 'Pals forever!' Then Daniel and Archie moved away after the Captain was killed, and Ash and Sidney and Albert were the only boys left.

Ash grew up to be a wonderful man. By the time he was eighteen he was occasionally sporting a military moustache, but otherwise he looked as he always had. He was nicely proportioned, with blond hair and grey eyes. He used to say: 'I am built for speed and distance. If you want someone to run to Wales and fetch you something, then I'm your man.'

When I bought a copy of Rupert Brooke's *Selected Poems* later on, I was stunned when I saw the picture of the poet at the beginning, and almost fainted away. I thought for a moment it was Ash. He was so beautiful that it gave you a kind of pain from which you might never recover. When I read Brooke's love poetry I always think of Ash. I used to have lines that went round and round in my head. '*Oh! Death will find me, long before I tire of watching you.*' '*Breathless, we flung us on the windy hill, laughed in the sun, and kissed the lovely grass.*' Unlike most people, I valued Brooke's love poems a lot more than the famous patriotic ones.

Ash and I were real sweethearts. He was so kind, so solicitous. If I was ill, he'd call round and sit in the morning room, where we had family prayers, and he'd just wait for the servants or one of my sisters to come and give him snippets of news about how I was. Whenever I thought of Ash, I would get a lurching feeling in my chest, and my throat would feel dry. Sometimes we would just stand and look at each other as if we were paralysed. If we touched, I would get a tingle down my spine and into my legs. By the time we were about fifteen our passion was so great that we couldn't even speak, and we communicated by little notes that went via the servants. I gave my notes to Cookie, who took them round to their cook, and then their cook would bring the replies round to Cookie. As the cooks were always borrowing things from each other, it was all terribly easy. Entering into little conspiracies with the servants, when people still had them, was one of the small joys of life. I keep Ash's notes and letters in a biscuit tin. I still read them sometimes, damaged though they are, and all the feelings come pouring back. Ash and I were engaged to be married when I was twelve and he was thirteen. Our first engagement ring was a brass curtain ring, so it was much too big to wear, and I keep that in the tin too. It was our secret, and anyone would have told us that we'd grow out of it.

We never did. On 29 May 1910, Ashbridge came round with a gramophone. He was practically the first to get one. We needed something to cheer us up after King Edward's death, and so he brought it round almost every day, to entertain us, and one day he stayed until it was 11.20. Sometimes my sisters and I rolled up the carpet and had dances. We'd suddenly realised that you didn't need to hire a pianist and violin player any more. It was when we were dancing to the gramophone that I truly had the chance to drink him in, to breathe him, to realise that I adored him so much that it would probably be impossible ever to love another. He used to look at me with his eyes so full of devotion that it made me shiver. The physical longing was almost too much to bear.

Just after war broke out in 1914, he came round to speak to my father. He had walked up the driveway singing 'I'm Gilbert the Filbert, the Knut with the Capital Kay'. It was Basil Hallam's song from the Palace Theatre that everyone had been singing before it was knocked aside by all the patriotic ones. Ash sometimes vamped it on the piano. He mostly liked to sing those sentimental plantation songs by Stephen Foster, like 'The Old Folks at Home' and 'Poor Old Joe' and 'Massa's in de Col' Col' Ground'. He had a lovely voice but the piano was always out of tune, and it even made sad songs sound comical. Father said we should get one with a metal frame, but we never got round to it. I think that poor Basil Hallam was eventually killed when he fell out of a balloon.

Ash and my father went into the dining room and shut the

door. I heard their voices, their laughter, and it was difficult to avoid the temptation to hover outside, because I knew what was going on and couldn't wait to hear the result. I went and sat in the drawing room with my mother and my sisters. They were talking about the war, but I couldn't think of anything except what Ash might be saying to my father. Bouncer was at my feet. He was an old dog by then and had completely lost his bounce. His muzzle was grey and his eyes rheumy, but he was still the same affectionate and not very clever dog, devoted above all to me and to my father.

My father was a clever Scotsman who went up to the City for three days a week, and stayed at his club. He made piles of money by thinking of things that needed to be manufactured, and buying and selling stocks and shares, and none of us ever really understood what he did or how he did it, apart from the steady stream of golf novelties that he came up with. He was regularly thrown into absolute dejection by losing all his money at once, but then he always managed to recoup his losses somehow, just in time to pay off the tradesmen. He put on an excellent show of being confident and jolly, but he was always mildly anxious and on edge. He used to say: 'I'd like to get out of this gambling business and actually make something, get into manufacturing properly. Can't think of anything that someone isn't already making, though.' At this time he was saying, 'Perhaps I can dream up something that might be useful for the war. Boots? Bridles? Bullets? Barrels? Other things beginning with B?' He did invent and sell several devices designed to improve one's golf, golf being the great passion of his life. He treated it like a patriotic duty.

When my father and Ash came into the drawing room, they were both holding a glass of whisky in one hand, and a cigar in the other. Ash never did smoke, and he was letting his go out. Father exhaled a big puff of smoke, and said, 'Wonderful news. Do you want to hear it?'

'Ooh, yes!' we all cried, except for Mother, who had a stern habit that she rarely let slip. She was the kind of mother who believed in exposing newborn babies on hillsides. Her favourite adage was 'Spare the rod and spoil the child'.

'Young Ashbridge here has requested my permission to ask for

Rosie's hand in marriage,' said Father, 'and I have given my consent.'

My sisters all squealed and applauded, my mother smiled faintly, and I believe I went pale. I could hardly prevent myself from trembling.

'I have asked him to turn Mahommedan and marry all four of you. I begged him to take you all off my hands in one big shebang, but sadly he has eyes only for Rosie. I even advised him against marriage altogether, but he is not to be deterred. What do you say, Rosie bairn?'

'But, Father, he hasn't even asked me.'

'Come on, old thing,' said Ash, 'I asked you when you were twelve. You have a brass curtain ring to prove it.'

'Ask her again!' cried Sophie. 'Oh, how impeachably romantic! Come on, Ash. Ask her again!'

Sophie was my youngest sister. She was sweet, and, until we knew better, we all thought her a bit silly because she muddled up her words very dreadfully sometimes. Mother said, 'Sophie dear, I think you mean "impeccably".'

'May I speak to Rosie in private?' asked Ash, but my sisters wouldn't allow it. 'Be a sport,' said Ottilie.

'Oh, go on, Ash,' said Christabel.

'What if I say "no"?' I said.

'That would be exscreamingly hard for poor Ash,' said Sophie. 'You know you wouldn't.'

'Well, Rosie,' said Ash, 'what do you say? Will you marry me?'

I was shaking so hard that I couldn't control myself. Suddenly I burst into tears and buried my face in my hands.

'I think that means "yes",' said Christabel.

Ash knelt down before me and said, 'Does it?' and I nodded. Everyone except Mother danced and capered. Mother paused in her embroidering, and said, 'My dear, I have always thought of you as a son, and now you will be!' My three sisters held hands and did an impromptu circle dance. Ash stood up and beheld the mayhem with amusement and affection in his eyes.

After the merriment had subsided a little, Ash sipped at his whisky, and said, 'There is something I do have to tell you all.'

We fell silent, realising that something ominous was about to be said. Ash cleared his throat and announced, 'I have enlisted with the Honourable Artillery Company. I feel that I have to go. To do my bit. I wanted to make sure I was really engaged to Rosie before I went.' He hesitated, and added, 'And Albert and Sidney have enlisted with me.'

My father was stunned, but my mother said, 'Good boy.' Sophie and Christabel and Ottilie exchanged horrified glances. As for me, I found myself standing up and saying, 'Of course you have to go,' but then I ran from the room, startled by the horrible wailing that I knew was coming from me.

4

In Which Ashbridge Attempts to Comfort Rosie

I ran out after her and found her in the room at the front where the family Bible is. She had collapsed on the window seat and was weeping in tremendous sobs. I picked her up in my arms and said, 'Rosie, Rosie, Rosie.' She laid her head on my chest and put her arms round my neck. I could feel her light body trembling.

'You don't have to go,' she said.

'I sure do, darling, I sure do,' I said. 'I've done the deed. I've taken the King's shilling. I had no idea you'd be so upset.'

'I thought we'd be safe,' she said. 'You're American. You didn't have to go. Or Sidney and Albert.'

'But we love it here,' I said. 'We come from New England, and we love the old one just as much, probably even more. We've lived here most of our lives. I've always been ashamed of my countrymen for turning traitor back in 1776.'

'No you haven't. You're always gloating about how you won and we lost. You think it's brave and clever to throw perfectly nice crates of tea into the sea, and you always forget how Canada and Florida wanted to stay British! Anyway, you've got to love Scotland too,' said Rosie, smiling despite her tears. 'Father's Scottish, remember? I'm half Scottish. You can't just love England.'

'I love both halves of you,' I replied, 'including any other parts from anywhere else. I've never been there, but I love Wales and Ireland too. And the Isle of Wight. And Croydon.'

'Why do you have to go away, though? Why can't you stay and work in a hospital or something? Why can't you drive a train or go and be a fireman? So many people have . . . so many have been killed already. What about Mons? And the Marne? And Flanders? Have you seen the death notices in *The Times*?'

'Don't forget the Angels of Mons,' I said. 'God's with us, not with them. We're defending the right.'

Rosie's weakness was God. She was always devout, even when she was a child. She was born with the kind of faith that you can't argue with. This time she stayed silent for a moment, and then she said quietly, 'We still had to retreat.'

'You are going to be an officer?' she said, and I knew what she was getting at; she was hoping there'd be a long period of training before I got sent away. I shook my head. 'I enlisted as a private,' I said. 'You get there a whole lot quicker. I was hoping I might be a gunner. They've got two batteries of horse artillery, and two ammunition columns, and a battalion of infantry, but the darned batteries are up to complement.'

She sat down on the window seat again, and looked down at her hands. 'I suppose I should be encouraging you,' she said weakly. I knelt and held her hands in mine. 'Rosie darling, it's the adventure of a lifetime. How could I possibly stay out of it? Do you think I could bear to live the rest of my life knowing that I hadn't done my bit? That I didn't heed the call?'

'Do you remember what he said, Sir John French? It'll all be over by Christmas, he said. But it won't be. The Boche have got Belgium. You could be away for months.'

I felt as if I was cajoling a child. I was fired up with excitement about going to war. I felt a deep happiness, a sort of elation, as if I had suddenly found my purpose in life.

I said, 'Every man who's never been a soldier regrets it when he gets old. I don't want any regrets.'

When we went back into the withdrawing room, Rosie was on my arm, still weak from her fit of tears, but she was managing to smile. The family got to its feet and applauded me. The sisters each kissed me on the cheek and hung upon my arms. I was very moved and touched. It was my greatest moment of glory, really. I gave Rosie's arm a little squeeze in mine, and she said, 'We'll get married as soon as the war's over. I'm sure it won't be long.'

'I'm bound to get some leave,' I said. 'We can be married when I'm on leave, if the war goes on too long. Would it be asking too much if Albert was best man?'

I went out and bought a little etching. It was by a certain L. Rust, and it was called *Adieu*. I wanted to give it to Rosie at Christmas, but if I had already gone, I would leave it for my mother to take round to her.

5

Hamilton McCosh Holds Forth in the Athenaeum

I can't tell you, old laddie, how completely dismaying this all is. First of all the bank rate went up. It was the 31st of July 1914. I'll always remember that date. To tell the truth I was quite delighted initially. I've got tidy sums deposited here and there. It went from 4 per cent to 8 per cent, and then to 10 per cent, and just when I was rubbing my hands with glee, the blighters closed the Stock Exchange. I didn't get invited to the conference with the Chancellor. If I had there would have been sparks flying, let me tell you. You couldn't get credit anywhere.

How was I supposed to earn a living? I have four charming daughters and a truculent wife. You're a man of the world, old boy, you know how these things happen, and I'm sure you're no different to me when it comes down to it, but I've got two mistresses current, and one retired, and they've each got a house and children to look after. The anxiety almost kills me. I got a note only last week – 'Dear Ham, please send money, the children int got no shoes.'

It was all very well, wasn't it, sitting around and saying, 'Well, what's Serbia got to do with us?' Now we know. It means less money supply, unemployment, unsaleable securities, a dearth of necessities. That's what it's got to do with us, damn it!

What on earth are the Huns up to? What on earth was the point?

Then there's the moratorium on debts, you know, the Postponement of Payments Bill. God help us. A lot of people owe me a lot of money. When am I going to get it? I don't owe anybody anything, so what use is it to me? How am I supposed to pay the tradesmen? Let's hope it never gets implemented.

Still, it was a bright day when the state insurance of merchant vessels came in. Did wonders for confidence. Actually it saved the bacon of my future son-in-law's father. What will he be then? A cousin-in-law? I never did understand how one is related to people. If I found out I was your second cousin three times removed, I wouldn't have a clue what it meant. He's in shipping, you know. The father. You might know him. The name's Pendennis. Anyway, thank God for that. It made everything possible again. Have you seen any of the new ten-shilling and one-pound notes yet? I just hope it doesn't undermine the currency. Coins inspire more confidence, don't you think?

The bank rate's back down to 5 per cent again now, more's the pity, but it shows what happens when the government promises to prop up the banks. I'm a businessman, it galls me, I must say, but the banks prop the rest of us up, so someone's got to prop up the banks, eh?

Have you heard what's happened in Germany? The whole damned system's collapsed. People are hoarding their small change. Runs on the savings banks. A hundred million lost overnight on the Berlin Exchange. Banks closing and refusing to hand over gold. Norddeutsche Handelsbank shut down. Can you imagine? Who would have thought it? Did you ever meet August Saal? No? A fine fellow, exceedingly clever. Went to his bank in Weimar and shot himself. What's that? Eugen Bieber? Yes, I knew him quite well. Met him in Potsdam, something to do with railways in Patagonia. We were in talks about the stocks. What? Killed his wife? And himself? Potassium cyanide? Lost thirteen thousand in two days? Oh good Lord. I hadn't heard about that.

Just goes to show, doesn't it? All you need is someone in charge who wants an empire and doesn't understand money, and the whole damn country goes to Hell in a handcart. And you can't make a mess in one country without messing up the rest. God save us from emperors, that's what I say. Makes you feel grateful for Asquith, eh? Never thought I'd hear myself say that.

Still . . . think what happened back at the end of July. Consols fell 4 per cent, Canadian Pacific fell 6½ per cent, Shell Oil fell 10 per cent, Malacca Rubber fell 17 per cent, De Beers fell 6½ per cent, and Russo-Asiatic fell 23 per cent.

I think there might be some opportunities here. I don't think I'd go for Russo-Asiatic at a time like this, and let's face it, no one needs diamonds in wartime. But think of all the vehicles they'll need for ferrying the troops around, and they say there are going to be huge numbers of aeroplanes involved, and war being war, a lot of these will inevitably be destroyed, and furthermore I hear they're beginning to build oil-fired battleships.

I'm going to buy into Malacca Rubber and Shell Oil, and I'd advise you to do the same. One should turn catastrophe to advantage. Another dram? If there's not a shortage already, of course. Canadian Pacific's an excellent bet too. The right time to buy, definitely.

Did I tell you, I've had an idea for a new kind of golf ball? I'm hoping it won't go rock hard after a few months, like the ones we have at present.

6

Millicent (1)

I am Millicent, if you'll excuse me, and I came to the McCoshes when I was a little mite of fourteen. It was expected that I'd go into service and I always knew that I would, so I'm not complaining. It weren't no good with me mum and dad anyhow, and Mum never got over coming down one day and catching the rats eating my baby brother's face. You couldn't leave a kid for a second where we was, on account of them rats. The baby died thank God and I don't remember him much, but me mum went half barmy and she never recovered, and now she's always ill anyway. Dad was on the docks and he was a big strong fellow. He didn't 'alf drink, but he wasn't barmy like me mum. I can read and write a little bit and had some education from the little charity dame school, and I know I left when I was only ten, but I think I done pretty well, considerin'.

It was a few days after the war got goin', and I went into Miss Rosie's room, thinking that she weren't there, but she was. She was crying her eyes out, poor thing, and I thought, 'Oh gawd, someone's been killed already,' and I said, 'So sorry, Miss Rosie. Shall I come back and do your room later?' and she said, 'I'm sorry, Millie. I didn't mean you to catch me like this,' and I said, 'Are you all right, miss? I hope nothing bad has come about,' and she said, 'It's the Pope. He's just died,' and I looked around and she had a candle all lit in front of a little statue of the Virgin Mary, and I said, 'Have you become a Roman papist then?' and she said, 'No, but the Pope's died, and he was a very good man, and I am so very upset about it. Silly of me, I know.'

I said, 'I don't know nothing much about it, miss.'

Miss Rosie said that this dead Pope said we was to renew all things in Christ, and that the best way was through the Virgin, and she said that once he filled up the Vatican with people what had been done in by an earthquake.

I didn't know what this Vatican was. I didn't like to ask, but I suppose it was quite big. Miss Rosie said, 'Don't tell anyone about this,' and she pointed at the Virgin and the candle. 'Mother and Father might be upset, because we're Anglicans.'

I said, 'I won't say nothing, Miss Rosie. Why would I?'

Don't ask me what she was on about. Our Miss Rosie always did have God pretty badly. We all went to church with the family in a big gaggle twice every Sunday, but us lot used to sit in the back, and I used to have a little sleep if I could. I was fair worn out usually.

It was better than a lot of families what made the servants go to a different church altogether, even if it meant they had to walk for bleedin' miles, and I heard that in the posh houses they make the servants turn and face the wall when there's family passing. Well, I wouldn't've put up with that. In them days you either were a servant or you had some servants yourself, and there was big houses where the grander servants had servants themselves, and every family had its own way, and ours was all right, if you ask me.

7

Now God Be Thanked Who Has Matched us with His Hour

I had felt a kind of loneliness, in amongst all that joyful and righteous patriotism. There didn't seem any chance of America joining in. It wasn't our scrap. I was a Yank from Baltimore, I was twenty-five years old and I hadn't made any mark in the world since leaving school. There I'd been brilliant, especially in athletics, but afterwards I'd never managed anything much. My father was in shipping, and I was working in his office with a view to taking over when he eventually packed it in. There was no sign of that. If he lived to be a hundred he would still be in charge. I was chaffing for some action.

My fondest memory of the outbreak of the war, however, was the reaction of Mrs McCosh. I came to The Grampians the morning after the ultimatum ran out, and she was in a considerable tizz. She was wringing her hands in the drawing room, exclaiming, 'We can't possibly be at war with Germany, we just can't, it's not possible. The Kaiser is the grandson of the Queen!'

Of course she meant Queen Victoria, not Alexandra or Mary. By 'the Queen' she always meant Victoria, and the other two were referred to as 'Queen Alexandra' and 'the present Queen'. She had a touching faith that royal alliances must inevitably prevent wars, unless someone along the line was mad. In retrospect I wonder if she was right; you'd have to be mad to plunge the whole of Europe into war quite deliberately. And the Kaiser was the son of the Princess Royal. He can't have had any family-feeling at all.

Like everyone else I shared in the ecstasy and euphoria when war broke out. Like everyone else, I went to Buckingham Palace and Downing Street and we cheered and sang the British national anthem until we were all hoarse. We sang 'For He's a Jolly Good Fellow' to the King when he appeared on the balcony. I sang my heart out even though I'm a Yank. He was dressed as an Admiral of the Fleet, and Queen Mary and the Prince of Wales came out too. We waved our hats and jostled each other, and men who were unacquainted shook hands and clapped each other on the back. I came over in a strange sweat of enthusiasm. The ultimatum was to expire at eleven, so we made our way to Whitehall, and I had my first taste of fighting. I got into a sort of jostling match with a protester just by Nelson's Column, who carried a placard saying 'This Is Not Our War'.

It was though. It was all very simple. The Kaiser had invaded France without even properly declaring war, and invaded Belgium. It was said that the Germans had brought in one and a half million men by rail. There wasn't any moral doubt in any of us. It was absolutely clear that Germany was in the wrong, and had broken a treaty it had signed up to a long time ago. We had to put a stop to them, and that was that. I don't think we would have been as pleased about a war that wasn't so obviously just, or against an enemy that hadn't done anything outrageous. We'd heard about the French officer they'd torn apart with horses. We'd all been insulted too, by the Kaiser saying that our offer to mediate between the Austrians and the Serbs was just 'British insolence'. It made us all want to go out and give him a bashing. It turned out that the Germans actually had a policy of terrorising the French speakers of Belgium; it was called 'Schrecklichkeit', but we didn't find out until much later.

No one came out of Number Ten when Big Ben struck twelve, and we all knew we were at war. We sang 'God Save the King' with heartfelt emotion, and then we dispersed, very much in a hurry to get home and share the news.

But more important to me than all this, was that I was in love with Rosie, and I will always be in love with her. I was going to marry her, and I wanted her to be married to a man she could be proud of, who was worthy of her. She was the kind of British girl who could cycle for miles without losing her wind, and would have taken on the Kaiser single-handed, given the chance. We always seemed to be surrounded by young men coming back on leave from distant parts of the Empire, like Archie, who had done wonderful things such as fighting off hordes of Pathans, armed only with a dead horse and a revolver, and here I was in my stiff collar, sorting out bills of lading, and impaling lists on a spike, when I really wanted to be an engineer, and had in fact got all the necessary qualifications. It made me feel unworthy of her, and it was no life for a fellow like me. I was created for leaping gates, winning steeplechases and repairing irreparable machines. I decided that I was going to enlist, come Hell or high water.

It was absolute chaos outside Armoury House. All the way down Finsbury Pavement there were thousands of men of all shapes and sizes and ages, all equally determined to get in and enlist. The playing fields were covered in tents and bivouacs, there were artillery pieces and gun carriages, and quite a few horses, all beautifully groomed and shining. Small detachments of men were marching in and out, because the infantry were going back and forth to guard all the public installations that the Germans might want to destroy.

We would-be recruits were almost fighting each other for the right to fight, and it was clear from the despondent faces coming out of the gates that an awful lot of people were being turned away. One older gentleman said to me, 'I gave thirty years of my life to the Honourable Artillery Company, and now they won't have me.' He was at least sixty-five years old, and he walked with a silver-topped cane. Another man came out, all ashen and haggard, and he caught my eye, and said, 'Buggered lungs.' In amongst the melee there were dozens of horses which had also been brought along in the hope of selling them to the HAC. A dejected Scottish vet in a flat cap was inspecting them near the gates, and arguing with some of the officers, who thought that most of the horses he was passing were fit only for the knackers, as indeed he himself was. To make things worse, there was a crush of wagons and carts that had been requisitioned, and arguments were going on as to what they might be suitable for. I watched an irascible wheeler-sergeant, tapping the wheels and axles with a hammer, and tut-tutting over the discouraging dings and clangs that resulted.

When I finally got in I was stood before a panel of officers, who shuffled my papers around and scrutinised my old school reports in turn. Colonel Treffry put his fingers together and said,

'Of course, you are off.·e. .a.cr.al.' He looked at me very kindly.

I replied, 'Am I, sir? Thank y .·.'

'A great many of the young men I have seen are officer material. But we are, as you know, a regiment of gentleman rankers. Our policy is to recruit all ranks from the officer class, and then to promote officers from the ranks. I expect you are aware of this. I am merely advising you that if you wish to become an officer in the more usual way, you should enlist elsewhere. In any case we need troops more than officers. A great many of our former officers have rejoined. So many that we have had to turn some of them away. They've been posted to other units.' He paused. 'Ideally you should be joining as a regular, and going to the RMC at Sandhurst. I have said the same thing to your brothers.'

He looked at me in the same way as before, and I said, 'But I've set my heart on the HAC. I wouldn't mind being a gunner. And I wouldn't be ashamed of being a private. In fact I would be quite proud of it.'

'Good man. I'm afraid that both the batteries are fully manned, though. We are hoping to set up some reserve batteries, but we'll probably have to go and see Earl Kitchener to get it done. I expect you know that the batteries are affiliated to the Royal Horse Artillery, but the infantry battalions are with the Grenadier Guards. I expect you've noticed the badge with the grenade on it. Would you be prepared to join us as an infantry private rather than as a gunner?'

'Infantry?'

'Yes, as an infantryman.'

'Would I get there sooner?' I asked.

'Very much sooner.'

'What did my brothers say? I didn't get time to ask them before I came in.'

'They are happy to go out in the same unit as you, as infantrymen.'

'There is just one thing,' I said. 'I'm afraid I'm an American citizen, and so are Sidney and Albert.'

The Colonel turned to the other members of the panel and

said, 'I didn't hear that. Did any of you gentlemen hear what Private Pendennis said? Did any of us hear the other two when they told us the same thing?'

They all shook their heads gravely, and the Colonel stood up and shook my hand. 'Welcome to the HAC, Private Pendennis. None of us has the slightest inkling that you are an American citizen. I am certain that you will be a credit to your nation, and I am certain that the King would wish me to convey his gratitude and appreciation. You will have to pass a medical, of course.'

I rendezvoused with Sidney and Albert and we shook hands, which was wasn't something we had ever done before. When we left Armoury House I said, 'Race you!' and we ran from Finsbury Square to Waterloo Bridge, just to give expression to the joy we were feeling. We ran past all the long queues for the banks, and I felt a guilty pang on behalf of my poor father. None of our ships were able to put to sea because no one would insure them any more, and the government had not yet stepped in. We faced ruin, just as Rosie's father did because of the chaos on the Stock Exchange, but none of that seemed important. I was so elated that I could have flown like an angel. Suddenly there was a point to everything, and there wasn't a medical in the world that would have failed me.

Running through London with my brothers beside me, I felt I had grown angel wings.

8

A Letter to His Majesty

The Grampians

15 September 1914

Sir, May It Please Your Majesty,

I am writing to beg you most humbly to intercede in the matter of my daughter's fiancé, who has recently had the honour and privilege of joining the Honourable Artillery Company in Your Majesty's service.

He is a very fine young man, most handsome and athletic, and he and my daughter Rosie have been promised to each other for a very long time. It would be true to say that they were childhood sweethearts.

In view of the reports of terrible casualties that have already been received I have the honour to ask you to if you would be so awfully kind as to ensure that he is posted somewhere quite safe once his training is completed, which I believe will be at Christmastime. The reason I ask is that I believe that my daughter's heart would be quite broken should he be killed, and she might never recover.

May I have the honour to repeat that my daughters and I would be most delighted to entertain His Majesty and Her Majesty the Queen at any time that they might be in our part of Kent.

I have the additional honour to submit myself, with profound respect, Your Majesty's most devoted subject and servant,

Mrs Hamilton McCosh, gentlewoman

9

A Letter from the Palace

Buckingham Palace

20 September 1914

Dear Mrs McCosh,

His Majesty asks me to express his gratitude to you for your kind letter of 15 inst. He asks me to inform you that he had the distinct pleasure of witnessing the First Battalion of the Honourable Artillery Company march past and out to war in his presence on the 12th of this month. He found them to be a fine body of men, most impressive in stature and demeanour, and he is conscious of the burdens and trials which they will imminently have to endure.

His Majesty asks me to express his pleasure in hearing from you again, thanks you for your kind invitation to tea, and asks me to remind you once more that whereas he reigns, he does not rule. That is, he has no powers other than to advise, to warn and to encourage, and is therefore unable to intervene in any executive decisions, such as the posting of individuals in time of war. This he leaves to his government and his generals. It is for the same reason that he was unable to intervene in the matter of the unreliable gas lamps in Court Road, Eltham, and in the matter of the lack of canine fastidiousness on the Esplanade at Ryde, as complained of in your two most recent letters.

His Majesty hopes most earnestly that the conflict will not be a long one, and that your daughter's fiancé (whose name you omitted to mention in your kind letter) comes through these difficult times unscathed. His Majesty has complete confidence that he will acquit himself with honour. You may be aware that even His Royal Highness Prince Albert has not been spared in the present conflict and is in service with His Majesty's Royal Navy. His Royal Highness Prince David has not been allowed to serve abroad with his battalion of the Grenadier Guards, but has gone to France nonetheless to serve as ADC

39

to *Sir John French, and frequently puts himself in danger whilst visiting the front line.*

I remain, madam, your humble and obedient servant,

Lt Col. Sir Frederick Edward Grey Ponsonby, Secretary to His Majesty

10

Rosie Remembers the Gypsy

On the day that the first bomb was dropped on London we were walking by the Tarn. We knew nothing about the bomb, though, until we read about it in the paper the following morning. The bombing of civilians made us hate the Boche even more. It seemed like absolutely ages since we had all been worrying about a civil war in Ireland, even though that had been only a few weeks before.

Ash was in khaki, and looked very dashing. All the training had thinned him a little, and there was a jaunty spring in his step. He and I were strolling in front, and my sisters were walking behind at quite a distance, in order to avoid being gooseberries, and give us some privacy. Ash's brothers Sidney and Albert were with them, charming them all at once. If they came out, it spared my mother the trouble of being a chaperone, and in any case it was better for Ash and me because my mother was very taken with him herself. She would monopolise the conversation, and even be flirtatious. If she was with us, she rather spoiled things. It was windy and cold, but I always did like clear autumn days. The golden leaves were drifting and lifting, and ripples passed across the surface of the water. 'The trees were weeping yellow leaves', as I wrote in one of my poems from back then. We had taken stale bread for the swans.

Ash and I sat on a bench, and Ottie, Sophie, Albert, Sidney and Christabel went to the other side of the Tarn. They had Bouncer with them, and he was a slow old dog by then, especially as he liked to stop and sniff at practically everything. We saw a gypsy girl approaching us. 'Oh darn,' said Ash wearily. It was obvious that she was going to importune us.

She was young, perhaps no more than fifteen, but she had a tiny baby wrapped up in a shawl and perched on one hip. The gypsies were a law unto themselves. They lived parallel lives that we knew very little about. When they turned up with their ponies and pretty wagons and their scrawny optimistic little dogs and their frightful hordes of wild children, you could expect a flurry of crime. Your milk bottles would go missing from the doorstep, and you'd lose your rake and even your brass doorbell. Ash was inclined to see the best in people, and said it was because the petty criminals in the locality took advantage of the fact that everyone would automatically blame the gypsies.

A lot of them were very useful people. The tinkers could mend almost anything made of metal, and they'd sharpen knives marvellously well. They had grinding stones that rotated through a trough of water, and they'd set them up in the street so that the scullery maids could rush out and get the cooks' knives perfect again. The gardeners would go out with their axes and sickles and billhooks. The didicois took away all the metal things that were beyond repair. There were people called pikeys as well, and they got most of the blame for the thieving. They didn't seem to have any other profession. The gypsies ran the funfairs and they travelled around picking whatever harvests needed to be picked. They always passed our house when it was time to pick the hops in the Weald, the men walking beside their ponies, leading them by the halter, and the children scampering in and out of the wagons.

This gypsy girl was a Romany. They had their own language and sometimes they'd stop speaking it the moment they thought you might be listening, or, contrarily, they'd tip into it so that you couldn't understand. She was dark-skinned, with shiny black hair, and big gold rings through each earlobe. Her eyes were so dark that you couldn't see how big the pupils were. She was wearing a loose scarlet dress embroidered in gold and black, and a waistcoat that matched. When Daniel showed me his photographs of India after the war, I was struck by how similar the Hindus looked to our Romanies. The girl looked wonderful and exotic, but she was obviously cold, and she was dirty too.

She stood before us, and held out a sprig to Ash. 'Good day to thee. Lucky white heather,' she said.

Ash looked at her a little ironically, and replied, 'Isn't it supposed to be in bloom? How do I know if it's really white heather?'

She screwed up her mouth vexedly, and said, 'Times is hard. I got a baby.'

'What's its name?' asked Ash.

'She's Sinnaminti,' said the girl, 'and I got another chavi called Nilly-Lisbee, and a chal by name of Awkie.'

We were shocked. 'But you're only a child yourself!' exclaimed Ash.

The girl blew a wisp of hair away from her mouth and shrugged. 'Even so, I loves them. There'll be more if God allow.'

You could almost hear Ash's heart melting. He was such a kind and gentle soul. He reached into his pocket and took out a florin. The girl's eyes lit up and she gave an involuntary start of joy. She took the coin hurriedly and secreted it somewhere about her waist. She pressed the heather into Ash's hand.

'Cross my palm with silver,' she said, 'and I'll read thy vast.' She saw his look of puzzlement, and she added 'hand', further adding, 'I got the gift. It came down the fam'ly. My old mother passed it down.'

'I just did cross your palm with silver,' said Ash.

'Indeed, sir, but that was for the heather.'

Ash reached into his pocket and brought out six pennies that had been bothering him with their weight and which he was glad to get rid of. She shook her head. 'It needs be silver.'

'Silver?'

'Pennies is copper. It needs be silver.'

'So if I gave you twenty guineas in copper farthings, you wouldn't take it?'

'I'd take it indeed, sir, but I couldn't read thy vast. I'd have to be pretending, sir.'

I rummaged in my purse and proferred the girl a silver threepence, which she immediately tucked away. She took my hand and traced some lines on it with her forefinger. I caught her scent. She smelled of something aromatic, but I couldn't place it. She looked at the bottom edge, and frowned. 'Thou'lt get to be middling old,' she said. 'Thou's going to beget two and half children, thou's going to be sick, but not fatal, and thou'lt have to take care of thy heart. Thy heart be weak, ma'am.'

'Two and a half children?' I cried. 'What on earth do you mean by that?'

The girl shrugged. 'I read what I read, ma'am.'

Ash looked at me tenderly, and said, 'How wonderful it will be to have children. We'd better start thinking of names.'

He held out his hand to the girl. She studied it intently for a few moments, and then, quite suddenly, thrust it aside as if it had burned her. 'I can't read it,' she said.

'Please,' said Ash.

'No, sir, I can't read it. Thou'ld best not ask.' She reached into her clothing and found the threepence, which she gave back to me. She hitched the child further up her hip, made a small noise in her throat that sounded like a stifled sob, looked up at Ash with teary eyes, and said something like 'Such a rinkeno coora-mengro. God save you both.' Then she hurried away, round the Tarn, straight past my sisters, who thereby escaped being sold white heather or having their fortunes told.

I looked at Ash, and he caught my eye and snorted. 'Two and a half children! Whatever next?'

'What do you think she saw in your palm?' I said.

'It's all stuff and nonsense,' said Ash. 'She didn't see anything at all.'

'Why would she be so upset then?'

'Because she thought she did. The superstitious are even handier at deceiving themselves than they are at deceiving others.'

We sat side by side in silence for a while. Leaves spiralled down into the black surface of the Tarn, and the ducks on the grassy bank shook the water out of their feathers. I shivered, overcome by sudden gloom, my heart heavy, and Ash said, 'Yes, it's getting cold. Let's go back.'

I'd recently bought a statuette of the Virgin Mary, and I kept it wrapped up in a cloth under my bed. I didn't want the rest of the family to know, because we were Anglicans, and they would have disapproved and thought I was becoming a papist. I loved the Virgin, though. Mine had a light blue robe with a gold hem. She had blue eyes, blonde hair and rosy lips. Her feet were bare. She was holding up the Christ child, who was also blue-eyed, blond and rosy-cheeked. He was holding a golden orb in his right hand, and looking very serious. His left hand rested terribly affectionately on the Virgin's wrist. Years and years later Daniel pointed out to me that the Virgin had actually been a Jewess from Palestine, and was probably quite dusky. I didn't say anything, but I think that the Virgin gives herself to you in any way that makes it easier for you to understand her. That's why I wasn't shocked when I saw a photograph of a black Virgin somewhere in Africa, and a Chinese one in Singapore.

That night I took my Virgin out from under the bed and stood her on my bedside table. I asked her to intercede for Ash and to save him from whatever the gypsy girl saw. I thought that I could protect him if I prayed for him every night, so I resolved to do so, even if I was too tired and even if it was too cold.

II

Ash Makes his Farewells

It was snowing when Ash came round to say goodbye on Christmas Day. The Christmas tree was lit up with candles, and the glass balls were glittering. The angel on the top was, after long service, terribly old and tatty, and had the forlorn air of better days gone by. The family had not opened its presents yet, because the rule was that it was always done after afternoon tea, and not in the morning after church as most people did. They called it 'the evening post', and the servants were told not to disturb them. They received their presents in the morning.

Mrs McCosh and Rosie's sisters very kindly waived propriety and left her and Ash alone in the withdrawing room, in front of the fire. Ash was in service dress, looking very dashing and smart. Rosie found the Honourable Artillery Company's cap badge rather curious. On that day Ash seemed to her to be particularly beautiful, and his grey eyes were sparkling with enthusiasm. He was longing to get going to the war. His movements were full of vigour and purpose, he smelled of cologne, and, as Homer would have put it of one of his heroes during their *aristeia*, seemed 'like unto a god'. He placed a parcel in Rosie's hands, and said, 'Happy Christmas.'

'What is it?' Rosie asked, although she could tell it was a picture from the feel of the frame through the paper.

'Open it after I've gone.'

She looked down at it and said, 'I can tell it was you who wrapped it.'

They sat opposite each other, leaning forward, holding hands, with their foreheads touching. Her tears were falling onto their hands, and he was whispering, 'Darling, my darling, darling, my darling.'

Rosie choked and suddenly burst out, 'I think you'll never come back.'

'I will, I will, I will. I will come back. I will never leave you. Even if I die I will never leave you. Even if I am dead I will come back, I'll find a way to be with you. I promise, I promise, I promise. I'll love you forever. Beyond death, beyond everything. Do you know that Arab proverb, about the ideal spouse being the keeper of your soul? I'll be the keeper of your soul, Rosie.'

'And I of yours,' she said. 'I will never love anyone but you,' and she looked into his eyes as the tears rolled down her cheeks.

He reached up, collected some tears in the cup of his palm, put his hand to his mouth, and drank them. 'You shouldn't say that,' he said. 'If the worst comes to the worst . . . I wouldn't want you to . . . you mustn't deny yourself. You'd be a wonderful mother.'

She looked directly into his eyes, which on that day seemed exceptionally beautiful, and said, 'I promise you, as if you had made me promise it, that there will never be anyone else but you. No one.'

'I promise you the same,' he said. 'But you mustn't promise it to me. I won't accept it. If I die you must have the chance to be a mother, to have a family, and be happy.' He stood up and beckoned her to follow.

They went to the conservatory at the back of the house, through the French windows in the withdrawing room. It had steps down into the garden. Ash stood Rosie where she could see the garden, and descended the steps. By then it had stopped snowing and the lawn was covered by a perfect, flawless, glistening crust.

Ash walked out into the snow, and lay down on his back. He stretched out his arms, and swept them up and down two or three times. Then he got to his feet carefully, dusted himself off, and came back up the steps into the conservatory. They stood side by side, looking down at what he had done.

She said, 'It looks like an angel.'

'It *is* an angel. It's a snow angel. We used to make them back home when I was a kid, in Baltimore. It's an American invention.'

'You think everything's an American invention.'

'Well, have you seen it before?'

'No.'

Ash indicated the angel with a toss of his chin. 'Always think of me as your angel. I'll be watching over you. The keeper of your soul.'

Rosie felt very uneasy, a little spooked. He said, 'I'd better go, my love. The train won't wait, and it's quite a walk with a back-pack full of razors and socks and field dressings. I'm meeting Sidney and Albert at the station.'

'We could send someone for a hansom,' she suggested, and he replied, 'No, it would take too long, and I reckon I should get myself in training. I'm mighty sure there'll be some long marches ahead. Before I go I want to recite something for you.'

'Recite something?'

'Yes indeed. I found it in that Georgian Poets book you love so much, and I memorised it, so I could say it at this moment.'

'Is it Rupert Brooke?'

'Uh-uh. See if you recognise it.'

He pursed his lips whilst he recalled the verse, and then recited:

> 'Breathe thus upon mine eyelids – that we twain
> May build the day together out of dreams.
> Life, with thy breath upon my eyelids, seems
> Exquisite to the utmost bounds of pain.
> I cannot live, except as I may be
> Compelled for love of thee.'

Rosie recognised it and took it up:

> 'O let us drift,
> Frail as the floating silver of a star,
> Or like the summer humming of a bee . . .'

'It's Harold Monro! What is it? "Child of Dawn"?'

'Yes, that's right. Now do you think you could breathe on my eyelids? Just so I can see what's so darn good about it?'

He closed his eyes and leaned down, and Rosie breathed on his eyelids. Suddenly he opened his eyes and said, 'It's not quite what Monro cracked it up to be. Might you allow a kiss instead?'

Eventually Ash went to say goodbye to her mother and sisters, and then they gathered to see him off at the door. Theatrically,

Ash affected French manners, and kissed each of the sisters' hands, and then their mother's. She did not know quite where to put herself. She said, 'I will write to the King personally to ask him to make sure that you are somewhere safe,' and the sisters smiled little secret smiles to each other. Mrs McCosh was always writing to the King, and was the fiercely proud owner of a little pile of polite and non-committal acknowledgements from his secretary.

Finally Ash took both of Rosie's hands and said, 'We'll get spliced on my first leave, then.'

She nodded, and said, 'I'll pray for you every day, especially before I go to bed.'

'Thanks, sweetheart,' he said. 'And long live the Pals.'

Rosie said, 'Pals forever,' and then he was gone, striding out into the snow with his baggage on his back and his cap on his head. He waved from the gate, and Rosie felt a little hurt that he so obviously could not wait to get away, and out into battle. That was how all the young men were, suddenly caught up by a very specific, important and tangible reason for living. Rosie could not blame him, and would later wish that she had had told him how proud of him she had been. The last she knew of Ash was the sound of him whistling 'Gilbert the Filbert', trilling the notes like a blackbird as he strode away.

After he had gone Rosie went to the conservatory to look down at the snow angel, and Sophie, Christabel and Ottilie followed.

'Ash said he was my angel. It was a funny thing to say.'

'Do you mean funny ha ha or funny peculiar?' asked Sophie.

'Funny peculiar, of course,' said Christabel on Rosie's behalf.

'Oh good,' said Sophie. 'I hate it when I don't understand jokes.'

After tea Rosie opened Ash's present, and it was an etching called *Adieu* by L. Rust. It depicted an old-fashioned infantryman wearing a shako, with a musket over his shoulder, on the point of stepping forward. A maid in a pinafore stood at his left side, on tiptoe, her arms draped about his neck and her eyes closed. Her attitude suggested depair and resignation and absolute devotion. Either he was kissing her nose, or was whispering something. Rosie thought it would have been something like 'I have to go now, I really do'. The contour of the girl's body exactly folded into that of the soldier. The effect of the picture was poignant, and it made her begin to cry. She took it upstairs and propped it against the wall on top of her bookcase, and then she retrieved her figure of the Virgin Mary from under the bed and put her in front of the mirror. She talked to her about keeping Ash safe, and then wrapped it up again, and replaced it.

She put on her coat and hat and muffler, and walked to the church. It was a freezing day, with the kind of raw cold that burns into the bones, but even so the church was full of women on their knees. She slipped into the pew beside Mrs Ottway, who had two sons at the front, and tried to pray, but could not help sniffling. Mrs Ottway put out a hand and took hers, and they prayed together. They said the Lord's Prayer. Afterwards 'Thy will be done' echoed and re-echoed inside Rosie's head, and she remembered the words that Jesus spoke in the Garden of Gethsemane, words that she would repeat to herself all through her life when she needed tiding through.

When she returned home, Bouncer was waiting on the other side of the door. During that night he howled inconsolably, and the whole house was reduced to helplessness. Everyone was down there by candlelight in their night attire, including the servants, trying to work out what to do, and in the end they shut poor old Bouncer in the conservatory and hoped that he would not perturb the neighbours too much. Mr McCosh thought that the dog might have had a stomach ache, but Rosie said that dogs howl only when they suffer mental distress. After that time Bouncer often howled at night.

As for Rosie, she longed with ever decreasing faith for the day when 'we twain may build the day together out of dreams'.

12

And the Worst Friend and Enemy
Is But Death

Regimental no. 1967
Rifle no. 1695
Pte Ashbridge Pendennis

Dizzy, sick and exhausted by the time we got to Kemmel.
Don't think I ever felt seedier. Trudged in full view of the
Huns up on the hill. No idea why they didn't mow us down. A
miracle.

Officers got told off. Came in cattle trucks, then buses that still
had 'London General Omnibus Company' on the sides, but then
it was slogging through mud and rain, mile after mile, with rifle,
ammo, a cape, a goatskin and supplies. Aching and shivering,
sweating and freezing. End of my greatcoat so soaked in earth
and water. Terribly heavy. Sidney and Albert and I ended up
almost carrying each other. Thank God they were there. Arrived,
slumped down and slept, without removing our webbing. Could
hear bombardment not far off. First time under fire, and too tired
to care. Am extra fit because of ribbing about being a Yank, so
always trained hard to be one and a half times as good.

Kept worrying about when I would get a chance to zero my
sights. Was thinking, 'What's the point of this gun if I aim it and
miss?' Other fellows had been developing the same obsession.

My gun quite old, but good. Nice feel to it. Obviously loved
by a previous owner. 'PLG' in tiny letters on the stock, and a lot
of wax or boot polish rubbed into the woodwork. Glows dark
brown. Barrel immaculate, not one pit. Bolt slides perfectly. Must
always look out for mud up the barrel, because then it could
explode in your hands. Took a tip and plugged the muzzle with
a tiny cork from a medicine bottle. Am almost as worried about
looking after that cork as I am about the gun.

Wonder who PLG was, and whether still alive. Think of him as a guardian spirit. If he's dead, hope he watches over me and his old Lee–Enfield. Fear that the first time I get a chance to take a potshot at Fritz, will feel sorry for him and funk it. Might aim at the ground, and made him skip.

You pick up on the lore of a unit almost as soon as you join it. The lore is one of the things that keeps you together. It's very like the stories that come down families, so that things that happened to your grandmother almost seem as if they had happened to you. Must write them down sometime.

Trenches taken over from the French. Just channels of slime. No wire, no sandbags, no proper parapets, no communication trench. Too shallow, so have to sit down in the mud, but if lucky might find the chest of a Frenchman to sit down on. Strange and disconcerting at first, but am already used to how dead bodies sigh if you sit on them.

Deep hole full of water in our trench, keep forgetting it's there. Sink into it up to your thighs. Good for thinning the half-inch of mud encrusting greatcoats. Hell to be made to march in great-coats. Some lads cut the bottoms off.

German lines higher than ours, only a hundred yards away. Huns always have the high ground, simply because they got there first. Always have the advantage of us in a firefight, but I think we lose just as many men to sickness, including our doctor.

Snowed and froze, but mostly rained. Work at night, so sleep in the afternoons, but sometimes sleep in snatches, just two minutes during busy times. You can't sleep wearing webbing and water bottle, but not allowed to take them off. Groundsheet isn't big enough, so you sleep sitting up, with your helmet on, so that drips fall away onto shoulders. In the front line we're not permitted to remove our boots and socks. Puttees leave horrible trackmarks round legs. Bad idea to take off boots in icy weather anyway, because they freeze solid. Can't get them on again.

Stand to on firing step at dawn every day. All night for prep-aration, so best time to attack. Fritz does exactly the same thing, of course, and no attack ever comes. All casualties from snipers and shellfire. Proper attacks rare as alligator feathers.

Regiment lost twelve officers and 250 men to enemy action,

exposure, exhaustion and frostbite, before I got here. Relieved by Royal Scots Fusiliers in December. Boys ate nothing but bully beef. You open the tins with a bayonet.

Thank God for rum ration. That navy stuff goes right down to your toes and heats you all the way back up again. Sincerely hate any NCO who tries to cream it off.

Rum and cigarettes; I guess that's what a soldier lives for. Swap my cigarettes for rum, and think it a darned good deal too.

Couldn't hold the line after middle of January. Lost too many men. Transport people volunteered to come and fight in place of our dead.

Began to think that there's something about a young man that makes him want to die, and die well, whilst still at the height of life, whilst still not tired of it. Or maybe war so terrible that the prospect of death entices. Is it a comfort not to have to face the future? We all end up discarded on the midden of time, so might as well be flung there now. Ain't I quite the philosopher?

Not thinking along those lines. I have Rosie to live for. Told her I was her angel, but really she's mine. Also knew that if I was killed she'd never have the chance to become disillusioned. She'd never get tired. We'd never have an argument. I'd be young, strong, handsome forever. Would never watch her grow old, either. No plans to die, but it might be a good thing before I let her down. If I die, the vision lives.

Impossible to imagine oneself being dead, because one is still there, imagining it. That's how we can watch our comrades die, and carry on. If I imagine myself dead, I'm still at Rosie's side.

13

Daniel Pitt to his Mother (1)

Somewhere in deepest darkest France

3 January 1915

Ma chère maman,

How lovely it was to spend Christmas with you on the South Downs, and quel plaisir *to go tobogganing with one's mother! It was cruel of you to make me drag both of our toboggans back uphill, though. How will I ever forgive? Perhaps time will heal.*

It was very sweet of you to come to the aerodrome to see me off. How marvellously you frightened the sentries and charmed the CO! and even his dog! I thought you were very brave, the way you held back your tears, but really, you didn't need to. Everyone was perfectly aware that you are French and have the perfect excuse to be emotional.

But, chère maman, *I do know how you feel. You saw my brothers off to South Africa, never to see them again, and we don't know what's going to happen to Archie out in Waziristan. You must be very lonely and worried. Even I am worried, a lot more than my fellow birdmen, none of whom seem to be older than eighteen. At twenty-two I feel a little less bulletproof than they do.*

I want to tell you why you shouldn't worry, but first of all I have to relate what happened on the way over. As you know, I came over in a gunbus, with another pilot in the front, and the plan was to collect a nice little Morane-Saulnier at St Omer. Well, the gunbus is a stout fellow, and a remarkably dependable and safe machine, but ours conked out not far from Gravelines. Broken ignition wire, it turned out. Ça se passe. *I can't tell you how frightening it was. I was fiddling with the instruments, almost in a blue funk, thinking I was going to have to ditch in the sea and get dissected by crabs and other molluscs, and the odd dogfish. But I managed to land right at the sea's edge, on the beach. Thank God it was low tide. The other fellow and I managed to drag it up the beach with the aid of stalwart fishermen who had been innocently beachcombing, and we telephoned through to Squadron HQ. Whilst waiting for the ack emma we got royally treated by the inhabitants of a bistro. I've never had such a good steak. I can tell that being a half-French birdman is going to be a huge bonus out here. I will have simpering girls draped off both arms, and have to check that there aren't any in my shoes in the mornings, as we did with scorpions out on the NWF. The weather leaves most of our flying days completely dud, so . . . more time for the fair maidens of France!*

Anyway, to the point. If you fly over France, you see beneath you a country of the most magnificent beauty. Where else are there towns like Fleurs, or Poitiers, or Abbeville? Where else are there lovely long avenues of poplars and infinitely long Roman roads? And rivers with such lovely curves? And elegant chateaux that were never made for war? And women who think you must be mentally deficient if you are not in love with them? Where everyone drinks wine and sings, but nobody's drunk?

The point is, maman, that I love France with all my heart and soul. She is my mother, as you are, and England is my father, as Father was. One loves one's parents equally, if differently, and I love France as I love you, with a sort of passionate aching tenderness.

Not far from here there is a strip, neither very long nor wide, where this exquisite land has been reduced to a hideous bog of brown mud, pitted with interconnecting shell holes full of filthy water, where there are no trees unbroken and no church or farm or house intact. It is already a vast grave-yard of the unburied. The gunfire is relentless and maddening. The front is an obscenity, maman, and this was inflicted on France by a madman who overran two neutral countries in order to get to it and bring about this wreckage. Only when it is covered with snow is purity restored to this land, and even then the trenches cut through it like cracks in glass.

At Westminster we had to learn reams of heroic poetry. It was beaten into us, did you but know it, but there's a verse I remember, by Lord Macauley, I believe, which goes:

> *'To every man upon this earth*
> *Death cometh soon or late:*
> *And how can man die better*
> *Than facing fearful odds,*
> *For the ashes of his fathers,*
> *And the temples of his gods?'*

Well, that's how I feel. Airmen don't live long, as you probably know. I may be lucky, or I may have the worst of luck and be maimed rather than killed. But if I am killed, I would like you to be fearsomely proud as you show my photograph to your visitors, and say, 'That was my son, mort pour la France.'

Ton fils dévoué,
Daniel P.

14

Rosie

Boxing Day of 1914 began very wet, and Rosie was awakened by the sound of rain on the windowpanes. Her face was cold, but her body was warm from being tucked under the covers. The coal fire, which had been banked up the night before, had burned itself out, and was giving very little heat. It was still dark outside, and she lay in bed thinking about Ashbridge in France. He would almost certainly be outside in the trenches, and she wondered how one could possibly cope with being there in weather like this. Rosie remembered that it was St Stephen's Day, and that he had been the first Christian martyr. She got dressed in bed.

The house was quiet now that all the male servants had gone. When she went downstairs the Christmas tree seemed lifeless with its candles unlit, and the presents gone from beneath it. She was the first of the family to be up, although she could hear Cookie and Millicent clattering in the kitchen. She sat in the drawing room watching the world become light outside, and felt helpless.

That morning she conscientiously wrote her thank-you letters, and then put on her coat and a sou'wester and went next door to see Mr and Mrs Pendennis. She found the latter very pale and agitated, but doing her best to be collected.

'My dear,' said Mrs Pendennis, 'I shall just have to resign myself, won't I? I've got three boys out there, and it's not very likely that they'll all come back, is it? Have you noticed that the parents of the dead boys have become a kind of club?'

'They do errands for each other,' said Rosie. 'It's nice in a forlorn kind of way, isn't it?'

'I'm worried about my husband,' said Mrs Pendennis. 'He's smoking an awful lot, and it's giving him a cough. He says it helps to clear his lungs, but I really don't think it helps at all.'

'We spend our time clutching at straws, don't we?' said Rosie.

On the next day, which was the day of St John the Evangelist, there was a terrible gale, and once again Rosie woke up feeling a kind of horror for Ashbridge, in case the weather should be like this wherever he was. Mrs McCosh, sensitive to Rosie's worries, tried to keep her busy, and despatched her to the post office, so that she came back drenched and windswept. Because Millicent was so busy, Rosie made up the fire in the drawing room herself and knelt in front of it to dry out. It was unbearable to think of Ash being shelled and soaked, with no real shelter and no fire to dry out next to. Rosie stared into the flames as if there were something to be divined there.

She tried to read, but could not concentrate. She wrote a letter to the Poetry Bookshop to ask when the next collection of Georgian poetry was due out, and then settled down with their anthology for 1911–12. She bypassed the rather overblown contributions of Lascelles Abercrombie and Gordon Bottomley, and turned straight to the five contributed by Rupert Brooke. How very strange to read a long poem written in Germany about nostalgia for one place in England. 'Grantchester' was a poem that could no longer be written. You could write something very like it in France, though. Rosie wondered how many of the soldiers were writing poems. It wasn't something that Ash was likely to do.

She read 'Dust' four times to herself, and then stood up and read it aloud as she paced about the drawing room. That poem was certainly about her and Ash, should one of them die. She liked the phrase 'The shattering fury of our fire'. That's what it was, this desperate passion. She read 'The Fish', and noticed how clever was that cascade of couplets, connected by so much deft enjambement. Rosie would have loved to write a poem as accomplished as that. 'Town and Country' was irrelevant because it was about the seeping away of love, and that was something in which Rosie did not believe. 'Dining Room Tea' seemed a little obscure and strange to her, so she went back and read 'Dust' again. Then she turned to page 71 and read Walter de la Mare's 'The Listeners'. Really, it was by far the best poem in the book, even better than 'Dust'. Rosie wished again that she could write poetry of such quality. She knew that somewhere inside her there was poetry waiting to come out. She had an obscure instinct that all she needed to do was read enough poetry with her eyes, and one day it would start coming out of her fingers. She went and fetched a paper knife from her father's desk, and eagerly began to cut the remaining pages.

In the evening Mrs McCosh, Rosie and Christabel went out to play bridge, and when they were coming back, Mrs McCosh's umbrella was blown inside out and wrecked.

On the 28th Rosie could not stand the agony of sitting around worrying, so she went to the YMCA hut to see if there was any way in which she could be useful, but there wasn't. What was she supposed to do with herself? She went round to see Mr and Mrs Pendennis again. Mrs Pendennis asked Rosie about the Pitt brothers who used to live on the other side of the McCoshes, wanting to know if she knew where they were these days. She said, 'No, but I expect Mama does,' and on the way home she remembered what a little scallywag Daniel Pitt had been, expert in all those horrible tricks and tortures that little boys love. He'd fired a rotten plum at her with his catapult, and it had splattered all over her dress. Still, she had been very fond of him. She remembered his brother Archie, who was older, and thought how nice it would be to see them again, after all these years. No doubt they were both caught up in the war too.

Rosie drifted through the 29th and 30th in a fog of numbness, but on the 31st it was raining violently again, and once more she was desperate with worry on Ash's behalf. That evening Mr and Mrs Pendennis came round for dinner, and afterwards they all played bridge until 11.30. As everyone does in wartime, they kept themselves distracted with conviviality. It was raw and painful having to sing the new year in with 'Auld Lang Syne'. Mr McCosh became emotional and stood up to recite Robert Burns. Then he sang 'The Flowers of the Forest' and the Pendennises went home feeling bleak.

The days of the new year dragged by. Rosie kept going down to the YMCA hut, but they never found any use for her. Her mother did the household accounts as usual at this time of year, and became irritable. Rosie went out to tea and people came to tea, she went shopping, she went to see Mrs Pendennis. On 5 January it occurred to her that the one thing she could do was to go and visit the Cottage Hospital, but she found it almost impossible not to get in the way, and felt very awkward with people who did not really want to speak. The sights and particularly the sounds were more dreadful than she could possibly have imagined. She knew that her horror was selfish, because she was never thinking of the victims before her, but only of the possibility that something like this could happen to Ash. Of course, she told herself, she would marry and love him anyway, even if he were blind and missing his legs, and even if he were covered in burns, but what worried her was how Ash himself might take it. Rosie was convinced that he would prefer to die rather than become some of the things that she had seen, whether she were to marry him or not.

On Friday the 8th of January, Rosie learned that Mrs Crow's husband had been killed, and so she and her mother went round to take her some black things to wear. She had been too distraught to go and get some for herself. Rosie felt helpless in the face of such abject despair, but she decided to go back every day for a while, if Mrs Crow were agreeable.

On the 11th it rained cats and dogs again, and Rosie remembered how Ash used to joke that English rain was more like horses and donkeys sometimes. Then on the 14th there was news that Mrs Burman's son Bill had been wounded and was in Lady Meynell's Hospital. Mrs McCosh became very excited about this, and immediately wanted to go there just in case she ran into Lady Meynell. They did not see Lady Meynell, but Bill Burman was in good spirits. He had a shattered knee and would always walk stiffly because the surgeons simply fused all the bones together. He was mainly worried about how it might affect his golf. Clearly, he would have to give up tennis. On the 17th Vera Burman came to tea and she told Rosie that Bill found her visits very comforting, and looked forward to them a great deal. Rosie told her that she would quite like to work in a hospital, because it was so awful to feel useless at times like these.

On Saturday the 23rd there was snow and fog, and Rosie had to break the ice in her jug in the morning before she could wash.

Mrs McCosh announced that it was as heavy as the great snow-fall of 1881. Christabel, Ottilie, Sophie and Rosie made a huge snowman in the garden, but had to keep coming back in to warm up in between forays. What if it has been snowing on Ash like this? Ottilie said, 'Don't worry, there couldn't possibly be any battles in weather like this.'

And then it thawed in the night and the lovely huge snowman melted away completely.

On the 25th Mrs McCosh went into Holders to ask about getting her violin valued and serviced. She only played it when everybody but the servants was out, and had long ago given up entertaining guests with it. She possessed genuine talent and a very romantic style, and the girls used to love it when they came home and were looking for their keys at the front door, and they would hear her in the morning room. She would prop the music up in front of the Bible on its lectern, and throw herself into pieces by Kreisler. Now that the war had got going, and she was particularly anxious about Ashbridge, she was playing more than ever, but only the servants had the profit of it. They knew every note of 'Schön Rosmarin'.

On the 27th Sidney Pendennis came home on leave and he said that Albert and Ash were bearing up well. He brought letters from Ashbridge, and a strange souvenir, which was a German bullet exactly stuck through a British one so that it made a St Andrew's cross. Everybody thought it a wonderful and strange thing, which indeed it was. Rosie put it in her jewellery box, next to the curtain ring that had been her original token of engagement from Ashbridge.

Another letter came from Ashbridge, in which he said that he had encountered Daniel Pitt, after how many years? He reported that Daniel was in the Royal Flying Corps now, but just a tyro, and had done a forced landing not far from Ash's trench, in between the lines. Apparently Daniel had had to hide in a shell hole until darkness fell, and meanwhile the Germans had completely wrecked his aeroplane with shells. Rosie thought about Daniel for a while, remembering how he'd once wrapped himself in a sheet and pretended to be a ghost in broad daylight, which had not been the slightest bit frightening.

On the 28th Rosie and her mother went to meet a huge convoy of Belgian refugees at Victoria Station, to assist in the general mustering and sorting. They were poor souls, miserable and confused, but also overwhelmed with gratitude for their friendly reception. Upon their return, Mrs McCosh learned that her violin was worth £90. It seemed an astonishing piece of good news amid all the gloom spread by the casualty lists. Rosie went to supper with Mr and 'Mamma' Pendennis. Between them they managed, for a couple of hours, to erect a thin facade of cheerfulness and optimism. Before Ashbridge left he had arranged a code, and from his latest letter they were able to work out that he had been in a place called Sanvic, but was now in Kemmel.

15

Daniel Pitt to his Mother (2)

A mysterious location not permitted to be revealed even to mothers,
but you know my squadron number anyway, so do write back
to that, somewhere near St Omer.

4 *February 1915*

Ma chère maman, elegante et magnifique!

You'll never guess who I've run into! I came down in front of the
lines – but worry not! It happens all the time and is only to be expected,
and I was unharmed, unlike my poor machine, a pretty little Morane-
Saulnier whose name was Florence, you may remember, and was imme-
diately shelled to smithereens by Fritz – and I managed to get into one
of our trenches, and guess who was in it! I'll write and tell you tomorrow.

Tomorrow. Same address.

It was Ashbridge Pendennis, he of two doors down when I was little
and you were even younger, the American boy with the two brothers who
was always mooning around Rosie McCosh, and she around him. He
and the aforementioned frères *are with the HAC, and he was 'mighty*
glad' to see me after all these years. He tells me that he is engaged to
Rosie. This information made me feel very forlorn, I have to tell you,
because I rather fancied her for myself. What lovely grey eyes! Or were
they blue? Such wondrous cascades of chestnut hair! Such touching freckles
and an adorable little nose!

I will tell you of my most recent escapades tomorrow.

Gee, it's tomorrow already.

I took a potshot at a Taube with my carbine and missed. Couldn't
get close enough to take a hack with my sabre.

We had the most enormous binge in the mess, which was of far greater
danger to me than Fritz is ever likely to be. I woke up in a ditch with
frost on my beard, if I had had one. We'd been playing Cardinal Puff
which is most lethal. Apparently there was a terrific rag after I passed

out, and now the mess looks as though a shell has landed in it. Please don't tell my mother – she would be very shocked. Nay, tell her that I have spent part of my spare time on my knees in church, and the rest reading the work of lady poets!

But why did we binge and rag? Chère maman, *it was because a Rumpler flew over the aerodrome yesterday, and dropped some eggs somewhat inaccurately, so yours truly ran outside with the aforementioned carbine, and took a potshot at him. By some miracle I got the pilot in the calf, and he had to land before he passed out. Ergo (and eheu!) one captured intact machine, and two disgruntled Fritz aviators! We packed the pilot off to the casualty clearing station in the tender, but the observer stayed for the binge and rag, and is now in the guardroom with all his regrets and the mother of all hangovers. So,* chère maman, *behold the hero of the hour!*

Heroically yours, grandes bises, je t'embrasse! *Any news of Archie?*
Ton fils dévoué,
Daniel P.

16

The Red Sweet Wine of Youth (1)

Rest camp at Sanvic. Have to lie down in ten inches of mud. Spend a lot of time unloading supplies in Rouen. Aching all over. Food was inedible. First fatigues moving hundreds of bales of hay. Second was loading tins of petrol. Empty tins end up as water vessels, so water in the front line always has the tang of petrol. My friend Hutch says he can tell from the flavour whether or not the can has been BP. Fun dropping matches into the cans to burn off the vapour.

Detailed to go and help in the bacteria lab. The Major extremely nice. Made specimens of bacteria for him taken from wounds. Let me see them under the microscope. Thanked me and asked me to come again. Told him I was really an engineer, and asked him what he thought I should do.

8th Jan. Pay parade and I got eight francs. Found a Frenchwoman with a tub and paid for a bath. Bought a fur coat made of a piebald goat. Not popular with pals – smells of former owner.

9th. Was sick, and so allowed to slack. An aeroplane came down between the lines, and after dark the pilot and observer crept up and dropped into the trench. We filled them up with tea, and damn me if one of them didn't turn out to be Daniel Pitt, an original Pal, who used to live the other side of Rosie's house! Had a good chinwag about childhood days. Said he'd crashed three times in the last fortnight. Par for the course, apparently. Feel envious of the birdmen, but by God, you have to be darned brave. They get colder than we do. Wouldn't catch me up there.

10th. Cookhouse fatigues. Felt very poorly. Probably flu. A lot of us got sick in the cattle truck. Thirty to a car.

12th. Some sweets arrived from my aunt. Extremely cold. This is a decent place. Lots of food locally. Enemy aeroplane dropped two bombs and didn't hit anything. Terrific noise, however. One of the men got run over by a lorry (five tonner) from head to foot. Thought he was dead, but just squashed into mud so had to dig him out. Contusions, that's all. That driver makes a custom of running people over.

This isn't the glamorous kind of soldiering we'd volunteered for.

13th. Marched seven miles in the rain. Glad to arrive. Quartered in a school. Shell burst five hundred yards away. A fine sight, my first real experience of shells. Grenade practice. A serious business. You light the fuse and have five seconds to throw it.

No idea where to go or what to do when we finally arrived. No plan, nobody came to meet us. Ruined village, heaps of engineers' supplies, knife rests, barbed wire, shovels, trenching tools, etc. Only intact structure was a grandstand with the paint peeling off.

Slumped on the green and smoked while officer went off to find someone who knew anything. Ended up distributed between least demolished cottages. With eight others in a tiny room with one shell hole punched neatly through it. Shell still lying there. Decided that it probably wouldn't explode. Hutch scrawled 'RIP' on it. I slept very well.

Dug latrines. Always the first thing to do. Don't even wait for officers to detail you. You arrive, unshoulder your weapon and shoulder your spade. Pulled up some leeks, dug a nice latrine. We pray, 'Dear Lord, please do not let a shell land in the latrines, because I am buggered if I am going to dig another one.' Ours has a horizontal pole to perch on. Nothing to clean up with. Can't bear to use Rosie's letters, so am using letters from anyone else, after memorising and replying. Post is extraordinarily efficient, considering. A lot of the lads forced to use their love letters. I don't smoke much, makes me feel dizzy, so use my cigarette ration to buy letters, as well as the extra rum. A sad fate for beautiful feminine sentiments.

14th. Went on fatigues to repair the road. Mud and water! Shovelled mud, sank in mud, breathed in mud. Felt like a fly on flypaper. Saw Albert, and he was the same dear brother, but very tired of it all. Plenty of shells.

Hutch found out that two old women still living in the village would sell us coffee and bread if we got there first. Like cartoon witches from a book of fairy tales. Found cans of Scotch broth just lying at the side of the road. Hooray! And they had a grand-daughter who was prepared to 'teach French'.

Hutch says that we are nobody's children. Don't know exactly what he means. Must ask. He keeps repeating it. Certainly, nobody seems to be in charge of looking after us, so we do it. Shot a rabbit. Last one in Flanders. Stewed it up with leeks. Bullet went through the ribs so no real meat was spoiled. Thought of how Rosie would have been upset by my shooting a rabbit. Such a big soft spot for animals. Expect she would have cried. Hutch made ripping little stove out of a biscuit tin and set it up in a niche. Call it 'the Savoy Grill'. The Major said it was just about the best in the battalion. He brought the anti-gas equipment today. Onward Christian soldiers.

15th. Re-dug a dugout that collapsed because of a shell. Spent all day in it. Stink perfectly horrible. Shells going overhead sound like carts on cobbles. Worked from 8.30 to 4.30 and then detailed to take bundles of wood to the Lancashires. Went in single file and fell in mud over and over. Bullets whizzed above us, and when they fell in the mud, they sizzled. Shell nearby made me jump, but already quite used to them. The Germans have extra-ordinary sniper. We put three sticks in a row poking up above the trench, and he snapped each in turn. Definitely don't approve of shrapnel. Fizzes and whizzes about like lethal metal bees. Causes one to execute a tactical narrowing of front, and keep it narrow thereafter. Rifles bunged up with mud and unshootable.

10 p.m. Hutch and a few others detailed to go and carry a pump from the chateau to the trenches. I was groaning in the latrine in the dark so was let off. Hutch brought back a spent bullet. Said it had been hell. Completely drenched and covered with stinking filth. You throw yourself down in the mud every time a star shell goes up, and Hutch fell straight into the corpse of a horse. Stretcher parties stumbling about in the dark, collecting the dead and wounded, because it can't be done by day. Continuous muttering of curses in the dark. Like the murmuring of nocturnal animals. Hutch said they finally delivered the pump and got cups of tea, only twenty yards from the Boche.

Morning. Cut off the bottom of my greatcoat. Did as he said.

We look like a tribe of vagabonds. The skin of that rabbit ended up under my helmet. Great joy over the arrival of balaclavas/gum boots. Collected pieces of string to tie faggots and little lumps of wood to my webbing. No fire means no warm food/no warm hands. Woke up covered with snow, clothes so stiff with frost they crackled when I moved. Bearded like the pard, and beard plastered with mudcrust, unlike the pard.

16th. Went on fatigues to build a shed for the horses, but mostly slacked. Shrapnel shell burst above a cattle shed and got men inside. Caught flea, big enough to use in a cockfight. Cracked it with thumbnail. Very satisfactory. Some of us getting mudbite. Difficult to sleep at night because of rats playing tag/British bulldog/other joyous games all over us.

Fatigues, dogsbody stuff, carrying sandbags. Ain't there no respect for territorials? Truth is that a soldier spends life digging and lumping things, shovelling mud and wreckage off roads etc. The ditches bridged by single planks, so at night you spend your time climbing out of the ones you fell in. Common knowledge that Army keeps us busy to keep us sane.

17th. My birthday! Package from Rosie! Sweets and a knife and fork, amongst other things. Detailed to bury a horse. You can tell by the smell what's died nearby. Donkey smells different from horse or fox, but I haven't detected any difference in the whiff of decaying Boche/Frenchies/Gonzoubris. A rat ran up my leg. Happy birthday, dear Ash, happy birthday to me. Another rumour death of Kaiser, German surrender imminent.

French bodies unburied everywhere. Stinks to high Heaven, even though January. God help us if summer comes. Corpses seem to watch you, especially at night.

18th. Snowed hard. You show up against the snow even at night. On parade 10.30 inspection.

New trench made for us by sappers. Classy affair, little cupboards cut into sides, proper parapet of sandbags, dugouts to curl up in. Duckboards, and sinks to collect the water, so that you can bail it out. Huns only a few yards away, invisible behind sandbags/ mounds of earth, apart from dead ones, with their short hair and new uniforms, lolling together in front, like sleeping drunks. Huns have annoying grenade catapults. Guard duty last night. Told to

68

fire off a round every ten minutes. Don't know why. Nothing to aim at, even if you could see. Perhaps it just keeps the guard awake. Important to make us feel we're doing something. You can poke your head above the parapet as much as you like in the dark. Pop it down again the moment a star shell goes up. I like the star shells. The strongest and blackest shadows. Violence of the light miraculous. Nice to have something flying about that doesn't explode. Wouldn't put it past the Huns to invent some kind of gadget for seeing us at night. Hope not to be the first one they try it on.

19th. Warmer, but everything soaking wet. The mud! Got into A Company and saw Albert. Lots of old letters. Birthday box from home. Thought about Rosie a great deal. Somehow she keeps me going.

Hutch said, 'Why do the Huns have a black sandbag every few yards?' Became quite a topic of conversation. Decided to find a German speaker who could shout very loudly, so that we could ask. Failed. Decided to shout question in French. Nothing doing, so still in ignorance. Probably just took a delivery of black hessian.

20th. 0400. Marched to Kemmel in the rain. Really ripping quarters in a school. I allow they're the best we've had so far. Wooden floors to sleep on! Rain rain rain. Received a hamper from Fortnum & Mason thanks to Mr McCosh. Shared it with section. Oh what a treat. Practically cried with joy. Hutch got cooked sausages all wrapped up, still wonderfully edible.

Hutch said, 'If I cop it, will you take care of my diary?'

I said, 'I thought you were writing letters.' He replied, 'Well, a diary is a kind of letter, isn't it?'

I said, 'Is it?' and he said, 'It's a letter to whoever's going to read it in the future. You might even read it yourself when you're old, and then it's like a letter to yourself.'

Asked him where it was and he said knapsack, wrapped up in bit of mackintosh. Asked if anything I'd like him to do, and I said, 'Go and see Rosie,' and he said 'What should I say?'

Said, 'Tell her I died well. Even if I died screaming with my legs blown off. Tell her to go ahead without me. Tell her that I was loved by my comrades,' and Hutch said, 'Well, that's true, even though you're a Yank.'

Gave him Rosie's address and he put it in the back of his diary.

Stood side by side, at the ready, and Hutch said, 'I love the smell of bacon in the morning. It takes you straight home.' Delicious whiff of impending breakfast washing over us from the support lines. Hutch nodded in the Fritz's direction and said, 'I wonder what that lot have for breakfast.'

Said, 'By all accounts it's sausage made from Belgian babies.'

21st. Still raining. Slack day. Truly needed it. Drank some red wine yesterday, and also water, and one of them has upset my stomach. Rosie sent sterilising pills and am going to use them in my H_2O.

22nd. Very cold. Germans shelled the hill as usual. Fatigues carrying bricks up to firing trench. Hell, absolute hell. Weight of bag about 75 lb. Fired on by snipers. Through mud up to knees. Cover behind dead animals etc. Dead French in dugout. One bullet missed me by a yard. Was glad to get back.

23rd. Aeroplanes. Shrapnel on hill as usual. Much brighter day. Started at 4.45. Finished at 11.45.

24th. Aeroplanes overhead. Daniel came and stunted. Marched to billets in school. Slept soundly.

Hutch watches the enemy shells flying over, to see where they'll land. Don't like that game at all. Have to duck down in a split second. German gunners spent the afternoon bombarding ruined farmhouse. Completely pointless, terrible waste of ammunition. Suppose they want to keep busy. I like the sound of Jack Johnsons, as long as they're at a decent distance. The sausages come over broadside on. Make the loudest bang conceivable. Rings inside your head. Hate the whiz-bangs at night.

25th. Inspection 10.30. Moved into church for the night, slept on chairs.

26th. Very wobbly service going on when I awoke. Parade 7 a.m. full kit – expected an attack by Prussian friends. Funeral service and baptism after breakfast. Rather weird experience. It was so barbaric – bells and Latin and incense. Concert in the evening. Very funny. Officers dressed as French tarts, down to a T.

Am getting ribbed because some of the rifle ammo is misfiring or not firing at all, and the guilty ammo is American. Do feel a little guilty about the American rounds. Huge task to find and remove them. A lot of our shells are duds. They go over and land, but no explosion. Daniel came and stunted again.

17

Rosie Waiting in Eltham (1)

On the 1st of February, it was turning very much colder, and it occured to Rosie that she could unravel old things and make new ones. She reasoned that if she were Ash, she would want a balaclava and mittens, so she set about dismantling an old scarf that had begun to fall apart on its own. Ottilie kept her company, turning some worn-out sheets side-to-middle so that the servants could have them.

On the 3rd of February there was such a fearsome gale all night that Rosie just lay in bed and shuddered. She could not sleep nor turn her mind off for thinking of what it must be like for Ashbridge. Even praying could not calm her agitation because all her prayers turned into desperate pleading.

Her mother was sixty on the 6th and she and her sisters went to a concert at the Queen's Hall. Rosie could not remember the programme. She was still visiting the Cottage Hospital almost every day, and was beginning to find it both more easy and more comforting than it had been, because nothing lifts one out of misery more effectively than being inspired by sympathy.

On the 10th there was good news, which was that Bill Burman was out of hospital. He came to dinner with his wife, and was obviously in severe pain. He grimaced and winced a great deal, and it was awkward to sit him down at table because the underneath of it was somewhat complex and he unable to bend his leg at the knee. Even so, he seemed quite cheerful. He said that he was glad he'd done his bit, and was just as glad he was out of it. He said he had seen things too ghastly to describe, and that he did not feel that he had really taken it all in yet. He said that the jitters often take a long time to arrive, according to the doctors. Now he had the worry of his brother Edward being out there. His golf club had appointed him their new secretary, apparently, and he was very pleased about that. It was quite a consolation. He had been thinking that he would help to set up a local firewatch, because the Germans were clearly very keen to wage war on civilians as well as on soldiers.

He and Rosie had a sparkling little dispute about whether it was time to give up thees and thous in modern verse. Bill said that there were so many words that rhymed with thee and thou that it would be a shame to give them up, because it would limit what one can say, and Rosie maintained that there was always another way to say the same things. They did agree that spelling rhymes ought to be disallowed. Bill asked Rosie if she would read them some of her verses, but she said that she did not feel she had written anything good enough yet.

18

Still May Time Hold Some Golden Space

27th. All sorts of inspections etc. Orders to stand to at half-hour's notice. Kaiser's birthday attack expected. Aeroplanes. Route march. Pay parade – fifteen francs!

Germans are using their dead to consolidate parapets. Stink abominable when wind shifts. Don't know how they put up with it. Bad enough casual bodies lying around in places where unretrievable. Out in front are two French officers, beautiful in scarlet and blue, bloating and rotting. Also three pigs and a cow. Always a point where you can't help vomiting. Then you get sent out at night, have to bury them with respirator on. Boche do the same. Unspoken agreement not to notice each other.

28th. Direct to trenches. Description of our trench. Rather wide, would be waterlogged, but thank God frozen hard. After passing through danger zone halt behind fire trenches then proceed across fields. Fired at. Little cave at the end of our trench. Nine men in a space six by four with brazier in middle. My, it was fine, though all had to go on guard at night for one hour. Stevenson was Rear Admiral today, got killed carrying latrine buckets up communication trench. What a way to go. Hutch just got there in time to give him a last puff on gasper. Hutch pleased about Players in the post. Slept well. Daniel stunted and dropped bottle of whisky on a little parachute.

29th. Water bottle frozen. 1200 approx. Fritz began shelling with lyddite five yards from trench! Again at 1500. Read almost all of *Quo Vadis* today. No good getting panicky. If they get you they get you, and much safer in a trench than not. Came back across fields as moon was too bright for usual way. Kemmel shelled. Killed twelve.

Can't help thinking about how nice it is when resting behind the lines. No stench except when the wind turns in the wrong direction.

And you can sleep. Slept for twelve hours once, all my webbing and equipment on, and my boots. The sergeant didn't have the heart to disturb me.

30th. Did not do anything but waited to be called as raid expected. Mother sent me Vest Pocket Kodak. Not supposed to have it but lots do, and nobody gets charged. Took picture of Hutch, with the stray dog we adopted when it was dug out of a ruin. Call it Fartillery because of productive guts.

Comradeship. Nothing like it in civvy street. Rises up out of your heart because so relieved to be still alive and temporarily safe. Sergeant from the South Lancashire Regiment turned up, when we were completely done in, with a huge jug of beer in his hands. Gave it to us, and went. Didn't have to do it, could have given it to his own boys.

31st. Fatigues cleaning up shelled houses for fresh billets. Shells certainly wreak havoc. So sad to see these homes empty and think that a few months ago this village prosperous and happy. At night did headquarters quad at chateau. Beautiful night, and imagined I was at home, i.e. bath then dinner with Mother, after dinner, study, and then bed. Boche interrupted with shells.

Hands need time to heal. Always blistered/cracked/bleeding so much labour, exposure frost and water. Delicious to ease boots off and waggle toes and just expose flesh to air. As usually on fifteen minutes' notice to depart, we're expected to sleep with boots on, but hardly ever do. The WOs don't want to sleep in theirs either, so conspire in pretence.

1st of Feb. Quite tired. Feet hurting for first time. Think it's rheumatism. Slept well in school. Rosie's packet arrived, and scarf from Mrs Beale. Dreamed of Mother, that she was out here with me.

Keeping us fit and busy marching us round the countryside. Choreographed tourism, get to see troops from all over the place, pleasant little ruined villages. We go to tiny place of Albertine and Emma, two fat/cheerful sisters who'll cook anything we bring. They make omelettes, and a kind of soup that ain't soup at all, milk with crumbled bread, and there's horrible vinegary wine, coffee, local beer (not bad at all). Always a scuffle to get near stove, blazes away like billy-o. Plenty of fuel in ruined houses. Five francs on pay day, enough for omelettes at Emma and Albertine's. Hardly understand a word they say. Make do with patois.

2nd. Warm today. Raining. Made hurdles all afternoon with sticks and string. Dreamed last night of Baltimore. Far away and long ago.

Re. lice: all been bedded down in church, and Catholic lice got into this poor Protestant's clothes, and poor Protestant clothes of brothers'. Quite enjoyed seeing Catholic services. Sort of barbaric magnificence.

Difficult to wash at best of times. Have to find an intact cottage and pay for bucket of hot water, then strip off in front of them and wash, because they want to guard their bucket. Aren't bothered by sight of naked soldiers, certainly do roaring trade.

Spent much time picking lice out of each other's hair, like monkeys, but then shaved heads completely. Seem to be different kinds of lice. Head kind, bedding and clothing kind, and the private parts kind, obtainable from naughty girls. Not got that kind, because well behaved, but plenty of boys say that you didn't need to be having fun to pick them up somehow. Then you get scepticism from MO.

Told not to scratch bites because diseases get in. Louse shit in the wounds. Skin comes up in weals and scars.

Instructed to soften nits with vinegar, then comb hair over and over with nit comb, then burn the nits. Else soak rag in paraffin, sleep with that on head, held in place with bathing cap. Before use of bathing cap again cook it in oven, if can find one. Total absence of bathing caps, paraffin and handy oven, however, so shave heads and make smelly bonfire of hair. Odour just like farrier shoeing horse.

Body lice little blighters survive washing pot unless most extremely hot. Don't actually live on you. Live in seams of clothes and visit just exactly when about to relax/feel a bit happy/composed. Then bite under armpits and round waist, fury of itching/scratching/swearing. Were told to soak clothes in Lysol and rub selves all over with paraffin and eucalyptus, and sprinkle inside uniforms with sulphur.

Hutch said, 'But, sir, we don't have any of those things,' and MO replied, 'Very true, Private Hutchinson, but I have been telling you what you ought to do, and not what you actually can do.'

Best thing to shave every single hair body, so nowhere to attach eggs, and then spend hours going through seams of uniforms picking out the lice/cracking them with thumbnail.

Think that lice good for morale. Companionable occupation when nothing happening, can sit on pediments naked/shivering, cracking lice/cracking jokes without thought of shells/shrapnel. Sometimes keep a tally. If male louse, call out 'Dog!' and if female, call out 'Bitch!' Boys scratch score on side of trench with bayonet. Always on mission break all known records.

If a purplish red one, means recently feasted, your own blood explodes over your fingers. Enjoy killing those ones most of all.

If infestation very severe, scrape them off with knife. Heard that in the hospitals they have lice infesting stumps of limbs.

19

Rosie Waiting in Eltham (2)

The 4th of February 1915 was beautiful, serene and sunny, and Rosie felt much happier, in case Ashbridge was also having a good day. She wrote two letters to him, one telling him that the garden was full of aconites, and mentioning in the other that Bouncer had cut his paw on a piece of broken glass.

On the 5th she and her sisters went to an exhibition of Modern Portrait Painters. Rosie was not impressed, but Christabel thought that some of them were very fine. Ottilie said how strange it was that civilisation just managed to carry on, even in wartime. Sophie said it seemed very anonymous, which puzzled the others until they realised that she meant anomalous.

That night was wild and wet, the wind lowing like a cow in the eves of the house.

On the 6th Rosie wrote a poem for Ashbridge, and then went to St John's to pray for him. She noticed for the first time the plaque on the wall commemorating the two Pitt brothers who had died in the Boer War. She wondered at herself, that she had been going there all these years and never noticed it before. The carving was wonderful, particularly of the drapery. It put her in mind of Archie and Daniel Pitt. She knew that Archie was in India on the North-West Frontier, trying to control the Afghans, and that Daniel had been there too, but now he was in France in the Royal Flying Corps. Rosie knew that his chances of lasting at all long were very poor indeed. She felt the same kind of lurch in her stomach as she did when she thought of Ashbridge being killed. It would be such a sadness, because he had been great fun as a boy and probably still was. How nice it would be to see him again, she thought, and smiled at the memory of him vaulting over the wall, and wondered if he still looked the same. He had very bright blue eyes, she remembered, and long legs and narrow shoulders.

Rosie did nothing on the 7th, because she was suffering from a deep lassitude born of helplessness, but on the 8th she went to the Cottage Hospital to see if she could be of any help there, and came back feeling not at all well. She blamed the fumes of Lysol, which made you feel quite drunk and heady.

On the 11th it turned out that Rosie's lassitude and reaction to Lysol had really been the German measles, and it was perfectly horrible. She hoped fervently that one couldn't get it twice, which is what people always used to say. Mrs McCosh moved her into the spare room because it was further from the rest of the bedrooms than hers was. The rash subsided very quickly, and Rosie's mother devoted the morning to reading her the poems of Mrs Hemans. In the afternoon Rosie got up, had a bath and dressed, but did not go downstairs. Rosie decided that she did not like Mrs Hemans very much, and, if you were going to read women poets, you would get a lot more out of Christina Rossetti and Elizabeth Barrett Browning, of both of whom Mrs McCosh disapproved. Rosie enjoyed Elizabeth Barrett Browning's experiments, and was slightly ashamed of not enjoying Robert Browning at all. She wrote to the Poetry Bookshop to complain that their 1911–12 anthology of contemporary Georgians did not contain one woman poet, saying that 'This cannot be because there are none of the requisite high standard; it must be because you have failed to take note of who they are, or have not troubled yourselves to find out.'

On the 12th and 13th Rosie got up and dressed, but stayed in the spare room, reading Coleridge and Keats. She felt considerably better, but still exceedingly weak and low in spirits. Mrs McCosh came up and offered to read to her but she declined, as she preferred to read to herself, and was not in the mood for any more Mrs Hemans.

On the 14th Rosie felt particularly desolate because it was St Valentine's Day.

On the 15th of February, the news came about Ashbridge Pendennis.

20

The Red Sweet Wine of Youth (2)

3 rd of Feb. Beautiful day. Nothing doing. Slept in church where lice caught. Daniel flew over, upside down at fifty feet. Wondrous.

Find can now buy huge meals of custard from what used to be post office. Made in big fish mould, so call it 'Kemmel Fish'. More people selling coffee. Impressive how adversity turns out entrepreneurs. Will always be someone clever enough. World proliferates with little Hamilton McCoshes.

Not supposed to be in village at all, so technique is invent reason to go to quartermaster's store/think up complaint that has to be dealt with by MO. Got put off when Boche started shelling village again. Killed nine men, but eventually Kemmelfishitis returns, and off we go.

4th. Awoke in church to find men kneeling all around me – weird. An old lady nodded to me, but after returning nod found was nodding and bowing to a saint. Slept well. Dreamed of Baltimore again.

Fond memories of worst trench. Had to get there in dark, and the ground frozen solid except covering of slime. Turnips poking out of soil so slipped and stumbled every step. Fell over French corpse, fell in ditch. Got snagged by brambles and thorns, panic because got left behind whilst trying to detach. Man in front whispers what's just happened so doesn't happen to one behind. Some ditches single plank across, always slippery with mud. Laden down like mules with equipment and provisions.

New trench an old one. Was German then French, shallow slimy one. Fritz hands and feet sticking out of parapet. Cuts in hands festering because nowhere to wash. Nearly vomited from stench. Hutch did. No sleep because of smell, so set about improving trench instead.

Realised couldn't deepen it. Ground too hard, so went behind lines at night, retrieved bricks from broken-down cottage. Bricks not best protection (shatter), but did raise/improve parapet. Sun came out morning, melted ground. Back in putrid stuff again.

Beautiful day, and was peaceful. I love to watch the aeroplanes. Daniel Pitt stunts almost every day on way back from patrol. Came in very low today, practically head height, bombed us with rotten apples. Completely mad, must have been fired at by every Boche machine gun within a mile. Those who stunt at low altitude don't last long, they say. Has painted 'Long Live the Pals' under bottom ailerons in bright red. Makes me want to cry. Good old Daniel.

21

Rosie's Poem, 6 February 1915, First Draft

Outside the winter wind is moaning,
Death is knocking at the gate,
The house, my heart, the world is groaning,
Cracked by tempest, war, and fate.

The bombs descend, the houses burn,
Death's thirst for blood we cannot slake.
I wring my hands, and, helpless, yearn
For one I beg Him not to take.

My Love's dwelling place is mud,
And rain and fire and sharded sleet,
And sudden hurt and bright dark blood,
Where Hell and Earth conspire to meet.

Now Christ protect him, bring him light
'Til all the enemy depart,
And Christ protect him through this night
Whose fearful tears,
Whose bitter fears
Tear and grapple at my heart.

22

The Sweet Red Wine of Youth (3)

5 th of Feb. Moved at night Lindenhowe where slept in barn near German lines. On guard and really splendid to see trees silhouetted against sky by German star shells. Last night a tenor in German lines sang Brahms's Lullaby just as sun went down. So beautiful almost wept. Not a dry eye in trench. How sleep the dead.

Had breakfast at brazier. Tinned salmon, biscuits, jam, big pot of tea. Young lad from Croydon, been cooper's apprentice, name Harold Rumthorpe. Can't say we were particular friends. War throws all kinds together, makes you comrades, not necessarily friends. HR was nineteen, six years younger than me, and I'm in shipping and he was tradesman. Don't know how he got in the HAC, wasn't exactly 'gentleman ranker'. Probably came out with his 'gentleman', like Hutch. Liked him, though never really had conversation. Just cursed/slogged along together.

HR spotted captive balloon. Were trying to work out if one of ours/theirs. He stood up to get proper look. Moment of inadvertence, no chance to get to him quickly enough. Next second, brazier kicked over and was spattered, glistening speckles red and white, and Harold fell in Hutch's arms. Hutch leaning back against parapet, repeating, 'Oh God, oh God.'

Took 45 mins to die. Pitiful noises enough to break heart. Bullet took off back of head, nowhere to lay him down in comfort. Orderly crawled over from next trench, but couldn't do anything, and couldn't get Harold out in plain view of enemy. Laid him on parados, and that night carried him back to ruined cottage and buried him in garden. Already five graves there, soldiers planted like vegetables, against the day of harvest. Plenty bullets whizzing. Several times had to wait for clouds to roll back across moon, and throw ourselves flat every star shell. Private who'd been ordained, recited burial service from memory, very loud and clear, so Huns would hear us. Boche tenor with beautiful voice responded, sang Brahms's Lullaby again. Had to cry. Hutch made cross of sticks.

Stark scene, strangest and most powerful ever experienced in my life. Will haunt me/make me think thoughts almost too large. Harold Rumthorpe, apprentice cooper of Croydon, farewell, laid to rest by his brothers, sung to rest by a Hun.

Will always hear those words of the committal ringing out into the night:

'Man that is born of woman hath but a short time to live, and is full of misery. He cometh up, and is cut down, like a flower; he fleeth as it were a shadow, and never continueth in one stay . . .'

That night went back to Kemmel, everyone wondering silently who would be next. Hutch said, 'Don't you wish you'd stayed at home?' Said, 'No,' and H said, 'Me neither.'

6th. After restful day returned to trenches. Lost 5/– at Crown and Anchor. Hutch lost 4/6d. Never again. Hutch now my trench-foot pal. I rub his feet in whale oil, he rubs mine. Have high hopes of success in avoiding it. Heard theory that all this rain caused by shells making water condense as fly through the air. Would have thought that friction would heat air up, not the reverse. So am not convinced, but Hutch believes it.

7th. Am writing about 9.45 a.m. Man yelling from shell hole. Sounds quite mad. Expect to be shelled. Last night brother Albert said he got excellent photos of star shells. Don't know how he knows, because when will he develop the film? After a sniper now, soon shall have a shot myself.

11.30. Poor Lampard just been shot through head as was observing rifle grenade fall. Died at about 1700 hours. Will leave big gap in our section – brother behaved wonderfully. Soldier in shell hole stuck fast by mud, finally stopped yelling, so suppose must have gone west. Once in, you can't get them out, not under fire. Suction incredible. Not even permitted to try.

Huns have our section covered by machine gun. V. dangerous to look over. Was glad to get back to town, slept like a boy. Our relief four hours late, mental strain on all of us awful. Brother Sidney in hospital with flu. Best out of all this. Humour running out. Fartillery hit by shrapnel, had to shoot him. Good friend and lots of fun during brief time we had him.

Spend much time making ruined houses into billets. Such a relief to stand upright/move like a man again. Most tiring thing about trenches is constant creeping, always bent double. Utterly wears you out. Then get sent on fatigues at night, carrying heavy objects thr. ditches and hedges, shell craters full of filth, hurry past snipers' alleys though can't see a thing. Always bogged down, falling, hands raw and split. Mine swollen so much can't put in pockets any more. Thank God for gumboots, otherwise God knows what would feet be. All look like vagrants/ruffians, rags in place of uniform, gaunt/hollow faces/stubble that grows for weeks before get hot water. But so goddarned beautiful, wash/shave faces and heads, drink hot sweet tea, put on new clothes, sleep! Never feel more contented.

Kept nerve, but beginning to give in to exhaustion. Would be content to be shot through head just to be relieved of it. Sometimes just slump down with all my kit on, soaking wet/trembling, so fast asleep might as well be dead. Only jerk awake when someone prods/says, 'Come on, Yank, fatigues to do! What bliss!'

Don't mind being called 'Yank'. Everyone suitable nickname. Anyone Scottish Jock, anyone Welsh Taffy, anyone Irish Paddy/Spud. Anyone bald Curly, and fellow with tight black curls Bogbrush, and fellow amazingly thin Wobbles. Charlie White called Chalky, Albert Black Snowy, Robert Quick Sluggish. Millers always called Dusty. Shortarses called Lofty.

After fitting out billet, found had to go back to same trench. Lampard's death smartened our ideas up, started filling sandbags by moonlight. Everything more intense at night. Perfectly beautiful. When wind shifts and reek of rotting meat vanishes few blessed minutes, can smell soft damp scent of countryside. Magnesium shells cast light so intense can see every detail that's out of shadow, nothing at all of what's in it. Whizz and buzz spent bullets, soft thump as they hit sandbags, sometimes zing of ricochet. Completely flattened bullet struck my webbing, have it in my pocket.

Sound of firing broke out to the north, started rolling down the line towards us, so manned the parapet/waited for order to fire. But no attack to repel. Another shitfight.

Dig and dig. Only way to get rid of water is dig ever deeper. Now got sumps every few yards, covered with doors fr. ruined houses, but never enough sumps to soak up rain, never enough sunshine to dry out ground. Winter bodies take longer to rot. No flies to lay eggs to make maggots. Bodies swell up with water. Stink in spite of cold. Only frost stops stink. Collect all corpses poss, but sometimes imposs. because too risky. Not long ago billeted in a barn, but perfume too retchingly bad. Turned out was full of dead Frenchies been there for months, just covered with straw.

Don't know if water or corpses, but all got diarrhoea at once, now resting behind lines. Turned nice respite into nightmare, have to scramble over each other in dark try to get to latrines, out in field down road. Fortunately been snowing, so enough light to see by. No fun falling into latrines. If not get there in time, scrub self off with snow. Been taking any number No. 9 pills, but not helping much. Put on show for Brigadier, very good one. Several unscheduled intervals as some made a dash for it. Even interval when Brigadier had to make dash. He is good old boy just as darned tough as we are. When turns up at trench borrows Hutch's rifle and pops up for snapshot. Hands it back, says, 'Thank you, private. An old dog's got to keep his hand in somehow.' Know for certain he got two Huns, because lieutenant saw it through periscope. Brigadier saw the South African war, oak leaves on his ribbons.

Got rum issued, keeps us going. Lifesaver, even settles stomachs a little. Oh, that lovely hot feeling spreads fire in insides and resets clockwork in skull.

Still not recovered and been sent back to Kemmel in pelting rain, carrying spades/rations/wire/trench stores. Man in front got bullet clean through knee, went down as if poleaxed. Wonder what chances being hit like that, randomly pitch darkness. Envious of stretcher-bearers, get chance to go back. We say that the bullet that gets you has your number on it, going to get you regardless. No point ducking, because might duck straight into path of bullet. Corporal nearly drowned in shell hole, but managed to pull him out after dumped his load. Worked by light of star shells. Fell into hollow then into ditch, both planks across it broken. Soaking wet, gumboots filled with water, will not get dry again for days. Hutch says, 'It's all right kicking sandbags to get the blood flowing again, but you can do yourself some damage without realising. It's better to kick thin air.' He's right. Effective as swinging arms in circle to get blood back into hands. Indescribable cold, extreme ache deep in bones. If any sunlight, even just moment, you look up at little gap in clouds/smile with pleasure, little glimpse Paradise. If don't get warm, start to feel lice, start wriggling/St Vitus's Dance. Written to Mother, asked her to send me Harrison's Pomade, but not arrived.

Think might have to stop writing diary. Palled on me/hands shake too much to write/read back what written. Nerves and cold put together, and pencil can write sodden paper not invented yet. Will try for while yet.

23

One Morning

One morning there was a nice view of a wrecked chateau and a dead German who was swollen up like an observation balloon, but we were only there until evening. Then two of us got hit on the way back at night, because of more random shots that weren't even aimed at anyone. Neither dead, thank God. Blighty wounds only.

Back at the breastworks on St Valentine's Day, when I was thinking of Rosie, the Senior Officer ordered five rounds of rapid fire at dawn. He just wanted to annoy the Huns, because that was his humour. There were no targets to shoot at.

In response the Huns began a barrage of high explosive and shrapnel, and we realised with dread in our hearts that our jovial little piece of mischief was going to have consequences a thousand times out of proportion. We watched the first shells land fifty yards away, and then begin to creep closer. They must have had a first-class observer. At last a shrapnel shell burst right over us, and for a second or two I was aware only of the overpowering ringing inside my head. My first thought was that I was going to be deaf. Hutch got a ball through his water bottle, and he was holding it up for me to see, when I noticed that I had got one through the stomach, and fell backwards, clutching myself, into a pool of filthy water. I remember thinking, 'I hope it's a ball and not a piece of shell case,' and then I passed out.

24

Naught Broken Save this Body (1)

I

Dearest Mother and Father,

*I've got a Blighty wound! I shall be with you in about two weeks' time.
Don't worry as I shall be quite well by then. Please tell dear Rosie that I
shall write to her soon, when I am a little stronger.*

Your own loving and devoted son,

Ashbridge

Passed by no. 1900 censor

2

No. 8 Clearing Hospital
British Expeditionary Force
France

15 February 1915

Dear Miss McCosh,

*Your fiancé (Private Pendennis of the HAC) thought you would like to
know that he was brought to this hospital today wounded. There is, we
believe, no need to worry – the doctor is allowing him to be quiet and restful
for a few days, and then we hope he will be able to go to the base, and
thence to you! Since beginning this note, I have seen the MO again, and
he repeats what he told me earlier in the evening, and so you must not worry
about him too much. From time to time I will send you a line telling you
of his progress, as long as he is here. You will, I know, do your part as well
as you possibly can. Keep up with the faithful earnest prayer and the cheerful
letters. That is all you can do. Let us keep him in God's hands. Be quite
sure that everything the staff and I can do for him we shall do. I have told
his mother that we are all near neighbours – my family live at Sidcup. Do
not worry – there is no need, and I will tell you exactly how he goes on*

89

day to day. He sends all that you would have him send to you. He is constantly thinking of you. Write at once, and above all, pray. I shall see him two or three times a day.

    Yours sincerely,

    H. V. Fairhead (Captain), Chaplain to the Forces

Passed by no. 1670 censor

3

No. 8 Clearing Hospital
British Expeditionery Forces
France

18 February 1915

Dear Miss McCosh,

    This is just a note to say that your fiancé is 'going strong', and the doctor reports well of him. Of course he is sure to have a few bad days, but he is very bright and patient. He is going to write you a line – we are trying to forbid him to write too much – and so you will see for yourself that he is by no means helpless. Keep him in God's hands, as we do here. I will send you a line tomorrow.

    H. V. Fairhead, CF

Passed by no. 1670 censor

4

21 February 1915

My darling Rosie and dearest Pal,

    Well, old thing, it looks as though I have bought a blue ticket home, having been here for just a couple of months!

    I expect you have heard already about me getting wounded, but I thought I should write to you as soon as I possibly could to tell you that I am doing well, and I was waiting to come home for a spell. I don't know if they will let me go back to the front or not (I suppose it depends upon how well I recover) but it looks as though I might soon be back in good old Eltham, at least pro tem. Won't that be swell? Perhaps I'll go into the fire brigade after

THE DUST THAT FALLS FROM DREAMS

all! I am disappointed that my time out here has been cut short, and that I have been here only in the most terrible weather, when it wasn't really possible to do a good job. I was looking forward to spring, so that the Boche and I could have a good old go at each other, unimpeded by continuous rain. It galls me that I might have been put out of action without even having taken part in a proper attack.

Still, I can't help feeling a little relief at the prospect of no more whiz-bangs, no more crumps, no more sausages of the exploding variety. I am looking forward mightily to the other kind. No more lice and Harrison's Pomade, no more woolly bears and Austrian armour-piercers, no more poisonous niffs, no more shaving with Vaseline to save water, no more falling into disused latrines in the dark, no more hot blasts from shrapnel shells, no more filling sandbags all night, no more rats running over my face as I sleep, no more being drenched for days on end. Hooray!

I'll miss Albert and Sidney. Leaving your brothers behind at a time like this is worrying. I won't be here to keep an eye on them! I'll miss my friends too. I've never known friendship like it. From time to time we hate each other, of course, particularly when exhausted, but there's something rather wonderful about sitting around a brazier, playing vingt-et-un *by the light of star shells, with a bunch of pals that you'd never get to meet in ordinary life. It cuts you to the heart when one of them gets killed, especially because most of the deaths aren't by any means as clean and quick as you might think if you weren't familiar with this kind of warfare, but you know that if the Boche get you, your pals will do everything they can to save you. They will go on even when they have not an ounce of strength left. They'll carry you on their backs through waist-deep mud if they have to, and if you sprain your ankle there's always a shoulder to put your arm around whilst you hop along. The comradeship is a beautiful thing. I'm sure hoping I will find it again with you, when we are facing life together, and having to be bold in the face of our difficulties. With any luck there won't be any!*

I'll miss the star shells too. They come in red, white and green, and they illuminate everything that one has to do at night, so one knows where to put that sandbag, and the Hun also unfortunately knows where to point. The thing about star shells is that they make everbody's faces look like the faces of ghosts. It's odd, having that feeling, being a ghost amongst ghosts. I like it, though. I feel at home as a ghost.

What happened to earn me my blue ticket was that on Valentine's Day, just when I was thinking of you, one of our officers thought it was a bit too damned quiet and ordered us to let rip with five rounds of rapid fire, even though we couldn't see anyone to shoot at. We thought we'd ginger up the Hun a little, and entertain ourselves at the same time, so we popped our heads above the parapet and blazed away for a few seconds.

They got very gingered up indeed, and replied with the first direct shelling I have actually been under, and just about the heaviest one imaginable. It was quite a nasty surprise, and not a very gentlemanly response to such a small and playful salvo. It was my valentine from the Kaiser, I suppose. I got yours, and treasure it. It's by the bedside. Did you get mine?

So here I am in hospital with a big scar across my stomach, and a ball or two of shrapnel in a glass jar on the bedside table. They look like old-fashioned musket balls, but smaller. They got twelve of us, but I don't know how many of the others have pulled through. I am happy to tell you, my sweetest darling, that I seem to have come through relatively intact, all affected organs have been stitched up and tucked back in, and here I am, propped up on pillows, albeit painfully, and able to write you a letter about my poor self and my little woes. I keep dropping off, but if I write a bit every time I wake up, I can get quite a lot down.

I don't know when I'll be sufficiently well to travel back, but I sure will be so pleased to see you that I think I may well swoon with the pleasure. Shall we be married at the very first available moment? Get someone to read the banns, I'm coming home!

I'm told they've stopped censoring our letters, so with any luck this will soon get to you intact, as shall I.

Your best friend and best husband-to-be,
Ash

PS Long live the Pals!

Passed by no. 1900 censor

25

Rosie in St John's (1)

Dear Lord, thank you, Lord, for sparing Ash's life and letting him only be wounded so that he can come home with honour but safe.

Thank you, Lord, for making our future possible, for sparing us any more the pain of separation, and thank you for taking away the terrible fear that's been my torment ever since he went, and thank you for this relief.

And I promise, Lord, that when he comes back I will be as good a Christian wife as it is possible to be, and I promise I shall care for him and tend to him and do all I can to make him happy, and I promise I shall strive to bring him closer to you by my own example and persuasion, and when we have children I promise I'll bring them up in the light of your countenance so that you will be their guide and comforter, and please let him recover soon and bring him back to me because without him I am nothing, Lord, and you know how desperate I've been.

26

Naught Broken Save this Body (2)

It was Ash's mother at the door, trembling, unable to speak or to control the muscles in her face. Mrs Pendennis had a piece of brown paper in her hand, folded in half. Millicent let her in, sat her down in the drawing room, and went to call Rosie, as if she knew by instinct what to do.

Rosie came running down the stairs and into the room. She liked to call Ash's mother 'Mamma' because she had spent so much of her childhood at the Pendennis house. Mrs Pendennis was seated by the window, fumbling in her handbag. She looked up, and silently passed the sheet of brown paper to Rosie.

Rosie took the telegram and read it several times. Her hands began to shake. She let out a small cry of agony and then stood quite still as the tears began to cascade down her cheeks. Then she put her hands to the side of her head and began to wail, her grief filling the far corners of that large, emptied house.

Ash's mother drew her down to the sofa and they clutched each other. Millicent came in, left them a tray of tea and biscuits, bobbed and went out. She returned to the kitchen, locked herself in the larder and began to sob. Cookie knocked on the door and demanded to know what was going on. Millicent unlocked it and just managed to relay the news before breaking down again. Cookie put her arms around her and they cried together, just like the women upstairs.

On the sofa, mother and fiancée embraced so tightly that they resembled a strange many-limbed creature. They locked together, rocking and sobbing, their world shrinking, contracting, distorting.

'It's all my fault,' sobbed Rosie at last. 'It's all my fault. Oh God, oh God! It was me, oh God, it was me!'

Mrs Pendennis said, 'How could it be you?'

'I . . . I didn't pray for him . . . the night before he was wounded . . . I was so tired . . . I thought, "Just once it won't matter" . . .'

'Oh, Rosie,' said Mrs Pendennis, 'don't, please don't. Do you think that I wasn't praying?'

27

Rosie in St John's (2)

How have we displeased you? What have we done? How can I live?

What am I supposed to do? What can I possibly do, now that he's gone?

Take me too. Let me die too. Please, Lord, take me too.

You've shut me out of the light. I'm in the dark, like one who has no eyes. All the days of my life, darkness and darkness and nothing but night.

O Lord, I can't get up, my cheek's on the freezing stone, and the tears won't stop, and I'm aching all over from weeping and Mrs Ottway and the priest and the other ladies are trying to raise me.

28

Safe Though All Safety's Lost

I

My dear Rosie,

I really don't know quite how to write to you about poor Ash's death, but first of all let me assure you that he died in no pain and that everything was done to save him. It happened just one week ago today during a bombardment, when a shell burst above the parapet and some balls of shrapnel struck him on the soft part of the hip and entered the stomach. I was just behind him and waited with him whilst the stretcher was brought. The details are awful, but as you loved him and he you, it is better that you know it all. We got him down to the dressing station. He was conscious most of the time and was quite cheerful. He never complained. He was sent at once to Bailleul Hospital where he was taken great care of. He died at 9.20 on Friday the 19th. I would have written before and would have gone with him but we were in the firing line and were not allowed to write or get leave even in such an extreme case. I was too late when I was released on the night of his death and did not get to Bailleul Hospital in any case because I could not walk owing to an ankle injury.

We buried him yesterday, Saturday the 20th, in Bailleul churchyard and on his wooden cross (which I will replace as soon as I can) is written 'Private A. Pendennis, died from wounds received in action 14 February 1915'. He was buried with full military honours and was carried by Ronald Heddewick, Leonard Hutchinson, Edward Burman and myself. The Reverend Captain Fairhead held the service.

Rosie, you can't imagine how sorry I am for you, but you must understand as he was my brother how I must feel, not only for myself and Sidney, but for my poor mother and father. In all your sorrow spare some sorrow for us. May God give us strength to bear all this. I have many of your letters to him. Shall I destroy them or send them back to you? If there is anything I can do for you out here, do not hesitate to ask me.

You have my heartfelt sympathy as you must know, and may God protect us so that if we meet again I can tell you every little incident of our life here.

Yours very sincerely, your old pal,
Albert P.

PS I saw Sidney yesterday and he is devastated of course, but he sends his fondest sympathy to you.

Passed by no. 1900 censor

2

No. 8 Clearing Hospital
British Expeditionary Force
France

27 February 1915

Dear Mr Pendennis,
Your letter arrived yesterday. No doubt your son's letter has reached you by now, giving details of Ashbridge's passing away. I meant to have written to you myself but after we had laid him to rest your other boy seemed anxious to tell you what there was to tell, so I left him to do it. Since, however, you have written, I can only repeat what probably the others have already told you. Ashbridge seemed to be doing really well for some days until the evening before his passing. Then he was restless, but the doctor overcame that and the next morning he seemed to be doing well again. It was only a few hours before he died that his condition caused any alarm, and even then the doctor hoped it was merely one of the bad times through which most of the wounded cases have to pass. But he became worse and I went to him. Though he was unable to talk much he was conscious. You were all very much in his thoughts and he sent you his dearest love and also to his fiancée. He said that he was perfectly happy. I pronounced the absolution over him and said prayers with him while he held my crucifix in his hand. I left him and later went to see him again. He was unconscious, and I commended him to

98

the love and mercy of Our Father and gave him the Blessing. Shortly afterwards he passed with the most peaceful expression on his face. May I say, in all sympathy and love, that of all those who have passed through the veil since I have been here, not one has passed into Paradise leaving behind in our hearts the certainty of that future life more fully and realistically than was the case with your dear boy. With all conviction we can say that he has passed into God's peace. Your son Albert came to see me in the morning and we arranged for the funeral to take place on Saturday afternoon so that he and some friends and an officer could attend. It was all most touching, and your boy was tremendously brave. In case you would like the particulars, the number of the grave is 331. On his grave there stands a plain wooden cross on which is inscribed his name, regiment and number, and also 'died from wounds received in action'. Nothing nobler could be said of any soldier, especially a civilian soldier, at a time like this. He has died nobly for God, for Country, for King, and you will bear your loss as I know he would have had you bear it, nobly too. And so we leave him 'til the Great Day. He will often be with you, closer than he has ever been before. I can sympathise with you so fully, dear friend. Only a week before you lost your son I was home on leave, and the evening before I returned to the front, my youngest and favourite sister (twenty-one years) passed away on account of a Zeppelin raid, and so it is with my heart full of sympathy that I ministered to him and have prayed for you and his dearest ones. But, thank God, our Christian Truth is a glorious thing. Your dear ones often come to cheer us and tell us of their present great joy and we are wrong to wish to rob them of that.

About the other matter of which you wrote. I have seen your son Albert since, and I have given him and his brother my open invitation to come and see me whenever they wish, and I think they may be coming to tea with me shortly. I trust that when you write to them you will say again, what I have already told them, that they must look upon me as a great friend and that I am anxious to be a help to them at any time.

In regard to the leave, I fear it has been stopped for the present, but I am writing to your son Sidney to ask him to call and see me, and perhaps a line to one of his officers may help to give him a few days with you all.

Please excuse me if some of the details of my letter hurt you somewhat – that is quite remote from my intention. What your loss is, one dare not say. I know that I have lost a real friend – we had become close even in the short time that we knew each other – and the whole staff realised that here had passed a man whom our country can ill spare. On their behalf I send sincere sympathy. Personally, I go further, and unite myself with you all a little more fully in your loss, if I may.

Commending you all to the comfort of the Divine Comforter, and in real sympathy, believe me yours very sincerely,
H. V. Fairhead, CF

Passed by no. 1900 censor

3

For yourself alone please

No. 8 Clearing Hospital
British Expeditionary Force
France

1 March 1915

Dear Miss McCosh
My heart has been with you in your awful yet glorious sacrifice since the evening of 19 February times without number. You have been in my prayers daily. I know, though so little, of the dreadful blank which must have come into your life, and I confess how much I have dreaded having to write this letter. If I did not sympathise so fully, it would not have been hard. Only one who really loves and has lately suffered severe bereavement, and has been face-to-face with the severest loss that this world can hold, can really sympathise, and I have been through it all. My heart aches for you, and I know how much you 'don't know how to live'. Oh, how I long to be some comfort to you, but one feels helpless when so far away. If I could only come and speak to you and tell you perhaps it would be easier for us both. You must have heard all the news from letters to Mr and Mrs Pendennis, but I must answer your questions.

Really and truly, Ashbridge was doing splendidly on the Thursday, and the surgeon was more hopeful on that day than he had been at all.

Ashbridge wrote his letters to you and gave them to me, and was most cheerful. On Thursday evening he was rather restless but settled down and had a fairly good night. The next morning he was bright. It was not until the afternoon that he appeared worse, and when I went to him in the early evening he was not so well. The surgeon hoped that it was only one of the little relapses that all the severely wounded have to pass through. However, he got worse, and I went to him again. I was with him also during his last moments of consciousness. It was then that I asked him whether I should give you any message if he did not pull through. 'Yes,' he said, 'give her all my love.' He was perfectly happy, he told me, and I remembered something he had said to me before, perhaps in jest, to the effect that if he should die you would at least always remember him as he was when he was at his best, and would never have the opportunity to grow tired of him! He drifted into unconsciousness at 8.45 on Friday, and he passed away not long afterwards. The exact cause of his death was the shrapnel wound in the abdomen, which pierced the bowel and set up peritonitis.

You have heard all about that touching service in the cemetery. I will not repeat it. You were not forgotten, dear Miss McCosh.

No, your wires did not reach here until the Sunday, I think, and I sent them on to his brother Albert, but somehow or other I seem to think – is it only my imagination? – that he received a letter or two. I wish I had known him better because we had become real friends in those few short sad days, and I admired him greatly.

Dear Miss McCosh, it is remarkable that by the same post by which your letter reached me, one also came from my mother. My favourite sister, Millie, had passed away in a Zeppelin raid the night before I left from my leave at home. Like you, she wrote to say that in her great grief she had had a dream that our dear one had come and talked to her and said she was very, very happy. It comforted my dear mother so much, and she is a different woman now. Our dear ones are very close to us, to cheer us, to talk to us, to inspire us, always present, always working for, always loving us. May your dream not mean that he wants to tell you that he really is living, happy, the same cheerful, loving soul that he was here on earth? I do believe it with all my heart. The spiritual is very real, and when you realise that he has not truly left you, but that he is with you only you cannot see him so easily now, I know how noble you will be, and how happy you will be too. It is not a long, long goodbye, dear friend, it is a goodbye for the time being. Will you read a book, or one chapter of it, if I ask you to do so? It is the Bishop of Stepney's new book In the Day of Battle. *Read the chapter on Our Father carefully. It has helped me no end.*

But you will be tired. I know it is no comfort that I give, or can give, only bald facts. With all my heart I go on my knees even now and ask Him, the Only Giver of Comfort, to send you the only source of comfort – the Divine Comfort – that He may help you bear the Great Sacrifice of love which He has called upon you to make for His sake and for Country's sake. Please remember it is in the spiritual life you will see him, hear him, be close to him.

With all my sympathy and kindest regards, yours very sincerely,
H. V. Fairhead, CF

Passed by no. 1900 censor

29

I Have Need to Busy my Heart with Quietude

The family were seated at breakfast. It was supposed to be one of those breakfasts where everybody drifts down in their own time and helps themselves to what lies within the chaffing dishes. Today Cookie had left kedgeree, devilled kidneys and scrambled eggs, and Millicent was going back and forth with pots of tea and hot water.

However, everybody had appeared at more or less the same time, attracted by the agreeable odours that had drifted up the stairwell, and they were now seated around the long table in the dining room, eating as quietly as they could, out of respect for Rosie's extreme grief, and out of respect for her latest decision, announced the night before.

Rosie had spent three days sitting motionless in the morning room, on the seat by the window, with its long blue cushion that went the length of the bay. Bouncer lay at her feet. Rosie stared at the gate through which Ash had gone to war, and relived again and again the sight of his retreating back, the jaunty wave as he disappeared, the angle of his forage cap over his eyes, the hitching of his haversack. It was as if she had received a violent blow to the back of the head, or been buried beneath an avalanche. She could neither think nor speak. She twisted and untwisted a small handkerchief between her fingers, looking out through the window at Ash's back disappearing, the turn, the jaunty wave.

Rosie's sisters and her mother felt next to useless, although they did their best. They came in and out bearing fresh handkerchiefs, and put an arm around her shoulder and kissed her on the cheek, saying, 'There, there, buck up, poor Rosie.' The trouble with all of them was that they were half English and half Scottish, respectable, and imbued with the powerful emotional restraint that those races have inherited somehow (via God knows what route) from the Spartans. It was a matter of self-conquest, refusal to show weakness, refusal to become a burden to others. This inheritance does not diminish one's natural sympathies, it merely makes them harder to express and to receive, and it is a legacy which it is extremely hard to unlearn. 'Come now, Rosie dear,' said her mother insensitively, 'no amount of snivelling is ever going to bring him back.'

Rosie went round to the house next door every morning, because Ash's mother knew how to weep, and that set Rosie off as well. Rosie felt a little ashamed as they clung to each other, but she desperately needed the release of their mutual tears. She felt, although this was something that she would never have admitted, that Mrs 'Mamma' Pendennis was more of a mother to her than her own had ever been.

In The Grampians the practical sympathy came from Millicent and Cookie. The latter sent up freshly baked biscuits and Millicent delivered them, saying, 'Cookie says please try some of these, and we're both so sorry for your loss, Miss Rosie, we truly are. We was very fond of him too, you know, miss. Please ring if you need anything. Would you like me to change the sheets in your room? And please let Cookie know if there's anything you'd partickerly like.'

Most surprisingly, Ash's death had brought out the best in her father. Hamilton McCosh was scion of a family that only two generations before had been destitute Gaelic speakers from the countryside north of Glasgow, but they had believed in education, hard work and ambition, and somehow it had come about that Hamilton had ended up in a large house in Kent, very convenient for London, with a respectable family. He had an infallible nose for taking advantage of the ups and downs of the stock markets, and a flair for marketable inventions. The family accent had slowly transmogrified into the cultured tones of Edinburgh, he had moved over to the Church of Scotland, and this year he was the captain of the golf club at Blackheath. He had played at Muirfield and at St Andrews, and he had fished for salmon and shot grouse with Lord Fermoy, who was a friend of the Duke of York. Hamilton McCosh had 'arrived', and he had made the most of himself. He had married a famous beauty, a high-spirited and slightly mad one, who had scandalised her friends by playing a vigorous game of tennis the day before giving birth to her first child, and campaigning vociferously on behalf of the Women's Tax Resistance League. Hamilton McCosh had caught her on the rebound, and now, with his daughters almost grown, he also supported a varying number of mistresses, and a few sports. Of all his daughters it was Rosie to whom he was most close.

He went to the Athenaeum less often these days, and came home to sit with her. It was a little awkward at first, his approach being instinctively biblical. 'Blessed are they that die in the Lord,' he said, and then, 'Greater love hath no man than this, that he lay down his life for his friend.'

'Oh, Daddy,' said Rosie, and he took this as a reproof.

'I'm sorry, Rosie bairn, but I dinna ken . . . it's hard to know what to say.'

She put her hand on his. 'Daddy, I believe all those things, but I know that you don't. It doesn't sound right when you say it.'

'Words never get to the heart of things, Rosie bairn,' he said after a while, and she squeezed his fingers. Then he said, 'Try to see what's left. It might not seem much. But if you build on it, it'll get bigger, surely.'

'Daddy, what shall I do?'

'I have always found,' he advised, 'that when everything goes agley and is as hard as you can bear, the most important thing is to keep busy. We are creatures who are born to work. Those who do nothing have lives that seem to go on forever and never come to anything. Between you and me, that is why I feel sorry for your mother, rather than vexed, as I should. This is wartime, lassie. We should all be busy. Do you know what I'm going to do?'

She shook her head.

'No, I don't either.' She laughed at this, and he continued. 'But I know I have to do something. It recently occurred to me that I should pay for some apprentices to learn how to make artificial limbs, and set up a workshop for them. I understand there's a shortage. It'll help keep us afloat, and do some good at the same time. What do you think?'

Rosie smiled. 'It's a lovely idea.' Secretly she was smiling at the way that her father's solutions to everything always involved making money. 'But you could volunteer to be a nightwatchman, or something.'

'The job should suit the man,' he replied robustly. 'I'd just be doing something that's better done by another. Talking of jobs suiting the man, I visited Graham White's aircraft factory recently, and all the workers are women apart from the foreman. I dare say I'd have a workshop full of women if I start making artificial limbs. Would that be dreadful, or would it be fun?'

Rosie said, 'Why don't you employ the wounded who've come back from the front? Someone with a leg missing would have a very good idea of what's needed, wouldn't they?'

'Rosie bairn, that's utterly brilliant. I shall do it straight away. I'm sure I can find a workshop, and the offcuts can be used in the braziers to keep the shop warm.'

There was a long pause, during which Mr McCosh vividly imagined everything that he would have to do in order to set up this enterprise, and then Rosie said, 'I want to go and nurse the wounded.'

'You do?'

'It's the one thing I can still do for Ash. And I've been visiting the Cottage Hospital an awful lot.'

Hamilton McCosh baulked. 'Your mother would never allow it. Soldiers get wounded in all sorts of . . . places. There would be . . . intimacies involved. You'd find it most distressing. All day, every day. The sights would be horrible. For a girl like you. And the noises.'

'And the smells,' added Rosie. 'But would you allow it, Daddy?'

He hesitated and looked into her wan face with its chewed lips and large wounded eyes. 'Yes, Rosie bairn, yes, of course I would.'

'Would you overrule Mama?'

'Gracious me, no man ever does that. When she tells God to send an earthquake, He sends an earthquake.'

'Please, Daddy. You're the only one she defers to in anything.'

He patted her hand and said, 'I'll do my best.'

'Anyway,' said Rosie, 'I think I know exactly how to get round her.'

Accordingly, Hamilton McCosh steeled himself for a confrontation, and marched into the drawing room, where, by the light of gas lamps, the women of the house were at their various occupations. Ottilie was sewing, Sophie embroidering, Christabel writing a letter, Rosie listening to her mother, who was reading aloud an edifying passage from a novel by Mrs Hunt.

'I have something to say,' announced Hamilton McCosh, positioning himself in the centre of the carpet, with his back to the fire.

'What is it, dear?' asked his wife.

He cleared his throat, and then spoke quickly so as not to be interrupted.

'Rosie has asked me, and I have given her my permission, if she can volunteer to go and care for the wounded, with the Voluntary Aid Detachment.' There was a collective gasp of shock and surprise, and then he capped it with a masterstroke. 'There is a war on,' he continued, 'and it is increasingly obvious that it will not be a short one. The freedom of all of Europe is in the balance. Luxembourg and Belgium have already fallen. It may be France or Russia or Italy next, and one day it may be us. We will never secure this freedom unless we all put our shoulders to the wheel. I expect every one of you to find something useful to do during these difficult times. I repeat, every one of you.'

'Including me?' asked his wife, quite horrified, and her husband nodded gravely, looking directly into her eyes.

Hamilton McCosh took advantage of the silence to stride purposefully from the room. Outside the door he encountered Millicent who had been listening surreptitiously. She bobbed, very embarrassed, and then said, 'If you don't mind me not minding my own business, sir, that was very well done, sir.'

'You're a bad lassie, Millicent,' he said, but kindly. 'In future, please refrain from eavesdropping. If my wife had caught you, I expect she would have dismissed you.'

'I'm ever so sorry, sir,' she said, adding, 'But I don't think she would, sir, not really.'

'You are indeed fortunate that I didn't catch you,' said Mr McCosh, and he bounded up the stairs two steps at a time until he reached his study. Somewhat breathless after his exertion, and feeling a little dizzy, he took a false book from the shelf and removed from it a small bottle of Bladnoch. He took one swig direct from the bottle, and then poured himself a little stiffener. He sat at his desk until he felt his heartbeat slow down. What mortification and inconvenience it was to live in such terror of one's wife, and to be obliged to stand up to her so often.

Back in the drawing room Mrs McCosh stood up, rearranged her skirts and sat down again. 'I absolutely forbid it,' she said. 'I will not have one of my daughters becoming a mere nurse. Ladies of our station do not enter such professions, any more than they dance the tango. They do not, indeed, enter any profession. Nurses have been at the forefront of the suffragists. They are a most reprehensible class of woman.'

Rosie protested, 'But, Mama, after campaigning with the Pankhursts, I would have thought you'd find a mere suffragist not remotely extreme enough! I don't wish to be contrary,' she said, 'but you are quite in the wrong.'

'Am I indeed? A mother cannot be wrong, and a daughter's duty is always to be in agreement with her. And I was campaigning because I want the right to vote Conservative. I am convinced that nurses are, in the main, not merely suffragists, but socialists. They are not of the class of women who would vote for Sir Kingsley Wood, now, are they?'

'A wife's duty is to agree with her husband,' said Ottilie drily, whilst avoiding her mother's gaze.

'Mrs Claude Watney,' persisted Rosie, 'has turned part of her house into a hospital. In Berkeley Square.'

'Mrs Claude Watney? Has she? Goodness me!'

'And Mrs Alice Keppel –'

'The late King's mistress? Please, Rosie!'

'And Lady Sarah Wilson and the Duchess of Westminster –'

'That's more like it!'

'– are setting up base hospitals.' Rosie paused for effect.

'I fear there may be more,' said her mother.

'Yes, indeed. Lady Esher is conducting a course on first aid and home-nursing at the Duke of York's Barracks.'

'And?'

'The Duchess of Teck is working voluntarily at Knightsbridge Barracks.'

'And?'

'Queen Amelie of Portugal has taken up work with the Red Cross.'

'A Portuguese queen is not to be compared with one of our own, of course,' said Mrs McCosh, with a knowledgeable air. 'In England and Scotland I doubt if she would amount to more than a duchess.'

'Nonetheless, Mama, you are quite wrong about ladies not taking such work.'

'It seems I am to be overruled by my betters, who in this case should know better, but apparently do not,' said Mrs McCosh with resignation. 'Where do you expect to find employment?'

'You get sent where you get sent, Mama, but I know you wouldn't want me to go to France, and I wouldn't want to be so far away, so I am hoping to get into something a bit closer, like Netley. In Southampton. Or Brighton Pavilion.'

'Southampton? Such a dreary place. At least you can get a presentable croissant in France. One hopes that hasn't changed, at any rate.'

'The hospital was founded by the late Queen, and she used to visit it several times a year when she was at Osborne House. She used to knit things for the wounded.'

'I see that you are quite playing upon my respect and admiration for the quality.'

'I've been praying and praying,' said Rosie, 'and I am sure that it's what God wants.'

'My dear, please, Queen Amelie and the Duchess of Teck are quite enough. To enlist God as well is simply *de trop*.'

'She's been most awfully clever, hasn't she?' said Sophie brightly. 'I wish I was as clever as Rosie.'

'You probably are,' observed Ottilie. 'Everyone suspects that you only pretend to be silly.'

'Oh no,' said Sophie, 'I have no brains at all. I am quite hebetudinous.'

'Sophie, my dear, I think you've just invented a word again,' said Christabel.

'Have I? You see, I told you I was silly.' She paused and put her forefinger to her lips. 'I think I will knit balaclavas, scarves and stockings for the troops. It's something I might be able to manage without causing distress or creating too much havoc. I'm just too trivial for anything as grave as nursing.'

'They also serve who only sit and knit,' said Ottilie. 'Apparently you can get all the patterns you need by sending off to the Queen's lady-in-waiting at Devonshire House. I've heard that they're asking for 300,000 pairs of socks.'

'Heavens, have I got to write a letter then?' exclaimed Sophie. 'How does one address a lady-in-waiting in the post?'

'I expect Mama knows,' said Ottilie.

'I shall find out,' said their mother. 'It is bound to be in one of my books of etiquette, or in the first part of my diary. If you have to write to Devonshire House, it may be that the Duchess is the lady-in-waiting concerned.'

'How amazing that you don't know,' teased Ottilie.

Later, as they strolled in the garden after tea, Ottilie said to Rosie, 'Guess what? I've already got a job at Brighton Pavilion. I'm going to be a VAD too!'

'Ottie, you're such a dark horse! You pipped me to the post! Have you told Mama and Papa yet?'

'Gosh, no. But luckily Mama doesn't know that the troops in Brighton Pavilion are from India. She would positively shudder at the thought of my pink little hands washing them and carrying off their bedpans.'

'I spoke to an Indian doctor once,' said Rosie.

'Did you?'

'Yes, he was most fantastically civilised. He made me feel quite the barbarian in fact. He told me that if you flay someone there is no way at all to tell what race they belong to. If you think about it, it must be true.'

'All God's children? Well, I think that if they're good enough to come here and die for us when it isn't really their war at all, then the least we white ladies can do is look after them when they get wounded. That's what I'm going to do, anyway. I had been wondering how to tell Mama and Papa. I did it all in secret. I was intending to leave a note and vanish, but now that Papa's ordered us to go out and be useful, the problem's disappeared.'

'All those trips to Barker's and Chieseman's and Gorringe's when you didn't come back with anything!'

Ottilie nodded.

'You are a dark horse,' repeated Rosie. She paused for a moment and said, 'All the same, don't you think it might be a bit difficult working with Indians? I mean . . . they're so different from us, aren't they?'

'Anything unfamiliar is difficult to begin with,' said Ottilie calmly. 'I have looked into it, you know, and I've talked to lots of people, and everyone says the same. After a little while you just stop noticing that they're different from us, and then you end up thinking they're exactly the same. So I'm sure your Indian doctor was right. To tell the truth, I'm more worried about how they will feel about me. I understand they are quite as ignorant and silly about us as we are about them. I expect the Mahommedans will be appalled to be cared for by an infidel harlot with her face showing.'

'Well, I won't tell Mama,' said Rosie. 'You can tell her. Or she can find out on her own. Tell Papa first.'

'I suppose you know what the soldiers call us?'

Rosie laughed. 'The Very Adorable Darlings.'

'Have you looked at the rules? They do everything they can to make sure we can't have any fun. That must be the reason our uniforms are held together by dozens of pins.'

'How can you talk of fun?' demanded Rosie. 'There's no fun any more. It's wrong.'

'I am going to have fun,' said Ottilie. 'I don't have your principles. You know, you are a bit of a puritan, Rosie.'

'It's the way I am,' said Rosie.

'Has Christabel told you what she's going to do?'

'No. Is she going to do something?'

'She wants to join the Snapshot League.'

'How perfectly wonderful! She hasn't got a camera, though.'

'She's just ordered one. She can even develop the film in the attic.'

'Mama isn't going to like her going to strange people's houses in all sorts of horrid places.'

'You know Mama. She's actually quite a sport, underneath. She says the first thing that comes into her head, which is usually quite shockingly crass, and then arrives at something more thoughtful later.'

'Sophie's already started to knit a pair of mittens,' said Rosie, 'with an elephant embroidered on the back.'

The following morning, whilst they were eating their smoked haddock and poached egg at breakfast, Mrs McCosh announced her intention to contribute to the war effort by having Belgian ladies to tea, and taking fruit to the Cottage Hospital. In the wake of this portentous news, Millicent came in with a letter for Rosie. She took it, and instantly knew the handwriting. She let out a small cry and began tearing at the envelope with trembling hands. The others watched her, their forks suspended midway to their mouths.

Rosie read the letter, turned it over and read it again.

'My darling Rosie and dearest Pal,
    Well, old thing, it looks as though I have bought a blue ticket home, having been here for just a couple of months . . .

She scanned and rescanned the phrases '. . . I seem to have come through relatively intact . . . Get someone to read the banns, I'm coming home . . . Your best friend and best husband-to-be . . .'

She jumped up, crying, 'He's alive! He's alive! He's coming home! He's only been wounded! He isn't dead! He isn't dead!' She began to laugh, but it was laughter that was strangely horrible and hysterical.

Hamilton McCosh reached out and took the letter from her. He looked at it briefly and handed it back. 'Look at the date on it, Rosie bairn,' he said softly. 'The telegram about the death was several days later than this.'

Rosie stared at him for a moment, and quite suddenly sat down and fell silent. Her father put his hand on hers, and eventually she looked up and announced angrily, 'He said he would come back, even if he was dead.'

She threw her napkin on the table and ran from the room. Upstairs in her bedroom she went down on her knees and groped frantically under the bed. She pulled out her plaster madonna and child, unwrapped it, sat on her bed and hugged it to her chest, rocking and keening.

Downstairs, Sophie said, 'Do you think perhaps that one of us should go to her?' and Hamilton McCosh said, 'I'll go. I'll give it half an hour, and then I'll go.'

'That's very good of you, dear,' said his wife, who had been hoping to be spared.

Upstairs, Rosie was startled by a knock on the door. 'Don't come in!' she cried, and Millicent's voice came back: 'I've brought you a cup of tea, miss. I'll leave it on the table on the landing.'

'Thank you,' said Rosie, choked a little further by this un-solicited act of kindness. She heard the voice of Ash, saying, 'Even if I am dead I will come back, I'll find a way to be with you.' For the very briefest moment, she thought she caught the manly scent of his cologne.

'Ash?' she said, looking up, but then she shook her head and sighed. She stared into the face of her plaster madonna, and then into the eyes of the somewhat adult-looking baby Jesus. She put the statuette down, and bowed her head.

30

The Volunteer

I

The Grampians

To His Grace, the Duke of Devonshire
15 March 1915

Your Grace,
I am writing to you because I understand that you have given over the ground floor of Devonshire House to the Red Cross, and am therefore hoping that you will be able to pass on this letter to the relevant authority.

I am seeking war work and am hoping that you may be able to assist me. I have no nursing qualifications, but feel that I may be of considerable use as a nursing assistant of some sort. I have set my heart on becoming a VAD. I am good with people who are suffering, I am prepared to work hard, and it is too much to bear having to stay at home at a time like this and not do anything important. My fiancé was killed in February, and you will understand that I feel I have a personal obligation to him to pull my weight, as he did, and to alleviate the sufferings of those who are suffering as he did.

I am not married, have no children, am of good reputation, and of the Anglican faith. I have the permission of my father to volunteer.

I am also writing to St John's Ambulance Association at Clerkenwell, to the War Office and to the International Council of Nurses in Oxford Street, in the hope of maximising my opportunities.

Thank you, Your Grace, and forgive me if I have not employed the correct terms of address. At the time of writing my mother is staying with friends in Bromley, and she is our expert on matters of form.
Yours respectfully,
Miss Rosemary McCosh

2

Devonshire House

18 March 1915

Dear Miss McCosh,
   Thank you for your letter, which I have had the pleasure of passing on to the Red Cross.
   I wish you the very best of luck, and every success in your patriotic and compassionate quest.
   I remain yours etc.
   Devonshire

31

Relics

There was a violent knocking at the door, and when Millicent answered it she saw, standing in the porch in a state of considerable distress, the young maid from the Pendennis house next door.

'Is Miss Rosie in?' asked the maid. 'I'm all alone with the mistress, and she's carrying on something terrible. Can you get Miss Rosie?'

Accordingly, Rosie found herself in the Pendennis dining room, where Mrs Pendennis had plumped herself down on one of the chairs and was weeping inconsolably. There was an abominable smell in the room, and on the dining table was a package whose brown paper, sealing wax and string had been opened carefully to reveal its contents.

Mrs Pendennis gestured towards the table and then continued to weep with her hands over her eyes. Rosie approached and took up the objects, one by one.

They were: Ash's fob watch, the one that had been given to him by his father on his twenty-first birthday; a bundle of Rosie's letters, tied up with string; another bundle of letters, from friends and family, also tied up with string; a Parker pen, with gold nib, a gift from his mother at Christmas; a water-stained notebook which had served as a diary, full of his writing, in pencil, which was beautifully neat at the beginning, and almost illegible by the end; a creased brown leather wallet embossed at one corner with 'AHP', containing a ten-shilling note, a ticket stub, and the hand-written words to 'Gilbert the Filbert' on lined paper, folded into four; *The Man of Property* by Galsworthy, in terrible condition, warped by damp and smeared with yellow mud, a tram ticket at page 43 serving as a bookmark; an unopened packet of Craven 'A' cigarettes, presumably for use as currency. There was a string of beads from a Christmas cracker, and a lock of Rosie's hair in a Three Nuns tobacco tin. There was a squashed bullet, and an extraordinary souvenir in the form of two bullets which had intersected in flight, making a perfect St Andrew's cross. All of these things seemed to radiate Ash's personality, as if he were present in what he had left behind.

Then there were the components of his uniform, much of it at first unrecognisable because of the mud and blood. His cap was torn across the top, as if ripped by barbed wire. There was a leather belt; his breeches had dark bloodstains where the balls of shrapnel had penetrated at the bottom right of his abdomen, and the tunic had the same holes and the same black patch of blood where it had hung over his breeches.

Everything was set solid in caked mud, a mud that was an unnatural shade of grey, and it was this mud that seemed to carry the stench that was so vile and overwhelming. Rosie tried not to breathe as she turned over the garments and looked at them, hoping to find some clues about Ash, something that she did not already know.

'How could they do this?' demanded Mrs Pendennis suddenly. 'How can they be so cruel? Why couldn't they wash them first?'

'The smell isn't Ash,' said Rosie dully. 'It's the mud. The mud's full of the smell of dead things. They've buried so many people that it's got into the earth. The mud's made of the dead.'

'Take them away. Please, let's burn them,' said Mrs Pendennis. 'I can't bear to have them. Take them away. Please take them away.'

'Mamma, can I keep the letters, my ones to Ash?'

'Yes, yes, of course. No one else should have them.' Rosie bent down and kissed Mrs Pendennis on the cheek. 'Thank you, my dear, you're a great comfort,' she said. 'Will you burn the uniform?'

Rosie nodded, because she did not want to lie out loud.

'Have you heard from Albert and Sidney?' she asked.

'Yes, they seem to be safe at the moment,' said their mother, and left it at that.

Rosie carefully packed the foul garments back into the brown paper, and went and put the package just outside the front door, in the porch, so that the stench in the house could begin to dissipate. She returned to find that Mrs Pendennis had moved to the drawing room, and so she sat next to her on the sofa, putting her arm around her shoulder. Mrs Pendennis began to sob again, and then wiped her eyes. 'I'm sorry,' she said. 'It's when somebody's nice about it that I can't help but cry. Yesterday it was the milkman, and the day before that it was the costermonger.'

'Oh, Mamma,' said Rosie, 'I'm just the same. It's the sympathy that's hard to take sometimes.'

'I haven't got any daughters,' said Mrs Pendennis, turning to smile weakly. Her face was shining with tears. 'I was hoping so much . . .'

Rosie kissed her on the forehead. 'Oh, Mamma, Ash was my husband even if we weren't married yet, and you've got a daughter as long as I'm alive. Really you've got four daughters. We've all been one big family since we were little, and there's always been the blue door.'

'Oh, the blue door. Thank God for the blue door. Hasn't it been a lovely thing? We were so lucky, weren't we? But it's you who's always been the real daughter. I mean the best daughter, out of you four.'

'I've always thought,' said Rosie, 'how nice it would have been if Albert and Sidney could have taken a fancy to Christabel and Sophie. Or Ottie.'

'Nothing is ever so neat, my dear.'

'The blue door has overgrown with brambles since the gardeners left. Have you noticed? It reminds me of that *Light of the World* picture, somehow. Maybe it's the thorns on Christ's head. I'm going to get some secateurs and open it up again.'

'It seems so long ago, doesn't it? When you were all children. Do you remember little Daniel Pitt vaulting over the wall, and running about pretending to be an aeroplane, spreading his wings out and roaring? And then one did fly over, and Bouncer went absolutely bonkers with barking at it.' She inclined her head and looked up. 'Do you know something, my dear? I've been thinking, now that Ash has gone, wouldn't it be wonderful if you and Daniel were to . . . you know . . . meet up again?'

'Mamma! How could you?'

'I can because I'm Ash's mother. You and Daniel always got on so well, and he obviously adored you.'

'Poor Archie adored me even worse,' said Rosie drily, 'and Ottilie adored Archie.'

'Shall we look in Ash's diary?' suggested Mrs Pendennis. 'Do you think that Ash would mind?'

'I think he was probably writing it for us anyway. How are we going to read it without crying?'

'Let's take it in turns to read it aloud, one entry each. I'll start.'

Rosie fetched the battered, mud-stained notebook from the side table and resumed her place at Mrs Pendennis's side. She flicked through it. 'It starts terribly smartly and ends up just a frightful scrawl.'

Huddled together on the sofa, Rosie and Mrs Pendennis spent the morning reading and rereading, often horrified, and just as often amused. 'Fancy eating a huge meal of nothing but custard! And having to use other men's love letters in the latrine!'

When they had read the last page, Mrs Pendennis sighed, got up and went to the window. She looked over to the blue door. 'The thing is . . .' she said. 'The thing is, he died like that. I mean, it wasn't in battle, it was just a shell that somebody fired for their own amusement. It's not the way he would have wanted.'

'I know, Mamma. I've had the same thought, but there's hardly anyone who gets to die the way they want, is there? I'm sure that I won't. I just want to ascend into Heaven like Jesus, or the Virgin. However I die, I'm quite certain it won't be like that. With any luck I'll just drop dead with a heart attack, but, you know, it can take weeks.'

'What galls me, my dear, is I just can't see the point of it. I do see the point of the war, of course I do, but that particular death . . . it didn't help anyone in anyway at all, did it?'

'It helped Ash. He went straight to Heaven without ever having to grow disillusioned, or sick and old. Whom the gods love die young. We all owe God a death. He who pays this year is quit for the next. It's true, isn't it? And Ash won't have to grow old, like us.'

Mrs Pendennis turned and saw the enthusiasm in Rosie's face. 'My dear, I so much envy you your faith. It must be such a wonderful consolation. Perhaps he went straight to Heaven. I hope he did. I hope he watches over us and comforts us without us even knowing. But he went there without becoming a husband or a father or a grandfather, without really ever having made anything of himself. That reminds me, we've had a letter from someone called Major Phillips. I expect you'd like to see it. He says that Ash's comrades called him "Yank" and that they loved him so much that they carried him to the clearing station under fire. I'll go and fetch it. I think I left it in the hall.'

Mrs Pendennis returned with the letter, and she and Rosie settled down to read it. 'It's a lovely letter,' said Rosie, her voice a little choked. 'That bit about *dulce et decorum est pro patria mori* . . . how he was prepared to die for a country that wasn't even his . . . and saying he was like Lord Byron, going off to sacrifice himself for Greece.'

Mrs Pendennis got up and went to the window, looking over towards the blue door. 'Well, my dear, he did actually love this country. One can perfectly well be a patriot twice over. I'm certain that the Pitt boys must love France just as much as they love England, and your own father must love England just as much as he loves Scotland, or he wouldn't have stayed here, would he? It wasn't so long ago when half of England seemed to be in love with Germany.'

The two women looked out into the garden, remembering how the world had been, back in the days of the coronation, when Bouncer had broken up the party, and Daniel Pitt had vaulted over the wall.

32

The Clothes

The following morning, Rosie and Millicent emerged from the door of the kitchen carrying a large galvanised dolly tub between them, and they began to go in and out with jugs of water from the kettle on the range, filling it with hot soapy water.

When Rosie unwrapped the clothes, Millicent stepped back and waved her hand in front of her face. 'Cripes, miss,' she complained. 'That's right niffy.'

'I'm sorry,' said Rosie. 'You really don't have to help me. I know it's horrid.'

'I will help, miss.'

Rosie had a washing bat, and Millicent a three-legged dolly stick. With these they stirred the mixture until a kind of loathsome scum began to gather on the surface of the water. They poured the water down the drain outside the kitchen and began the process again. They washed the uniform three times before the scum began to clear. 'Why don't we get clean water and leave 'em to soak?' suggested Millicent. 'We can have another go tomorrow. We're both all of a lather, in't we?'

'Just think,' said Rosie, wiping the perspiration from her face with a handkerchief, 'we used to have a permanent whitster to buck the clothes. How times have changed.'

'Well, now we all have to do our bit, don't we, miss? You didn't used to know how to wash clothes at all, miss, and now you're no different from anybody else.'

'I think I prefer it like this,' said Rosie. 'The only thing worse than having too much to do is not having anything to do. I much prefer being busy.'

'Me too, miss, but me and Cookie don't half have to do a lot these days.'

The following morning the uniform was washed again, put

through the mangle, and hung out on tenterhooks on a line inside the boiler room. Rosie was ashamed that she had broken her promise to burn it, and did not want Mrs Pendennis to see it drying on the line outside.

In the warmth of the boiler room the clothes dried out, and even acquired the pleasant aroma of coal. Rosie inspected them where they hung on the line, and stroked the fabric. She put a forefinger through a shrapnel hole and thought about how Ash must have crumpled and fallen. The bloodstains had not entirely gone, but now they seemed bearable. Later on, in the light of experience, she would understand more deeply how fabric carried into a wound could set up complications, and how the mud that was carried into a wound by that fabric was purulent and lethal because it was made of corpses.

Rosie went into Eltham on the omnibus and bought a very small suitcase at Elliot's. Into it she put Ash's uniform, his memorabilia, his diary and their letters to each other, and then she slipped it under her bed, next to her statue of the Virgin.

She often took the suitcase out and stroked the bloodstains, putting her fingers through the holes and holding the fabric to her face.

33

Daniel Pitt to Rosie

6 April 1915

Dear Rosemary,

I heard recently on the grapevine that Ashbridge Pendennis was killed in February, at Kemmel. I am in the RFC now, and met him in the trenches, as I expect he told you. Thereafter I used to go and stunt for him. Anyway, I got the news from an HAC man that I came across at a CCS near here (not allowed to give locations) when I was delivering an airman with a head injury.

I know that you two were engaged to be married, and so I just wanted to tell you how very sorry I am about this terrible loss. You must be inconsolable, so what could I say to console you?

I have been out here a few months now, and have seen many terrible things. It is very hard to justify them, but I realise that in a way this war has nothing to do with Great Britain or America. I mean, Great Britain could simply have disregarded its treaties and stayed out. Ashbridge was American, and had even less to do with it.

But I am half French, and so this war means everything to me, and I am incalculably grateful to Ashbridge and everyone else who has come out to here to help us. What I am trying to say, on behalf of France and myself, is 'thank you' to him, and to you for your great sacrifice.

Our liberty, when it comes, will be his everlasting monument.

Yours ever, je vous embrasse,

Daniel Pitt

34

Spikey

Rosie arrived at the hospital an hour early. It had its own railway station, and so her trunk had been sent in advance, containing all fifty-one items stipulated, which included even a lantern, galoshes and a collapsible rubber basin. Everything had been assembled at some trouble and expense, and she felt with all these articles she could probably survive for months. Slipped into pairs of stockings and wrapped up carefully inside her apron (white), her apron (coloured), her wool dress and dust skirt, was her plaster statuette of the madonna and child, and her mending bag contained the battered New Testament and Psalms with which she had once been sent off to school.

As she was too young for Foreign Service, she had been posted, just as she had hoped, to Netley. She had arrived courtesy of a first-class travel warrant, and had read the regulations over and over on the train. She was entitled to seven days' leave in the first six months, and was to be paid twenty pounds for her first year's service, which was just two pounds more than Millicent earned at home as a housemaid, and she would receive two pounds and ten shillings in uniform allowance, which she had already spent during a rather sober spree on the ground floor of Selfridge's, now entirely given over to nursing supplies.

Although much bolstered by the happy thought that, almost identically equipped, Ottilie was at the same moment making her way to Brighton Pavilion, Rosie was confounded by the vast size of Netley. She stood by the sentry box before its grand facade thinking that it must be several times larger than Buckingham Palace. Built by command of an empress, the place was on such a scale that it could have belonged only to the greatest empire on earth. It had been constructed to echo the style of Osborne House, just across Southampton Water, whence the late Queen had frequently ventured forth to visit her wounded troops, of whom she kept photographs, and for whom she had knitted shawls which became so highly prized that no one dared or wanted to use them.

At its centre was a copper dome, green with verdigris, and to either side stretched wings of granite, brick and Portland stone, set up in the classical style, with Italianate turrets and spires. Hundreds of windows were set into walls that were 440 yards long. On the greensward of the grounds hobbled or sat the wounded in their blue uniforms, and all seemed peaceful and orderly. Here and there a VAD with the red cross on her breast supported an elbow or strode forth on a mission.

She plucked up her courage and entered the building through the vast double door. She found herself confronted by the stupendous skeleton of an elephant, whose bleached bones had been set up in the lobby. There were alligators and crocodiles mounted on the walls, row upon row of snakes preserved in formaldehyde, and fish were set into the plaster of the walls in imitation of a shoal. Vast sets of horns and antlers were set up by the hundred, as if this were not a hospital but the country house of an implacably bloodthirsty aristocrat.

Rosie was just emerging from the museum, and wondering where to report, when mayhem suddenly broke loose. There was a great commotion as people began to pour out of the building – doctors, nurses, VADs, FANYs, stretcher-bearers. As if drawn irresistibly by their collective purpose she followed them, still carrying her valise, only to realise that a hospital train had come in.

Nothing could have prepared her for this, although she would soon become familiar with it. As the wreckage was unloaded onto the platform, the doctors scurried from one man to another, injecting morphine into those who would certainly die and so require no other attention.

She stood, fixated by horror. There was a stink of excrement and putrefaction that grew steadily worse as the bodies were laid out on the platform. She saw heads bound up with filthy bandages, white faces with black gaping mouths and wild eyes, black and green rotting stumps bound with improvised tourniquets, flesh bubbling up with blisters that gave off poison gas. She saw wounds patched with field dressings that had not been changed for days, and great pools of dried black blood across chests and stomachs. She saw faces without jaws, and skulls cracked like eggs. She saw bellies bound up with bandages that she somehow knew were retaining bowels, scooped up and thrust back into their cavities. There was a low moaning like that of cattle being driven from one field to another, interspersed with sharp shrieks, whimpering and keening. She heard prayers, appeals to mothers and sisters, the curt orders of doctors as they detailed the nurses and the stretcher-bearers. Some stalwart souls, eyes bulging with pain, made no sound at all.

Astounded by this horrible tumult, and sickened by the pall of smoke and wet sooty steam, it was a few moments before she realised that an officer was standing next to her, his arm in a bloody sling, one of the luckier ones. 'You should see the ones who didn't get this far,' he said, in a strangely deadened voice. 'I saw a man with his head compressed into his chest by a shell. The crown of his head was just poking out at the top.' He paused, said, 'Major Frederick Arbuthnot, Irish Guards,' and fell silent, leaving Rosie wondering whether that had been the name of the casualty, or whether he had been introducing himself. 'Better get to the sawbones,' said the officer, and he set off on foot towards the hospital.

Rosie knew that she had to do something. She knelt by a doctor who was checking a soldier for signs of life, and said, 'What can I do?'

'VAD?' asked the doctor without looking up at her.

'Yes.'

'Trained or untrained?'

'Untrained. Just arrived.'

'Well, the first thing you do is ask "shrapnel or bullet". Treatment depends entirely upon which one it is. Now just find someone who's dying and hold his hand. Say prayers. Say what you like. Just don't get in the way.'

Rosie knelt by a skinny runt of a boy from the East End. He was breathing stertorously, and no one was tending to him. She took his hand, which was cold, clammy and limp. At first she could not see what was wrong. As she looked at his face, overwhelmed by pity, the tears began to roll in huge drops down her cheeks. Suddenly he turned his head and looked at her, holding her gaze. 'Don't cry for me, miss,' he said. He began to convulse and shudder, then closed his eyes.

35

News

The Grampians

19 June 1915

My dear Rosebud,

   I am writing to you with bad tidings, but I did think that you would like to be amongst the first to know.

   I am very sorry to have to tell you that both Sidney and Albert Pendennis were killed on the 16th of June in the same engagement at Hooge, where they were caught by machine-gun fire, side by side, as they went over the top. Half of their battalion apparently perished with them.

   I do not know many of the details. Mrs Pendennis came round to tell us, and, as you can imagine, the poor woman can hardly speak and is utterly prostrate with grief and despair. I shudder to think of the agony of those who lose all their sons. You may remember that the same thing happened to two of the Pitt brothers, who perished in the South African war, when Daniel and Archie were fortunately too young to join them. As you may know, the Springfields have lost all their sons, and so have the Baskervilles and the Revells. I have never regretted only having daughters, and even less do I regret it now.

   Please do write to Mr and Mrs Pendennis, should you find yourself with a spare moment. I expect it would be consoling for them, and they would like to feel that even though all their sons have gone, they still have a daughter of a kind.

   Let me repeat, dear Rosebud, how proud I am of what my brave and pretty bairns are doing in this war. If it were possible for a father's pride to bear his daughters up, then you would be shoulder-high.

   Your loving and grumpy and proud old daddy,
   Hamilton McCosh

PS The new workshop for making artificial limbs is up and running in Woolwich. Just as you suggested, I have largely employed the wounded, and a marvellous job they are doing too. I am going to set up another workshop to make the wooden struts for aeroplanes.

PPS My idea for a new kind of golf ball has made a wee bit of progress, but of course it seems frivolous under these circumstances, and I don't have much enthusiasm for it at present.

36

Hutch (1)

The world was still absorbing the shock of the *Lusitania's* sinking. In Stepney a mob was setting fire to the shop of a German-born baker, and stoning the policemen who had arrived to intervene. Rosie was with Bouncer at her station at the window seat, as usual, watching life go by in the street outside. She was exhausted from her work at Netley, and was taking advantage of a weekend off, having managed to coordinate matters with Ottilie so that they would both be at home at the same time. The casualties from Artois had not yet begun to come in. The rag-and-bone man had just gone by in his cart, his head bowed down with drowsiness and drink, but every few minutes he would raise it and call 'Raggabone! Raggabone!' Rosie always felt sorry for his horse, a ruined old grey, and she had told the servants that if ever they took something out to the cart, they should take the horse a carrot. It had not occurred to her that the rag-and-bone man himself was equally in need, and that he and his horse were starving together.

A short, stocky man in khaki came to the gateway, stood for a second, confirmed that he was at the right address, and strode up the drive. She listened to the man's hobnails on the stone steps, and then for the tinkling of the brass bell. She wondered if she should call someone to answer the door, but the footman had gone to war, and there was no way of knowing where Millicent was, so she answered it herself. War had changed even the protocol of answering doors.

'Can I help you?' she asked the soldier, before noticing that he wore the insignia of the Honourable Artillery Company.

'Yes, good morning,' replied the soldier, removing his cap. He pulled a handkerchief from his cuff and mopped his brow. ''Scuse me, miss, but I've been going at a right old trot.'

He put the handkerchief back in his cuff, and held out his

hand. 'Leonard Hutchinson, corporal. Well . . . acting corporal. Might you be Miss Rosemary McCosh? Or might you be one of her sisters?'

'Yes, I'm Rosemary.'

'Then it's you I'd be wanting to speak to, if you can see your way clear.'

'Is it about Ash?'

'It is, miss.'

'Then you'd better come in. Can I get you some tea?'

'That would be very congenial. Thank you, miss.'

'Come through to the drawing room. Shall I take your cap?'

'That's very good of you, miss. I don't want to cause you no trouble, though.'

'It's no trouble at all. I understand that you were one of the men who carried Ash to the first-aid post. I have been wanting to thank you. And anything I can do for you is no trouble, I do assure you.'

Rosie rang for Millicent, and she soon appeared with a small trolley.

'I've never seen such dainty teacups in all my born days,' said Corporal Hutchinson admiringly, as he sipped at his tea. He had horrified Rosie by heaping mountains of sugar into it.

He was ruddy-faced and strong, with a crease across his cheek that must have been left by a bullet. His ears and nose were coarse, and his lips somewhat out of kilter, but the overall effect was pleasant, giving the impression of good humour and kindness. She noticed that his hands shook when he picked up his teacup, and that sometimes he steadied it by drinking with both hands.

'I've come about Ash,' he said.

'Yes, you did say so.'

'We had an agreement. I'd go and see you if something happened, and he'd go and see my lot if something happened to me.'

'He gave you a message?'

'Not so much a message. He wanted me to tell you that he was loved by his comrades and that he died well.'

'I do know how he died. His mother had a letter from Major Phillips, and she showed it to me, and the Reverend Captain

Fairhead has written to both of us several times. He didn't die well. Not as he would have wished. It wasn't a soldier's death, was it?'

'Course, it was, miss. We die in hospital as well as in the field. More of us do, I'd say. He weren't killed outright in a charge, if that's what you mean. A soldier's death, it don't often happen very quick. And most of us is got by shells. You know, splinters and shrapnel. They say that there's many more die of sickness than wounds. Anyway, the other bit's true.'

'The other bit?'

'The bit about being well loved by his comrades. That's why I'm here. We loved him, miss. He was a right good comrade, and there was no man braver. And he was mighty strong. He carried me half a mile once, when I did me ankle in, and that's with all our kit. And he always won the sandbag-filling competitions. In the end there was no point betting.'

'Where are you from, Corporal Hutchinson?'

'Walthamstow, miss. It's a long way out. Just a village, really. Close enough to enlist with the HAC, though.'

'How did you get in, if you don't mind me putting it so bluntly?'

'I don't mind, miss. You mean I'm not a gentleman ranker.' Hutchinson looked up at her and explained. 'I was chauffeur to a gentleman, miss, and so we went out together. You'll find many a gentleman and his valet, or his gamekeeper, or his chauffeur. Mine said he wouldn't come if I wasn't allowed, so they allowed. They always do, miss. Anyway, he's gone now. Killed straight away, pretty much. Caught a moaning minnie.'

'I am sorry. That must have been terrible for you.'

'It was, miss. It's hard to get over, that kind of thing.'

'Is it true that you called Ash "Yank"?'

Corporal Hutchinson nodded. 'He didn't mind a bit. Some of the lads called me Rabbit.'

Rosie looked puzzled, so he explained. 'Hutchinson . . . Hutch . . . Rabbit. One-a these days they'll be calling me Bunny, I just know it.'

'Is it as bad as they say, in the trenches?'

'It's a lot worse, miss.'

'Is it?'

'You couldn't possibly imagine, miss, even if I explained it.'

'Isn't there anything good about it?'

Hutchinson pondered and said, 'The friendship.' He reached up his right hand and showed her his forefinger and middle finger side by side. 'Yank and me were like that. Best friends. We would've been best friends all our lives. And you know what? I'm nobody from nowhere and he was a toff from round here. That's one good thing. Then there's other things.

'Sometimes the Huns have little concerts in their trenches. They've got these brass bands. You can listen to it when there's not much else goin' on, and it's a right treat. They play lovely, things, miss, sad things, and it's not all blasted out and soldierly at all. Sometimes we give them a clap. And there was a Hun who used to sing, when the sun went down. It was a lullaby, really lovely, sent a chill down your spine, it did, miss, but we in't heard 'im for weeks. Must have been got, I suppose. And then, when you go to occupy a trench, someone's always drawn a cap badge on a piece of paper and stuck it up, so you know who was there before. And once we got lovely parcels all put together by a girls' school, and every parcel had a card in it with a message. And it's nice watching the Zeppelins and the aeroplanes, and if you can't sleep the star shells at night are exceeding pretty. And the Very lights, they're not as strong as magnesium, but they're still pretty. And it's nice thinking of home. And the concerts are very jolly. You get officers dressing up in frocks and doing daft songs. And there's going to *estaminets* for egg and chips when you're behind the lines. And I saw some violets growing where you wouldn't expect it. And there's Flying Corps types who come and do stunts for us, and I think you know one of them, miss. Lieutenant Pitt who used to live next door. He wrote "Long Live the Pals" under his wings, so we'd know it's him. And it's even quite nice when we're just chatting.'

'I expect you do get a lot of time to talk to one another,' observed Rosie.

'No, miss, I mean chatting is getting together round the brazier and delousing.'

'Oh my goodness!'

'You can run a taper up the seams and then scrape 'em out dead, but you might burn the stitches, so you got to watch out. Or you can dig 'em out and crack 'em, with your thumbnail. If it's icy you can turn your shirt inside out and let 'em freeze.'

'I used to send Harrison's Pomade to Ash,' said Rosie 'He was always asking for it.'

'Funny stuff, that. You rub it on, and the little blighters come running up the seams and out at your neck, and you have to catch 'em as they pop up out the top.'

'Lifebuoy soap,' said Rosie. 'At Netley we use Lifebuoy. The lice can't take it if you rub it along the seams.'

'Really, miss? I didn't know that.'

'I'll give you some before you go. I'm sure we've got some in the kitchen.'

'That's very good of you, miss.'

Rosie went and called down to Millicent, and then she returned to her armchair. 'You were telling me what's good about it.'

Hutchinson fell silent for a second, and then said, 'Sometimes you can turn bad things into good things. I mean, the rats are something terrible. Bloody terrible. Millions of 'em, all huge, like this –' he stretched his hands apart – 'and they run over your face at night, and they nick your food no matter how you try to hide it, and they even eat the candles after lights out. I swear those rats know how to open an ammo box. But it's damn fine, excusing me, miss, to go on a rat hunt. You block up all the holes with cordite, all except one hole, miss, and then you light it, and when they come rushing outta that last hole, you whack 'em with a trenching tool, but you mustn't whack 'em with a rifle butt 'cause they break, and then you're in big trouble, and sometimes when it's quiet you take a potshot at the ones between the lines, and it don't matter if you miss because the bullet's going in the right direction to catch a Boche if you're lucky. Those rats eat the corpses, miss, which is why they get so huge, and that's one reason why we hate 'em, and they eat out the bodies inside and then they live in the ribcage, millions of 'em, all squeaking. And I'll tell you something else, miss. Rats is cannibals. Throw 'em a dead one and they'll strip it.'

'We get rats in the cellar sometimes, and now that we've got chickens we've got them at the end of the garden too,' said Rosie, so overwhelmed by this information that she had no sensible response to it. Millicent entered, and Rosie told her to find some Lifebuoy soap, and wrap it for Corporal Hutchinson. She took a moment to inspect the guest, and their eyes met. Millicent felt her heart leap in her chest, and he perceived her shock. He gave her a little wry smile, and nodded his head almost imperceptibly. She went out and leaned against the wall beside the door, before scurrying away to find the soap.

Hutch resumed his monologue, as if the chance to talk had liberated his tongue at last.

'Sometimes the Gonzoubris are right nice to us, the French ones, not the Dutch ones. The Dutch ones want the Huns to win, but no one gets told that at home.'

'Gonzoubris?'

'The locals, miss.'

'Why on earth are they called Gonzoubris?'

'Search me, miss.'

'I'm sorry, I interrupted you.'

'You can't get salad because the Gonzoubris all have pet rabbits,' continued Hutchinson. 'They don't eat it themselves. They just give it to the rabbits. If you want salad you have to crawl around at night and nick it from the bunnies. And the local beer's complete muck.' He paused. 'There was a sweet little girl, though. Can't tell you how sweet she was, a proper little darling. She'd come and sell us vegetables. But in the end she was got by a shell. Couldn't even find the bits. That was sad, that was.'

'I hear the men talking to each other in the hospital,' said Rosie. 'They don't often tell me anything. A lot of what they say is hard to follow. It's like a different language, you know – crumps, whiz-bangs, woolly bears, archie, flaming onions, moaning minnies, sausages, coal boxes. Of course they explain if you ask. But they don't tell me what it was really like. I glean it from what they say to each other.'

Millicent came in once again, this time bearing a plate with four scones on it. She glanced at Hutchinson coquettishly as she left, and he caught her gaze, smiling at her.

'Corporal Hutchinson?' said Rosie.

'Yes, miss?'

'Please can you tell me what a death yell is?'

Hutchinson put down his tea and wiped his brow with his sleeve. 'It's like nothing you ever heard,' he said at last.

'Yes?'

'It's the scream of a man who's already dead, but he just keeps screaming.'

'Already dead?'

'First time I heard it, it was a man who got a bullet and it took the back of his head off. You know, when a bullet gets tired it starts to tumble, and that's the worst kind to catch. He was dead, no mistaking, but he kept up that yelling. It was the worst thing I ever heard. I heard it two or three times since. You don't want to dream about it night-times, I can tell you.'

'How awful,' said Rosie, blenching.

'It's a pretty stiff order, miss. You know what bothers me, miss? What really upsets me? It's the horses.'

'The horses?'

'It's terrible, the way they scream. I counted once, miss, at the roadside, a place we called Suicide Corner, and I reckoned there's a horse killed for every two men, give or take. It's awful, miss, you can't help 'em in a gas attack 'cause you're trying to get your own mask on and how do you get a mask on a horse that's in a panic, even if you had one? And what use is a mask when it's mustard gas and they're just one big horrible blister? And you've got no stables so they freeze all night and they're all covered in ice in the morning, and when they get shelled you can't hide 'em and there's guts and legs everywhere, and they don't understand what's happened, they're still trying to stand up on legs they haven't got. And you know what, miss? When you can't talk to your mates you can always talk to a horse. That's what the blokes do. They go and tell the horses how bleedin' frightened they are, and that way they don't have to tell anyone else. And those horses, miss, they ain't Boche or British or Froggy. They're just horses, they don't know a damn thing about the Kaiser or the bleedin' King of the Belgians. They're innocent, not like us, and they're out there being cut to pieces and slogging their guts out and not understandin' any of it.' Hutchinson paused and looked out of the window. His lips were working, and Rosie could see that he was fighting back tears. 'I'm sorry, miss,' he said. 'I didn't mean to go on about it.' He fell silent for a minute, wiped his eyes with the back of his hand, and added, 'I always used to work with horses, before, when I was a kid. A lot of 'em ain't very bright, but they're lovely, you know, inside. My dad was a drayman.'

Millicent came in bearing a cake of soap wrapped in brown paper. She presented it to Hutchinson and let her fingers rest briefly in the palm of his hand. She held his gaze for just a moment, looked down coyly, and then offered to fetch more tea.

After she had gone out there was a long silence, and then Rosie asked, 'Do you happen to know the Reverend Captain Fairhead?'

'Yes, of course, miss. He was good when Yank died. He's good when anyone dies. There's two types of padre. There's the kind that comes forward into the lines, and there's the kind that don't. Captain Fairhead's up with us quite a lot, miss. Have you ever heard of Woodbine Willy, miss? Well, Captain Fairhead's that kind of padre. He's little but he's tough. He'll take over from a stretcher-bearer when one gets knocked down, and he don't give up.'

Mrs McCosh came in, and stopped abruptly when she saw her daughter alone with a strange man. His uniform reassured her slightly. Corporal Hutchinson stood up, and Rosie introduced them. 'Mama, this is Corporal Hutchinson. Corporal Hutchinson, this is my mother, Mrs Hamilton McCosh.'

Mrs McCosh held out her hand in a somewhat regal fashion, and the corporal was slightly baffled as to what to do with it. He took it lightly in his own and gave it a small shake. 'Delighted, I'm sure,' he said. Sensing Mrs McCosh's *froideur*, he turned to Rosie and said, 'Well, miss, I've told you everything I came to say, and a little bit more besides. I'd better be on my way.'

'Please don't let me keep you,' said Mrs McCosh.

At the threshold, Rosie asked, 'When do you go back?'

'On Monday, miss.'

Rosie took his right hand between hers and looked into his face. 'Do come and see us again when you're home next. And thank you for coming and telling me about Ash. I'll pray for you.'

He was visibly touched, and hardly knew what to say. 'No one's ever said that to me before,' he said finally. 'That's a first, that is. By the way, miss, I wanted to thank *you.*'

'Thank me? What for?'

'Bein' a VAD. You girls, all the men love you. We couldn't manage without. I thought you'd like someone to say it.'

As he was making his farewells, Millicent took the opportunity to emerge from the top of the stairs that led down to the kitchen, bearing a dustpan and brush, in case any crumbs had been left on the floor. He said, 'Goodbye, Miss Millicent, and thank you for looking after us so well. I'm very pleased to have made your acquaintance.'

Their eyes met and she said, 'Good luck. Out there.'

Hutchinson felt his feet carrying him through the door without his consent, and Millicent suppressed the urge to go out after him.

He strode towards Mottingham Station, repeating 'Damn, damn, damn!' to himself, and Millicent went back down to the larder and rested her forehead against the cool white wall. It was the first time that she had ever met a man who had affected her in quite this way. She felt something like hunger, and the weakness that accompanies it.

After Hutchinson had gone, Mrs McCosh, who, despite her husband's strictures, had not found any real war work, nor even looked for any, but had had many Belgian ladies to tea, said reprovingly, 'My dear, you should not let such men into the house. I will not have it. I hope you didn't let him use the sit-upon.'

'Such men? Mama, whatever do you mean?'

'He is very obviously common. His speech is uneducated, he has an accent, he is probably from some ghastly place like Sheffield, and he carries himself in an ungentlemanly fashion, and he's probably something perfectly frightful like a Primitive Methodist. I will not have such people coming to this house and bringing down the tone of it, and I will not have you associating with them. We – you – have a certain reputation to conserve, a certain position in the world.'

Rosie raised her eyebrows in a manner that her mother rightly construed as insubordinate. 'That was Ash's best friend, and he came here to talk to me about Ash.'

'Best friend? He isn't even an officer!'

'Mama! Ash wasn't an officer! The HAC is a regiment of gentlemen rankers. None of his friends would have been officers. They must have thought he was a natural gentleman or they wouldn't have taken him on. And Corporal Hutchinson's not from Sheffield, he's from Walthamstow.'

'Gracious me!' exclaimed Mrs McCosh. 'This all just too bad for words. He's not even from a place I've heard of!'

Rosie went to fetch her bonnet, and as she put it on she said, 'Honestly, Mama, you're enough to turn anyone into a raging socialist.'

'How dare you? What a perfectly dreadful thing to say! And where are you going?'

'To the church, Mama. Corporal Hutchinson returns to the front on Monday, so I am going to pray for him.'

'I don't like you wandering off on your own like this. It is quite uncalled for. A young lady doesn't go out on her own. You should take one of your sisters. Who knows what might befall you? God listens just as well in your own bedroom, you know.'

'I'll be back in time for tea,' said Rosie, ignoring her mother's strictures. There would be other women in the church, and she liked to be with them, all of them either heartbroken or anxious. Praying together was better than praying alone, whether God listens or not. Mrs Ottway had lost one of her sons in Mesopotamia, killed when a horse had panicked and bolted with a limber. She might say the Lord's Prayer with Mrs Ottway.

She had a choice. In the end she walked across the golf course to Holy Trinity, even though it was a bit further than St John's. There was always the chance that her father might be playing a surreptitious round instead of attending to his work in London, and it would have amused them both if she had caught him out. Sometimes, too, one came across a lost ball in the rough, and he was always delighted to be presented with it. Once she had been walking past a rabbit hole when a ball had been suddenly ejected from it, an amusing little miracle, whose recollection had always made her smile.

37

Millicent (2)

I waited 'til Miss Rosie stopped praying before I knocked. I always knew when she was praying because she made these muttering sounds and you could just hear it if you put your ear to the door, and then you heard her wrapping that Virgin and putting it back under the bed.

I went in and said, 'Pot of tea, Miss Rosie,' and she said, 'I didn't ask for one, Millie,' and I said, 'No, nor you did, but I thought you might like one,' and she said, 'You're turning into a mind-reader.'

I didn't know how to bring it up and so I didn't say nothing but I just sort of lingered there, and then Miss Rosie said, 'What are you waiting for, Millie?' and then she said, 'Why are you blushing?' and I said, 'I'm all sort of confused, miss. I'm all of a doodah.'

'Confused, Millie? All of a doodah? Whatever about?'

I didn't know what to say, and I was right embarrassed, and then she said, 'I did notice, you know. I've never seen anything so obvious. His name is Corporal Leonard Hutchinson, and he was my fiancé's best friend at the front.'

I said, 'Oh no, he's not at the front. Oh cripes.'

Miss Rosie said, 'They don't all get killed.'

'Sometimes it's worse,' I said. 'I seen 'em, all blind and burned and things. It's horrible, miss.'

'I know,' she said, 'I look after them every day at Netley.'

'Excuse me askin', miss, but will Mr Hutchinson be comin' back here?'

'I'll try to make sure that he does, Millie.'

I said, 'Thank you, Miss Rosie,' and she said, 'You know you can't carry on working here if you get married?' and I said, 'Who's talkin' about getting wed? And anyway, this war's changed every-thing round, hasn't it? Nothing's normal any more, is it, miss? I mean, a lady like you workin' in a hospital and lookin' after young men like that, that didn't used to be usual, did it? And now it is,' and she said, 'We can't look ahead any more, Millie. Thank you for bringing the tea. It was very thoughtful of you.'

'That's what I like about you, miss,' I said. 'You're always thanking me and there's many that don't, not naming any names,' and Miss Rosie laughed 'cause she knew who I was meaning. In them days Miss Rosie and the master were the only two what treated me like I had feelings like a human.

'We all get taken for granted sometimes,' said Miss Rosie.

38

Two Paschal Letters

I

Dear Miss McCosh,

You will I am sure excuse a hurried note but I did want you to know that I shall be thinking of you at Eastertime and praying that the Resurrection joy may be yours in all its fullness. Your dear one will be very near to you, and the certainty of it at Eastertide is beyond all description. I am sure that all our stricken hearts will be really comforted. May God's Blessing and Comfort be yours through Jesus Christ Our Saviour and Risen God.

With very kind regards, yours very sincerely,
H. V. Fairhead, CF

Passed by no. 1900 censor

2

The Grampians

10 April 1915

Dear Reverend Captain Fairhead,

Thank you so much for your recent letter at Eastertide. I must say I am astonished that you are able to keep up such a rate of correspondence when by now you must have attended hundreds of deaths. If you are writing to every bereaved family at the same rate as you are writing to ours, then yours must be a life entirely without sleep. I would beg you not to deplete yourself with overwork.

You may know Corporal Leonard Hutchinson, who was my fiancé's best friend. I met him recently, and he spoke very highly of you.

I do know how busy you must be, because I am now working at the Victoria Military Hospital at Netley, in Southampton, as a VAD. Everybody calls it Spike Island, or 'Spikey' for short. The work is gruelling and relentless. One sees and hears such truly ghastly things that it is sometimes hard to keep control of one's own sanity, a whole universe is too small to contain the tears that one could shed, and I know that if our chaplains wrote as frequently and conscientiously as you do, they would very quickly be exhausted. I cannot but think that your friendship and bond of brotherly love with Ashbridge must have been unusually intense for you to be so preoccupied by his death in particular, when you have to deal with so many, and when you have been so grievously wounded by the loss of your own dear sister.

I would be most honoured and grateful if you could find the time, when next on leave, to call in and see us. I would wish to meet with you and converse in person. There is much that I would like to discuss with you. There are soldiers in the hospital who tell me the most extraordinary things. I have, you may rest assured, clung most tenaciously to my faith — how else could I have survived? I would otherwise have died of heartbreak and loneliness — and despite the hideousness of what is being done to the lives and bodies of our beautiful young men, I cling also to the faith that Ashbridge died in a worthy cause. The death of your poor sister in an attack from the air, explicitly directed at civilians, proves that we are confronting a terrible evil, and have no choice but to do so. I know that Ash would never have thought that it was vain to lay down one's life at a time like this.

I have read the Bishop of Stepney's book, as you recommended, and I did find great comfort in it.

I look forward to meeting you in person one of these days.
Yours most sincerely,
Rosemary McCosh (Miss)

39

An Interruptor

Sophie came into the drawing room and flopped down on the sofa next to Christabel. 'Look!' she said. 'My fiftieth hospital bag!'

'Fifty!' exclaimed Christabel. 'Why, Sophickles, you've turned into a positive factory. I don't know how you do it. And every one with a cheerful little elephant embroidered on it.'

'It's my last one,' said Sophie. 'I really can't face making any more.'

'What are you going to do now?'

'I've hatched a plot, a very ingenuous plot.'

'Ingenious?'

'Ingenuous and ingenious. I've joined the Women's Legion Auxiliary! I'm going to be a driver for the Royal Flying Corps, I hope. And I'll learn how to mend engines and things. It'll be topping. Ain't I a kink?'

'Sophie, you're priceless! What will Daddy say?'

'Oh, I spoke to Daddy, and he said, "Gracious me, Sophie bairn, what will your mother say?"'

'Is that all?'

'Daddy likes spunky girls,' said Sophie happily. 'He said, "What if they send you to France?" and I said, "I'm starting at Suttons Farm," and he said, "But you have no idea how to drive tenders and mend engines," and I said, "Daddy, you didn't know anything about gas masks and artificial limbs until you started manufacturing them."'

'Well, you know what Mama will say. She'll say, "Oh, you can't possibly! I absolutely forbid it!'

'I won't tell her until after I've gone. I shall write and tell her that I am living in a compound with high walls, and any man attempting to enter will be shot dead by one of our fearsome lady guards. Mama doesn't really care about anything but telling us to keep our legs crossed.'

'Sophie!'

'Well, it's true, you know it is. She wouldn't mind at all if we were footpads and murderers. Anyway, I've no intention of having babies until I'm married, and then I'm going to have dozens and dozens. Positive plenitudes of them.'

'Where are you actually going to live?'

'In a nice little farmhouse. They're going to build us some special huts later on, I think. Won't it be fun? I'm terribly braced. No more balaclavas and hospital bags. Hooray! And if I get sent to France I shan't mind at all.'

'You'll have to cut off your fingernails.'

Sophie held up her hands. 'Already have! I have been most prescient and not at all nescient, if not omniscient. And I was frightfully good at French at school. I got the prize for dictée and conversation. I could be an interrupter. I shall wax Molièresque.'

'Interrupter?'

'You know, French into English and English into French, that kind of thing.'

'Oh, you mean an interpreter!'

'Do I? Silly me.'

'With your love for messing about with words, and scrambling them up, I think you'd better stick to driving. Just think, you might fall in love with a pilot! Wouldn't that be romantic!'

'Frantically. But they do get killed an awful lot. Better not, really.'

'The trouble with love,' observed Christabel, 'is that one really has no choice as to who one falls in love with.'

40

Now that April's Here

'Rupert Brooke's died,' said Ottilie.

'Oh,' said Rosie, 'he hasn't, has he? Why? I mean, how?'

They were sitting in the tea room of a hotel on North Street, Chichester, having met halfway between Brighton and Southampton on an afternoon off. They were waiting for Christabel, who was coming down by train. Outside, a light rain pattered on windows that overlooked a garden that was coming to life as if there wasn't a war on.

'He wasn't shot or anything. It was an infected mosquito bite, somewhere near the Dardanelles. I think he got bitten in Egypt.'

'What a thing to die of! You'd think that God would've been kind enough to let him die of something else. Something more glorious.'

'I don't know how you've clung to your faith,' said Ottilie.

'Why?' said Rosie. 'Haven't you?'

Ottilie looked straight ahead and said, 'It doesn't come naturally any more.'

'I couldn't live without it,' said Rosie. 'I would die of the horror and loneliness.'

'I do know what you mean.'

'There's a VAD at Netley,' said Rosie. 'She can see the souls of the dead as they leave their bodies. She discovered it by accident, and she says that after the war she's going to be a medium.'

Ottilie looked at her sister sceptically.

'She isn't mad,' said Rosie. 'She's quite normal. She says that when you die there are people who come to fetch you away, sometimes one, or two, or three. And there was a soldier who told me that on the battlefield there are hundreds of angels collecting the souls of the dead. He said that lots of people see them.'

'I've heard soldiers say all sorts of things,' said Ottilie.

146

'I've watched a lot of men die,' said Rosie. 'You have too. You know what it's like. The moment they go, they don't even look like themselves any more. You can tell the body's uninhabited, that's someone's left it behind. It's just discarded.'

'I've noticed that too, but, Rosie, it doesn't tell you anything about God, does it? They could be leaving to go on to something else, but it doesn't mean there's a God at all. If there's an afterlife, it might be like going to stay in Hastings or something.'

'How can you have an afterlife without God?'

'Well, why can't you?'

Rosie was stuck. This possibility had never occurred to her before. 'All I know,' she said at length, 'is that God looks after me and answers me.'

They looked out over the lawn again. It all seemed too peaceful. 'I am worried about Mama and Papa when the Zeppelins and Gothas come over,' said Ottilie. 'Mind you, they seem to be bombing anything and anywhere, don't they? It could just as easily be us.' She looked sideways and saw that her sister was crying silently. 'Oh, Rosie, whatever is the matter? Is it Ash?'

Rosie hung her head and wept, her thin shoulders heaving. 'I'm just so tired,' she said. 'I'm so exhausted. I could sleep for a year. I only wish I could.'

'I know what it's like,' said Ottilie, 'I really do.'

'They work us so hard,' said Rosie. 'We get up so early and we aren't allowed to sit down all day, and we work so late, and I'm still in a tent because there's no accommodation, and one of the other women snores, and it's so cold that when you undress all you actually do is take your shoes off, and I never seem to get a decent wash, and the trained nurses are so horrible to us and call us amateurs and pretend nurses, and say that we're under-mining their profession, and the doctors treat us like vermin, and I'm spending all my time polishing brasses and sweeping floors when I want to be helping properly. Ottilie, it's just too awful, and you see all those beautiful boys mutilated and dying or going mad, and they've got a whole ward for men with syphilis and everyone calls it "Hell" because it really is hell. And I got into big trouble because I said to the matron that officers and men shouldn't be treated separately, but they shouldn't, should they?'

'The Pavilion is quite nice,' said Ottilie, 'but everything's governed by caste and religion. It drives you mad. We have to have lots of separate kitchens – we've got nine of them – and separate water for Hindus and Mahommedans, and different loos, and the notices have to be in Hindi and Urdu and Gurmukhi, and all the laundry's done by untouchables who have to live in a tent on the lawn. If it worries you separating the officers and men at Netley, you can't possibly imagine what it's like for us in the Pavilion. One has to have the expertise of an anthropologist. Do you know what the worst thing is?'

'No.'

'It's the Mahommedans. They think that they can't get to Paradise if they're missing a limb. If you have to do an amputation the grief and hysterics are quite dreadful to cope with.'

'How very silly,' said Rosie, 'to think that God would care about a missing leg.'

'They get over it,' said Ottilie. 'In the end they're grateful to have a bit more life.' She paused, and added, 'And the Hindus think they can't go to Heaven until they've had a son, so if they haven't got one yet, they positively refuse to die, even when it's absolutely inevitable. They die in a kind of spiritual agony. It's dreadful.'

'We've got ghats at Netley, for burning the Hindus. You know what the best thing is?' said Rosie. 'Do you know why I couldn't give it up, no matter how awful it is? It's the gratitude of the men. It makes me want to cry every time I think of it. When they leave they write messages in my scrapbook, and poems, and then they write me letters.'

Ottilie nodded, and they looked out over the lawn again. Christabel came in, throwing her bag down and collapsing theatrically on one of the chairs. She closed her eyes and said, 'My darlings, I'm absolutely fagged.'

'Too much snapping?' asked Rosie.

'In the last few days I've been all over London and to Guildford and Petworth and Reading and every town and village known to man. I can't tell you how many buses and trams I must have got in and out of. Why can't they come up with lighter cameras? What about papier mâché? I swear my shoulders are getting a permanent sag.'

'But you must meet lots of nice people,' said Ottilie.

'Everyone's nice,' replied Christabel. 'They're always so grateful.'

'We were just saying that,' said Rosie. 'It keeps you going, doesn't it?'

'The sad thing is that by the time the photographs get to the front line, a lot of the recipients are probably dead already.'

'Oh, don't say that!'

'It's true, though.'

'The soldiers at Netley love their snaps more than practically anything else,' said Rosie. 'And another thing, even the ones who aren't Catholics have rosaries and pictures of saints.'

'Do your Indian soldiers have photographs?' asked Christabel.

'No, they don't. I can't think of any.'

'Shall I come along to Brighton and take some snaps for them to send home?'

Ottilie put her hands together eagerly. 'Oh, wouldn't that be wonderful? We'd have to ask the matron, or someone.' She paused. 'You'd absolutely love Brighton. The Pavilion's a hoot. They put all the Indian soldiers in it because they thought the architecture would make them feel more at home! Can you believe it? Most of them grew up in villages, in huts! When they come to the Pavilion they think they've all become maharajas.'

'I wonder how one would light them,' said Christabel. 'I've only ever done pallid folk like us before. Any news of Sophie?'

'Just a cheery message from somewhere near Amiens, saying that she got shelled and had to change a tyre, and suddenly crowds of men emerged from nowhere and changed it for her. She says she's driving French officers around on liaison missions and has become quite the interrupter.'

'Good old Sophie. Have you heard her latest Sophieism?'

'No,' said Rosie. 'Do tell.'

'She wrote and said that the number of women working in France was expanding excrementally!'

The sisters laughed, and Ottilie remarked, 'I never really know if she does it on purpose.'

'Well, of course she does,' replied Christabel. 'And did you know that Papa's gone to Leeds?'

'Leeds? What on earth for?'

'He heard about a certain Honorary Colonel Professor Smithells at the university who's come up with some new ideas for an anti-gas respirator, so he got in touch and off he went. Apparently Professor Smithells is the government's chief adviser on chemical warfare.'

'Papa's fabulous, isn't he?' said Rosie. 'He helps mankind by helping himself. It's quite a knack. He's making parts for Sopwith's now.'

'Guess what!' said Christabel.

'What?' echoed the sisters.

'Millicent got another letter from Hutch. I had to read some of it for her. Hutch has got terrible writing, and Millicent isn't as good at reading and writing as she thinks she is. I helped her a little with replying.'

'How sweet,' said Ottilie. 'I just hope that he gets through, that's all.'

'Send him a snap of Millicent,' suggested Rosie.

Christabel started laughing to herself, and Ottilie said, 'Do tell us!'

'Oh, it was something that happened yesterday. It was too funny. I needed a few pennies to pay the cats' meat man, and I thought Cookie might have some, so I shouted down the stairs, 'Have you got any coppers down there?' and Millicent's little voice came back up: 'There's three, Miss Christabel, but it's all right 'cause they're all my cousins except the one what's my brother.' It turns out that we are quite the little staging post for weary peelers on the beat. No wonder we're always running out of tea and sugar.'

'It's been going on for ages,' said Rosie. 'I've been dreading Mama finding out.'

'It couldn't have happened when we had a footman,' observed Ottilie.

'Yes, it could,' said Christabel. 'Servants just adore getting into conspiracies and seeing what they can get away with.'

That night a dud bomb fell through the roof of Swan & Edgar, and the McCosh conservatory was destroyed by a small Zeppelin bomb that fell on the lawn and sucked all the glass from the windows. It remained a veranda until 1919, and in the interim Mr and Mrs Pendennis next door adopted the few surviving plants. Mr McCosh toyed with the idea of converting the crater into a fishpond, but was overruled by his daughters, who wanted the lawn to revert to being a tennis court after the war. 'After the war' was a phrase on everybody's lips, especially those of lovers. Millicent and Hutch wrote letters to each other in which it seemed to be repeated in every sentence . . . after the war . . . after the war . . . after the war . . . after the war. It was a phrase that went well with 'forever'. I'll love you forever, after the war.

41

The Harmony of the Wires

Down below in Bailleul lie the sodden bones of Ashbridge Pendennis and his two brothers, entombed in mud and marked with wooden crosses made from the slats of ammunition boxes. High above them, oblivious, Daniel Crawford Pitt hurls his Sopwith Camel around the sky for the sheer exhilaration and joy and love of it.

Having survived many months at the front as an observer, and having brought down several enemy aircraft, he has won his ticket at the Central Flying School in Upavon, and has gone on to win the wings that are now sewn onto the breast of his tunic. He has kept the winged 'O', however, as he is proud of it, and no one has told him to remove it from his upper left arm, where he has sewn it without permission. He has learned to fly in a 'Sociable', the kind invented for Winston Churchill personally, and flown an Avro 504, and even the Flying Coffin (otherwise known as the Clockwork Mouse), and some other types too. He has flown the delightful Sopwith Pup as a pilot, and now he is mastering the Camel, which was terrifyingly unflyable at first, but has become an extension of his body and his spirit. It is August 1917, and Bloody April is receding into memory. Down below, the French are just about to break the German line at Verdun, and the British are about to gain a few hundred yards of mud at the third battle of Ypres. On this day, twelve German aircraft and twelve British ones have been lost. In Russia the new government is at war with the Bolsheviks, and the Tsar and his family are rumoured to have been sent to Siberia.

It was intimidating enough trying out a DH2, because that had a natural spin, and the Sopwith Pup was unnervingly responsive at first, but he had got used to it. It was strange how each type of machine was so different from every other, and with each machine it was like learning to fly all over again. You could stall a Pup on purpose, but it was practically impossible with a DH2. You put the nose up, it stalled, the nose went down level. It climbed again, stalled, put its nose down level.

Nothing has prepared him for the Camel, however; he has already crashed one, and half of those training with him have been killed or injured.

The strain of flying it is appalling, because the torque of the engine means that it won't do a left-hand spin, but puts it into a right-hand spin that is irretrievable on take-off. Most of the casualties are caused by right-hand spins. To stop it spinning you wrestle with the controls from the moment you begin to taxi, and you wrestle with them until your fuel runs out some two hours later. You are always on left rudder, but you use rudder as little as you can. The plane always wants to climb, and always wants to sideslip, to drift sideways, which turns out to be miraculously useful when there's a Hun on your tail. He opens fire and you're suddenly not there to be fired at. When you get home you are sometimes too weak to climb out, and all your limbs are shaking. How different is an SE5a, with its in-line engine! And how much more cosy and warm! You can set the controls for a distant destination, and arrive there without doing much else. You don't make your kills in a dogfight, as you do with a Camel. You dive and zoom. A Camel fights like a cat, an SE5 fights like a shark.

The Camel pilots complain that the aircraft has a low ceiling, so you seldom have the advantage of height, the *sine qua non* of a conventional attack. It is useless above 15,000 feet, and it isn't fast enough to chase and catch a fleeing enemy, and in any case you can't go far over Hunland without worrying about not having sufficient fuel to batter back against the prevailing wind. God is perhaps on the Huns' side, because the Huns have the wind to carry them home, and the Huns don't stray over the lines anyway, so you are forced to go to them. Only at night do the Huns come over in their bombers, and then the night Camels go up, but Daniel doesn't know who they are and doesn't envy them either. It's cold enough in the daytime.

Daniel knows better than to complain. McCudden has tinkered with his own engine and carburettor so brilliantly that he can get his SE5 up to 22,000 feet. One day Daniel visits 56 Squadron, and Mac lets him take his bus up. At 21,000 feet Daniel gets hypoxia so badly that he falls delirious, does something stupid and unaccountable with the controls, and nearly spins to earth. The cold is utterly unbearable and makes his bones ache to the marrow. When he comes down he has hypothermia and has to be collected in the squadron tender. When he returns two days later to collect his bus he says to McCudden, 'Think I'll stick to Camels. Don't know how you do it.' McCudden claps him on the shoulder, and says, 'Well, old fruit, you wouldn't catch me in a Camel. Each to his own. One day someone'll come up with a better engine and you'll be upstairs with us. Can't you get hold of a Bentley?'

The Camel pilots complain of having to do too much ground-strafing, because they can't ascend very high, but they are unaware that everyone else is also having to do it, including those who can get to 22,000 feet. Even the Dolphins are receiving the same unwelcome orders. It's a far cry from the scouts' original job, protecting their own two-seaters and destroying those of the enemy. Like everyone else, Daniel longs for the old days. It's actually a relief to go into combat with an enemy you can see, to have a proper duel, after days of strafing. A curse on those who worked out that an aircraft can also be used for mowing down soldiers.

So Daniel is content to keep a watch on his back for Huns coming out of the sun, knowing that when he dives his wings almost certainly won't fall off, and knowing that the moment a Hun attacker arrives, his machine guns popping and the tracer zinging past his ears, he can split-arse the Camel with such instantaneous virtuosity that he can turn twice for every once of the foe. Nothing will worry him until the Fokker DVII arrives, too late to make enough of a difference, and the Fokker pilots themselves not realising for several months how good their new planes really are.

Now Daniel, having dropped his eggs on a transport column and somehow become separated from his flight, plays with the clouds. High above Albert he hits a heat bump and suddenly ascends vertically for four thousand feet. It is like going up in a lift, with exhilaration thrown in. He is stunting around the towers and chimneys and battlements of the cumulus. He pretends he is landing on the flat parts, and scoops his undercarriage through the vapour. It is sparklingly bright up there. Every detail he sees is in sharp and glistening focus. He zooms up a vertical wall and loops, blipping the engine when he sees the cloud beneath him again. He loops once more, half rolling at the top so that he is horizontal again. He dives until he is going faster than two hundred miles an hour, and the wires are singing. Here is a crevasse, a cathedral, a cave, a chimney, lilac shadow. He pulls back the joystick steadily and carefully, and he is level again. He has to pump the oil pressure up by hand, and switches to gravity for a moment. His compass spins, his ears are aching almost unbearably. Up he loops once more, and barrel-rolls at the top, straight over the gleaming summit of a cloud. He flies between the sun and the cloud, and looks at the exquisite double-rainbow nimbus around the shadow of his machine. He goes into a falling leaf, then centralises the controls and comes out of it. He goes into a spin, turns off the petrol, gets through that horrible moment when the controls go limp, pushes the joystick forward to convert it into a dive, and gets out of that too, Gosport fashion. He remembers the full horror of his first spin, and smiles grimly. It had happened because he had stalled in a loop, and for a few seconds he had foretasted the bitterness of doom. He sings loudly to himself: 'If you want the sergeant major, we know where he is, we know where he is . . .'

He nips down into a valley of dove-grey shadow, and hurtles back out of it. He all but stalls the machine, it hangs on its propeller for a second, and then he drops it back down to follow the dunes and ridges. It is like tree-hopping and contour-chasing at altitude. The beauty and clarity is not of this earth. Nothing is more sublime and ineffable than this. He crashes through a white wall into greyness, and sees nothing until he emerges through the other side and realises that he is almost upside down. He goes fully upside down, and feels the straps straining against his shoulders. He holds hard onto the spade grip of the joystick, because he has no parachute, and no one really trusts the straps.

He pushes the stick over and then centralises it again so that he does a long vertical turn, like a loop on its side, and he watches the cloud and the visible patches of earth going round in a circle. He is so high above the devastation that he is beyond the distress of it. The Western Front is surprisingly narrow. It is a long scar of brown and yellow earth, cutting through verdant countryside. It's the right-hand vertical turn that the Huns can't cope with and can't follow. Do it long enough and they have to give up in despair. The Camel is a damned swagger machine.

He remembers the occasion when he was stunting up in the cumulus, and came round a majestic stack of pink and golden vapour just as the sun was about to set, and beheld in front of him a whole flight of German Albatroses enjoying their own last bout of stunting before returning home. There is a rumour that the Germans are ordered to return home after a set number of minutes, which is why they often seem to abandon fights unexpectedly. These ones must have been using up their last minutes by having fun. He had decided to bank vertically into a pillar of cloud before they spotted him. He did not have enough fuel left to take them on, so he had let them have their fun. One of the odd things about the Germans is that they disapprove of looping the loop, so you never see them doing it.

He rolls one and a half, pretends he has an enemy on his tail, and immelmanns. He gets on the tail of his enemy and then waggles his wings in wild exaggeration. He banks and follows the contours of a feathered canyon. An SE5 appears out of nowhere, and he realises that it is McCudden. They play hide-and-seek for a while, dipping in and out of the gaps between the clouds, chasing each other round and round a funnel, and then McCudden waves and disappears.

At this point Daniel realises that his voice has gone hoarse from too much gleeful shouting and singing, and that he has no idea where he is. He descends in a shallow dive. He once had his engine stop in a cloud, because of moisture in the jet, and ever since he has worried that it will happen again. You have to come out cautiously too, because you do not know what might be underneath, and without a horizon you can easily end up flying upside down. At forty-five degrees the rudder becomes the elevator and vice versa. You can make horrendous mistakes. He cuts the engine with the button switch and glides down through the cloud, keeping an eye on the bubble of the spirit level, listening excitedly to the harmony of the wires rising in pitch and volume as his speed increases. You can tell how fast you are going, because of the harmony of the wires. These wires were made originally for pianos. And ploughshares shall be beaten into swords. The pristine white clouds are wisps of drifting and swirling ghostly greyness inside. It is one of life's small disappointments. He notices that, as always seems to happen with Camels, his right foot is drenched in engine oil.

Underneath, to his absolute chagrin, he spots an enemy two-seater, taking photographs over Poelcapelle. It is a Roland Walfisch, which once upon a time had been Daniel's favourite German aircraft. It is dumpy, with a window on either side for the observer, and has the upper wing lying across the top of the fuselage, just as the Dolphin does. If you turn it over, you support the entire weight of the aircraft with your head.

It is obsolete, and Daniel has not seen one for months. It occurs to him that this might be the last one left in service. He feels a bitter contempt for whoever it was that ordered this machine out on a mission. Then he suspects a trap. He switches his engine on.

He turns and blots out the sun with his thumb. He sees nothing. He glances around for the flash of wings, for tiny silhouettes in the distance, and again sees nothing. The British archie notices him and stops firing at the Roland, so now the crew of the German aircraft know that there must be an Allied craft nearby. The observer spots him and cocks his Parabellum. He taps the pilot on the shoulder, the pilot looks round and up, puts the nose down and streaks for home.

He hasn't got a chance, however, because Daniel has the advantage of height and can dive at whatever speed he likes. Even on the flat he can outrun a Walfisch. He curses. Who is this demon who throws a spanner in the works when you're just out harmlessly stunting in the clouds? He is not in the mood for killing after so much fun.

Nor is he in the mood for being killed. A scout should not attack a two-seater on its own, even an obsolescent one, unless it can surprise it by coming up from underneath. For a good observer, a scout coming from above is a sitting duck. Daniel thinks of breaking away. If he has the wind up, it is the rational wind up.

He opens fire from a hundred yards, too far away to be effective. The observer fires a short burst, and Daniel sees the streaks of tracer passing between his wings on the starboard side. 'Damn, damn, damn,' he says between gritted teeth, as he presses on.

The tracer stops, and he is within killing range when he sees that the observer is struggling with his machine gun, which has jammed. The observer is in a rage of panic and frustration. Daniel is only a few yards away and is certain of an easy kill. The observer thumps the gun with his fist, and then, amazingly, furiously wrenches it from its mounting and hurls it overboard.

Like an executioner testing the edge of his axe, Daniel does not open fire as he easily follows the weaving and diving of the Roland. Daniel notes that this is the kind of Walfisch that has no forward-firing gun. He draws alongside, and the pilot looks at him wonderingly. Daniel stabs his finger at him and puts his own arms up briefly to signify that he is demanding surrender. You don't take your hands off a Camel's controls for any longer than you have to.

The pilot looks round at his observer, and nods, and the observer puts his hands up. Daniel fires a brief burst to signify that he demands cooperation, and then points in the rough direction of his aerodrome. The pilot nods and they fly side by side at eighty miles an hour. The observer is dejected and sits with his face in his hands. Daniel reflects that the day hasn't been spoiled after all, and for some reason he begins to think about the lovely house in Eltham where he used to live, before his father was killed. There were four girls living next door, Ottilie, Christabel, Sophie and Rosie. Rosie with the startling blue eyes and chestnut hair. She had been his ideal girl when he was a boy. He thinks, 'I wonder if they're still there? If I get through this, I'm going to call on those girls.' He gets a warm feeling in his guts thinking about them. A house with four girls!

Back at the aerodrome the squadron leader, Major Maurice Beckenham-Gilbert, known as 'Fluke', emerges from his hut, and all the ack emmas, pilots and ground staff come out to admire the captive machine, which has landed first. Daniel comes in second, blipping his engine and side-slipping to reduce speed. He volplanes into a perfect three-pointer, which is just as well in front of so many people. Everybody shakes hands with the German crew and has their photographs taken with them and Daniel in front of the Walfisch.

The crew are taken into the mess and offered tea or cognac. They choose cognac. Daniel says, '*Sprechen Sie Englisch?*' and the two men shake their heads. '*Français?*' and they both say, '*Oui, un peu.*' The pilot supplements this with '*Un très petit peu.*'

'*Je suis content de n'avoir pas eu le devoir de vous abattre.*'

'*Abattre?*' questions the observer.

'*Tuer,*' says Daniel.

'Ah,' says the observer. '*Nous aussi. Mais vous avez eu beaucoup de chance, n'est-ce pas? Que la mitrailleuse n'a pas marché?*'

Major Beckenham-Gilbert interrupts. 'Daniel, be a good fellow and translate, unless you can get them to talk in ancient Greek. Latin would do.'

'I said I was glad that I didn't have to kill them, and they said I was lucky that their guns were jammed.' He turns back to the two Germans.

'*Oui, j'ai eu de la chance. Je trouve que votre machine est très beau, j'ai toujours aimé le Walfisch. Je n'aimerais pas détruire le dernier. Ça serait triste. Plus tard je veux bien l'essayer.*'

'*Oui,*' answers the pilot.' *Elle est belle mais elle est vachement vieille. J'espère qu'elle est la dernière. Je n'ai pas offert de me suicider.*'

'I said yes I was lucky, and I think the Walfisch is a lovely bus, one of my favourites. I said I was glad not to have shot it down, and I'm going to give it a spin later.'

'Me too,' says Beckenham-Gilbert. 'Might be a good idea to paint out the crosses, though, and splash on some roundels. The last person to take a captured machine up for a spin got shot up the arse by a French farmer with an antique rifle.'

'And the pilot said,' continues Daniel, 'that it's too old, and he'd never volunteered to commit suicide, and I am going to reply that we all offer ourselves up for suicide every day. *On s'offre à la suicide chaque jour.*'

'*C'est vrai,*' said the pilot. '*Mais quand même . . .*'

'*Elle est la dernière?*'

'*Peut-être.*'

'*Alors, elle est un trésor. Il faut la preserver.* We said it might be the last one left, and ought to be preserved.'

'Wouldn't mind it as a run-about,' says the Major.

One of the prisoners gestures towards Daniel's Camel. '*Cet avion . . . le Camel . . . il est absolument incroyable . . . il est là, il n'est pas là . . . qu'est-ce qu'on peut faire contre un avion comme ça?*'

'*En anglais on dit "split-arse",*' says Daniel.

Major Beckenham-Gilbert understands that they are talking about the Camel, and interjects, 'Damned bloody split-arse.'

'Damt blutti split-haus,' repeats the German pilot.

'*Qu'est-ce qui se passe maintenant?*' asks the observer. His face is pale and worried.

'*Vous êtes tous les deux prisonniers, naturellement. Demain vous partez, mais ce soir vous dînez au mess avec nous. Je dois vous avertir qu'à la fin du repas, nous nous levons pour porter un toast au roi. Vous ne devez pas porter le toast, mais vous devez vous mettre debout. Compris?*'

They nod, and their faces light up at the thought of a meal. They have heard that the British have plenty of meat. Daniel offers them cigarettes. Camels, courtesy of the Americans. The two Germans look at the packet and smile. Daniel gives them the entire packet. He says to the Major, 'I told them they could dine with us tonight, and they'd have to stand up for the loyal toast, but wouldn't have to drink.'

'Seems a shame not to drink. Mind you, I wouldn't toast the Kaiser. Well, I might do so, but I'd take the opportunity to wish him a stiff case of haemorrhoids.'

'*Pour vous la guerre est finie,*' says Daniel to the two captives.

'*Finie,*' they nod, wondering what emotion to feel. They have a sense of let-down, anticlimax, relief, fear of the future, extreme weariness permitted at last. They feel a bond of affection and gratitude for this British airman who has changed their lives by making the future possible, and who seems simultaneously to be French.

'*Si vous avez besoin de quelque chose, avertissez-moi dès que possible, d'accord? Je vous donnerai le numéro de téléphone ici, et j'écrirai une lettre comme espèce de renseignement. Je vous donnerai aussi l'addresse de ma mère. Après la guerre, si je suis toujours vivant, on va se rencontrer et dîner ensemble. Je vous invite.'*

The pilot is touched. He says sincerely, *'J'espère que vous survivrez. Dieu vous prête la vie. Je vous remercie de nous avoir épargnés. Je vous souhaite le bonheur et prospérité et des jolis enfants.'*

'*Et moi aussi,*' adds the observer. '*Nous vous devons la vie.*'

'I told them to keep in touch,' says Daniel. 'They thanked me for sparing them, and wished me lots of pretty children.'

'Seem like a decent pair of fellows,' says Major Maurice Beckenham-Gilbert. 'Now I come to think of it, I think that they might be the two blighters who nearly shot my rudder off, over Arras.'

42

The Telephone (1)

Millicent was standing on a chair dusting the frame of the portrait of Mr McCosh's grandfather with a feather duster, when the telephone rang. 'Oh bother!' she exclaimed, and hopped down. She ran to the apparatus and lifted the earpiece off the hook. She put on the most aristocratic voice she could manage, and recited the words that Mrs McCosh had once made her repeat fifty times, until she had got it quite right: 'Eltham 292. The Grampians. Millicent speaking. To whom would you like to speak?'

'Ah, Millicent,' said a warm voice from east London. 'You don't 'alf sound posh. It's you I'm after, as a matter of fact.'

'Who is it? Is that you, Hutch?'

'What if it wasn't? How many boyfriends have you got, my girl?'

'About fifteen, but only four is serious. Where are you? Are you home?'

'I'm home. I've got two weeks. When are you off?'

'After church. On Sunday.'

'Can I come and see you? I want to ask you to marry me.'

'What?'

'You heard.'

'Hutch! You can't just ask me on the phone! All casual!'

'I haven't. I'm going to ask you on Sunday. We'll go down to the Tarn.'

'You won't find a dry place to kneel.'

'Stuff that, sweetheart. I've been sodden for years. But I'm not going to ask if you're not going to be accepting.'

'Oh, Hutch! Well, what do you think?!'

'Is that yes, then?'

'Oh, Hutch!'

The telephone began to bleep, and in the few seconds left, Hutch said, 'Got no more pennies. See you Sunday, sweetheart.'

Millicent sat down on the chair beneath the portrait that she had been dusting, and blew out her cheeks. She felt the most wonderful sense of jubilation, and began to laugh. Rosie came out of the drawing room and found her there, apparently idling, and Millicent sprang to her feet in embarrassment. 'Oh, Miss Rosie, I wasn't slacking. I wasn't, I promise!' Rosie looked a little sceptical. 'I wasn't, miss! I was recovering! I just had news!'

'Happy news, by the looks of it.'

'I'm going to get married, miss! Hutch is coming on Sunday, and he's going to ask me. Down by the Tarn.'

Rosie stood silent for a second or two, absorbing the news.

'Why are you crying, miss?'

'Oh Millicent, I'm so happy for you. I'm sorry. I can't help it. It's such wonderful news.'

Millicent realised at that moment that Rosie was perhaps also crying for herself. She reached up her hands helplessly, as if to embrace Rosie, but knowing that it could not possibly be done. Rosie saw the gesture and reacted naturally to it. She reached out her own hands and the two women found themselves in each other's arms, both in tears.

Eventually Rosie detached herself, wiped her eyes with the exiguous handkerchief that she kept up her sleeve, and said, 'I bet that's never happened in this house before.'

'Nor never will again, most like.'

'Millicent?'

'Yes, miss?'

'Can I be your bridesmaid? For Ash's sake? Because Hutchinson was his best friend?'

Millicent was horrified, and flushed hotly. 'But, miss, no gentlewoman has ever been no servant's bridesmaid. What'll Mrs McCosh say?'

'Everything's changed, Millicent. Before the war Ash and Hutchinson wouldn't have got to be friends, would they? And there's absolutely no need for my mother to know. I'll go as the family representative. If you accept, of course.'

'But, miss, I got four sisters.'

At last Rosie perceived Millicent's agitation, and felt ashamed of herself.

'Oh, Millicent, I am sorry. I didn't mean to put you on the spot. It was thoughtless of me. It's just that I'm fond of you. And I'm really not a snob any more. But I can quite see that it would seem awfully strange for your family if I were there. I am sorry. I shouldn't have asked.'

'It was nice of you to ask,' said Millicent. 'I don't honestly think we'll have any bridesmaids at all, though.'

'May I come to the service? I'll sit at the back, if that's all right.'

'Course it is, miss.'

'Thank you.'

43

Autographs

One of the nurses in Rosie's tent had bought an autograph book and was filling it with inscriptions by the wounded soldiers in her care. The fashion had caught on because the men loved having something to do, and for many it was a chance to show how grateful they were to the nurses, to make up rhymes that lurched to scan, often didn't rhyme very well either, and even to make oblique declarations of affection. Rosie went into Southampton and bought a very nice one at the stationer's. It was bound in soft black leather, and the paper was thick and watermarked. Rosie had wanted a book of high quality in order to demonstrate to the men how much she valued them.

The first man to write in it was Able Seaman Devonshire, who turned straight to the last page and wrote: 'By hook or by crook I'll be the last in this book.' G. Grimble of the Machine Gun Corps wrote: 'When on this book you look, when on this book you frown, think of the one who spoiled your book by writing upside down.' Private Shaw 12367 of the 1st Battalion Scots Guards left his address in the hope that Rosie would get in touch with him at a later date. Private Humphrey 2021, 3rd Battalion the Queen's Regiment, stuck a small photograph of himself into the book. He decorated a whole page with writing that looked as if it were done in relief. He did it with his left hand.

Lieutenant Collier of the Yorks and Lancs drew an elaborate cartoon of some German soldiers being frightened by tanks. A. Hilberry of the Inniskilling Dragoons drew a cartoon of a sailor and a bulldog, and Private Francis Love in hut 19 drew some brooms and a carpet sweeper, subtitled 'Some Mine Sweeping Equipment'. Bombardier Hood drew an ivy tendril in flower, very beautifully. Master Sergeant Montgomery of the 4th CMR wrote:

Think of me when you are lonely,
Cast on me one little thought,
In the depths of thine affection,
Plant one sweet forget-me-not.
You are my friend, my friend forever,
You may change but I will never.
Though separation is our lot,
Dear Old Pal forget me not.

12767 Joseph Webber of the 2nd Suffolks stuck in a photograph of himself straddling a chair backwards, with his arms resting on the back. He drew an immaculate picture of his cap badge, and wrote:

The best of luck I wish for thee,
The best of all good things,
The best of happiness and joy
That fortune ever brings.

Private Edwards of the 14th Battalion Durham Light Infantry,
wounded at Ypres.

'May your life be free from sorrow and care, may fortune always attend you, and may your days be filled with happiness is the sincere wish of Wm. J. Allen, 2nd CMR BC Canada.'

V. Buxton wished VAD Nurse McCosh the best of good luck from her little Aussie, and wrote a strange rhyme about a kangaroo that she couldn't decipher.

Another little Aussie, Pte ME Obrien of the AIF, wrote:

The Netley Red Cross Hospital is the first that I've been in,
And the way that we've been treated, I'll long to be back
again.

Though you may be wounded badly, there is no cause to
fear,
For you're sure to recover quickly with the nurses they have
here.

Although Australia's far away across the briny sea,
I'll not forget the hospital where the nurses were so kind
   to me.

Impressed by his own talent, he wrote 'Some poem!' obliquely
across the bottom of the page.

The waggish HM of hut 19 wrote:

> Mary had a little lamp,
> It was well trained no doubt,
> For every time her sweetheart called,
> That little lamp when out.

At Christmas 1916 Sergeant J. J. Hennessey of the Rifle Brigade
(Prince Consort's Own) reflected that: 'As the stormiest days
frequently end in the most gloriest sunset, so we hope and pray
that out of this time of sorrow and strife may issue a nobler and
better world than has been yet.'

148928 MTASC, EAEF wrote:

> Little dabs of powder, little daubs of paint,
> Make a girl's complexion look just what it ain't.

Rifleman Frank Neale of the Post Office Rifles wrote out all
of Portia's speech about mercy, from memory.

On and on they went for three volumes, the rhymes, cartoons,
reflections, words of gratitude, some beautifully done, some semi-
literate, all sincere. As her life went by Rosie spent many hours
alone with her autograph books, remembering the cheerful young
men in the photographs, trying to picture those whose images
had been slowly fading, admiring the immense talent of common
soldiers from all over the Empire who could paint immaculate
pictures of flowers or dogs, or bottles of whisky. To her they
remained as young and cheerful as they had been back then, frozen
in time by fond memory as old lovers are. These wounded young
men who had left traces of their spirit in ink and pencil, verse
and adage, were signals of the time in her life when she had been
doing the most important things it would ever befall her to do,

when experience was most intense, when the immensity of her grief and exhaustion made the plasticity of the world shimmer before her eyes like the heat haze on a summer road, when the whole universe seemed to smell of carbolic and Lysol and surgical spirit.

The contribution to which she unfailingly returned was the entry by Private J. C. Grundie of the Argyll and Sutherland Highlanders, who had taken a particular shine to her because she was half Scottish. On 9 April 1918 he drew a picture of a young woman wearing a sun hat, with a trug basket in the crook of her arm, and a rake over her shoulder. Behind her was a picture of a steamer and a submarine, and from each corner of the page grew tufts of what looked like tropical fern. In the middle of these surreal juxtapositions he had written, in tiny italic script:

When the war is done we'll recall the fun —
The fun that conquered the pain —
For we'll owe a debt (and we'll not forget)
To the jokes that kept us sane:
How the wounded could laugh and bandy their chaff
And kick up a deuce of a row!

It may be in peace, when the sufferings cease,
We'll be sadder, aye sadder, than now.

Rosie learned these prophetic words by heart, and hoped that for Private J. C. Grundie she too would remain forever young, with chestnut hair on her head, freckles on her face, and so much grief to cope with that she smothered it in work, and kindliness, and jokes.

44

The Metamorphosis of Mrs McCosh (1)

Mrs McCosh adored Folkestone. Every Whitsun she travelled down by train from Victoria to stay with her friend Myrtle, who liked to style herself Mrs Henry Cowburn, after the fashion of the day. Mrs Henry Cowburn lived in a dilapidated four-bedroomed house not far from Little Switzerland with her husband, a former yeomanry officer and local solicitor, who was infinitely more interested in playing golf than in practising law, and liked to play with Mr McCosh whenever he had reason to come up to London, and with Mrs McCosh when she came down to visit his wife. He had served in the South African war and his intestines had never quite recovered from the dysentery that had nearly killed him, and had, indeed, done for most of his comrades far more efficiently than the guerrilla tactics of the Boers. Before setting off to the golf course he would take great pains to ensure that nothing gastrointestinal was likely to happen to him. Fortunately the green of the ninth was near the clubhouse, and he could usually manage until then. He ate prodigious quantities of eggs and bacon, in the belief, current at the time, that they had a binding effect. This diet certainly made an outdoor life in some ways preferable, but now that eggs were fivepence and bacon was one and eight, he had discovered to his delight that a more normal diet actually improved the state of his bowels.

Folkestone had been greatly changed by the war, at first becoming somewhat dismal. It had been designated a prohibited area because of its proximity to France and its vulnerability to naval bombardment. All the Austrian and German waiters had been interned, and the hotels and boarding houses had fallen into desuetude. The Metropole and the Grand were barely ticking over, and the band no longer played its exuberant music on the Leas. The young men had gone into the navy or the Buffs, and their place had been taken by abject Belgian refugees, with their tales of atrocity and rape, and their hopeless penury. Myrtle was on the Committee for Belgian Refugees, and her three spare rooms were taken by three elderly musicians from the same orchestra who had all fled together. Her house was filled with melancholy chamber music played on borrowed instruments that were not nearly as good as the ones they had had to leave behind, as they often reminded her. On three days a week she manned the soup kitchens at the fishmarket. Major Cowburn was on the Emergency Committee, and was one of those in charge of destroying anything useful to the enemy in the event of invasion. He had a list of everything useful in the town, and detailed plans as to how to destroy it. In his garden he had prepared a large ziggurat of kindling so that a bonfire might be lit at short notice.

Not long after the commencement of the war, Folkestone had begun to fill up with tens of thousands of Canadian recruits. On St Martin's Plain were acre upon acre of tents, shops, huts, cinemas and canteens. Practice trenches reconfigured the landscape and became a hazard for drunks and unwary sheep. Millions of men had marched proudly down Slope Road, and many fewer were later to march wearily back up it.

Mrs McCosh's luggage had been sent on ahead. When she left the station she was somewhat displeased by the present appearance of things, and wondered with whom she might have a stern word. She felt the onset of a letter to His Majesty. To begin with, the coming and going of so many military vehicles had turned the roads into a sea of chalky mud that clung to one's shoes like treacle, and furthermore, the empty houses were already falling into disrepair, giving the town a forlorn aspect that Mrs McCosh felt was certain to be bad for the general morale.

Myrtle had come to meet her at the station, and they had exchanged embraces and delighted giggles as if they were still schoolgirls. Myrtle was slender, despite the approach of middle age, and her eyes were still bright with the humour and interest of youth. She always dressed, even in winter, in such a way as to give the impression that she was a fairy draped in diaphanous gauze. Mrs McCosh, on the other hand, dressed stylishly and expensively without in any way standing out from the crowd.

'My dear, you look most scandalously well,' said Myrtle to her friend. 'It's terribly unbecoming in wartime, don't you think, to be so much in the pink?'

'You're becoming a poet,' replied Mrs McCosh.

'It's so lovely to see you,' said Myrtle, 'I was inspired to rhyme quite accidentally. I do think you're most frightfully brave to come. One lives in constant fear of a raid. It's rather a jar.'

'Oh no,' replied Mrs McCosh, 'in that, you are quite wrong. Everyone knows that Folkestone is perfectly safe.'

She was referring to the widely held belief that the Germans would never attack Folkestone because in the recent past the local people had saved hundreds of German sailors from drowning after a collision between two warships, and it was certainly true that even though Dover and Ramsgate and Margate had been bombed, Folkestone itself had been spared.

Myrtle was sceptical. 'My dear, these people have invaded Luxembourg and Belgium, and think nothing of killing civilians. Why, I believe they even think it's a good thing! And they invented that ghastly warfare with gas. I do hope you're right though.'

'I am always right, my dear,' said Mrs McCosh drily. The two women set off gaily, receiving the respectful greetings of many a Canadian officer on the way. 'I do love these Canadians,' said Myrtle, 'the way they sweep off their caps and even bow, and I don't believe it's the slightest bit ironical. And it's amazing how many of them are sort of French.'

'Sort of French?'

'Sure, it's quite like being in Brittany sometimes. They gabble away to each other in such a strong accent that it's quite hard to follow. Of course, if one addresses them in proper Parisian French, they simply reply in English.'

'Did you say "sure"? I do believe you are becoming a Canadian yourself.'

'Oh, you should hear us all,' said Myrtle. 'Dear Henry almost has an accent. Oh, and I must tell you, I have three Belgian musicians in the house at present, so please don't be alarmed if you come across poor shambling folk on the landing. They are nearly ghosts, but not quite. Two of them have very kindly agreed to share during your visit, so you shall have your usual room over-looking the sea.'

'How lovely,' said Mrs McCosh with evident insincerity, a little worried about having to be in the vicinity of unknown foreigners. She had not bargained on any such thing. 'Of course, I have been having Belgian ladies to tea quite a lot myself.'

'Don't worry, they are perfectly sweet,' said Myrtle. 'They have such a glum air that it makes one want to tickle them.'

It was a beautiful day in May. The sky was clear but for some tiny clouds, and the sea was Mediterranean blue and flat calm. A small breeze was bringing the aroma of kelp and salty water to the promenade, and Mrs Hamilton McCosh and Mrs Henry Cowburn walked along it in a daze of contentment and well-being. They had been friends for a very long time, despite being so far removed from each other temperamentally, and it had been Mrytle who had seen Mrs McCosh through that terrible period that the latter always thought of as her 'Dreadful Disgrace' or 'Awful Scandal' when it had been revealed in the press that the Lord to whom she was engaged already had a wife in a lunatic asylum in America. She had felt humiliated and shamed by it even though she and everybody else had known perfectly well that she had not been remotely at fault. She had destroyed all her personal diaries that covered that period, and moreover His Lordship had recently died, so that Mrs McCosh finally felt completely free of him. She had been utterly grateful and aston-ished when one day Hamilton McCosh had proposed to her, although she had been slightly mortified when he had added, 'And I have nothing but cobwebs in the attic.'

They reached home at exactly the same time as Henry Cowburn himself, who was dressed in plus fours and was carrying one golf club and a new box of golf balls. He was returning from the monthly match of the Mashie Club, in which each player was only permitted the use of one club for the whole round. He had learned to putt left-handed so that the negative loft of the back of the club put a marvellous topspin onto the ball and sent it unerringly into the cup. The other members liked to josh him that he could only win by cheating, and win he did, every time. As the prize was always a box of half a dozen golf balls, he now had a fair store of them in the cupboard under the stairs, and was hoping to send Mrs McCosh home with a box or two for her husband.

'Welcome to Little Toronto!' he exclaimed, and Mrs McCosh held out her hand.

'Did you win again, dear?' asked his wife.

'Absolutely!' he replied. 'Or should I say "sure"?'

'You could but you shouldn't,' said Myrtle in her best Canadian accent, '"cause it ain't good English.'

That evening they and the musicians dined on the rabbit that Henry Cowburn had bagged himself from the rough on the fifteenth. They agreed that the war would already have been lost but for rabbits, and afterwards the musicians played the famous andante by Vinteuil. It was soothing and sad. Mrs McCosh retired to bed feeling serene, not missing her own family one little bit.

The following morning the elderly musicians convened in the conservatory, where they played Beethoven amongst the bromeliads and pelargoniums. Major Cowburn went to his office, where he intended to do as much work as possible in the morning so that he might be released to the golf course in the afternoon, and the ladies went for the first of the day's promenades, firstly in Radnor Park, where they watched some girls playing tennis, and then to the cemetery, where Myrtle took her companion to visit the graves of her departed friends and acquaintances. She wiped her eyes at each, and told Mrs McCosh anecdotes about the occupants, all of which Mrs McCosh had heard many times before. 'Just think, my dear, one day I shall be in here with them,' she said, adding, 'and on a beautiful day like this I don't think I'd mind a bit. It's such a nice place to rest in forever, don't you think?'

It was indeed a perfect day. Despite the war and its losses, shortages and inconveniences, it was impossible not to feel a little joyful.

They lunched at the Grand Hotel where, because the sole alternative was whale meat, they had to eat rabbit again, spent the afternoon drifting amongst the shops, and stopped twice for tea and cake, laughing and chattering the whole time, even though the cake had almost no sugar in it, and was hardly up to scratch. Certainly, her own daughters would have been much astonished to see their mother in such a frivolous, light-hearted and girlish mood.

It was at the second of these tea houses that an acquaintance of Mrs Henry Cowburn informed her in tones of breathless excitement that not only were Gosnold's of Tontine Street selling fine lace at two shillings and three farthings a yard, but Stoke's in the same street had a large supply of potatoes. 'Oh, lace and potatoes,' exclaimed Myrtle. 'Goody-goody. How could one live without them?' She turned to her friend. 'Why don't you go for a wander? There's no point in both of us queuing for hours.'

'There's a little shop I'd like to visit in Dover Road,' replied Mrs McCosh, who had never had to queue for vegetables in her life, and had no intention of starting now. 'I'll come and find you in half an hour and we can go to Gosnold's together.'

'I fear you might have to allow more than half an hour,' said Myrtle. 'The queues can become frightfully long. Luckily one always runs into friends, and it's just like a party, but without the drinks and canapés, and with all sorts of delightful common people that one wouldn't normally come across. It's quite a leveller, I do declare.'

The friends separated, and Myrtle almost skipped to Stoke's grocery shop, where she found a large, patient queue that included children playing football, babes in arms, dogs and even horses. There were very few young men, but plenty of elderly ones, all of them engaged in discussing how lovely the weather was, and saying how well it boded for Whitsun.

A series of explosions began in the near distance, coming ever nearer, and people reassured themselves that it was the Canadian soldiers getting into practice with their gunnery.

The twenty gigantic Gothas had set off with the intention of bombing London, but had been foiled by dense cloud. Although crudely built, they were magnificently invulnerable because they could fly higher than any Allied aircraft, and had a gun port in the rear that faced downwards so that it was impossible to attack them safely from below as one did with any other kind of bomber. None of the aircraft sent up against them were able to get within three thousand feet.

They were flying in diamond formation so as to maximise mutual defence, and intended to break it only to circle as they released their bombs. Their crews were brave and patriotic young men who loved the way that their engines sang, and deceived themselves into thinking that they were achieving military objectives when they had no very clear idea of what was beneath them and no way of accurately aiming their bombs. The Kaiser had in any case decreed that it was legitimate to bomb civilians because this reinvention of total war would demoralise the population and so bring about an earlier peace, which is what any civilised person would want. The thought did not occur to him that this might provoke the British to retaliate in kind. As he greatly valued *Kultur*, he magnanimously forbade his bombers to attack ancient monuments, and as he valued his family he sentimentally forbade any attacks on the property of the royal family.

Frustrated by the failure to attack London, the twenty bombers turned for home, and followed the railway line to the Cinque Ports. They killed a sheep at Marden, another one at Mersham, and an eighteen-year-old girl at Ashford. A dud landed in an open grave at Belsingham, and eighteen Canadian soldiers perished at Shorncliffe Camp. They killed a middle-aged man in his garden in Cheriton, Dorothy Bergin, who was sixteen, and Francis Considine, who was five.

Myrtle thought the bombers looked beautiful as they circled above her. The sun was sparkling off their white wings, and everyone in the potato queue was craning their neck upwards and pointing, confident that the planes were theirs. They still thought that the explosions were from the training camp, even though they were now coming from the West End, and Radnor Park and Bouverie Road.

Myrtle watched a single bomb fall from one of the Gothas, the tiny black speck growing ever larger. She clutched her bag to her chest and held her breath as she and forty-four others were annihilated instantaneously, and seventeen more began their agonising and indecent journey into death.

Mrs McCosh had been watching the bombers like everyone else, thinking how pretty they were, and had not tried to take shelter. It was 6.22 when she saw the black speck leaving the

Gotha, heard the crash of the explosion, and saw the column of debris and smoke rising up into the air over Tontine Street.

Carefully she put her bags and her shopping down in a doorway, and for the first time in many years began to sprint, shouting, 'Myrtle! Myrtle!' as she rushed round the corner from Dover Street.

What she beheld stopped her in her flight, and she walked slowly into the killing ground. A great sheet of flame from a gas main rose into the air with a whoosh, like the finishing touch to a portrait of Hell. There was a stink of blood and flame and explosive.

Mrs McCosh searched amongst the carnage. She pushed aside the rubble and severed limbs with her feet, peered beneath the mangled bodies of horses and into the tangled heaps of the dead. There was a woman, recently in pursuit of lace in Gosnold's, with blood pouring from wounds in her head as she attempted first aid on those still living. Three of the dead lay in a cart, and there were many to whom humiliation had been added to obliteration because their clothes had been blown from their bodies.

Mrs McCosh tried to ignore the disassembled corpses of all the little children, because to have done otherwise would have been more than she could have borne. But then her gaze fell on the golden curls of Florence Norris, whose severed head lay gazing up at her from the step of the Brewery Tap in a puddle of blood. She was two years old. Tears came to Mrs McCosh's eyes, and she bit her lip in rage and pity.

She found some bits and pieces that she thought might have belonged to Myrtle and gathered them in a heap.

The Canadian Red Cross ambulance arrived, then the firemen and the police, and she helped them wrap the limbs up in blankets for transportation to the hospital, and then, dishevelled, exhausted, weeping and drenched in blood, she went to fetch her bags, which had remained undisturbed on the doorstep where she had left them.

On the way back to Tontine Street she encountered Major Cowburn, who had been striding down Dover Street to see if he could be of any assistance. He had been enraged by a bomb that had left a large crater on his beloved golf course, and was wondering if Myrtle would allow him to re-enlist, if the army would accept a man who was too old, and always running for the lavatory.

He stopped suddenly in his tracks when he came face-to-face with Mrs McCosh, who was drenched in blood. 'Oh my dear,' he said.

Mrs McCosh put down her bags and silently clutched him, laying her head on his chest. He patted her back in embarrassment. She had about her the familiar smell of war. He murmured something inane that seemed to be all he could come up with.

Eventually Mrs McCosh managed to calm herself a little, and drew back slightly.

'Oh, Henry, I am so sorry,' she said.

'Sorry? Sorry?'

'I did my best, I really did. I looked everywhere, but I just couldn't find it. I tried so hard, I did Henry. She was so pretty, oh, Henry, she was so pretty.'

'I am sure you did,' said Major Cowburn, realising that he would have to bide his time.

No one found it, and so it was that in Cheriton Cemetery on 30 May, amongst dozens of others, a coffin was lowered into the ground containing what were probably the torso and limbs of Mrs Henry Cowburn, without her head.

45

The Metamorphosis of Mrs McCosh (2)

Windsor Castle

15 June

Dear Mrs McCosh,

His Majesty graciously requests that I should thank you for your kind letter of 5 June.

It is indeed true that there are no regiments of women on armed active service, although there are of course many women playing important roles as, for example, the drivers of fire engines and ambulances.

His Majesty asks me to remind you that he has no direct control over Parliament or over the Ministry of War, and that the issue as to whether or not women may go on active service is a matter for them.

His Majesty feels that even were there such units of women on active service, you may yourself be of too mature an age to endure the rigours of battle, and he therefore recommends that you consider preparing yourself for any invasion that may occur in the unlikely event of defeat on the Continent.

If you have friends in the country you might like to consider a visit sufficiently long to learn the use of a hunting rifle and shotgun from one of the gamekeepers or the man of the house.

In the meantime you may consider the acquisition of an air rifle, which may safely be used in the garden, and which would provide invaluable preparation for the mastery of a more powerful weapon. With an air rifle you will be able to practise on rats and pigeons those arts which would become most useful were the war to come to Eltham, since the elementary skills employed in the accurate use of an air rifle are identical to those required in the use of a Lee–Enfield, just as an air pistol would provide admirable apprenticeship in the use of a revolver. His Majesty advises that shooting with a rifle is at its most accurate when performed from the prone position.

His Majesty offers his sympathy over the loss of your dear friend in the recent atrocity in Folkestone, and asks me to convey his admiration for your determination to use this loss as further inspiration for patriotic action. As you have not been in touch for several months recently, he asks me to inform you that he is pleased to find you are still vigorous.

On behalf of His Majesty,

Lt Col. Sir Frederick Edward Grey Ponsonby, Secretary to His Majesty

46

The Metamorphosis of Mrs McCosh (3)

Mrs McCosh took a morning out to go to Swan & Edgar, reluctantly making the journey by omnibus. As she entered its doors she made it immediately clear that she was not just another tabby by collaring a shop walker. 'I wish to be taken immediately to whichever department it is where I may be able to acquire an air rifle,' she said.

The walker was not unduly surprised by this, since there has always been a certain type of Englishwoman who is prepared to brain a burglar with a poker or take potshots at an invader with an airgun, and in wartime the number of them greatly increases.

An hour later, having tried out everything they had, and listened to many lengthy technical explanations, she had bought a Brittannia, a strange-looking weapon because it had the compression chamber under the stock. It was, however, powerful and accurate, and you could adjust the compression so that you could use it on half power, for greater safety in confined spaces. She had also bought a supply of fifty targets, one thousand pellets and a metal target holder.

She wrote out her cheque and dictated her address so that the items might be delivered, and then she went to the toy department and purchased ten painted lead soldiers that together proved to be surprisingly heavy. There were no models of contemporary German soldiers, so she bought Napoleonic infantrymen on the grounds that an old enemy was better than none, Entente Cordiale and present alliance notwithstanding.

Two days afterwards Mrs McCosh walked boldly into the clubhouse of the Blackheath Golf Club. Her husband, who was supposed to be conducting business in London, was fortunate to spot her as she came to the door, and darted out of the back of the building, concealing himself behind an artisan's shed.

She addressed the assembled elderly gentlemen who had until that moment been tapping the dottle out of their pipes, reading the *Morning Post* or *Punch*, or idly watching the putting on the green outside.

'Are there any old soldiers here?' she demanded.

Thus it was that Major Butterworth, fifty-five years old, veteran of the Sudan and former regimental shooting champion, found himself in the garden of The Grampians supervising Mrs McCosh's education, with Mrs Pendennis knitting in a deckchair nearby, for the sake of probity.

Mrs McCosh lay on a tartan rug and learned to shoot in the prone position, then she learned to shoot kneeling, and then from behind a wall, and then standing. She quite undeniably had a knack for it, achieving tight groups at the upper edge of the bullseye almost every time. Major Butterworth regretted never having met her when he was younger, before Hamilton McCosh had snapped her up. He very much enjoyed their lessons, and acquired an air rifle of his own, setting up a shooting range on the upper landing of his house, much to the dismay of his housekeeper. He cut out pictures of the Kaiser and of liberal politicians from newspapers, glued them to pieces of card, pinned them to a large wooden board, and took pleasure in obliterating their heads every day for a quarter of an hour after breakfast. This catharsis greatly increased his personal happiness, and the happiness greatly improved his golf.

When Rosie next came home she found no one in the house to answer the door, and so she went round into the garden and stood and watched in wonder as her mother, one by one, knocked ten Napoleonic lead soldiers off a packing case from a distance of twenty yards, attended by Millicent, who was bearing the tin of pellets.

A week later Mrs McCosh was upstairs when she heard the unmistakable clattering of wood pigeons as they mated in the tree outside the landing window, which had been opened on account of the warmth of the day. She had always strongly disapproved of the shameless public promiscuity of pigeons.

Ten minutes later she appeared in the kitchen below stairs and laid a dead bird on the table, the scarlet blood still purling at its beak. 'Please remove the breasts from this bird,' she instructed Cookie, 'and put the rest in the stockpot. I will have the breasts sliced and fried with onions and bacon for lunch tomorrow, when I shall be dining on my own.'

'Yes, madam,' replied Cookie. 'Without it being hung at all?'

'I have never acquired the taste for rotten meat,' said Mrs McCosh with grandeur.

After she had gone, Cookie looked at the beautiful bird and said, 'Poor little sod.' Then she began to pluck it, still warm in her hands, because a warm bird is easier to pluck by a long mile.

At about teatime it occurred to Cookie that there may be a further use for Mrs McCosh's marksmanship, and accordingly she went to her and said, 'Madam, did you know that since we've had chickens, 'cause of the war an' all, we've had rats something chronic down the orchard? They're nicking the scraps. I thought you might like to, you know . . .'

'Deal with them? Certainly, Cookie. I shall imagine they're the Boche.'

Mrs McCosh soon learned the art of sitting extremely still, partially concealed behind an apple tree, and then she learned the hard way not to shoot at rats when a chicken was in the same field of fire.

A few nights later the air-raid maroon went off, and the immense engines of a Zeppelin were heard overhead. The air filled with the strong, aromatic odour of their kerosene. Mrs McCosh hustled the servants from their top-floor rooms down into the kitchen. Her husband announced his intention to die comfortably in his own bed, and refused to leave it.

Mrs McCosh found her air rifle and her tin of pellets, and went out onto the terrace that had been a conservatory before its conversion by a bomb. She beheld the airship above, caught in searchlights. It was quite inconceivably vast, and seemed to fill the whole sky from one side to the other. She stood still for a minute, awestruck. It was outrageous that this leviathan could come so far and rain bombs on the innocent, but, equally, it was a very beautiful sight, majestic, effulgent in the cross lights. The night fighters were up, their engines buzzing and clattering in harmony with the roar of the Zeppelin. Because the night fighters had arrived, the anti-aircraft batteries fell silent.

Mrs McCosh loaded her air rifle and shot at the Zeppelin. She knew that the pellets would fall thousands of feet short, and wished she had a real weapon, but she shot at the airship because this was the best she could do for Myrtle Cowburn, the best she could do to assuage her unassuageable hatred and indignation. When the airship had sailed sedately away and the bugle was blown for the all-clear, she went to the kitchen and told the servants to return to their beds.

In the morning she read that the Zeppelin had been shot down in flames near Enfield, and in the withdrawing room she danced triumphantly to the inaudible music of joy with her bemused husband, before allowing him to go to work.

On 20th June she attended the funeral of the eighteen little children killed by bombers in Poplar, and sniffled into her hand-kerchief as the horses drew the flower-laden hearses by. She left a wreath in the town hall, along with some five hundred others. The stories were known all over the nation; how a father was able to identify his five-year-old daughter only by the Egyptian medal round her neck; how an engineer identified his headless daughter in the mortuary by means of a freshly sewn-on button; how of one child, nothing remained except her boots.

There was no room in the church, so she did not hear the bishop read out the King's message. The bishop said that after two thousand years of Christianity, it was inconceivable that war was now being waged against women and children. Mrs McCosh followed the hearses to East London Cemetery, and watched as the strong young sailors carried the tiny coffins to their communal grave. Then she went home and shut herself in her room, devastated all over again by what had happened to Myrtle.

The next day Mrs McCosh went to Charing Cross Station and joined the sympathetic crowds who gathered there in order to welcome in the wounded. This she continued to do almost every day until the end of the war. She needed to have something to do, now that her daughters had left home, and there were so many horrible images and sounds that cluttered up and confused her mind.

47

Daniel Pitt to his Mother (3)

No fixed address

6 April 1918

Ma chère maman,

We are, as you know, in the middle of the most hideous German push. I like to think it's their last desperate effort, but we've had to move airfields twice, and now we're moving again. I have been sleeping in a leaky tent with a waterproof blanket that isn't.

But, chère maman! Light in the darkness! I have had the immense good luck to shoot down a Gotha! The Gothas come over quite often, but normally they are too high for us to reach them. This one was flying over the airfield quite low (11,000 ft) when I was coming back from an OP on my own, because the other two in my flight had developed dud engines and gone home early, and I nearly decided to run and hide in a cloud, because the damned things are impregnable. Discretion is the better part etc.

But I didn't, and I came down out of the sun, and got the observer in the back before he even saw me, overflew, immelmanned, and got the pilot on the second run. He managed to crash-land in a field and the bus didn't catch fire, so we got the pilot out and the other two crew, but the pilot died a few hours afterwards. Mimimal blood on my hands, though: it could have been four. The Gotha is vast, but not as big as a Handley Page.

And so . . . I have joined a tiny elite of Gotha-busting Hun-punchers! I am very fortunate, except that I had spent the previous day with the fitters, zeroing and fine-tuning my guns.

Fluke (my squadron leader) has put me up for an MC, and then he sent off a letter to Paris to tell Pétain that he'd damned well better give me the Croix de Guerre.

I can't tell you, maman, *what a stupendous rag and binge we had in the mess. My head will never be the same again.*

Ton fils dévoué et vainqueur,

Daniel P.

48

Hutch (2)

On 11 November 1918 Lloyd George read out the terms of the armistice to the assembled House of Commons, and then the entire House adjourned for a service at St Margaret's. A copy of the terms was posted at eleven o'clock on the railings of Buckingham Palace, and a great swell of people assembled at the Victoria Memorial.

The factories closed and the workers poured out into the streets. Anyone in uniform was hoisted onto people's shoulders and jubilantly carried along, seldom in the direction they had been hoping to take. Bonfires blazed and fireworks crackled from Land's End to Dover to Holyhead to Benbane Head to John o'Groats. Policemen had their helmets whisked off their heads and set on top of lamp posts at humorous angles. Soldiers overturned taxis and set them on fire. The crowds surged and cheered. At exactly eleven o'clock the maroons went off all over the country, and church bells swung vigorously and joyously in their towers. If there were no accordion to dance to, folk stood and clapped out a rhythm as youngsters and oldsters alike capered in the streets. The shop girls in Harrod's opened the windows, climbed on the roofs, and waved their handkerchiefs and flags above Knightsbridge. A bus drove by bearing a sign 'To Berlin, only a penny', its over-crowded passengers singing and whooping.

The King emerged on the balcony in the uniform of an admiral, accompanied by Queen Mary. The guard presented arms, a band played the national anthem, and after half an hour the King returned inside, only to be summoned forth again by an irresistible cry of 'Good old King George! We want King George! We want King George!' Someone began 'Rule Brittannia', and the whole crowd joined in. They sang the 'Old Hundred', and the Marseillaise. Somebody began the chant of 'Speech! Speech! Speech!' and the King thereupon made the shortest speech of his life, perfectly aware that nobody could hear it. The crowd sang 'Now Thank We All Our God' and afterwards the King joined in with the cheering. The crowd, drunk with relief and happiness, called for the King to re-emerge, and expressed no ill will when he didn't, until at half past three he and the Queen drove out in an open carriage, accompanied only by four mounted policemen. They passed in a great circle down the Mall, the Strand, Fleet Street, Ludgate Hill, Queen Victoria Street, Holborn, Oxford Street, Shaftesbury Avenue, Trafalgar Square and back down the Mall. It rained but the people would not disperse. When it grew dark the King and Queen came back out on the balcony in a halo of electric light that dazzled the crowd.

In the meantime the Prime Minister had made a speech in Downing Street, and then the people demanded another speech, so he had to come to the window and address them again. The cheers resounded to Westminster. 'We have won a great victory,' he declared, 'and we are entitled to a bit of shouting.'

The city suddenly blossomed with colour, like a garden in spring when the tulips come. The blackout curtains were torn down, so that lights blazed once more from windows. The French tricolour and flags from all over the Empire were hoisted on broomsticks and curtain poles lashed to chimneys and drainpipes. In every town and village the Boy Scouts were sent out on their bicycles to sound the all-clear for the last time. Incoherent fanfares blared from hunting horns and bugles, even inside people's own houses. The pubs were drunk dry, and those that were not stayed open in defiance of their licences.

The merrymaking continued all night. Military lorries laden with roaring loads of multinational servicemen lurched around the streets. The Savoy Hotel was overturned by officers of the Royal Air Force, led by a young ace waving a stupendously large French flag. It was a Monday, and the celebrations carried on all week. At 1 a.m. Mrs McCosh came home by taxi, dishevelled, wet, hungry and exhausted. She hammered on the door, unable to find her key, and Millicent in her night attire let her in, shocked to discover her mistress smelling distinctly of brandy. Mrs McCosh was mainly inebriated, however, by having seen the King so many times in one day. As for him, he spent the night writing letters of thanks to his ministers and to the personnel of the army, the navy and the air force.

Amid those who cheered and danced in the streets there were many who neither cheered nor danced. There were those, wiser than before, who remembered with a sense of retrospective amazement that four years earlier they had taken part in scenes of celebration almost identical to these, when war broke out. Very nearly all of them, however, thought that the war had been worth it.

On 7 November Hutch had gone with Lieutenant Simmons and seventy-one other ranks to establish an advanced GHQ in an abandoned train near Valenciennes, in the tiny village of Iwuy. On the 11th he had been one of the unlucky ones who had had to remain on guard duty whilst his comrades went on a spree to celebrate the news of the armistice.

Nonetheless, a few days later he was on his way home on leave, in part a recognition of the extraordinary fact that he had survived the entire conflict in one regiment, in one theatre of war.

As he travelled home across the English Channel he found that he did not really know how to feel. A part of him seemed numbed. He slept well at night but his dreams were populated by the dead. He saw their faces and heard their voices. Oddly enough, he often remembered more vividly the faces of dead enemies than those of his friends. It is impossible to forget the amazement on the face of a soldier who doubles over, grasping at the muzzle of your rifle as he tries to pull out the bayonet that you have thrust through his abdomen. The army's policy of keeping you relentlessly busy even when you are exhausted had made the war go by in a blur of activity and extreme fatigue. He had mastered the soldier's art of snatching a few seconds of profound sleep, whenever the opportunity arose, even when he was frozen and soaked, and lying on a bed of duckboards.

There were many things he remembered with great pleasure, such as the sun glistening on frost shortly after dawn, or the brilliance of the stars on a clear night, or the way that birds sang louder when they were competing with guns, or how the larks sang high above when battle ceased, or the German tenor who used to sing a lullaby, or the wondrous black shadows thrown by the intense light of star shells. He remembered well-loved faces lit up in a dugout by the light of candle stubs, the smell of damp wood burning, the fountains of mud hurled up by shells, the mad few days of leave when he had lived at the rate of a day a minute. He had loved watching aeroplanes. He remembered the pleasure he had taken in witnessing the heroism and cheerfulness of the upper-class lady ambulance drivers who had deserted their comfortable estates in order to drive vehicles donated by their fathers, slogging through the squelching mire to carry the injured away to their makeshift hospitals that were always on the move because of the shifting boundaries of the front, and where they worked all night during offensives. Those women were the salt of the earth, in his estimation. He remembered too the wild and hilarious football matches behind the lines when they were resting, the ribald songs, the stupid jokes, the playfights. He remembered standing with Ash looking at a huge hole blown through the wooden sides of a bunker, and Ash saying, 'Looks like we've got rats.' He remembered an officer getting a large hamper from Fortnum & Mason, who had then been hit by a fragment of bomb from a Halberstadt when they had been relaxing in the relative safety and comfort of their billet at Mont St Eloi. 'Sergeant, I bequeath you my hamper,' the young officer had said, a moment before he died, and the warrant officers had shared it out, drinking the champagne out of tin mugs and proposing toasts to the memory of their benefactor. Hutch was still wearing his boots.

Hutch had kept going not least because of his passion for Millicent. There was never a time when he was not thinking about seeing her again. He thought constantly of what he would say, and of the things that one day they would be able to do, after the war. He had spent time with her on every occasion that he'd been granted leave, spending less time with his family than he rightly should. Rosie, who tried to coordinate her leaves with Hutch, had admirably connived in this, finding false errands for Millicent that would allow her out of the house. Hutch had a steadily growing bundle of letters that Rosie had helped her to write, and read them over and over again even when they spoke only of the weather and of how you could hardly get sugar.

Nonetheless Hutch was exhausted, so exhausted that he did

not even know it himself. He was two stone below his natural weight, his bowels were either in flux or blocked solid, and often he ached all over without really knowing why. His rank had meant that he had had at all times to be tougher and more energetic than his men, because no soldier respects anyone above him who cannot do what he does, or does even better.

He went home briefly to Walthamstow to check on his mother and father, and then set off by train for Eltham. He was feeling a little out of sorts, or 'seedy' as people liked to say in those days, but put it down to the strangeness of being at peace. Now that the 15th had passed, the universal joy and relief were beginning to be tempered by a mood of counting the cost, and there was an atmosphere of uncertainty about what might happen next.

Something new and as deadly as the war had gathered momentum. It was said that six million had already died in India.

Dressed in civvies, and wondering whether he should turn back and go home, he knocked on the kitchen door of The Grampians, and it was answered by Cookie, rolling pin in hand, with her sleeves rolled up to reveal her florid, powerful forearms. 'Oh, it's you!' she cried, adding, 'I was just making pear-and-apple pie.'

'Good to see you, Cookie,' said Hutch.

'Come in, come in,' cried Cookie, 'Millie'll be so pleased.'

At the kitchen table, cradling large mugs of milky sweet tea, were the two policemen who called in on most days and were refortified by Cookie at elevenses, their feet already hot and a little swollen from pounding the beat. 'This is Corporal Leonard Hutchinson,' announced Cookie, 'what's going to marry our Millicent one of these days.'

'I'm a sergeant now,' said Hutchinson. 'Everyone calls me Hutch.'

'Not "Bunny" then,' said one of the policemen drily.

'Not yet,' replied Hutch, 'and no one'd better start either.'

'Well, I'm Police Constable David Miller, and this here is Police Constable Ernest White.'

'Known as Chalky and Dusty.'

Hutch shook their hands, and quite suddenly a wave of nausea shot through him, causing him to buckle at the knees. He made a grab for the back of a chair and gasped, 'Oh, Cookie, I'm not well.'

The two policemen stood up and eased him down into a seat. Cookie ran to the tap to fetch him a drink of water. 'Thank you,' he said feebly, as he sipped at it. He set down the glass and put his hands to his temple. 'My head,' he complained.

It felt as though his brain were swelling and pulsing inside his skull, and now his back and his arms and legs were beginning to hurt too. 'I'd better get home,' he said, and stood up, whereupon he fell unconscious to the floor, folding like a rag doll.

'Bleedin' heck,' said Cookie, kneeling down next to him. She put her hand to his forehead and said, 'He's burning up. We'd better get Miss Rosie.'

'Can't be us. We're not supposed to be here,' said Dusty, so Cookie dashed out, and up the stairs, finding Rosie in the morning room, where, having taken the heavy family Bible from its lectern, she was reading it on her knees at the window seat.

Rosie's heart sank when she knelt down at Hutchinson's side and realised immediately what the illness was. It had peaked just at the turn of the month, but hitherto her own family had avoided it by the simple expedient of not going out, apart from Ottilie, who was still down in Brighton nursing her Indian troops. She herself had returned the previous day from Netley, and had not been much exposed.

'What is it, miss?' asked Chalky, having forgotten that he and his companion had no particularly good reason for being in the kitchen of the house.

'Spanish influenza,' said Rosie, straightening up and trying to think quickly and precisely. 'Fetch me three tea towels, will you, Cookie?'

She bade the two policemen tie the tea towels across their faces and, then did so herself, saying, 'It's probably no use, but it's better than nothing.' She knew that if Hutchinson were to sneeze he would fill the air with microbial droplets. The two policemen heaved the body upstairs to the spare room, left their masks there, and then retired to the kitchen to recover their breath and drink another pint of tea. Rosie had told them to wash their hands thoroughly, and now they and Cookie sat in gloom, smelling somewhat carbolical, speculating about the possibly fateful results of their encounter.

'Mostly gets the very young and the old, don't it?' asked Dusty.

'And the sick,' said Cookie, 'and them that's weak. That's why it's got so many soldiers, they're that wore out.'

'God help us,' said Chalky.

When Millicent found out from Cookie that her fiancé was in the house, gravely ill, contradictory emotions of joy and anxiety overwhelmed her. Rosie had decided that she was going to look after the patient on her own and that she and Hutch would both be in strict quarantine. She soaked towels in Lysol and hung them from the walls and from the architrave of the door. She made Millicent stand in the doorway with a muslin cloth across her mouth and nose, and did not permit her to come one step closer. She stood there with her face in her hands, whimpering and repeating, 'He will be all right, won't he, miss?' until Rosie wondered how may more times she was going to have say, 'I really don't know, Millicent.'

Mrs McCosh was not pleased. Refusing to wear anything across her face, she positioned herself down the corridor and expected Rosie to have a conversation with her by calling from the doorway.

'You must get him out straight away and down to an infirmary,' she instructed her daughter.

'What infirmary? The Cottage Hospital?' replied Rosie. 'You can't take him into a hospital, he'll infect the other patients, and a lot of them will die.'

'But he's going to kill us all!' cried Mrs McCosh.

'Stay away, Mama, and he'll only kill me.'

'How can you say such dreadful things? Don't you mind dying? He's not even a gentleman. What do you think people will say when they hear you have been immured in a room with a man to whom you are not even related?'

'He was Ash's best friend,' said Rosie, bridling, 'and I've spent the whole war looking after men who weren't gentlemen.'

'Heaven knows what it might have done to your morals,' replied her mother, whereupon Rosie went back into the room and re-emerged with a long-necked Wedgwood vase, which she hurled at her mother with extraordinary force, so that it shattered on the wall, next to her head. As Mrs McCosh looked at her, wide-eyed with astonished outrage, Rosie said coldly, 'What do you say of the morals of someone who did practically nothing for four years while millions of young men died?' Then she went back into the sickroom, slamming the door behind her. Mrs McCosh sat down in a chair on the landing and said to herself, 'But I got a gun after Myrtle was killed. I went to welcome the wounded at Charing Cross. I had Belgian ladies to tea. I took fruit to the Cottage Hospital.' She would never have dared confront her own mother in such way when she had been young, and now she was quite uncertain as to how to comport herself. It was true that she had greatly provoked her own mother, but now she was helpless in the face of her own angry adult daughter. One thing she knew was that it was no good expecting her husband to take her side. 'I am quite alone,' she said, and decided to write to the King.

Rosie sat at Hutch's bedside, not worrying about whether or not she was going to catch the Spanish influenza. Hutch was almost her last connection with Ash, now that his brothers were also dead, and his parents paralysed by grief. She fetched her madonna from under the bed in her own room, and put it under that of Sergeant Hutchinson, and she brought in her Bible and her prayer book, and the rosary that nobody knew she had, and which she had learned to use from a Roman Catholic missal that she had bought at Westminster Cathedral. Fingering the beads, she repeatedly told the Mother of God that she was blessed amongst women, and her muttering certainly seemed to have a calming effect on her patient.

Hutch was running an extremely high temperature, he was coughing drily in his stupor, and his tongue was coated in a thick grey fur. His eyes and nose were running, and when he awoke it was almost impossible for him to talk, so sore was his throat. Rosie knew that it was quite unrealistic to expect him to eat anything, so she gave him honey from a spoon for his throat, tea and weak vegetable soups, planning to add milk and eggs when he began to recover.

In a hospital, Hutch would have been given mustard baths, but Rosie was not strong enough to carry him to a bath on her own, so she propped him on the side of the bed and made mustard baths for his feet, which he did enjoy when he was lucid. Millicent ran up and down stairs with bowls of freshly boiled water, into which Rosie stirred Friar's Balsam, so that the air in his room could be kept moist in appeasement of his cough.

For his throat, Rosie made a cold compress of methylated spirit and water, and poultices of linseed for his chest and for the space between his shoulder blades, to relieve the pains. She realised all over again that she actually enjoyed the extreme fatigue of caring for a desperate case. To help him sleep profoundly she gave him a weak solution of potassium bromide, and to his recumbent and sterterous body she read the poems of Rupert Brooke, as if by reading to one of his comrades she could reach Ash's shade. As he was unconscious, she also read her own poems, and this gave her a strange feeling of excitement and agitation. 'I should work more at this,' she thought. 'This is something I really do want to do.' She had no idea whether her verses were any good, but it was like a forefinger prodding her in the small of the back. She thought that, even if she were not particularly good at present, she would eventually become so.

In the meantime Mr McCosh sent a telegram to Netley to inform them that his daughter was fully engaged in looking after a sick soldier in Eltham, and requesting leave, which was shortly granted, since the flow of new casualties to that hospital had abruptly slowed to a trickle after 11 November. He sent another telegram to the police station in Walthamstow, asking them to locate Hutchinson's family and tell them the news, and he sent yet another telegram to Armoury House to reassure them that their soldier had not deserted but was in fact gravely ill.

Millicent was in an extreme state of distress, brought on by helplessness. She knew that Rosie was right to exclude her from the sickroom, but at the same time she could not bear it, and could scarcely concentrate on her work. She made frequent mistakes, and was inclined to run sobbing from the room at short notice. Cookie found herself with a greatly increased workload, and grew bad-tempered, so that when Mrs McCosh unwisely accused her of deliberately spoiling the food, she inadvertently prompted a resignation crisis that Mr McCosh was only just able to avert by means of charm and his considerable ability to cajole.

'Don't ever do that again,' he said to his wife, 'I practically had to offer to marry her.'

'The servants are the concern of the lady of the house,' she replied, to which he responded, 'And the lady of the house is the concern of its master.'

After four days, it became evident to Rosie that Sergeant Hutchinson's disease had become malignant. She saw a strange heliotrope cyanosis developing, there was discharge in his ears, and he had terrible pains in his abdomen and chest that reduced him to breathless spasms. When she listened, she was sure that he was developing pleurisy, and when he began to cough up something sticky and bloody, she knew he had got pneumonia.

At this point she did what she should have done before, and called Dr Scott. He himself had just recovered from the disease, which he had caught in mid-October, and was now suffering from a kind of depression both in body and spirit that made it very difficult for him to work at all.

He examined the patient and listened to Rosie's account of what she had done, and her apologies in case she had proved inadequate. He looked at her sadly and said, 'My dear, you couldn't have done better. You've done exactly what any doctor such as myself would have recommended. I have always had the greatest admiration for what you and your sister Ottilie have done in this war, and indeed, I would nowadays, after everything I have seen and learned, go so far as to say "Piffle" to anyone who asserts that a woman cannot make a good doctor. However, he now has pneumonia, as you have rightly found for yourself, and against a bacillus there is absolutely nothing one can do. It will certainly be some kind of pneumococcus. I wouldn't be surprised if nephritis has also set in. I would have to take a urine sample, of course. I fear that his heart has been considerably weakened.'

'Is there no hope?' asked Rosie tearfully.

'He's going to drown,' said the good doctor. 'It is, at least, a peaceful death. Was he a man of faith? I think you might do well to call in a priest.'

'Oh!' exclaimed Rosie. 'After getting through the whole war! It's so unfair!'

'He didn't get through the war, my dear. He has been exhausted by the war, and this is how it's got him after all.' He paused and sighed. 'We all die, my dear, some soon and some late, but we all die. One might even feel a little envious.'

'I know what you mean, Doctor,' said Rosie softly.

Sergeant Leonard Hutchinson, as so many do, waited until dawn before he died, whilst Rosie was asleep beside him in her chair, her Bible open at the Book of Job. Her former colleague might have seen angels in the form of his comrades coming to carry him away, but there was no one to see anything. He breathed less and less often, more and more shallowly, until there was a pause that seemed to last for minutes, and then he breathed one last rasping breath.

When Rosie awoke, she leaned over him and kissed him on the forehead. Before leaving the room she turned the mirrors to face the wall, then she went down the garden to Bouncer's grave and sat in the smoke-fogged air until she grew too cold.

At his funeral in Walthamstow, where Mrs McCosh surprised everyone by her wailing, shots were fired over his grave, and the shell of one more valiant soul was swallowed up by the ravenous earth.

Millicent was prostrated by grief and by the collapse of her beautiful dreams, and it was the sisters and Cookie who carried her through it. Rosie learned very quickly not to offer her the consolation of religion. The first time she tried, Millicent turned on her with fiery eyes and said, 'No! No!' running away with her hands over her ears. It was God she blamed for the theft.

Oddly enough nobody in the family was infected by the influenza until the second wave struck in late February. On the day that France proposed the idea of setting its frontier with Germany at the Rhine, the whole household, including Cookie and Millicent, were abed, helpless with fever, whilst Rosie struggled to look after them, although herself most terribly ill. It was only when they were beginning to recover that she took to her bed and slept in a fever for three days, tormented by strange dreams about weddings, and about the wounded men she had attended at Netley.

49

Rosie Waiting for the Cats' Meat Man

Rosie was waiting for the cats' meat man. She was perched on the window seat of the large room at the front of the house, where the family Bible lay open on a lectern. Here, each evening, her unbelieving but respectable father would read the next chapter, and then they would all say the Lord's Prayer together before going into supper in a modest and humble frame of mind. They called it 'the morning room' even though it had no clearly discernible connection with mornings and did not receive the full light of the sun until the afternoon. It overlooked a classical porch, painted white, and a neat gravel driveway devised in the form of a crescent, so that carriages might have no trouble coming in and going out. This crescent contained a patch of lawn planted with the young walnut tree whose leaves Mr McCosh loved to see turning yellow in the autumn.

Rosie was not busy. There was a limit to the amount of time one could spend sewing or reading, or playing Ezra Read on the piano, or walking down to the Tarn to watch people throwing tennis balls for their dogs, or thinking about all the people who had been killed, or just looking at the rose beds, and now she was fretting with boredom. It was utterly horrible to have nothing to do after having been frantically busy for years. When she was bored, her mouth filled with a metallic taste, as if she had been sucking on a copper penny. She had the tune of 'Gilbert the Filbert' running through her mind, as she seemed to have done ever since 1914. It had become so much a part of her stream of thought that she barely even noticed it any more.

Although the room faced west, it received plenty of light even quite early in the morning, because its windows were very large. Sometimes Rosie and her sisters just sat on the bench that had been built into the bay, and watched the world go by in the street outside. It was upsetting to see so many amputees, but on the other hand it was nice to watch the costermonger with his barrow full of apples, and the fishmonger who brought his fish up from Brighton in dog carts that dripped with melting ice. Rosie did not know what kind of dogs they were, but they were lean, powerful and shaggy, and clearly enjoyed their gruelling job.

Best of all was the cats' meat man, a strong, roaring Irish fellow in his late forties, with a patriarchal ginger beard, who passed up the street every other day with a basket of horseflesh on his head, fresh from the knacker's yard. Unlike the other mongers, he varied his cry from day to day, and it was always amusing to hear whatever he came up with next, but it was usually a variation on keeping your cat on the mat happy and fat.

So Rosie sat on the long blue cushion with nothing to do but wait for the cats' meat man, even though, despite being an inveterate rescuer of abandoned and lost cats, she did not at that time have a cat at all. Before he could pass by, however, a Phelon & Moore with sidecar turned into the driveway trailing a pretty plume of blue smoke. It came to a halt, the driver fiddled with the levers on the handlebars, and the machine gradually died, with a series of putterings and small percussions that sounded like petulant afterthoughts. The driver was wearing goggles and a leather flying helmet, and before he removed them, Rosie had the exciting but impossible idea that it might be Ash, not dead after all. There was something very similar about his personal atmosphere. She leapt to her feet, her heart fluttering, and put her hand to her lips. He dismounted, flexed his shoulders as if he had been riding a long time, came up the steps to the door and rang the brass bell vigorously.

No servant came to answer. There was no footman or butler any more, and the two female servants who were left were down in the kitchen and the scullery. Rosie hesitated. She was reluctant to open the door in case the visitor might think that she was a servant, even though she was far from being attired as one, and in any case, the sight of the young man who might be somewhat like Ash had made her feel nervous and apprehensive. She felt that she just wanted to go to the back of the house and out into the garden.

Nonetheless she took the few steps to the door and opened

it. She could not help but giggle a little at the sight of the young man, because he was wearing enormous fug boots, a Sidcot flying suit, and looked somewhat like a panda in reverse, his face black with travel dust, and the rings around his eyes perfectly white.

'I do believe it's Rosie!' exclaimed the young man. He removed his cap, and held out his arms as if to embrace her, but then remembered himself, and extended a hand for her to shake. 'Remember me?' he asked mischievously. She noticed that he smelled not unpleasantly of castor oil.

Nonplussed by his informality, she hesitated before exclaiming, 'Daniel? Daniel Pitt? From next door?'

The young man smiled. 'We haven't seen each other since we were about ten, I wouldn't think.'

'I did get a little news about you from Ash, at the beginning of the war. It was never quite the same after you and Archie moved away. The Pals were very diminished.'

'Well, we couldn't live in our former style, unfortunately, after Father was killed. We found a little place in Frensham, and then we moved to Sussex, to Partridge Green. And now I'm calling in to see my old playmates. How is Sophie? And Christabel? And Ottie? Are you all well? And your mother and father?'

'All well,' said Rosie, 'but everything's changed such a lot, as you can imagine. The servants have gone, and my mother is really not herself any more. She was caught in the Folkestone raid, and she's hasn't been the same since.'

'Oh, I am sorry. And Bouncer? I suppose he's long dead by now. I loved wrestling with him. Such a nice dog.'

'He's in the orchard, with a rose climbing out of him, and up a Bramley.'

'I must go and pay my respects. I remember when you found him and brought him back. Your mother wasn't best pleased.'

'No, she wasn't. It's been the same with all the cats, but she comes to love them in the end. Do come in. It's a great surprise to see you. I'm very pleased, of course,' said Rosie, and she stood aside to let him in. 'I'm very sorry that I didn't reply to your sweet letter about Ash. About being grateful on behalf of France. I was . . . well, I was too . . .'

'Please, I do understand. I wasn't expecting a reply. After I sent it I wondered if you'd even remember who I was. Where shall I put my motorcycling paraphernalia?'

'Oh, just leave it in the morning room. There's no one to take care of it just now. We don't have servants any more, just a cook and a maid.'

'It'll take care of itself,' he said, and he unfastened his flying jacket, laid it across a chair, and put his goggles and helmet on top of it.

'I've just remembered the last time I saw you,' said Rosie.

'Yes?'

'You came round to say goodbye, and you gave each of us a little box wrapped up in newspaper, with string instead of ribbons, and we opened them after you'd gone.'

'Oh gosh, I do remember.'

'Inside mine was a frog, and you gave Christabel a toad, and Sophie had a newt, and Ottie had some kind of fat little golden-coloured snake. It was so horrid of you. You can't imagine the panic, particularly when Ottie opened the box and saw the snake.'

'It was a slow-worm. It actually isn't a snake at all. It's a kind of lizard without legs. If you pick it up by the tail, it drops off.'

'I remember,' said Rosie. 'Believe me, I remember. Our footman picked it up, and he was left with a tail writhing and wriggling in his hand, and the rest of it went to hide under the chaise longue.'

'Did you all scream?'

'We certainly did.'

'I was only ten. My sense of humour is a little more sophisticated these days. Making girls scream plays a very small part in it.'

'You put a worm down my front once.'

'Did I really? Oh dear. Would you like me to go?'

'Oh no. Do stay and have some tea. I'll ring for Millicent. I expect she's in the kitchen. I'm afraid that Sophie and the others went for a stroll down to the Tarn.'

'Oh, I remember the Tarn. Everyone said that it was so deep it had no bottom.'

'They still say that, and it's still not true.'

As Daniel sipped his tea and munched his way through a plate of shortbread, Rosie took her chance to see what he was like these days. He was not like Ash at all. His hair was black and shiny, he had penetrating and worryingly blue eyes, and he wore a thin military moustache. He spoke with the slightly languid drawl that officers liked to affect, but did not exaggerate it as some did, and he did not, thank God, wear a monocle. He was long-legged and slenderly built, which gave him the misleading air of being even taller than he really was, and there was something vigorous about him that appealed to her. She was an active person herself, but these days she seemed condemned to spend far too much time as a sedentary.

'How are you? How are things?' asked Rosie.

Daniel laughed softly. 'A perfect mess, as always.'

'And how is your dear mother?' asked Rosie, and Daniel laughed again.

'She hardly changes. A little grey and lined, but still elegant and very naughty. She still pokes people with a parasol and flirts with the postman. She's as French as she ever was, and only speaks English if she has to, except that sometimes we speak a truly dreadful kind of mishmash of French and English at home. She can now pronounce the "th", though. No more zis and zat.'

'I'd almost forgotten you were half French,' said Rosie.

'*Maman* never lets me forget it. She insists upon pronouncing my name the French way.' He paused. 'It turned out that being francophone was quite useful during the war.'

'I imagine it must have been.' She sipped her tea. 'Oh, you might be just the man! Can you read something to me?' Before he could assent, she dashed out of the room. He heard her footsteps on the stairs, ascending and then descending. A little breathless, she came into the room and handed him a very prettily bound book with a soft leather cover that had 'Autographs' inscribed in gilt italic writing on the front of it. She took it from him again and flicked through it. 'Here we are,' she said, and handed it back to him. He began to read: '*Quittant sa douce canadienne, le gars se fait soldat —*'

'No, no,' interjected Rosie. 'Can you translate it? My French isn't terribly good.'

'Oh, I see. Sorry. It says "Leaving his sweet Canadian girl, the fellow makes himself a soldier in the English army in France where the fighting is. When leaving he said softly to himself, 'Canada, I will love you always, the woods, the rivers and the fields. But I also love the Canadian girl, faithful in the country where she waits for me."'

'Oh dear,' said Rosie, her eyes welling with tears. 'Poor man. That was Corporal Larvière. He got septicaemia.' She reached out her hand and took the book, flicking through it to find another passage. She handed it back and he saw '*Chantons soldat chantons même si les blessures saignent . . .*' He translated: '"Let's sing soldier let's sing even if our wounds bleed and if our voices have to rise higher than the highest torment louder than the cannons even if the wounds bleed and the heart breaks sing of hope and implacable hate by this beautiful autumn sun and the pride of remaining kind when vengeance would seem to us so good."'

'That's extraordinary,' said Daniel. 'No punctuation but it makes a beautiful kind of sense.'

'He was called Georges,' said Rosie.

'Gone west?'

'No, but there are things he'll never be able to do. He would have been a wonderful father, I expect.'

'This is a tremendous book,' said Daniel. 'I'd like to read all of it one of these days. Such lovely cartoons. All the cap badges and photographs, the silly rhymes, the fond messages. It's a treasure.'

'I've got three,' said Rosie. 'I look at them and it makes me think that those years of hard work really were worth it. Quite a lot of them say that they love me and will never forget. I mean love in the proper sense. I loved them too. They were my boys.'

'Did you know that both my older brothers died in South Africa? Only just after my father?'

'I see their memorial every time I go to St John's,' said Rosie. 'What happened?'

'Enteric fever got one and an ambush got the other. You can imagine how dreadful it all was for my poor mother after what happened to my father.'

'I can imagine,' said Rosie. 'What regiment are you in? I'm not sure I recognise your uniform.'

'This is the important bit,' said Daniel, pointing to the wings above his left chest pocket. 'Royal Air Force. Personally I preferred it when we were the Royal Flying Corps, but reorganising everything is a military passion, I'm afraid, and they decided to bung us together with the Royal Naval Air Service. We have completely incompatible habits and traditions, even in the manner of toasting the King. They sit and we stand. The rest of the uniform is Service Corps. Not very glamorous, but it's what I could scrounge when I came over, and all my proper Royal Flying Corps stuff is being laundered, and we haven't got our RAF ones yet. It's a bit complicated. By the end of the war none of us was wearing anything that was related to the unit he was with. I had a wonderful Sikh uniform, but I left it behind. The soldiers at the trenches all looked like tramps, tied up with bailing twine and wearing captured hats. And boots without socks or puttees.'

'I remember,' said Rosie. 'What did you mean by "came over"? From where?'

'I was in India. North-West Frontier, busy with all those tribesmen who want to kill each other and us too. I was in Rattray's Sikhs, but then I volunteered for the Frontier Scouts. My brother Archie was out there with me. I expect you remember him. He got in the papers once.' She nodded, and he continued. 'Anyway, I did a very disgraceful thing.'

'Did you?'

'Yes. I deserted.'

She put her hand to her mouth in horror.

'I didn't want to spend the war involved in some sideshow, so I deserted. We had three months' leave per annum anyway, so I took ship home and immediately volunteered for the Flying Corps. By the time they caught up with me I was back in uniform and serving in France.'

'What happened?'

'They didn't know whether to shoot me or pat me on the back. In the end they lost the file, quite accidentally on purpose. I did turn out to be reasonably useful, I like to think. I don't suppose that Archie will ever forgive me. I left him in the lurch in the middle of one of our amateur dramatic society productions. We were doing *Iolanthe*.'

'You've got some medals,' she said, looking at the row of ribbons on his chest.

'One or two. Nothing very special. I'm thinking of leaving the air force now. Everyone says there are going to be huge opportunities in civil aviation. I'm looking into it, just sniffing around. Now that the show's over we're all going to have to look for something else.'

'What does the "O" with a wing on it mean?'

'That means I qualified as an observer. The one with the Lewis gun and the camera who has to try and land the plane if the pilot gets hit. You don't get the O until you've survived an engagement.'

'An engagement? I don't follow. What's being engaged got to do with it.'

'An engagement with the enemy, not a marital contract.'

Rosie leaned forward, patted his arm and laughed. 'I know. I was just being silly.' She paused and said, 'I was with the Voluntary Aid Detachment. That's how I spent the war. And now it's horrible having nothing to do after all those years of frantic hard work. I just find all the things I saw . . . and the sounds . . . going round and round in my mind, and I can't get rid of them. I'm sure you know what I mean. I'm probably as mad as poor Mother is. Or soon will be. You must find the same, sometimes.'

'I do. I have a bad dream that keeps coming back. Wakes me up in a sweat every time. It's an endless parade of the dead.'

'I keep hearing "Gilbert the Filbert", and it won't go away.'

'So, you were a VAD?'

'Yes, at Spikey.'

'Spikey?'

'That's what we all called it. Spike Island. I don't know why. Everyone else knows it as Netley.'

'I know people who came through Netley. You must have known them too.'

'Netley's absolutely vast, so I probably didn't. We had tens of thousands of patients.'

What about Edward George, from the Buffs? Got sent to 46 Squadron?'

'No, I'm afraid not.'

'He lost his legs. And he has to wear a mask when he's out. Poor man. He's back in Lincolnshire with his family now. He made a perfectly good landing, and then the undercarriage collapsed.'

Rosie hung her head and fell silent for a very long time. Suddenly she burst out, 'It was so awful, I just had to do something. That's why I went to Netley. Mother wouldn't have let me go to France, and actually I didn't want to go there either. I love it here. Going away is such a wrench. But I couldn't do nothing, could I?'

She looked up, and he saw that she was trying to be cheerful. 'Do you remember that day when you and Archie did that wonderful thing, at the coronation party?'

'When I vaulted the wall and Archie did a somersault? Gracious me, we must have been utterly mad. I can't imagine why my parents let us do it. The pole wasn't even the real thing.'

'You were brought up to be Spartan warriors,' said Rosie, 'and that's what you became, really. It was at that party that Ash . . .'

'Yes?'

'That Ash . . .'

Daniel looked at her with concern. Her shoulders had started to heave, and she had put her face into her hands as she sobbed. He hesitated, and then knelt before her. She dropped her hands to her lap, and he took them in his, pressing them to his cheek and kissing them. As the tears flowed more freely in response to his sympathy, he felt that he ought to put his arms around her, but realised that it would not be appropriate. Then at last he decided to follow his instincts, and hugged her to his chest, murmuring, 'My dear girl, my dear girl.'

50

Daniel Makes an Impression

A month or so after their recovery from the Spanish influenza, and not two weeks after his reappearance in the lives of the McCosh family, Daniel came to tea, and found himself in the drawing room, making conversation whilst Millicent scurried in and out bearing drop scones, Eccles cakes, gingerbread, and refills of hot water for the pot. After so many years it felt strange to be back with these sisters and their eccentric mother, none of whom had really changed very much in the intervening years, except that Mrs McCosh was clearly becoming more 'unusual' with the passage of time. Daniel and Sophie soon realised that they had in fact seen each other occasionally, but without recognition. She had used to bring the Wing Commander on his regular visits to the airfield when she was a driver.

Conversation was relatively easy, because all the company were agog to hear of what it had really been like in the Royal Flying Corps on the Western Front. Daniel was quite used to this, and it seemed that he had to endure the same questions and conversations, over and over again, wherever he went. Most people just wanted to talk about the aces. He had to suppress his natural instinct to say, 'What about all the rest?' modestly forgetting that he too had won many more than five victories.

He also liked to put in a word for the PBI. He had never forgotten visiting the front line in the squadron tender, and seeing the legs of the dead protruding from the trench walls, still wearing puttees and boots. That was a far more vivid memory than the stench and the shell bursts. He remembered taking refuge with Ashbridge Pendennis's unit after spending all day in a shell hole, and being astonished when Ash had pointed to the sky and said, 'I don't know how you do it. You wouldn't catch me up there.'

'Did you know Albert Ball?' asked Ottilie.

'I did know Albert Ball,' he said. 'He was utterly reckless, and apparently fearless. He had an SE5 for going out with his flight, but he kept a little Nieuport for going out on his own. He'd charge a whole circus on his own and pepper the lot of them. Hawker was like that. His order was always "attack everything". Arthur Rhys Davids was exactly the same. He was a classicist, you know, a wonderful boy. His hut was full of books. Ball was his flight commander for a while, so I suppose he got the madness from there. It was a lot to live up to. The strain steadily gets worse and worse, and one of the symptoms is recklessness, without a doubt. It's the effect of incremental fear on a brave man. And there's a part of you that would like to get it all over with, I think. It's like a devil's voice in your ear, you know, like in Hamlet's soliloquy, where he wonders whether quietus might be the most desirable thing after all.

'I knew McCudden too. He was the exact opposite to Ball and Rhys Davids. Meticulously careful, and scientific, and considered. Billy Bishop I met once. He was another Nieuport man. Raided an airfield on his own and got the VC for it.'

'What about those French aces?' asked Christabel. 'You know . . . Guynemer . . . and Nungesser?'

'No, I never knew Guynemer or Nungesser, or Rickenbacker. I expect you've heard of Mick Mannock. He was Irish. I never met him either, but I wish I had. He worked out how to do deflection shots, apparently, and that accounts for his tremendously high score. That's when you work out how far to shoot ahead of an enemy so that he flies into your bullets. Most of us couldn't do that. We just got on their tails and fired from point-blank.'

'It's a bit of a miracle you got right through the war, isn't it?' observed Ottilie. 'Four years in the air. That must be a record.'

'Well, in some ways I was lucky. I wasn't there for the Fokker Scourge in '15, I was on Home Establishment. Of course people remember Immelmann for that. And I missed Bloody April for the same reason. I was instructing.'

'And what about the famous Red Baron?' asked Christabel. 'Was he really such a brilliant flyer?'

'Hmm, I often think that the only German ace that anyone wants to talk about is von Richthofen. He was unquestionably a great flyer – I came up against him a few times – but he did tend to attack in vast formations, always diving with his circus behind him, so he had lots of protection. He wasn't a lone wolf like Ball. Funny thing is, when he was killed, the first rumour was that he'd been shot down by the observer of an RE8. That would have been an anticlimax, eh? Not remotely glamorous. Luckily they eventually decided it was a Camel, but a lot of us suspect that actually he was done for by machine-gun fire from the ground, like Mannock. One often doesn't know who the real victor is, and the figures are all poppycock anyway. If four Brits got a victory between them they got a quarter each. We often used to draw cards for a victory, or toss a coin. The Americans and the French gave all of them one each. And then you have flyers of real genius, with masses of victories, that no one's ever heard of, like Collinshaw. There was Fullard, Little, McElroy, Thompson, McKeever, Beauchamp-Proctor, and that's missing out the Canadians, the Belgians and the Italians. I absolutely fail to understand why people have only ever heard of Albert Ball and von Richthofen. It's tiresome, and all the other flyers feel the same. The Huns had just as many aces as us. Boelcke for example, and Müller and Bohme. And Udet.'

'So who do you think was the very greatest,' asked Mr McCosh, 'if it wasn't von Richthofen?'

'Who was the greatest? Of the Huns? To my mind it was Voss. Flew a Fokker triplane like the Red Baron, but his wasn't red of course. I had a scrap with him once. Six of us against one of him. Those little triplanes couldn't dive because the wings came off, but they could go up like a lift. Every time we thought we had him he nipped upstairs and then came down on us again. He could have got away quite easily. I got a tight group of five in my empennage – Empennage? Oh, sorry, that's the tailplane. We all got a few holes. He did things I've never seen before or since, things you can't do with an aeroplane, things that aren't in the manuals. It was perfectly astounding. Then some of his friends turned up and some of ours turned up, and it just turned into general chaos without any casualties, but I swear he was deter- mined to kill all six of us on his own, and might well have pulled it off. To my mind there's never been anyone to touch him. When

I heard he was dead I felt as if I'd swallowed stones. Rhys Davids was pretty sorry for pulling it off, as I understand.'

'And was it really like being a knight of the air?' asked Rosie. 'Everyone made it sound so romantic.'

'Ah, the chivalry! Well, there wasn't as much as people think. It's still cold-blooded murder much of the time. You dive on a two-seater out of the sun and down it goes, sometimes in flames, and you know you're as guilty as Herod, and you've just got to face up to it and then go out and do it again. A flamerino makes you feel sick to the heart, and you just hope they were dead already. And let no one tell you that von Richthofen was chivalrous. He wasn't. He followed Hawker down and shot him in the back of the head when he had to turn home after a long dogfight that had been honourable up to that point. And during Bloody April, twenty-one of his kills, or thereabouts, were defenceless and obsolete old two-seaters and wounded stragglers. He was doing his duty, and I've done the same, but it's nothing to do with honour and chivalry. It's plain old-fashioned murder. Every one of us has to live with the knowledge that we were murderers. It's true! It's true! And von Richthofen was a braggart who claimed kills that belonged to his pupils. Mannock did the exact opposite and gave his kills to his pupils. If you want a hero of the air, give me Mannock any day, but he was no knight either. I hear that he took to machine-gunning planes that were already down. After too much fighting, what with the tiredness and the strain of it, you can get more than a little mad. That's when they send you home to be an instructor for a while. I had to do it twice, and that's why I survived, thank God.

'And something else. The Huns always had a defensive approach to war in the air. They didn't come over our lines in daylight, so we always had to take the fight to them. It was against the rules of war to use dumdums and incendiaries on other planes. We didn't use them. If we'd crash-landed on their side, and been caught with them, we'd have been court-martialled and shot. But as the Huns did always crash on their own side of the lines, they didn't have to worry about being court-martialled and shot, so they used incendiaries against us. There's no other explanation for why our planes caught fire so easily and theirs didn't. There was nothing that gave us the wind up more than the thought of being burned alive in a plane, and they knew it, because they were just as frightened of it themselves. So much for chivalry. Obviously one enjoys being thought of as a "knight of the air", but I sometimes have to remind myself just how brutal it often was.'

'So when you get a victory, does that mean a kill?' asked Christabel. 'I've often wondered.'

'No, no, we counted victories, not kills. If you've got twenty or thirty victories, a lot of them will have been forced to land and so on. I killed hundreds of men by mowing them down in ground attacks, flying six feet above the ground and going straight at them, and I have no idea how many I killed with bombs. People don't think about this, they only think about single combat, knight against knight. It comes from reading the papers. But yes, of course a little bit of chivalry occurred from time to time. We had a problem with jammed guns almost every time we went out. They said it was caused by deformed rounds that shouldn't have passed inspection. We had to carry a hammer in the office – that's the cockpit – and we'd spend half of every fight bashing the cocking levers with it. The frustration and rage was beyond imagining. I remember once my guns jammed in a dogfight and the pilot I was up against saw me struggling to clear them, so he flew alongside and waved and laughed at me whilst I hammered at the damned – I mean wretched levers . . . Anyway, I couldn't clear them, and he just gave me a little wave and peeled off and flew away. That was a Fokker DVii, and I was in a Camel. He could have got me with no bother at all. I always wish I'd had the chance to fly a DVii. Once it happened again, and this time it was the Hun's guns that jammed, so I repaid the favour, and let him go.'

'Was it the same Hun?' asked Christabel.

'No, no. It wasn't the same one. And then another time a courteous Hun waited for me to clear my guns and then he renewed the attack, so we had a good scrap, and I shot him down over Arras. I took him a bottle of cognac and some cigarettes in hospital, and we shook hands, but he got peritonitis, rather like poor Ashbridge, and died a few days later. I was very sorry about that. I always felt less awful when I could force someone down intact.

'And once I lost my flight, somehow, and then I saw them not far away, slipping into some light cloud, so I caught up and came out the other side, and lo and behold, I was flying in formation right next to a little posse of Pfalz. The Hun beside me caught my eye at exactly the second that I caught his, and after a moment of complete mutual amazement, he laughed and signalled to me to fall back and creep away, and that's exactly what I did. Mind you, even a whole posse of Pfalz would have had a struggle against a Camel. Much faster, but too slow on the turn.

'So there was a little bit of chivalry from time to time, yes, there was; but what I remember the most is mowing down those columns of men and horses, seeing them topple, and fall, and being thankful that I couldn't hear them because of the engine. Once there was a platoon up to its neck in water, but keeping going. You could use water to test the accuracy of your guns, because of the splashes. I strafed them and then came back for another go, and the brown water had turned red.'

There followed a long silence as they reflected on the horror of this, and then Daniel said, 'Lots of strange and inexplicable things happened. Once, when I was shot down between the lines and managed to get to our trenches after dark, I discovered that the PBI believed that there was a magnificently wild and fearless scout pilot who did the most amazing feats of acrobatics and daredevilry right over the lines, almost every day. The troops used to look out for him and watch him, and he never got shot down. They were full of wonder and admiration. They called him "the Mad Major". He really bucked up the troops an awful lot, and they used to cheer him on. Lots of the boys used to go and stunt for the infantry, just to keep their peckers up. There was a Naval Air Service fellow called Christopher Draper, used to fly under bridges and so on, and so did Gwilym Lewis. I did it too, particularly after I found out where Ash and Albert and Sidney were, but I happen to know, and so does everyone else who has checked up on these sightings, that a great deal of the time there wasn't, technically speaking, anyone there at all. In other words, according to all the logs there was sometimes nobody there when the Mad

Major was stunting above the lines. I have often wondered . . . well . . . do you suppose there can be ghosts who appear in the daytime? Was it . . . something like the Angels of Mons? Or can one be in two places at once, but unaware of it?

'Shall we talk about something else?'

51

My Heart Is Sick with Memories

The Reverend Captain Fairhead arrived at exactly the appointed hour, having previously left his card in the old-fashioned, orthodox way. He was a small man, very neatly turned out, with a precise moustache. His hair was sparse and gingery, his lips were thin and straight, and his face had been aged before its time by the sights that he had witnessed.

He was wearing gloves, and an officer's warm over his uniform, which Millicent took from him after she had let him in. She greatly admired its fur collar and double-breasted front, thinking that Hutch would have looked grand in such a garment.

Rosie would have preferred to have met him at the door herself, but somehow it had seemed more correct to sit in the drawing room on tenterhooks, pretending to be doing something. When Millicent ushered him in she rose from her chair to greet him, and he said, 'Oh, please don't get up.' His voice was quiet. 'You must be Miss McCosh.' She nodded and smiled, and he said, 'Reverend Captain Fairhead. I am very pleased to meet you.'

'Please do sit down, Father,' said Rosie, and to Millicent, 'Would you bring in some tea and scones?' To Fairhead she said, 'It's nice to have scones again. What a novelty it is to have enough sugar!'

Captain Fairhead sat in an armchair but perched himself on the front of it, as if to show that she had all his attention. 'I used to dream of scones. At the front. Jam and cream, scones still warm from the oven. That and a decent jug of beer.'

'I hope you had a good journey here,' said Rosie.

'I did indeed. You should see all the women at the polling stations. Whoever would have thought it would happen at last? I dare say we'll all get used to it.'

'One has to be over thirty,' Rosie reminded him. 'So we sweet young things aren't to be credited with wisdom yet.'

'Bound to end up equal, though, isn't it?' said Fairhead. 'I mean, what's the point of a halfway house?'

'My mother has just voted for Sir Kingsley Wood,' said Rosie. 'She is immensely pleased with herself. She was in the WSPU, but then she handed in her membership when it became violent. Now she feels almost insufferably vindicated.'

'Quite rightly,' said Fairhead. 'I am very much looking forward to meeting her.'

'She didn't actually want other women to vote, though. She really only wanted it for herself. She took not being allowed to vote as a personal insult, and not as an affront to womankind in general. It's good of you to come,' said Rosie.

'Felt I had to,' replied Fairhead. 'I am visiting a fair number of people, when I get the opportunity.'

'But there must be so many!'

'Thousands actually. Obviously I kept notes, but the rate of attrition was so high that one simply couldn't keep track. It's a blur of faces and wounds and short conversations and trying to listen to last words. I do remember Ashbridge very well, though. He was one of my first.'

'I hope you're not just visiting the relatives of officers.'

'Good gracious, no. Why would you think that?'

'It was only officers who got in the papers when they got killed. I always thought that was very shocking,' said Rosie. 'At Netley I got into masses of trouble for saying that officers and men shouldn't be treated separately.'

'I think I agree with you,' said Fairhead, 'but it's never been done like that. Old habits die hard. And you're forgetting that Ashbridge wasn't an officer.'

Rosie put her hand to her mouth. 'Oh, I am sorry. Of course he wasn't. But he was a gentleman, you know, officer class.'

'There are man-made gentlemen and natural gentlemen,' observed Fairhead, aware even as he said it that it was something of a cliché. 'Ashbridge would have been the latter if he hadn't already been the former.'

'His friend Hutchinson was a natural gentleman,' said Rosie. 'He said he'd got to the front by coming out with a real one.'

'Yes, I was very sorry to hear about what happened to him.

Such bad luck after getting through the war, don't you think? I hear you were most kind to him in his last days. Yes, er, he came out with a gentleman, and the gentleman concerned wouldn't agree to go to war without him. I forget his name, one of those Frenchy names, de Soutoy or something. I remember him quite well, tall and confident, had hampers sent out, used to say "dash it" whenever his monocle fell out. He got a bullet through the face that took the back of his head off. That used to happen rather a lot.'

'And Hutchinson stayed on?'

'Too valuable to let go,' replied Fairhead. 'He was an excellent soldier, and he felt he owed it to the gentleman he'd lost. Nobody asked him to go back home, but he would have refused, and no one would have gainsaid him, so that was that, and he stayed on, out of loyalty.'

'What was it about Ashbridge?' asked Rosie. 'Why did you write to me so many times? There must have been so many other bereaved to attend to.'

'I wrote thousands of letters, all in pencil and all on pages torn from notebooks. I wrote them in dugouts and field hospitals and trains and carts. That was my war, comforting the dying and writing to their relatives. All the same, Ashbridge was special.'

'He was to me,' said Rosie.

'I think you want to know why he was special to me.'

'I do, Captain. I would very much like to know.'

'Because he was so beautiful.'

Rosie looked at him, a dark suspicion arising in her imagination. 'Beautiful?' she echoed.

Fairhead stood up and went to the window, as if looking out over the wintry garden might make it easier to muster his thoughts. He watched a magpie and a rook, engaged in a tug of war over a crust of bread.

'War destroys everything,' said Fairhead. 'That's obvious and well known to us all. But I have always felt that what is beautiful is especially sacred, that the loss of something beautiful is more tragic than the loss of something banal. As a Christian, I am quite sure that I shouldn't feel this way, but I do. I was most affected by Ashbridge because he was the Greek ideal, if that makes sense to you.'

'Of course it does.'

'Athletic, bold, humorous, congenial, courageous, intelligent, honourable, stoical . . . one could go on and on. He was an Apollo.'

'Have you ever seen a picture of Rupert Brooke?' asked Rosie.

'Yes!' exclaimed Captain Fairhead. 'The similarity struck me at once. The photograph of him with his left index finger up the side of his face, and that enormous tie, or is it some kind of cravat?'

'I adore Rupert Brooke,' said Rosie. 'I read him every day, especially the love poetry.'

'His poems are somewhat irreligious,' said Fairhead. 'They have a sort of pagan barbarousness about them.'

'Do you mean the funny one about how fish think that God is a fish?'

'No, no. I find that most witty, although I am sure I shouldn't be amused. There is a sensuality I don't feel comfortable with. How can I put it? It sometimes seems forced, or perhaps a little posed.'

'Well, I know he was irreligious, and a socialist too, but actually I think there's something quite religious about his irreligiousness. Does that make sense? Do you remember the one called "Failure"? The poet goes to Heaven to confront God "Because God put His adamantine fate/Between my sullen heart and its desire"? And it turns out that God's throne is empty and everything is overgrown with moss. I think one would have to be very religious to have written that, to be so very disappointed with God. And there's that one about angels carrying God's dead body. Why would you write that if you weren't terribly religious, deep down?'

'I'll have to think about that one. In fact, I have to confide in you, Miss McCosh, that I have come out of the war with the gravest doubts. You may recall the absolute faith and confidence of the first letters that I wrote to you. I'm afraid it fell off rather greatly as time went by. I would very much like to go to Heaven and question the Lord.'

'Doubts, Father?'

'Of course there were many times when I felt I was carried

through on the shoulders of Our Lord, that it was the Lord who bore me up.'

'I felt the same after Ash died, and then at Netley,' said Rosie eagerly.

'I am sure you did. You must have seen many of the same things as I did. One cannot manage such horrors unless one is carried by the Lord. All the same . . .'

'Yes?'

'I am sorry to say this, but I have been forced to question my vocation. I kneel to pray, and find myself accusing Him. I want to know why such things are tolerated; why they are tolerable to Him. I can't help thinking of my sister, and of Ashbridge, of course, and then the many thousands of others.'

'You receive no answer?'

'Not as yet. I will wait.'

'I do hope an answer comes,' said Rosie.

'Don't you have doubts?' asked the Captain.

'Ottilie and Christabel do. My sisters. Sophie is either so silly or so bright that I never know what is really happening in her head. But I don't have doubts. I don't think about philosophical things. Not because I can't; it's because I don't need to. I know that Jesus said, "I am with you always." He is here, and I know that Ash is too. He promised, before he left. And I almost feel I know Our Lady personally.'

'You're lucky, Miss McCosh – luckier than I am. Do you know what helped me to soldier on?'

'Do tell me,' said Rosie.

'It was the parable of the Good Samaritan. If I lose my faith entirely, if I decide that God is a delusion, I will always have that parable as the epitome of what is worth believing and what is worth acting upon.'

'Yes?'

'I mean the idea that all men are our neighbours, and that one must love one's neighbour as oneself. The rest of Christianity can go to hell, if push comes to shove. I hope I don't offend you. Everything I did in the war came out of that belief. I learned it whilst tending to the enemy wounded.'

But Rosie was following her own train of thought. 'One of

the nurses at Netley could see the souls of the dying leaving their bodies.'

'You believed her?'

Rosie was already thinking of something else, and did not answer. 'I want to confess something to you.'

'What? As in a confessional?'

'No, no. I mean I have a burden and it troubles me very greatly, and I'd like to tell you.'

'Please do,' he said. 'A trouble shared is a trouble halved, as they say.'

'Captain Fairhead, I promised Ash I would pray for him every night, and I always did. Except the night before he was wounded.'

'Oh,' said Fairhead glumly, understanding at once, 'that's awful for you.'

'I can't help it, I know it's silly. I can't help feeling that if I had remembered to pray, Ash wouldn't have been killed.'

Fairhead reacted almost angrily. 'My dear Miss McCosh, you completely misunderstand the nature of God. I am the last person to say that he understands what God is up to, but I do know that prayer is not the same as casting a spell.'

Rosie felt unable to explain to him that she had a special relationship with the Mother of God. For her the Virgin was like a human being, who could be forgetful if not frequently reminded. It was the Virgin's intervention that she'd sought every night.

'Do you think there's any point in praying to saints?' she asked.

'I don't know,' said Fairhead. 'I don't know if saints have the power to intervene. Roman Catholics think they do. But we're Anglicans, Miss McCosh. It seems to me that we're a kind of halfway house between Luther and the Pope. We do assume that we have a direct line to God, though, so there really isn't any point in praying to saints, even if it does no harm. Why talk to a minister when you can go straight to the King?'

'I suppose you're right,' said Rosie. 'Do you know "The Wayfarers"? By Brooke?'

'No, I can't say I remember it.'

Rosie went over to the sideboard and came back with a slim book. She leafed through it, and presented it to Captain Fairhead at an open page. He took it to the window and read aloud:

'Is it the hour? We leave this resting-place
Made fair by one another for a while.
Now, for a god-speed, one last mad embrace;
The long road then, unlit by your faint smile.
Ah! the long road! And you so far away!
Oh, I'll remember! But . . . each crawling day
Will pale a little your scarlet lips, each mile
Dull the dear pain of your remembered face.

. . . Do you think there's a far border town, somewhere,
The desert's edge, last of the lands we know,
Some gaunt eventual limit of our light,
In which I'll find you waiting; and we'll go
Together, hand in hand again, out there,
Into the waste we know not, into the night?'

'How beautifully you read that!' said a playful voice from the doorway. It was Sophie, returned from the Tarn, where she had been throwing stale bread for the ducks. The chaplain strode towards her, extending his hand, feeling unaccountably delighted. 'Sorry about my cold hands,' said Sophie. 'I got quite perished at the Tarn and am probably going to die of ammonia. How fortunate to have a priest in the house!'

After he had left, with a light step and an invitation to return for tea the following Tuesday, Sophie said, 'Did you notice that he has the ribbon of the Military Cross on his tunic? I do so wonder what he did.'

'He had an oak leaf as well,' said Rosie.

'An heroic clergyman!' exclaimed Sophie. 'How marvellously anonymous!'

'Anonymous?'

'Oh, is that wrong? I mean that word which means that something doesn't quite fit. I'm always getting them muddled up.'

'Anomalous?'

'Well, it's almost the same.'

'Think of all the martyrs. Hooper, Ridley and Latimer. People like that,' said Rosie. 'It's not unusual at all.'

'But that was such a long time ago,' said Sophie. 'The Church of England simply doesn't do saints and martyrs any more. Not since we were in the caves.'

'Mary Tudor lived in a cave?'

'Surely not,' said Sophie, 'I am quite certain we must have been in grass huts by then. Probably with wattle and daub and a hole to let the smoke out.' She reflected a moment, and asked, 'How did we burn people at the stake before the invention of matches?'

'Tinder and flint,' said Rosie. 'I hear that birch bark catches very easily. I suppose that if you wanted fire you knocked on people's doors until you found someone with something in the brazier or on the stove, and you lit your spill and rushed home with it. Or to the pyre. I did hear of a case where all the local people put out their cooking fires so that some martyrs couldn't be burned. I wish I could remember where it was. It might have been Spain.'

'What a dreadful fag, having to make sparks. It would certainly put me off trying to burn anyone. And how do people catch fire anyway? One isn't exactly comestible.'

'Combustible, Sophie!' Rosie's face fell dark. 'Actually, people are highly combustible. The fat catches fire. It's utterly horrible. You don't usually die of being burned though. You die from inhaling the fumes.'

'I do so admire you, being a nurse,' said Sophie quietly.

52

Captain Pitt's Dream

He is standing on a steep and stony hillside above a road that is curving downwards, round to his right, where it enters a wide tunnel whose mouth is shaped like a half-moon.

He is clutching a small ginger cat to his chest, and is looking out over a mountainous landscape that is all the several shades of charcoal grey and indigo blue. He has never seen the world in these colours before. Even the air and the sky are blue-grey, like the ugly ink supplied by schools for dip pens. He makes no note of the temperature and has no idea of the time or the season. He is in a world without temperature, time or season, but he is in shirtsleeve order with no cap on his head. He does not know why he is there, but is not puzzled about it either. He just stands and looks down at the road, with the ginger cat in his arms. Nothing is happening and the universe is still.

Suddenly there is a grinding and shrieking of metal, a roaring of engines comes from the tunnel, and two Mark IV tanks emerge. The khaki paint has been burned off, and now their partially rusted metal is of the same hue as the rest of this world. They are going at high speed, even though they are both burned out and smashed, and one of them has no tracks on the side facing him. They produce no exhaust. He watches in puzzlement as they pass. He thinks, 'They should not be able to move at all.'

The small ginger cat panics, struggles and resists his attempts to hold on to it. It scrabbles out of his arms and hides between two rocks that are behind him. He makes a note of where it is, because he wants to be able to find it when the hideous noise has ceased.

Behind the tanks a squad of men emerge, leaning into the ropes with which they are dragging the wreck of a flying machine. He thinks it is an Aviatik, and the pilot is still seated in it, one arm over the side, and his head lolling. Along the fuselage he sees a neat and gently curving line of bullet holes. The propeller is broken. He hears the scraping noise as the plane is dragged along.

The men drawing the plane are like those who emerge from the tunnel after them, marching in endless streams together in lines of four abreast. They are dead men, in all the many states of decomposition. It is difficult to discern their nationality because their uniforms are as decayed as they are, but he thinks that the Germans are coming first, and then the Italians, and then the Turks. He knows without being told that these Italians died on the Isonzo, these Germans at Cambrai, these Turks in Mesopotamia. He wonders where the French and British are, but just now it is the horses that are emerging from the tunnel, shire horses, hunters, cavalry horses, pit ponies and cobs. They too are dead, and he wonders how it is possible for so many men and horses to be passing by when they have legs missing, or no legs at all. He thinks it strange that there is no stench, and that the bones do not creak as they rub.

He watches the march past of the dead for what seems like hours, and is transfixed by the infinite number of them. He worries about the cat.

More tanks and aeroplanes pass by, and the burned-out skeleton of a Zeppelin, two hundred yards long, pulled through the stones by those who must have been its crew. It should not have fitted in the tunnel, but somehow it did.

The dead have taken no notice of him. He tries to identify anyone he knew, perhaps Ashbridge and his brothers, perhaps those who left empty chairs in the mess week after week for months.

Suddenly one of the corpses turns its head and looks at him. Perhaps it is someone who knows him, but is unrecognisable with so few patches of dried leather left on the bones.

Death has looked at him, and he is abruptly terrified. 'This is a dream,' he tells himself, 'you must wake up now.' It is the rational part of himself intervening to save him from the horror and terror, as it always does when this nightmare strikes.

'This is a dream, you must wake up now,' says his rational soul, but he cannot wake up. All night, on the side of a stony hill in an indigo-and-charcoal world, he watches the dead emerge from the mouth of the tunnel. The march past is ceaseless, and has not ceased by the time he wakes.

When he does wake, still worrying about the small ginger cat, he thinks, 'I have not seen them all yet. I can't stop until I've seen them all. Tomorrow night perhaps I'll see the rest.' The fear has left him, and been replaced by curiosity. He wonders how many more there are, how many more nights will pass before all have been counted in.

53

Captain Fairhead Proposes an Outing

Captain Fairhead and Sophie got on so well that Rosie very soon lost her dark suspicions about Fairhead's attachment to Ash.

Sophie was not a conventionally pretty girl. She was slight and had little bust to speak of, she was small and energetic, and her legs did not seem to come out of her hips at quite the right angle. She had a pointed face with thin lips, and her head was framed by an impressive bush of frizzy hair that was impossible to control in the manner of the times. In old age, when it would become as white as snow, it would grow into a magnificent and refulgent halo that made her seem like a frail creature from Faery, but at the time when Captain Fairhead fell in love with her it had the same shiny chestnut colour as Rosie's. Fairhead was not such a fool as to think that love is only a matter of compatible souls, and he often wondered what it was that so attracted him and kept him awake at night with terrible longing.

'The tip of your nose moves when you speak,' he said to her one day, 'and it moves in a slightly different way according to your facial expression.'

'You've been observing me,' she said. 'How very underhand. From now on I shall make every effort to become invisible, except when you are not looking.'

She smiled at him mischievously, and he realised that what made her adorable was that she was more than the sum of her parts. She was animated and funny, and had the natural transient radiance of youth, of course, but she had developed an entire language of facial expressions that was perpetually amusing and interesting. She would pull a face to express whatever emotion she intended to convey, but she did it as a good actor would when mimicking a bad one for the amusement of other actors. She rolled her eyes, waggled her head, stuck her tongue out and flared her nostrils. She had a completely charming gesture which consisted in putting the tip of her forefinger to her nose when adopting a puzzled expression, and another one when looking into the distance, when she would put her circled fingers to her eyes in imitation of binoculars. She liked to hold conversations between her left and right hands, ventriloquising with her mouth whilst her fingers and thumbs took it in turns to talk. Captain Fairhead was enchanted. It made him feel happy just to be in her presence, and at night when he tried to sleep he was no longer tormented by the looming faces of the countless dead that he had seen off across the Styx, but was taken over instead by recent happy memories of Sophie and her quirky ways.

One day he was seated with Rosie in the conservatory, as it was not quite pleasant enough to be out on the lawn, and he said, 'Miss McCosh, may I ask you a question?'

'If it's one I can answer, I shall,' replied Rosie.

'It is a somewhat delicate matter. I hope you don't mind.'

'It's about Sophie, isn't it?'

'You are very astute, Miss McCosh.'

'I think that in private you should begin to call me Rosie. In preparation for the future.'

'The future?'

'Well, forgive me if I mightily jump the gun, as Ash used to say, but I am certain that if you asked her, she would say yes.'

'Gracious me! Certain?'

Rosie nodded. 'Don't ask me how I know. I wouldn't want to divulge things said in confidence and in private. But I have had conversations.'

'Conversations?' repeated Fairhead.

'Yes. Conversations.'

'I am completely overwhelmed. I hardly know what to say. I am ten years older than she is, and not one fraction as amusing. Do you think I can make her happy?'

'I am sure you can, dear Captain, but whether you actually will or not is another question. And don't forget that you have to ask Father.'

'Do you think he will be . . . sympathetic?'

'He'll ask you to become a Mahommedan and marry all of us.

That's what he said to Ash. He loves his old jokes. He likes to pretend that he's longing to get us off his hands. Your quest for Sophie's hand has caused you to be here so often that he has become immensely fond of you. As we all have.'

'Dear me, I've been coming too often.'

'Of course not. We knew perfectly well what it was all about.'

'I've brought a book for you,' said the chaplain. 'It's been quite the rage for some time. I thought you'd like to read it. It might give you much consolation. I trust you haven't read it already.'

Rosie took the book and looked at the front cover: *Raymond or Life and Death* by Sir Oliver Lodge.

'He's a formidable scientist,' said Fairhead. 'Nobody's fool. When it came out in 1916, everyone was talking about it. And more recently that one by Sir Hereward Carrington. Do you know it? I'll lend them to you if you like.'

'Thank you, I would like to read it.'

'I have been very impressed by Lodge's book,' said Fairhead. He paused. 'It gives us the strongest grounds for hope.'

'We have the promise of the Lord,' said Rosie, mildly reproaching him.

'I know this may be somewhat unorthodox,' said Captain Fairhead, 'but I have heard of a very successful medium in Merton, and I wondered if I could interest you and your sisters in accompanying me. As I say, it might be very consoling.'

'I don't think I should. I'm sure the rector would forbid it.'

'Why should you ask him? I am a priest myself. What could be better for one's faith than proof of the afterlife?'

'Well,' said Rosie, 'it seems to me that the kind of afterlife supposedly proved by a medium isn't the same as the one promised us by the Lord. I fear it may be very bad for one's faith.'

Later on, at sunset, Rosie looked out of the window from her bedroom on the first floor, and saw shadows at the far end of the orchard, underneath the tree where Bouncer was buried. She opened the window softly, and heard giggles and hushings. She felt a wave of pleasure coming over her, to think of Sophie finding happiness with such a good man, and at the same time she felt a painful nostalgia for the time when an equal happiness had been in prospect for herself and she and Ash had been clasped together under that same tree, when Bouncer still lived. She also thought about the time when Daniel Pitt had taken her in his arms to comfort her, and how nice it had been to be embraced again.

Under the Bramley Sophie was covering Captain Fairhead's face with bold kisses, and he was entering into a kind of delirium, that strange elation brought about by the impossible becoming the inevitable.

Later on, sitting side by side in the conservatory in the semi-darkness, Sophie said, 'I love this time of day.'

'You enjoy a little crepuscule.'

'Oh, very much. Do you know, dear, that when you first started coming here we all thought you were after Rosie?'

'I'm very fond of Rosie. I can quite see why Ash adored her, but she's really not quite my type.'

Sophie raised an eyebrow.

'I know this will sound strange, coming from me, but she's just a bit too religious. I find that kind of absolute and uncompromising faith a little hard to take. I keep wanting to say "but . . . but . . ." Do you know what I'm getting at?'

'You mean she's a fanatic?'

'I wouldn't be as hard as that. I just don't think it's normal, somehow, not to have any doubts. After what we've been through.'

'I do know what you mean,' said Sophie. 'I think it's a bit peculiar. She's always been like that, though. Don't tell anyone, but she keeps a madonna wrapped up and hidden under her bed. And she's got a rosary. She thinks we don't know. Well, Mama doesn't. We wouldn't tell her, of course. Imagine the fuss she'd make. Quite a hoo-ha.'

'One thing that doesn't seem to fit is her passion for modern poetry. It doesn't go with being religious in such an old-fashioned manner.'

'Wasn't Christina Rossetti something of a religious fanatic?'

'Almost morbidly so, I'd say. If a priest is allowed to say such a thing.'

'It seems unseemly. Anyway, the thing about people is that they are all inexhaustibly peculiar. Apart from me.'

'Well, my darling, it wasn't her I fell in love with. It wasn't her keeping me awake at night because I couldn't stop thinking about her.'

She took his hand and squeezed it.

'After we're married, do you think I should stay in the army?' asked Fairhead.

'Do you still have enough faith?'

'I have a vocation. It's a different thing, but it has the same way of leaving one without choices.' He paused, and then broke the silence by saying, 'Besides, we're never going to be rich. That's one thing I can promise. No servants for us.'

'Servants are so Parsee these days,' said Sophie. 'I couldn't bear to be unfashionable. Before the war this place was so cluttered with servants you could hardly avoid falling over them. It's so much more peaceful now.'

'The word is "passé",' said Fairhead automatically, and Sophie smiled to herself.

54

The Drunk

It was only the third time that Daniel had called by, and he had not yet rung the bell because a rowdy game of British bulldog was going on in the street, and he was watching it with fond memories of his own schooldays. A posse of ragged urchins had wandered up from Mottingham, and were using the pavements as Home, and the road as their battlefield. It had begun because one of them had found a tennis ball that must have come over the wall of one of the wealthy houses, and a tennis ball was exactly what one needed to start a game of British bulldog.

The children had stood with their legs wide apart in a big circle in the middle of the street, and the ball had been tossed into their midst. It went through the legs of a little girl wearing a crushed bonnet on her head, and much grime on her face, and so she was 'it'.

To cries of 'British Bulldog, one, two, three!' a magnificent hurly-burly of rushing, grabbing and throwing to the ground began, in which knees got grazed, noses bled and torn clothes were rent yet further. The little girl had managed to catch a tall child with a wall eye, and the two of them had caught two more, until at last there was only one very fast girl left, who had no chance against twelve bulldogs all in a line.

She became the first bulldog of the next game, and was standing in the middle of the road ready to begin when a new AC Six hove into view. Its driver was wearing an expensive herringbone tweed coat, goggles and a deerstalker hat, and was clearly neither skilful nor experienced. The car lurched and staggered as he crashed it into the wrong gear and pressed down on the accelerator too much or too little. Daniel and the children watched it with fascination, and the fast girl who was the new bulldog ran quickly to join her friends.

Just as the vehicle was about to pass, it swerved out, and then back again, mounting the kerb and sending two children spinning into the wall of The Grampians. The crack of a head hitting the wall was clearly audible above the screaming and the belated sound of the motor's klaxon. The children began to wail and panic, running about and crashing into each other. The AC came to a halt twenty yards up the street, and the driver merely sat there, blinking and muttering. The car began to roll slowly backwards, and Daniel ran forward, leapt into it and engaged the handbrake.

The screaming had caused many doors to open, and, running back, Daniel saw Rosie and Ottilie coming out onto the steps of their house. He waved at them to come down.

The two women dealt with the children as best they could, fortunate to have had those years of nursing behind them. Daniel ran indoors to call Dr Scott and an ambulance, and then ran out again. He instructed the children to fetch mothers and fathers, anyone to whom the injured children might belong, and they scattered in the direction of Mottingham, like a small flock of ragged birds.

It was at this point that the driver of the car clambered out. Unsteadily he went round to the nearside and inspected the bumper. When Daniel realised that he could do nothing for the broken children that the sisters were not already doing, he came up beside the driver. The latter gestured towards the bumper. 'Damned shame,' he said. 'I'll have to get it straightened. Only had the damned thing for two weeks, and it's dented already.' He pulled a fox hunter's pocket flask from his coat, took a swig and offered it to Daniel.

Daniel waved a hand in astonished refusal. The driver was a man in his forties, portly and prosperous, with the red-veined face and watery eyes of a drunk. Once he had evidently been handsome and virile, but he had clearly been unmanned by alcohol for quite some time.

'Come with me,' said Daniel, taking his arm.

'Steady, old boy,' said the drunk, as Daniel frogmarched him down to where the injured children lay.

'I'm making a citizen's arrest,' said Daniel. 'You do as I bloody well tell you, or I swear I'll break your neck.'

Rosie looked up with tears in her eyes. 'I don't think this one'll live,' she said. Daniel looked down at the cracked skull that was oddly flattened on one side, with its caking of dark blood in the blond hair. He was a beautiful little boy, despite the dirt and poverty that had been his lot, and was no more than six years old. Tears flowed down his cheeks from bright speedwell-blue eyes that stared at nothing, and his mouth worked silently.

The little boy that Ottilie was tending was lying flat on his back, howling with pain, his fierce sobs seeming to echo from the walls of the houses. 'Both legs broken,' said Ottilie, when Daniel leaned down. 'I don't know if they'll ever be straight.'

Daniel turned to the drunk and said fiercely, 'One child dead and one maimed. Are you proud of yourself?'

'Damned little hobbledehoys, fourpence a dozen. Would have grown up thieves. What about my bumper? That's what I want to know. Doubt if I can get their mothers to pay for it. Probably haven't got fathers. Too many damned brats, anyway.'

'Pay for it?' repeated Daniel, astonished.

'Expensive things, motor cars,' said the man.

By now several people had come out of their houses, or stopped in passing, and were as outraged as Daniel. 'You are a drunk, and a murderer,' he said.

'Steady on,' repeated the man. 'Let's try to keep things decent, eh?'

'Decent? Decent?' Daniel felt the rage rise up in him, hatred mixed with contempt, and instinct overtook him.

He took the man's throat in his left hand, pulled his right fist back past his ear, and drove it straight into the drunkard's face. There was an explosion of blood from the man's nose, and he put his hands to his face. Daniel kicked his legs from under him, and he went down on the pavement.

Constable Dusty Miller appeared at that point.

In those days policemen were numerous and ubiquitous, and were able to summon other policemen by blowing vigorously on a whistle. Many was the mischievous child who possessed an Acme Thunderer, with which to decoy the police for the entertainment of their friends.

Dusty Miller had happened to be in the kitchen of The Grampians, drinking tea kindly supplied by Millicent and Cookie. When he had realised that there was a fracas on the street outside, he had been faced with a dilemma: either to get there quickly and give himself away as a covert tea drinker in a forbidden kitchen, or to find a long way round that would save face, but possibly allow the fracas to get further out of hand.

He chose the latter course and ran down to the end of the garden, where he scrambled over the wall, turned right and sprinted round up the alleyway, appearing on the scene, breathless and red-faced, thirty seconds later, just in time to see Daniel felling the drunk.

'Stand back! Stand back!' he ordered, wearily resigning himself to having to intervene in a fight. It was the one thing he least liked to do. Keeping calm was impossible, and conquering one's own fear never became any easier. Fortunately there was no fight. The crowd had gathered round Daniel and the fallen man, wondering with admiring horror what Daniel would do next.

'What's all this about?' demanded Constable Miller, and Daniel gestured towards where the children lay by the wall.

'One child almost certainly dead, and another with broken legs,' said Daniel, panting, 'because this cretin ran them down when he was drunk.'

The policeman hurried to where the children lay and knelt by them. 'Oh my word,' he said. 'Has anyone gone for an ambulance?'

'We have a telephone in the house,' said Ottilie. 'We've called for one. And Rosie and I were both with the VAD.'

'Well, thank God for telephones,' said Constable Miller. He got to his feet and turned to Daniel, who was flexing his fingers. 'You were committing an assault, sir. You should know better than to take the law into your own hands. I ought to be arresting you.'

'He got what was rightly comin',' said the cats' meat man. 'Poor little kids. He's a feckin' murderer, that's what he is. No doubt about it.'

There was a murmur of agreement, and a respectable woman dressed in a fur coat and a hat with a prodigious feather sticking out of it said, 'You can't arrest him, Constable. There aren't any witnesses.'

'No witnesses?' repeated the constable. 'What? With all you lot here?'

'We didn't see nothing,' said the gaslighter.

'I saw it,' said the policeman.

'No, you didn't,' said the muffin man. 'None of us saw sod all, including you.'

'Help me, help,' whimpered the drunk, and the policeman prodded him in the ribs with his boot. 'You shut up,' he said. 'And get up.' He took out his notebook. 'I need names and addresses of all you lot who saw what happened when the kids got hit,' he said. 'And as for you, sir, I don't care if you're the King himself, you don't take the law into your own hands. Do I make myself clear?'

Daniel nodded, feeling ashamed. He had not previously realised that he had so much anger and stress pent up inside. 'I'm sorry, Constable,' he said, 'I'm afraid I lost control.'

'Well, sir, it's understandable under the circumstances. We'll let it pass, shall we?'

A motorised ambulance arrived. The drunk was led away by Dusty Miller, who propelled him along to the station with frequent prods in the small of the back, and gradually the little knot of people dispersed. Ottilie and Rosie insisted on going in the ambulance with the children, and were not resisted, since ambulancemen did not defy middle-class women who had the habit of command, and vital nursing experience to go with it. They came back two hours later with the news that the little ragged blond boy who looked like an angel had died an hour after admission. Millicent and Cookie cried in the kitchen, and the sisters wept in the drawing room. Daniel went for a walk at high speed, three times around the perimeter of the golf course. Upon his return he started up the AC and parked it in the driveway. Ottilie cut flowers from the garden and laid them on the front wall at the scene of the accident, and Mrs McCosh went to her bedroom. The whole thing had reminded her too greatly of that awful day in Folkestone, when she had seen the child's severed head looking up at her from a doorstep.

That night, having sobbed again over the death of the boy, Rosie lay in bed clutching her plaster statue of the Virgin, thinking about what Daniel had done. She had found his violence frightening and repulsive, but completely understandable. She had watched it with fascination, and done nothing to stop it. Despite herself, she could not help but admire his moral outrage, his energy and strength. She thought that for him there must have been some catharsis after so many years of strain. She realised that she hated that driver as much as Daniel must have done, and found herself hoping that something a lot worse than a broken nose would happen to him. 'Sometimes I'm not really a very good Christian,' she thought, and she fell asleep wondering if Ash or Hutch would have punched the drunk.

55

The Rescue

Rosie went down to the Tarn to sit on her own and think about things, and on the way home she heard a pathetic mewing as she passed one of the houses near the church. At first she could not locate it, but when she peered over the low wall, she saw a hessian bag in the darkness between the wall and the laurel hedge. It was too far to reach by bending over, and she was reluctant to go into a stranger's driveway.

She looked around hastily, saw nobody, put her bag down and, without thought to her clothes, clambered onto the wall. By lying along it, she could just reach down a hand and lift the bag out. She just had it in her right hand, when a voice said, 'Are you all right, miss?'

Rosie hastily got off the wall, very abashed, and dusted the moss and grit off her front. 'It's all right, Constable,' she said, looking up. 'I was just rescuing these kittens.'

'Kittens, eh?' repeated Dusty Miller. 'Let's have a look, then.'

Rosie struggled with the knot in the neck of the bag, and gave up. 'You have a try,' she said, handing it to him.

Dusty Miller could not untie it either, so he handed the bag back to Rosie and fetched his penknife from his pocket. He cut the bag as Rosie held it, and said, 'What have we got here, then?'

He took the two tiny creatures out and held one in each hand, showing them to Rosie. Their eyes were only just open and their ears still flat on their heads. There was a ginger-and-white short-hair, and a silver tabby that was clearly going to be long-haired.

'I just don't know how people can be so cruel,' said Rosie. 'They're so sweet. How can anyone just throw them away and leave them to die?'

'I've been a bobby for ten years,' said Dusty Miller. 'There's no limit to human wickedness, miss, believe me. There's nothing some folk won't do for sixpence.'

'What are we going to do?' asked Rosie.

'One for you and one for me,' said the policeman. 'We need a new mouser down at the nick. The old one's got past bothering.'

'My mother'll kill me,' said Rosie. 'I'm always coming home with cats. We do find homes for them, though.'

Constable Miller gave them to Rosie and took a look under their tails. 'One boy and one girl,' he announced. 'What do you fancy, miss?'

'I like the ginger,' she replied. 'That must be the boy, I assume.'

'I'll have the girl, then. I expect we'll call her Fluffy.'

Rosie smiled and said, 'Constable, don't you think you should go for something more original?'

'Original, miss? What's the point? The cat don't know any better, do she?'

He tucked the tabby into the pocket of his uniform, and hurried back to the station, leaving Rosie to carry hers in her cupped hands back to The Grampians.

Mrs McCosh was less delighted. 'Another kitten? My dear, this is too much. Why do you keep coming home with kittens? You brought back five once. The mayhem! It was like being overrun with tiny mad horses, all practising for the Grand National.'

'Rosie's very serendipitous when it comes to kittens,' said Sophie. 'The rest of us never find any. Do let's call it Caractacus.'

'Caractacus?' repeated Mrs McCosh. 'Whatever for?'

'It's full of cat sounds. There are three "a"s and three "c"s, and a "t", and it even rhymes with "puss". Couldn't be better.'

'It'll just end up being called Cracky or Cracker,' declared Mrs McCosh. 'A cat needs a name with dignity, with *cachet*. We should call it Prince.'

'Oh, Mother,' cried Rosie, 'that's a dog's name!'

'Let's call it Rover then,' suggested Sophie, 'and teach it to bark. It could be Eltham's premier guard cat.'

'I perceive I am outnumbered as usual,' said Mrs McCosh.

'No one's to call it Ginger,' said Rosie.

56

The Séance

The Reverend Captain Fairhead and the four sisters arrived at the house in Glebe Avenue with a quarter of an hour to spare. Rosie was having deep pangs of doubt, and kept repeating, 'I'm sure that we shouldn't be doing this.' Sophie was saying, 'What fun! Isn't this naughty of us? So apprehensible!' Fairhead was keeping a grave and thoughtful silence, and Ottilie and Christabel were arm in arm for mutual reassurance.

They were shown into a sort of anteroom by an elderly maid who radiated a powerful sense of disapproval, and they sat on hard wooden chairs in a ring around the walls, in the company of six other nervous characters who all carried with them on their faces the stresses and losses of the last four years. The air was heavy with cigarette smoke.

The sour-faced maid served them with tea and langue de chat biscuits served up on delicate porcelain that was decorated with pink roses and sprigs of greenery. They stared dumbly at the dark green flock wallpaper as outside the rain began to patter against the windows.

'Turned out wet again,' said one of the six strangers, and everyone nodded in wise agreement and sipped at their tea.

'Been raining for days,' offered someone else.

'The garden needed it,' offered another. 'It was about time.'

Christabel thought, 'Well, what are you supposed to talk about when you're hoping to talk with the dead?' and decided not to contribute. She felt sombre and subdued. She had dilemmas of her own to worry about.

At last they were shown into a wide, dark room, at the centre of which was a large round mahogany table that had clearly been distinguished in its time, but which had become scuffed and scratched. The same could be said of the Chippendale chairs that surrounded it. In one corner of the room stood a cello on its stand, with Ernest Bloch's *Schelemo* open on the music stand before it, and propped against the back of an armchair was a violin. Against the wall was an upright piano, with the names of the notes written on the white keys in thick blue chinagraph crayon.

The moment they were seated, Madame Valentine entered, exuding a heavy scent of lavender. She was a voluminous woman with a bust so massive that, had she ever attempted to walk down a mountain, she would not have been able to see her feet. She was dressed in swathes of gauzy and floaty chiffon, and upon her head she wore a pink turban with a white cockade exactly in the middle, above her nose. On her fingers she wore enormous rings in silver and gold, with topaz and ruby predominating amongst the stones. Her long nails were painted crimson, the same shade as her lips, and her cheeks were highlighted with rouge, somewhat hastily applied.

She would have appeared comical, the mere stereotype of a medium, had it not been for the dignity of her bearing and the authority in her voice.

She seated herself, put her hand to her mouth and coughed for silence.

'Welcome to you all,' she said. 'First things first, for those of you who have not been before. I regret to have to tell you that I cannot charge fees for what I do. The spirits forbid it. However, should you wish to show your gratitude, I am free to accept offerings that may be placed on the tray which is on the table in the hall. I will not be present. Fortunately for me, enough people have been grateful for me to be able to continue to operate.'

'What would be the normal contribution? Is there a sum that you recommend?' asked Fairhead, to the surprise of the assembled folk.

She glared at him a little balefully. 'The most I have ever received is twenty pounds, two shillings, and sixpence, and the least is nought pounds, nought shillings, nought pence and two farthings. If you should wish to contribute, it is entirely at your discretion. Measure your wealth against your gratitude and your credence. And in case you may be tempted to think that I am nobler than

I truly am, you should know that we workers in the spiritual world generally believe that to accept payment for our services would cause us to lose our powers. This may or not be a superstition, but I am not prepared to risk it.'

'Thank you,' said Fairhead, feeling a little cowed.

'In addition,' she announced, 'the spirit world, is, I'm afraid, somewhat overpopulated by jesters, mimics and mischief-makers. It is sometimes very hard to know which ones to take seriously. I generally find that a prayer before we start is a good idea.' She looked at Fairhead severely. 'Perhaps you would be so kind as to oblige?'

'Me?'

'You are a clergyman, are you not?'

'Yes, but . . . how could you have possibly known that?' He had come without his dog collar, strange though that felt, and had believed he was in disguise.

She looked at him and replied, 'Would you be so kind as to oblige?'

Somewhat disconcerted, Fairhead could not think of anything except the blessing. He bowed his head, and the company followed suit. 'The Lord bless you and keep you, the Lord make His face to shine upon you and be gracious unto you, the Lord lift up the light of His countenance upon you and give you peace. In the name of the Father and the Son and the Holy Ghost.'

They all intoned the 'Amen', and Rosie noticed that Captain Fairhead was blinking back tears.

'Thank you,' said Madame Valentine. 'Shall we begin? I expect we shall have rapping noises to begin with. We normally do. Lights off, Spedegue.'

The morose and disapproving servant left the room and switched off the lights as she went. 'Join hands,' said Madame Valentine, and the company meekly did as it was told, although with great unease, as the British are not natural hand-holders.

'Come! Come!' demanded Madame Valentine in the darkness. After a few moments there was a sudden violent rap right in the middle of the table, and Rosie was one of those who jumped in her seat with startlement.

'To whom do you wish to speak?'

There was one more rap, and Madame Valentine sighed with impatience. 'Whoever it is does not wish to speak to anybody,' she said. 'Please leave, whoever you are. Now, I would ask you all to concentrate. If there is someone with whom you desire communication, kindly picture them in your mind and try to call them. If they arrive, they will do so through me.'

Rosie began to concentrate her mind on Ash, and Ottilie thought of a nursing friend in Brighton who had quite suddenly collapsed and died whilst changing sheets. Fairhead's memory was so full of the dead that he was quite unable to focus. Sophie sat, full of wonder, thinking that this was all great fun, and Christabel was wishing that she had asked permission to take photographs. She had a Kodak Brownie with her in her bag, but only because she always carried one, just in case an interesting subject should pop up out of the blue. All of the others were thinking of brothers and sons.

It was then that a series of fantastic and extraordinary events began to take place. Madame Valentine started to moan in a manner that struck some of the married people as positively sexual. The sitters' eyes had by now accustomed themselves to the darkness and they could dimly see the room and its contents.

The table at which they were sitting lifted slowly from the floor and floated, swaying like a rowing boat at harbour. They were still looking at this in amazement, when the piano too rose in the air and then suddenly crashed to the floor with that cataclysmic noise of which only a falling piano is capable. Then the cello and the violin rose into the air and sailed above the table, where they began to play a very discordant, gypsy-like and sarcastic, but entirely recognisable version of 'There's No Place Like Home', followed by 'Gilbert the Filbert', which made the hairs on Rosie's neck prickle. The most wondrous thing was that they could all clearly see the pale disembodied hands and fingers that were plying the bows and pressing the strings.

A large fireball emerged from the wall above Madame Valentine's head and hissed across the room, disappearing through the wall above the door through which sitters had entered, followed by several smaller ones that swerved wildly past their heads and forced them to duck.

A woman who had come in the hope of a message from her son, who had been dematerialised by a high explosive shell on the Italian Front, became hysterical with fear and began to wail and sob, at which point the manifestations abruptly ceased. Madame Valentine emerged from her trance, looked around as if in extreme confusion, and Spedegue re-entered the room and turned on the light. Sophie, never a woman to be unnecessarily inhibited by custom, put her arms around the unfortunate hysteric and cooed soft words of comfort into her ear.

'Oh Lord, what happened?' asked Madame Valentine, whereupon she was subjected to the excited babble of the company as everyone tried to tell her at once. She listened in dismay and said, 'Oh dear, I am most terribly sorry. This is too awful.'

'Too awful?' said Christabel, who had been mightily impressed.

'I had no intention . . . One has these powers, you know . . . sometimes it can't be helped . . . I was hoping we would have a nice quiet time talking to the departed . . . and then this happens again.'

'I fear my prayer was ineffective,' said Fairhead a little drily.

'I fear it was,' agreed Madame Valentine. She got up and went to inspect the piano. 'It's very odd,' she said. 'It never gets damaged one little bit.'

'Perhaps you should move it to another room,' suggested Ottilie.

'You still get the grand piano smash,' said Madame Valentine. 'That's what I like to call it, "The Grand Piano Smash". Even if you move it out, you still get the noise. I wonder if I can get the house exorcised, then I could make a fresh start.'

On the way out Fairhead had a brief private conversation with Madame Valentine, and left a half-crown on the plate even though he had received no messages. Rosie and her sisters left a florin each, and the woman who had been so frightened left a one-pound note, as if in apology for bringing about the termination of the séance.

The five walked towards Colliers Wood in a loose gaggle, Ottilie and Christabel arm in arm, Rosie at the front, and Fairhead and Sophie bringing up the rear.

'What a terrific show!' exclaimed Christabel. 'What are we to think of it?

'Lord knows,' said Fairhead. 'Do you really think it was just a show?'

Christabel stopped and turned, and everyone else stopped walking too. 'Don't you?'

'No,' said Fairhead. 'The fact that it all went wrong and out of control indicates to me that she's genuine. If everyone got a nice message about being all right and not to worry from a relative with an "e" in their name, you could be certain she was a run-of-the-mill fraud.'

'If she could do all that in daylight, I'd be a lot more impressed,' said Ottilie seriously.

'It was horrid,' said Rosie, her eyes shining with anger. 'She's an illusionist. She's putting on shows and just taking advantage of people!'

'You think she's a charlatan?'

'What else could she be?'

'Why would she be upset, then?' asked Sophie.

'It's all part of the deception, obviously.'

'Silly me,' said Sophie cheerfully, rolling her eyes.

'I don't think you really believe what you're saying,' said Ottilie to Rosie. 'I remember Ash was always whistling or singing "Gilbert the Filbert".'

Rosie did not reply, but addressed herself to Fairhead. 'Why were you upset when you said the blessing? I'm sorry to ask. I just can't help being curious.'

'Oh, you noticed. Well, it's just that I've said that blessing hundreds of times, at the final moments. It suddenly occurred to me that forever and forever that blessing will remind me of all those dying boys. I shall always be trying not to let it show.'

A week later the Reverend Captain Fairhead called by and the door was answered by Christabel. 'How's the new darkroom?' he asked.

'Up and running,' she replied. 'I have pictures drying on lines all over the attic. It's murder trying to keep the kitten out. He seems to be able to be everywhere at once. I see you've arrived exactly at teatime.'

'Purely a coincidence,' he replied. 'I do hope Cookie has made scones.'

'Flapjacks,' replied Christabel. 'Bad luck.'

In the drawing room Mrs McCosh, Rosie and Ottilie were playing mah-jong, with Rosie being two players at once, and Sophie and her father were seated at a small table, playing spillikins, exclaiming every time that a stick moved or was successfully lifted. They were suffering terrible interference from the kitten, who was darting in and pouncing on the sticks the moment they moved. 'Daddy, you're such a gregarious cheat!' Sophie exclaimed as Fairhead came into the room. The kitten chose that moment to hurtle up the curtains and perch on top of the pelmet.

'Ha ha, I've got the masterstick!' said Mr McCosh, brandishing it in the air.

After tea, Captain Fairhead said to Christabel, 'I would very much like to see some of your photographs.'

'She's quite the professional these days,' said Sophie. 'She did a photographic portrait for the Fermoys, and they paid her squillions.'

'All thanks to the Snapshot League,' said Christabel. 'Who would have thought? I'll go and get the new ones, they should be dry by now.'

'Do be careful how you go up that ladder into the attic,' said Mrs McCosh.

'I'll make sure no one is standing underneath,' said Christabel.

'Ladies should not use ladders at all,' said Mrs McCosh. 'Who knows what might happen?'

'The Queen of Serbia used a ladder recently,' said Sophie. 'She climbed up a ladder against a wall so that she could have a peek at Romania. I saw it in the papers.'

'Did she?' asked Mrs McCosh. 'Well I never.'

'It's all right, she was wearing culottes.'

'Culottes? Gracious!'

'Oh, Mama, she's teasing you,' said Rosie. 'I don't think the Queen of Serbia is wearing rational dress.'

'Rational dress!' exclaimed Mr McCosh. 'Have you seen the photographs? Thoroughly peculiar people wearing the most absurd things. Give me irrational dress or let me go naked.'

'Hamilton!' exclaimed his wife reprovingly, much to his satisfaction.

Christabel returned a few minutes later, and carefully laid out her pictures on the dining-room table. 'There are one or two duds,' she said apologetically. 'There always are. I have absolutely no idea what this one is. I don't even remember taking it.'

She indicated a blurred photograph in which a young woman in a wide hat was smiling shyly into the camera and waving with her right hand. 'Whoever she is, she's very sweet.'

Fairhead fell silent and started to tremble. He put his hand to his forehead and looked as though he were about to faint.

'Are you all right?' asked Rosie, looking at him with concern.

'Did you take your camera to that séance?' he asked.

'My Box Brownie?' said Christabel. 'I take it everywhere in my bag, just in case something good comes up. Why?'

'That's my little sister,' said Fairhead.

57

Daniel and Ottilie

Daniel found Ottilie alone in the middle of the drawing room. 'My, this is strange, isn't it?' he said, waving his hand to indicate the absolute emptiness of the room.

'It's what we always do,' said Ottilie. 'It doesn't matter how careful he is, the sweep always fills the room with horrid black dust and soot. Draping everything with sheets just doesn't seem to be enough, so we always empty the rooms out completely. It's funny what turns up sometimes. We found Papa's magnifying glass under an armchair, and we have absolutely no idea how it got there all the way from his study.'

Daniel went to the window and clasped his hands together behind his back. He remembered vaulting over the wall, and smiled. 'Ottie?' he said.

'Yes?'

'Do you mind if I ask your advice?'

'Advice? What advice could I possibly give you?'

'Well, I find myself in a tricky spot.'

'Do you? How irksome for you! But how can I help?'

'It's Rosie.'

'Oh well, I suppose I might have known.'

'Have I made it that obvious?'

'It's obvious to me and Christabel and Sophie. We've been gossiping about it for ages. You've been turning up just like Fairhead when he was after Sophie.'

They went into the conservatory, as if it gave them more privacy, and Daniel asked, 'What do you think I should do?'

'I think you should spend a very long time becoming friends with her before you even think of anything like a proposal. You should take her to the moving pictures, and smoking concerts, and art exhibitions, and if it's freezing you must take her skating, and Mama taught her to play golf, so you might get her interested in that again. You have hours and hours to get to know each other whilst you're looking for balls in the rough.'

'Two months? Do you think that two months would be enough?'

'No, Daniel. A year at least.'

'Oh God. A year? It seems unbearable. I'm on such tenterhooks.'

'You love her that much?'

'Absolutely smitten.'

'Daniel, my dear, you do know all about Ashbridge?'

'Well, of course. We were all Pals, weren't we?'

'Rosie is the kind of woman who only ever has one grand passion.'

'Hmm, that's not what I wanted to hear, really.'

Ottilie came over and tucked her arm through his, squeezing it reassuringly. She smiled up at him, her dark eyes rich with conspiracy.

'You know, Ottie,' said Daniel, 'you're a real little darling. If I had any sense I'd have fallen for you.'

'Well, you know me. I'm a dark horse. My great passion was Archie. I expect you remember.'

'Of course I do. And he had eyes only for Rosie.'

'Don't you think he might be a little upset if you were to marry her?'

'But he hasn't seen her for years! I doubt if he thinks of her once a month.'

Ottilie thought, and said, 'Daniel, I do believe that if I had any sense, I'd fall for you too.'

'You can be my sister,' said Daniel. 'I never had one, and I really wish I did. Boys with sisters are so lucky, don't you think? Will you be my honorary sister?'

Ottilie stood on tiptoe and kissed him on the cheek. 'Of course I'll be your sister. And hope to be your sister-in-law. And I'd love it so much if you could make me an aunt. Fingers crossed.'

She held up her right hand with forefinger and middle finger crossed.

'Yes, fingers crossed,' repeated Daniel. 'You really think it'll take a year?'

Just then there was a sudden crash as a long pane of glass shattered, throwing shards all over the conservatory, and a golf ball landed at Daniel's feet.

'Oh my goodness!' exclaimed Ottilie, clutching her hand to her breast. 'I've never had such a shock in my life!'

Daniel went to the window, and saw Mr McCosh striding up the lawn with a golf club in his hand. 'I think we've found the culprit,' he said.

Hamilton McCosh hurried up the steps of the conservatory. 'Damn it!' he said. 'So sorry. Must have given you a wee surprise! Anyone hurt?'

'Daddy, aren't you supposed to shout "Fore!"? And what on earth do you think you're doing whacking golf balls at the house?'

Hamilton McCosh was abashed. 'It's my new golf ball,' he explained. 'I realised there was a need for a decent ball you can use for practice in the garden. It would have to weigh the same as the real thing, behave the same in flight, and travel about a quarter as far. I think that this one travels a little too far.'

'I think it does, Daddy. But why did you have to whack it in this direction?'

'Well, lassie, I didna want to hit it over the fence, did I? Imagine losing your prototype! I've only got the one.'

'Is this one of your projects with Professor Smithells?'

'It is indeed.' McCosh looked at Daniel, and explained. 'He's a professor at the Victoria University. We came up with a good gas mask once.' He held up the ball. 'We're going to call it the Gardenrite.'

'Well, at present, Daddy, it seems to be the Gardenwrong.'

McCosh waved his hand to indicate the shattered glass. 'Don't tell your mother. I'll get on to Beasley straight away, and with any luck she'll never find out.'

'Scout's honour,' said Ottilie, and Daniel handed the offending golf ball over to Mr McCosh.

'Ah, thank you, Daniel. Very kind. We'd better get Millicent to come and clear up the mess. Did I tell you I've come up with a new golf club? It's made of a telescopic steel tube so that it compresses down to almost nothing, and the head is adjustable, on a ratchet, so you can make the loft anything you like. Hey presto, you only need one club! No more lugging round a bag of seven!'

'It's a brilliant idea,' said Daniel cautiously. 'But I rather like my bag of seven. Having lots of them is part of the fun. They each have their own character.'

McCosh's face fell, and Daniel felt he should console him. 'It would be marvellous for travel, though. And of course, I'm only a beginner. What are you going to call it?'

'The McCosh Patent Universo.'

'How it trips off the tongue,' said Ottilie drily. Turning to Daniel, she said, 'Daddy just invented a kind of bellows where you hold it in one hand and wind a handle with the other.'

'Mmm,' said Daniel. 'Does it work better than the usual kind?'

'Not at all,' replied Mr McCosh, 'but it looks very smart in dark green enamel, and you can fit the handle on either side, and the name is picked out in scarlet paint on the casing. People don't buy things because they're better, Daniel, they buy them for the novelty and because they look nice. Novelty's the thing! Novelty and niceness!'

'What are you going to call it?'

'The McCosh Patent BlazoBrite Mechanical Bellows,' said Ottilie, on her father's behalf. 'Another masterpiece of simplicity and economy. Bound to catch on.'

58

Christabel and Gaskell

Now that the Snapshot League had been dissolved, Christabel was wondering what to do with her time. As with her sisters, the years of strenuous activity during the war had given her a taste for doing something useful and creative, and she could not envisage herself sitting at home in the drawing room, embroidering and making conversation until the right man turned up. Accordingly she devoted much time to looking in the Situations Vacant pages of newspapers and magazines. It was in one of these magazines that she found that there was an exhibition of war paintings being put on at a small gallery in Dulwich, not far from the school. It was well reviewed, but, since she could not persuade anyone else to accompany her, she went to see it on her own.

There were ten paintings occupying the whole of one wall, and they were very striking indeed. One was of two soldiers, one German and the other British, each with a cigarette in his mouth and a bandage about his forehead, sitting side by side and arm in arm against a low wall at a casualty clearing station. They were grinning and waving as if it were a holiday snap. Another picture showed an expanse of glutinous mud with a few broken trees and a smashed limber. Christabel was convinced that the artist had pounded real mud into the oil paint. Another showed a French officer standing smartly to attention in his red-and-blue uniform. His head, however, was a skull, depicted in the most extraordinary detail. Christabel shuddered. There was another, very like the famous Singer Sargent painting, that showed soldiers with bandages about their eyes, temporarily blinded by gas, each with a hand on the shoulder of the man in front. These soldiers were of all nations, however. There was a very lovely painting of a rifle, propped casually in the corner of a room, and another of a nurse at a table improvised out of ammunition boxes, slumped in exhaustion over a half-drunk cup of tea.

Christabel became aware of someone standing next to her, looking at the same pictures. 'What do you think?' asked the stranger. Her voice was low and melodious, with a hint of an aristocratic drawl.

'These are the best pictures in the whole exhibition,' said Christabel. 'They've got so much . . .'

'Pathos?'

'Well, I was thinking personality rather than pathos. Of course the pathos is very obvious. You'd have to be an idiot not to see that, but what I like is, well, they're not at all conventional.'

'The work of a truly individual artist?'

'Absolutely. And technically they're quite brilliant. Do you have any idea who it is?' She leaned forward to read the signature. 'Gaskell.'

'I can introduce you if you like.'

'Oh, would you? Is he here?'

The woman laughed, turned to face Christabel, and held out her hand. 'Gaskell,' she said.

Christabel looked at her in astonishment. She was extremely tall, with short black hair slicked back with pomade, and was dressed as a man in a tweed suit and brown brogues. In her left hand she carried a long holder with an unlit cigarette in it, and a monocle dangled on a cord from the buttonhole of her jacket.

'Your eyes!' exclaimed Christabel, and Gaskell laughed.

'My best feature,' she said, with an air of proud satisfaction. Her eyes were a rich and bright emerald green, and fixed on Christabel with a beautiful, sincere and humorous intensity. 'Let's go out and have a cup of tea and a piece of cake,' she said.

They sat and chatted, and then went for a walk, getting on so well that they decided to go to the West End and see a play. In the interval Christabel found a telephone box and phoned home. It was answered by Rosie. 'Where are you? We've been worried sick!'

'Actually, I'm in the West End, and I'm going to stay in Kensington tonight.'

'Kensington?'

'I've made a new friend. She's marvellous. You'll really adore her. Anyway, I'm going to stay with her tonight. She says that her flat is frightfully bohemian, and –' She was interrupted by the bleeping of expiring time, and the last Rosie heard was 'Gaskell, have you got another penny?' before the telephone was cut off.

Gaskell's rooms were really a fully functioning studio, with canvases propped up against chairs and walls, pots of paint lined up, and brushes decongealing in jars of turpentine. The smell was intoxicating. Gaskell had been using the walls to try out colours, and you would have had to look up to see that they had once been white. There was a marvellously vigorous multicoloured patch where she had been cleaning the excess oil from her brushes, with strong diagonal strokes that had built up into thick contours. There was a large new canvas, still at the charcoal stage, which was going to be of a dead horse.

The two women drank sherry out of teacups, ate anchovy-paste sandwiches straight off the table, and talked about photography. 'I always take lots of photographs before I do a painting,' said Gaskell. 'Otherwise it's terribly difficult to sketch things quickly enough, or get anyone to pose for long enough.'

'The dead horse would have been easy,' pointed out Christabel.

'Very true, but that particular one has been dead for two years, and by now it would be quite a different thing to paint. I took lots of pictures of it. Of course, I had to make notes about the colours.'

'Will you teach me how to take photographs artistically?' asked Christabel. 'I think it might be my vocation, but I have such a long way to go technically.'

'Why don't we do joint exhibitions?' suggested Gaskell. 'Photographs and paintings together would double the potential, I would think.'

'I think you'd better wait and see if I'm any good,' said Christabel.

They killed the bottle of sherry between them, and Gaskell fetched Christabel a glass of water, saying, 'Better drink this, or you'll have a head in the morning.'

That night Christabel lay wide awake in Gaskell's bed, her head swimming with alcohol, and Gaskell tried to accommodate her long frame on a sofa, covered only by a rug. It seemed that they could not stop talking, no matter how they tried to get to sleep.

They had forgotten to stack up the grate, and it grew very cold. At two o'clock in the morning, Christabel said, 'Aren't you absolutely freezing?'

'I wouldn't say I'm toasting,' replied Gaskell.

'Come and get in with me and we'll keep each other warm,' said Christabel.

'I'm not sure . . . well . . . I mean . . .'

'Oh, come on, it'll be like being at school again. And I often cuddle up to my sisters when it's cold.

'Isn't this nice?' said Christabel happily, as they matched contours, and began to warm up deliciously.

'You smell just like a puppy,' said Gaskell, putting her arm over Christabel, and tucking up.

59

The AC Six

After a few weeks had passed, the AC Six was still in the driveway, and Mr and Mrs McCosh were beginning to find it a nuisance.

'Why doesn't that fellow come and get the damned thing?' Mr McCosh demanded frequently.

'In case Daniel's here and gives him another thrashing,' said Ottilie. 'I wouldn't come back if I were him.'

'He's probably too ashamed,' said Rosie. 'I would be.'

'He might be in prison,' said Christabel. 'He's a murderer, if you think about it.'

'A manslaughterer, at the very least,' said Mr McCosh. 'I hope he's sewing up mailbags for many years to come. But what are we going to do about the damned AC? The hackney carriages can't get round the crescent and have to drop us off outside in the road.'

'It is too humiliating to be dropped outside in the road,' said Mrs McCosh. 'Just imagine if Their Majesties were to come by, and had to be dropped in the road. It would be too mortifying.'

'Or the Shah of Persia,' said Ottilie.

'Indeed,' concurred Mrs McCosh.

'Or the Maharaja of Morvi,' said Christabel.

'Or the Grand Panjandrum of Mysorebaksyde,' said Mr McCosh.

'Thank you, that's quite enough,' said Mrs McCosh. 'What does one have to do to be taken seriously? What are we going to do about the horseless carriage?'

'One of us should go to the police station and try to find out what's going on,' suggested Rosie. 'We can ask the police to sort it out.'

'Your idea,' said Ottilie. 'You do it.'

'I'll do it if you come with me,' said Rosie.

The two sisters walked to the police station and found a sergeant at the desk, who was not at all interested. 'Once it's been there for ten years, I think I'm right in saying that it's yours,' he said, 'but I might have made it up. Better ask a lawyer.'

'Can't you give us the man's name and address?' asked Rosie. 'Or ask someone from the station nearest to his house to go and see him and ask him to dispose of it?'

'I'll see what I can do, miss' said the policeman wearily. As the British police, then as now, measure out their lives by the intervals between cups of tea, he resolved to deal with the matter at a quarter past eleven.

Thus it was that one week later Constable Dusty Miller arrived at the house and presented Rosie with a handwritten message stating that the gentleman concerned had jumped bail and apparently absconded abroad in a Vickers Vimy. Furthermore, he had been fined £600 during the war for hoarding. 'He was an all-round nasty piece of work,' concluded the constable.

'Gracious me, what shall we do with the car, then?' asked Rosie.

'If I were you, I'd just use it, miss. I don't think 'e's coming back. 'E's probably sipping gin in Rangoon. I'd get it insured, though.'

'Hmm,' said Rosie doubtfully. 'Oh well, thank you so much, Constable, and do call in at the kitchen. I'm sure Cookie will give you a cup of tea.'

'Thank you very much, miss, that's very kind, miss.' This was something he had been intending to do anyway, but it was certainly congenial to have permission. 'How are you getting on with the cat, miss?'

'He's always climbing the curtains. It drives my mother mad. Then he reverses down with great difficulty. He's growing terribly quickly.'

'Ah, a curtain climber. Fluff mostly stops us writing our reports. She likes to sit on the paper and play with the pens. She knocked over a pot of ink last week. And she turned over the milk jug.'

'We were going to find a home for Caractacus,' said Rosie, 'but I don't think we will.'

'Well, that's the trouble with cats, miss,' said the constable wisely.

60

Rosie and Fairhead

Out by the side of the house, on a freezing day, the Reverend Captain Fairhead, dressed in his officer's warm, was watching with interest as two dozen bags of coal were borne from Freemantle's large cart by four men who were themselves as black as the coal that they carried, as were the enormous dray horses which stamped and snorted in the shafts, their breath hanging like plumes of smoke in the frozen air. The coal dust had been worn and compressed into the coalmen's leather aprons and jerkins, their caps, the felt of their donkey jackets, and into the skin of their hands and faces. Shining and gleaming, the coalmen were like creatures from another universe. Not for the first time, Fairhead felt a kind of gratitude that he had been born to a lighter fate.

He bowed his head for a second, though, when he remembered how backbreaking it had been to be at one end of a stretcher, struggling through mire, or attempting to carry a wounded man over one's shoulders. 'I have something in common with them after all,' he thought. Fairhead remembered how intense physical labour can keep you more than warm on an icy day. He saw how much they enjoyed tipping the coal down the chute into the cellar. They always stood for a second and watched it go. It went down with a wonderful rumble on the wooden boards, and arrived at the bottom with a satisfying soft crash. He wondered what kind of life the coalmen could have at home. Perhaps they left their clothes at the door, stepped naked into their houses, and stood in a tub while their wives went back and forth with jugs of hot water. Perhaps they spent their evenings and Sundays as white as the lamb.

Fairhead became aware of someone standing beside him, and he turned his head. 'I love it when the coal comes,' said Rosie. 'When you're inside the house you don't expect it, and when it starts, my first thought is "Oh no, it's an earthquake!"'

'I was thinking about the lives of these people, these coalmen,' said Fairhead. 'I was trying to imagine it.'

'I often look at people with what seem to be intolerable lives, and then I can't help but notice that they're really quite happy. Just as happy as us, anyway.'

'Are you happy, Rosie? I can't help noticing that you and Daniel have become constant companions. Moving pictures, skating, art exhibitions, smoking concerts, dancing . . . Do we have grounds for hope?'

'Hope?'

'Come, Rosie, I'm sure you catch my drift.'

'Well, I wanted to ask you about it. I want your opinion. As a man of God. Shall we go inside? It's perishing.'

They gave up their coats to Millicent, and sat either side of the drawing-room fire, shivering now that they were warming up a little.

Rosie said, 'I won't beat about the bush. The thing is . . . Daniel has asked me to marry him. Several times. He is very insistent.'

'I take it from what you say that you haven't accepted him?'

'No. Not . . . I'm very doubtful. I'm in two minds. It's not like you and Sophie . . .'

'But you do get on terribly well. Let's come straight to the point, shall we? Do you love him enough to marry him?'

Rosie hung her head. 'This is what I don't know.'

Fairhead leaned forward, pressing his fingertips together. 'Look, Rosie, I don't have any experience to speak of. But one thing I do suspect is that you should not marry someone if you are not dedicated to their happiness rather than your own. Are you willing to dedicate yourself to his happiness? And are you sure that he will be more interested in your happiness than in his own?'

'I'm certain he would be a good husband,' said Rosie sincerely, 'and that's what makes it so tempting. But I do know myself. I might very well say that I will always put his happiness before mine, but will I, when it comes down to it? I don't trust myself, the way I would have done with Ash.'

Fairhead nodded, and said, 'Go on.'

'The thing is, I had thought of him as my husband since I was about, what? About twelve years old? We got engaged with a curtain ring. I promised I'd love him forever, even beyond death, and there'd never be anyone else, and, you know, how can I put it? It feels as though my heart is closed, and will always be closed. And there's another thing.'

'Yes?'

'You know how important my faith is to me?'

'How could I not? It puts mine to shame, in every way.'

'Well, Daniel has no faith.'

'He doesn't not have faith. I mean, he's an agnostic, not an atheist. He has perfectly defensible philosophical doubts. It would be strange not to, after such a terrible war. I've had some very interesting conversations with him.'

'I don't think I could live with someone who doesn't share my faith.'

'Did Ashbridge have faith like yours?'

Rosie blushed and looked a little horrified. At length she admitted, 'I honestly don't know. We never really talked about it much. He called it my "weakness", and teased me about it. And back then, before the war, it wasn't so important. We lived in a nice golden cocoon, didn't we?'

'Mmm, yes, it was lovely being Edwardian,' said Fairhead. 'That was our little golden age.' He stood and looked down at her sympathetically. He picked the poker out of its stand and rattled at the coals in the grate. 'Listen, my dear, you should not count very much on my advice. My certainties are really very small, when it comes down to it. But first of all come and look at the Bible with me, will you?'

They went into the morning room, and Fairhead turned to the Book of Romans. He loved the smell of the expensive slightly damp paper, and the elaborate red-and-gold illuminated lettering at the beginnings of the chapters.

'Here it is,' he said, pointing with his forefinger. 'Read that.'

Rosie read: '"For the woman which hath an husband is bound by the law to her husband so long as he liveth; but if the husband be dead, she is loosed from the law of her husband."'

She took this in, and then turned to look at him. 'But I promised.'

'Knowing him as I did, I'm prepared to bet that he told you to find happiness with another if he was killed.'

'Yes, I think he did,' confessed Rosie, 'but I didn't want to hear it, and now I think that maybe I didn't. What I remember is the promise to love beyond death, forever.'

'But of course you can love him forever. I'm certain you will. But you can't love him as a husband when he's dead. You know, life isn't a romantic poem, Rosie. You're alive here. We believe he is alive somewhere else. But this is where you must live.

'And I must tell you what St John the Divine said. He said that God is love. He said that therefore anyone who loves is of God.

'Now, Daniel loves his mother. He loves animals and children. When we go down to the Tarn he throws sticks for dogs he's never met before, and he goes down on his knees to play clapping games with little ones, and lets them ride on his back while he pretends to be a horse. He loves your sisters, and Gaskell too, that's plain. He loves your father. He loves his friends and his dead comrades, and he still loves his brothers and his father who died so long ago. He adores you, Rosie, it's absolutely obvious, and it isn't very much distempered by commonplace desire, as far as I can see. He doesn't importune you, does he? Rosie, a man who loves so much and so liberally may not know God. But Daniel is of God. And if I were you I'd talk it over with Ottilie. She is much the wisest of us all, don't you think?'

61

Rosie and Daniel at the Tarn

On a cold and windy day in late winter, not long after Rosie's conversation with Fairhead, she and Daniel, muffled up in heavy coats and scarves, sat on a bench and looked out over the water. 'Why do coots have white foreheads?' asked Rosie.

'Because they hope to join the Band of the Royal Marines,' said Daniel. 'And I have a question: why are moorhens called "moorhens" when they don't live in moorland, and they aren't hens?'

'They got thrown off the moorlands at the time of the enclosures,' said Rosie. 'By wicked landlords.'

'That must be it. What shall we do on Saturday evening?'

'Let's go and see the new Charlie Chaplin. Mama went to see it and hated it. She didn't think it was funny at all, so I expect it's hilarious. And on Sunday there's a church parade of Boy Scouts going down Court Road, so I'm going to turn out and be appreciative. I expect you'll be going to your mother's on Sunday, won't you?'

'Yes, that's the plan, but do let's see the Chaplin on Saturday. You know, I never did join the Boy Scouts. I wanted to at first, because I always longed for a sheath knife. Then I got one anyway, so there was no longer any point. I could make dens and camps and cook up tins of beans any time I wanted, with Archie. Once we made a walkway that connected about six trees, fifteen feet up. I did have a copy of the Scouts' Manual. It fell to bits from so much reading.'

'It's a pity the Pals got broken up, isn't it?' said Rosie. 'Such a shame that your father died, and you had to move. It went very quiet after you and Archie left. No one flying over the wall any more like Sunny Jim, and staging fights with sticks, and making bows and arrows. It was such a lovely childhood, all of us in our little false paradise.'

'It wasn't false! That was real, and it all did happen. And you still had the Pendennis boys after we left.'

'I know. But Ottilie did so love Archie, didn't she? And I was terribly fond of you.'

'Ash was the one, though.'

'Yes, Ash was the one.'

'Such a shame.'

There was the sound of people crying out, not fifty yards away, and the two of them were jerked out of their reminiscences. It appeared that a woman was getting very agitated on the bankside, and calling out to someone in the water. It was not a person, however.

'There seems to be a dog stuck out in the water,' said Daniel.

'Oh dear, perhaps we'd better see if we can help.'

Daniel rose and ran the fifty yards. He saw that there was indeed a large black retriever in the water, apparently unable to keep itself up, and beginning to drown. A woman of about thirty, accompanied by a small boy, was calling, 'Sheba! Sheba! Come on, girl! Come on! Oh, come on. Please come on! Swim! Swim!'

The little boy was in tears, and the woman was clearly desperate. Daniel bent down and untied the laces of his shoes, kicking them off. Then he removed his coat, jacket, shirt and socks but left his vest. The others watched him in amazement and hope. He sat on the bank and lowered himself into the water, exclaimed at the coldness of it, and struck out. The dog was fifteen yards out, and by now struggling so feebly that Daniel was only just in time to stop it going under altogether. 'Come on, girl,' he said, grabbing its collar and trying to work out how he was going to get it back to the bankside. There was no bottom beneath his feet, and that it made it all immeasurably difficult. The dog struggled hopelessly, and Daniel managed to get it almost onto his chest so that he could swim backwards with it. He felt so weighed down by the water in his trousers that he wondered whether he would make it back himself. At last his feet found the bottom, and he felt its horrible slimy mud squelching up between his toes. He picked the dog up and waded to the edge, depositing it on the bank, and scrambling out himself by holding onto a wooden post that had been driven in near the edge. As he came out he was overwhelmed by cold, made much worse by the sharp wind, and could not control either his shivering or the chattering of his teeth.

'Thanks, mister,' said the little boy. 'I was only throwing sticks. She loves fetching sticks, doesn't she, Mum?'

By now Rosie and Daniel were kneeling at the dog's side. It was very old, perhaps fourteen, and its muzzle was entirely silvered over. It was breathing jerkily and its eyes were glazing over.

'I'm very sorry,' said Daniel, 'but she's obviously dying. I really don't think there's anything we can do.'

'I'm sure she's had a heart attack or a stroke,' said Rosie. 'They often happen at the same time. It might be both.' She stood up and addressed the distraught woman. 'I think you should just take the opportunity to say goodbye. While you still can.'

'What can I do? What can I do? I can't leave her here, can I? I can't just leave a dead dog at the Tarn, can I?'

The little boy knelt by the dog, and put his arms around its neck, saying, 'Don't die, girl, don't die, please don't die.'

'Do you live nearby,' asked Daniel, 'and do you have a garden?'

'We've got a tiny one, and we're in Chapel Farm Road.'

'That's very near,' said Rosie.

'Look,' said Daniel, 'I'll go back to The Grampians. You wait here and see Sheba off. I'll be back as soon as I can.' With this sat down on the grass and put his shoes and socks back on.

'What are you going to do?' asked Rosie.

'I'm going to run back because that's the only way I'm ever going to get warm again, and I'm coming back with the AC.' He put his shirt on over his wet vest, rose up, still shivering, and sprinted away.

'Gracious me,' said the woman. 'That's . . . I mean . . . what can you say? . . . What a wonderful man, wouldn't you think?'

'Oh, he is wonderful,' said Rosie. 'He'd do anything for anyone. Let's see what we can do for poor old Sheba.' She took Daniel's abandoned jacket and placed it gently over the sick animal. 'She must be very cold.'

Twenty minutes later they heard the sound of the AC outside the Court Road gate, and Daniel reappeared, in dry clothes, carrying a rug. 'Wretched AC!' he exclaimed. 'Thought it would never start. Practically wrenched my shoulders off. How is Sheba?'

'Almost gone,' said Rosie.

'So she is. Poor old thing. Let's get her into the car. What if I put her on the back seat? Rosie can go in the back along with her, and you, madam, could perhaps sit in the front with your little boy on your knee?'

'I want to go in the back with Sheba,' protested the little boy.

'Then you shall,' said Rosie. 'We'll just have to squeeze.'

Daniel knelt down and scooped the retriever up in his arms, saying, 'Rosie, my dear, could you go ahead and put the rug on the back seat? I'll lay her down on it, and we'll wrap her up.'

Rosie sat in the back with the dog's head on her lap, and the little boy perched on the edge of the seat. By the time they had travelled the few hundred yards to the house, Sheba was dead.

The woman stoked up the fire and made them tea, which they drank together in her small shabby drawing room. The whole house smelled of old, damp dog, and there was a ragged blanket in front of the fireplace where Sheba used to sleep.

'I'm not house-proud,' said the woman suddenly. 'I sort of don't see the point now that it's just me and my Bertie. I lost heart.'

'He was killed, was he, your husband?' asked Rosie, nodding towards a photograph on the mantelpiece of a smiling man in sailor's uniform.

'Jutland.'

'I'm so sorry.'

'And now the dog's dead.'

'Bertie's the point, isn't he?' said Rosie gently. 'He seems a very sweet little boy.'

'Yes, I suppose you're right. All the same, it's hard to carry on sometimes. He's just like his father, you know.' Then she added, 'He's only seven, the poor little mite.'

'I wanted her to live forever and ever,' said the little boy.

'Would you like me to help you bury her?' asked Daniel. 'Do you have a spade?'

Out in a derelict rose bed overgrown with clumps of grass, Daniel dug a pit four feet deep, soon striking heavy yellow clay that came out in lumps like bricks. He went back to the house and fetched Sheba from where he had laid her on the doormat of the garden door. He called into the house.

The others stood as Daniel lowered the dog into the grave with the rug, and then let it remain there with the body.

'Don't you want your rug back?' asked the woman.

'I'm certain we can spare it,' said Rosie.

Daniel spoke to the little boy, whose lips were working, his eyes welling with tears. 'Say goodbye to Sheba, Bertie. Would you like to be the first one to throw some soil on her? It's what you do when you bury someone you love, so I think you ought to go first.' He bent down and handed Bertie a lump of the yellow clay.

Bertie solemnly let the clod fall into the grave, and then Daniel began to backfill it as the others watched. Rosie found herself crying in sympathy with Bertie and his mother, even though this was the first time she had ever met the dog.

Whilst Daniel was washing his hands in the kitchen, the woman said to Rosie, 'I can't thank you enough, I really can't. Would you and your husband like to come round and have tea sometime? In a week perhaps? I can make some scones.'

'We're not married yet,' said Rosie. 'But we'd love to come round for tea, and see how you and Bertie are getting along.'

Before they left, Daniel bent down to talk to Bertie face-to-face. 'Listen, little fellow,' he said, 'don't be too sad. Sheba had a lovely life. When you get another dog, and I expect you will one day, just remember that dogs don't live as long as we do, so you really have to make the most of every minute. Do you agree?'

Bertie nodded, and Daniel held out his hand for him to shake. 'Brave boy, Bertie,' he said.

On the way home in the AC Rosie wondered at herself. She had actually said 'We're not married yet.' What was this 'yet'? It was as if she had made a decision without consulting herself.

62

Gaskell and Christabel at the Tarn

They sat side by side on the same bench, well wrapped up in heavy coats, looking out over the water. 'They say the Tarn has no bottom,' said Christabel.

'Like love,' said Gaskell gloomily.

'It has no top either,' replied Christabel sensibly. 'If you think about it, love isn't a three-dimensional thing, is it? Space words can't apply to it.'

'Oh my gosh,' said Gaskell, 'you're immune to the power of metaphor.'

'What's the matter, darling?'

Gaskell shrugged. 'I can't help thinking about us.'

'And?'

'I can't help thinking that, no matter how wonderful it is, one day you're going to leave.'

'And so might you.'

'And so might I. But it's more likely that you will.'

'Really? Why?'

'Because you're not entirely like me.'

'Aren't I?'

'One day you'll start wanting to have children, and you'll meet a nice man, and then you'll be off.'

'Don't you want children?'

'Of course I do. But I'm not going to have any, am I? It's not in my nature . . . to be able to bring it about. I absolutely couldn't bear it, in fact. And I think that you could.'

'I don't want to think about it, darling. We have such fun, don't we? And we're such a success. We're filling the galleries already! We're kindred spirits. I don't want it to end, ever.'

Gaskell tucked her arm through Christabel's. 'I don't like to talk much about the past. I like there to be a clean canvas . . . but I've been in love twice before.'

'And?'

'They both gave me up for a man, because they wanted children.'

'Were you heartbroken?'

'Of course. Both times. You're very like them. You see, I can only love women. I think you're the kind of woman who can love either. I just happened to come along first. Aren't you often attracted to men?'

Christabel thought, and then nodded. 'But with me it seems to be the person that counts.'

'I thought so,' said Gaskell. 'That's why I'm down in the dumps.'

Christabel said, 'You have the most fascinating and beautiful eyes I have ever seen. I could live inside them. I really don't think I could ever give them up.'

They looked out over the water, its surface rippled by smart gusts of wind. 'Don't you envy the ducks?' said Gaskell. 'Such a lovely simple life.'

'No one to judge them, or make them feel ashamed.'

'Mind you,' said Gaskell, 'they do get crunched by foxes.'

63

The Interview

Daniel was as nervous as he had been the first time he flew solo. He was in the dining room with Mr McCosh, who was in a good mood because his investment in Argentine railways was paying off handsomely. He had Caractacus, now half grown, in his arms.

'I thought it wise to seek your advice,' said Daniel. 'I feel I'm on shaky ground.'

'You certainly are,' said Mr McCosh, stroking the cat's head.

'Yes?'

Mr McCosh indicated a chair and said, 'Do sit down. Cigar?'

'No, thank you, sir.'

'Very wise. I am beginning to convince myself that they're toxic. I dare say I'll be giving them up one of these days. After I smoke one I often feel a mite dizzy, and I can feel my heart fluttering.' He paused. 'You do realise that she was engaged to Ashbridge from next door?'

'Everybody keeps reminding me. A childhood friend, if you remember. We were "the Pals". I saw him briefly in the trenches, early 1915, and he told me then that he and Rosie were engaged. I was very fond of him.'

'As were we all. My wife refers to him as "our lost son". But Rosie was utterly devoted to him. She thought he was made in Heaven specifically to be with her. When he was killed, well, she hasn't been the same since. She has become increasingly strange.'

'Strange?'

Mr McCosh looked out of the window. 'What do you think about God? Religion?'

'I have nothing to do with it to tell the truth. I've never seen any sense in it.'

'Well, you would be quite incompatible with Rosie. She adores

Our Lord more than she adores anyone, perhaps even more than she adored Ashbridge. The Bible is her reference for deciding absolutely everything and anything. She's almost a Roman. It wouldn't surprise me if she became one. How can I put it? Her religiousness is altogether vehement. I don't see how you two could possibly get on if you're a sceptic. You may not have realised it yet, Daniel, but a couple can't get on if they don't have the same assumptions. You would irritate and bewilder each other. I might add, she has a strong puritanical streak, which is completely absent in you, and she does things out of duty even when she knows they're not right.

'Furthermore, my good wife, Mrs McCosh, adored Ashbridge just as much as Rosie did. You must realise that you would have to displace him from the hearts not of one woman, but two. I scarcely think it can be managed.'

'Are you opposed to the idea of having me as a son-in-law?'

'Absolutely not, but you should have taken a fancy to one of the others. You cannot possibly be happy with Rosie, or she with you. Do try Ottilie or Christabel if you want to be married. Ottilie is quiet, but there is a wonderful, courageous and very womanly woman smouldering away inside, and Christabel is vigorous and in many ways rather magnificent. She would make a superb companion for the more adventurous type of man. You could take her salmon fishing or climbing in the Himalayas, and she'd catch the biggest fish and get to the top of the mountain several hours before you.'

'But if Rosie accepted? If I keep proposing, and one day she accepts? I do have the feeling that she's coming round to the idea. We have a lot of fun together, and she hardly ever turns down my invitations.'

'I wouldn't forbid it. Of course not. I merely advise strongly against it. I do very greatly approve of you personally – how could I not? – but she will make you unhappy, Daniel. Be sure of it.

'We have become exceptionally good friends. She's a wonderful companion. I haven't had such fun since I first joined the RFC.'

'And how do you propose to provide for her?'

'I'm in the RAF. I have my officer's salary.'

'Don't count on the RAF, old boy. They'll send you packing the moment they find they have more men than they need. It's the same in any industry, and at the moment war is an industry in recession.'

'I want to stay in aviation,' said Daniel. 'I love flying more than anything.'

'There are thousands of aviators left over from the war, and you all love flying. Have you thought of motorcycles?'

'Oddly enough, I have,' said Daniel.

'I am assuming that the motorcycle will be the preferred mode of transport for those who cannot afford a motor car for a great many years to come. Thousands of servicemen learned to ride them in the war, and I am certain they will wish to continue to do so. I know the people who run Henley. It's a new company in Birmingham. I understand they make very fine machines. Until such time as everyone can afford a motor car, I would venture to prophesy that the motorcycle has a very profitable future. Would you like me to have a word with them?'

'Yes, sir, thank you, sir.'

'And another thing, Daniel.'

'Yes, sir?'

'My wife is not herself. Ever since the Folkestone bombing, it seems to me that her behaviour is becoming increasingly peculiar. We put up with it, of course. We either ignore her or humour her, and she certainly isn't mad enough to lock up. I wonder, however, how much you will be able to put up with it all. A mother-in-law like her might be a very real strain for someone like you.'

'I imagine we'd be moving away into our own quarters,' replied Daniel. 'And I'm very glad that you would allow me to marry Rosie.'

Mr McCosh put down the cat and went to the window, gazing out at the hydrangeas, his hands behind his back. 'Ah, but please don't,' he said. 'I will regret it very much when I am proved right. My advice is to go abroad for several months. You'll find that eventually all your passion turns into a pleasant memory. And perhaps you should talk it over with Ottilie. She has a very good head on her.'

Daniel laughed. 'Everyone tells me to talk to Ottilie. I already have, sir.'

'And what does she say?'

'She tells me to wait, and become friends first.'

'Wonderful girl, Ottilie,' said her father. 'She'll make a splendid wife one day. Why couldn't you have fallen for her?'

64

Madame Valentine

Spedegue answered the door with her usual ill grace, but Fairhead gave her the time of day very civilly, and handed her his hat and coat. These days a good maid had become as hard to find as a bag of sugar in 1918. The war had taken them away into jobs that were better paid and offered them more liberty, and afterwards they had not come back, and neither could many people afford them anymore. Fairhead assumed that Madame Valentine owed Spedegue a debt of loyalty, and no doubt they had a certain long-standing allegiance to each other that was unsoured by such drawbacks as mere grumpiness.

'Madame is in the séance room,' said Spedegue, saying the word 'séance' as if she were handling it with tongs. She did not announce him or show him in

The sound of a cello piece was coming from that very quarter, and Fairhead pushed the door open gently so as not to disturb the music. He stood very still whilst Madame Valentine finished playing, and then coughed politely after she had had a few moments to savour the aura of the finished piece. Suddenly aware that someone was present, she looked round, and rose to her feet. 'Oh!' she exclaimed.

'I am sorry to have disturbed your practice,' said Captain Fairhead. 'You do play very beautifully.'

'You can't go wrong with "The Swan",' said Madame Valentine. 'It's not too difficult, and it does carry one away. Sometimes I think I could play it all day and all night. Of course, one does need a pianist, ideally, or one gets very rusty in the timing department.'

'Have you never thought of playing professionally?'

'Oh, I did. I was in a quartet, but the other three were men. Passchendaele, Jutland and Cape Helles, I'm afraid. I hardly have the heart to start again. Such lovely boys. Nowadays I just teach.'

'You teach?'

'Don't be surprised. I'm not a professional medium, you know. Just a very good one. On a good day. Do find yourself a place to sit. I expect that Spedegue will bring tea.'

Fairhead settled into a high-backed chair and Madame Valentine did likewise. He hardly recognised her. Gone were the theatrical trappings of mediumship, and she was dressed entirely like any other large middle-class woman with respectable acquaintances and aspirations.

'I barely recognised you,' said Fairhead.

'One has to dress up,' replied Madame Valentine. 'Butchers butcher better in their aprons, soldiers march more smartly in uniform, and no one takes policemen in plain clothes at all seriously. I see you have your dog collar on this time.'

'I do.'

'No doubt you know what I mean.'

'My fiancée says it's just a normal collar put on backwards. It does seem to have an effect, though, not least on me.'

Spedegue entered with a rickety wooden trolley covered with an embroidered cloth, upon which she had already spilled a few drops of tea. There was a plate of Shrewsbury biscuits which Fairhead soon discovered to be soft.

He produced a small brown paper bag from the inside of his jacket, and took out a photograph, which he handed to Madame Valentine. It showed a young woman smiling and waving at the camera. 'How did you do this?' he asked.

'Who is it?'

'My little sister. She was killed in a Zeppelin raid.'

'I don't know anything about it. What are you asking exactly?'

'One of the ladies who came here with me had a camera in her bag. When she developed the film she found this picture. It is unmistakably my sister.'

'Gracious,' said Madame Valentine. 'And what's this? There's something behind her that looks very like an obelisk.'

'That,' replied Fairhead 'is, also unmistakably, the obelisk of a large and impressive grave a few yards from hers. Major Goodhorn, lawyer and Territorial Army officer.'

'Gracious,' said Madame Valentine again.

'I am thinking of submitting it to the Society of Psychical Research. Would you cooperate if I did?'

'Cooperate? In what way? I was quite unaware that anything like this had happened.'

'Do think about it,' said Fairhead. He paused. 'But that isn't the reason I'm here.'

'No?'

'I want to ask you about the afterlife.'

'You're the clergyman,' replied Madame Valentine drily. 'Surely you must be the expert?'

'I suspect that things may be other than the average Christian supposes. I was at the front for several years. I saw many things. Heard many stories. I have for some time been in doubt. And the odd thing is, the Bible says practically nothing about it. The Jews thought you gibbered away in a place called Sheol, and the more reprehensible souls smouldered on a rubbish dump outside Jerusalem, called Gehenna. The Achaean Greeks apparently thought that you wandered about in a diminished state, with absolutely nothing to do.'

'And you want to know what really happens? You want to know where your sister is?'

'I do. And all the dead boys.'

'All I can tell you is what I think. I have no proofs except circumstantial ones.'

'Go on,' he said quietly.

'What I think is that we do survive death in some form, and that we remain almost exactly as we were. A man who smoked a pipe when he was here smokes a pipe in the next world. I don't know how long the afterlife lasts, or if there are other deaths to die later or if any of our deaths are final.'

'One assumes that the hereafter is eternal,' said Fairhead.

'There is no reason to,' she replied. 'People assume that one becomes omniscient as well, but I have never encountered a spirit who knew much more than when he was alive. Death doesn't seem much of an improvement in most cases. I have encountered ones who were extraordinarily foul-mouthed. It doesn't even make you polite.'

'Heaven and Hell?'

'Probably not. I think there are levels of existence that you can ascend or descend, like a ladder. Once someone goes a long way up, they can no longer communicate with us. It's like trying to talk through thick glass. There are those who are very sad, and those who go on quite jauntily. And I often suspect that there are many kinds of entities one has to deal with, everything from mere scamps and scallywags right up to creatures as angelic as angels. It's the scallywags who infest the drawing rooms of planchette players.'

'And what about coming back again?'

'Reincarnation? I have never come across it, but there are those who have, it seems. My opinion is that it is optional. A choice one can make.'

'Really?'

'It's only an opinion.'

Fairhead sat in silence and sipped his tea. It was tepid and oily, and Spedegue had obviously made it with hot water from the tap. He wondered again what the bond was between the two women.

'She is a poor soul who needs caring for,' said Madame Valentine suddenly. 'Her mother was a complete brute who drove her father to suicide. Apprently she was exceptionally violent and he was too much of a gentleman to defend himself.'

'Who?'

'Spedegue. You asked me about her.'

'No, I didn't. I was just thinking about her.'

'Oh, I must have picked up on it,' said Madame Valentine matter-of-factly. 'She's utterly hopeless as a servant.'

'You're telepathic, then?'

'I can't do it on purpose.'

'You're a most interesting woman,' said Fairhead. 'What do the dead say about the afterlife?'

'Very little. It's as if they're not allowed to. They mainly want to say that they're all right. Sometimes they want to tell you where to find something. Like a key. Or a will. I sometimes fear that the hereafter is extraordinarily banal. I did come across a spirit who said that she'd seen Jesus.'

Fairhead perked up, reassured. 'Really?'

'But she might well have been mad or deluded,' said Madame Valentine. 'She was when she was alive.'

'Oh,' said Fairhead, disappointed.

'I fear I have not enlightened you very much,' observed Madame Valentine.

He shrugged. 'One always asks too much.'

'"Seek and ye shall find,"' she said, 'but more importantly, in your case, "Knock, and it shall be opened unto you."'

'That's your advice?'

'Oh yes, you really should go ahead and give it a try.'

'You really are extraordinary,' he said gratefully.

'Do come and see me again,' she said. 'I think we have much to say to each other, and I do thank you for showing me the photograph. It helps to convince me that I am not a fraud. Sometimes I look down on myself and feel utter contempt, because one can't help having one's own suspicions. More often than not everything goes haywire. I do wish I didn't bring on all that bashing and crashing and mad music when one only wants a quiet conversation. Evidence like this brings me great joy, believe me. And the strength to carry on.'

'You really should,' said Fairhead. 'I am sure you are a very good thing.'

She laughed and smiled sadly. 'Not so long ago I would have been burned at the stake.'

'Perhaps you were, in a previous life.'

'Oh, don't! This life is bad enough! I did have the most awful dreams about it for a time, though, not being able to close my eyes because the lids were burned off, and hearing my own blood hissing in the flames. Do you suppose that's what used to happen? I always thought that the heat would dry one's blood up.'

At the door, Fairhead asked her, 'All those spectacular occurrences . . . can you do them in daylight?'

She was surprised. 'I've never tried. I don't do them on purpose anyway.'

'Why don't we come back and have a session with the lights on?' suggested Fairhead.

'It might be more peaceful,' said Madame Valentine. 'I wonder if I'll be able to get into a trance, though?'

'You could wear a mask over your eyes.'

'Gracious, what a good idea. Do telephone. You have my number.'

65

The Curate

Rosie stood in St John's Church reading some of the memorial plaques that were left over from the previous building, and the one to the two Pitt brothers. The new edifice had not existed long enough to have become sanctified by time. It had not settled into its foundations or soaked up the necessary centuries of prayer, although it had received a good start during the war. The church was empty now, but Rosie remembered how there had always been mothers and sisters praying here, and comforting each other.

She knocked on the door of the parish office at the western end of the church, above which hung the royal coat of arms, a relic of the former building. She had been hoping to speak to the priest, but it was the curate who answered her knock.

He was a nervous and slightly effeminate young man of the kind who has always been able to find refuge in the Church, and was much admired for his skill at skating on the Tarn when it froze over in winter. His flamboyance and panache were extraordinary, and Mr McCosh had often remarked that it was indeed a pity that one was quite unable to earn a living by it, because otherwise the curate would have been wealthy indeed. Off the ice, the young man reverted to his normal epicene self.

'Ah, Miss McCosh,' he said, upon seeing her, his discomfort quite visible. 'Can I be of any service?'

'I had been hoping to see . . .' began Rosie, but then realised that he might take this as a slight. 'I had been hoping to ask a question, a theological question. I wonder if you could help.'

'I will if I can, of course. Shall we sit in the nave? And shall I make you a cup of tea? We have a small stove in the office.'

Sensing his awkwardness at being alone with her, Rosie said, 'It's such a lovely day. Shall we sit outside?'

They sat on a bench and watched the traffic go by.

'It's awfully noisy with all these motor vehicles,' said the curate. 'I do think it was much pleasanter when we just had horses.'

'And the dog carts,' said Rosie. 'We used to buy fish from the dog carts. The dogs were simply enormous, do you remember?'

'I do, I do,' said the curate, mopping his forehead.

'On the other hand,' said Rosie, 'I do sometimes like the smell of the petroleum. It's aromatic, isn't it?'

'It does indeed have an aromatic quality,' said the curate hopelessly, 'but I also very much like the smell of horses. What was it you wanted to ask me?'

'I wanted to ask a clergyman about communicating with the dead,' said Rosie.

'Communicating with the dead? Spiritualism?'

'Not necessarily spiritualism. You know, communicating with the dead in general. Planchette, Ouija, mediums, all of that.'

'Yes?'

'Is it allowed? By the Bible? By the Church?'

'No, it isn't,' he said. 'Some people don't even think it's possible, because strictly speaking the dead are supposed to be fast asleep until Judgement Day. For some reason, these days people assume that you go straight to Heaven or Hell, but it doesn't really matter in this case because trying to communicate with dead people is strictly forbidden in the Bible. I'll just go and fetch one.'

He retreated into the church and returned shortly with his own Bible, a gift from his parents at confirmation, and flicked through it rapidly.

'Deuteronomy 18, beginning at verse 10,' he said. '"There shall not be found among you any one that maketh his son or daughter to pass through the fire, or that useth divination, or an observer of times, or an enchanter, or a witch. Or a charmer, or a consulter with familiar spirits, or a wizard, or a necromancer. For all that do these things are an abomination unto the Lord." Necromancy is getting in touch with the dead. And there's another passage, let me see, Leviticus, I think. Ah yes, here we are, 19, verse 31. "Regard not them that hath familiar spirits, neither seek after wizards, to be defiled by them." And then there's 20, verse 27. "A man also or woman that hath a familiar spirit, or that is a wizard, shall surely be put to death: they shall stone them with stones.'"

'Gracious,' said Rosie, thinking of poor Madame Valentine subsiding to the ground plumply, with a series of little shrieks, whilst being stoned to death. 'You must admit, the Old Testament is awfully extreme and peculiar in places. There's a bit where it says that if you are cutting wood and the axehead flies off the handle and kills someone accidentally, you have to flee to the city, and that's why there are three cities. Did Christ say anything about it? About communicating with the dead? I would really like to have a more up-to-date opinion than Leviticus and Deuteronomy.'

'I don't think Our Lord said anything about it. Not as far as I know. However, it is definitely forbidden, and always has been.'

'But why? It's such a comfort.'

'I don't really know why,' admitted the curate, 'but I have heard it said that it's because there is no way of checking whether the communicating spirit is really the one that you hoped to speak to. What if they are demons, or mischievous spirits? You know . . . impostors.'

'Surely there are ways of telling?'

'Perhaps there are. I can only tell you what the teaching is. You may remember that in *Faustus*, Helen of Troy is really a devil doing an impersonation of her. That's always been the worry.'

'Have you ever tried it?'

'No, Miss McCosh,' lied the curate, who had been devastated by the loss of his younger brother, and had, coincidentally, also gone to see Madame Valentine. He forgave himself with the thought that he had to do the right thing by his congregation, whatever his own errors.

From that time on Rosie gave up receiving messages from Ash, and the others persisted without her, bringing back the news of the séances, which Rosie doggedly tried to ignore.

66

The Proposal

One evening not long after the episode of the dog at the Tarn, Rosie went into the morning room, to consult the family Bible, which lay open upon the Book of Romans. She read briefly that all is vanity, before closing it, and then closing her eyes.

She opened the Bible again, put her finger on the page, and opened her eyes. She read the verse upon which her finger had settled. It was the verse that Fairhead had quoted: 'For the woman which hath an husband is bound by the law to her husband so long as he liveth; but if the husband be dead, she is loosed from the law of her husband.'

She read it several times, and it seemed to her that it could not have been a coincidence that this particular passage had appeared so opportunely before her eyes, even though she knew perfectly well that a book tends to open naturally at a page where it has previously lain open. She reflected for a moment, and then returned to the drawing room, where Daniel was anxiously pacing up and down with his hands behind his back.

'I will marry you,' she said.

Daniel had already asked her many times, almost to the point where she began to feel that she was being nagged, and on each occasion she had temporised and prevaricated. At this moment, however, because she believed in divine intervention rather than in chance, she felt herself absolved from her vows to Ash. It was, in its way, a liberation, and for a moment she enjoyed the relief of it. She had been contemplating a life of spinsterhood, not because so many of her marriageable contemporaries had been killed, but because she and Ash had made promises that were binding forever. She could hardly recall anything that Ash had said on the subject of what she should do in the event of his death, because in her own mind she had bound herself to him in perpetuity. She had told him so many times, and she had told herself the same thing for so long, with such vehemence, that it seemed inconceivable that she should ever be attached to another. In her own mind she was married to him, and always would be, but just now these words of St Paul had come to her at a pivotal moment. If she had read on she would have found that he was elaborating a metaphor about the marriage of Christians to Christ.

As for Daniel, he was in love. He had a general feeling about the right time in life to do certain things, an urge to settle, to make something of himself, to relax into domesticity after all the excitement and turbulence of war, to know the sweetness of the marital embrace and the pleasure of having children that one can love and of whom one can be proud. In truth, in that frame of mind he might have chosen any respectable and reasonably attractive young woman. He might have settled on one of the other sisters, and prospered if he had done so.

He had not been able to stop thinking about Rosie, and he could not prevent himself from imagining vividly what it might be like to share a bed with her. Everything about her kept him awake. He lay in bed, sweating and turning, his brain whirling with all the things he wanted to say to her. His impulse upon seeing her was to clasp her to his breast and kiss her neck. In the daytime he would suddenly go into a dream and stop doing whatever it was that he was engaged in. The sky seemed bluer than before, the taste of water more metallic, the thrill of flying more thrilling. His friends remarked, 'Got a spring in your step, old boy. Nice to see.'

It is often given to people to believe that they are in love, and it is only later that they say, 'Oh, I was obsessed . . . It was nothing really . . . I was fooling myself . . . I made a mistake . . .' This is how nature deceives us into the higher vocation of caring for children. In the case of Daniel Pitt, it is true that some of his love for Rosie consisted of sympathy. There was something about her obvious sadness and persistent distress that made him want to protect and comfort her. He was the kind of man whose heart goes out to the wounded, who feels that the natural role of a man is to be a protector and consoler of women. His mother had brought him up with firm ideas about the sanctity of womanhood, but he had had no sisters, had been to boys' boarding schools, and then spent his life in adventure. He had no great understanding of women, or of the ways in which they are different from each other. He knew that he loved them in general, that they were attracted to him, and that he wanted this one in particular to be his Beatrice.

Rosie, on the other hand, had already known a very great love, a love that was not temporary, and it was not temporary because its object was no longer there to disillusion her. Her beloved had become an angel, perfect and pristine forever. Even as she said 'I will marry you' to Daniel, her little burst of happiness and relief had turned sour in her mouth, and when he had clasped her to his chest, muttering joyful endearments, she had inhaled his fragrance of tobacco and cologne, and remembered that Ash had been much stockier, and smelled only of cologne.

67

Wondrous Things

S hortly after a séance with Madame Valentine, when the whole
tribe was gathered at The Grampians, Christabel arrived,
accompanied by her friend Gaskell.

Christabel was a very tall girl with a large nose and a florid
complexion. She had stiff golden hair that settled at her shoulders,
and typically wore long blue dresses and a slightly old-fashioned
bonnet. She moved with lovely physical grace, and had triumphed
in every athletic event at school. Her father greatly admired her
Amazonian nature, and said to her, 'My dear lass, I do believe
you may be the ideal woman. A beautiful lassie who can run as
fast a horse and throw a javelin is an ideal to which few men
may aspire. I should have named you Penthesilea. Do let me
encourage you to take up golf. You'd become a champion in no
time.'

'Daddy, we've played golf hundreds of times. And I am hardly
beautiful.'

'Of course you are. You know there is a kind of person who
does not seem beautiful at first sight, but the moment you know
them, they are transfigured. You are beautiful after two or three
minutes. Everybody says so.'

'Who is everybody?' she demanded.

'Everybody. *Tout le monde.* The common crowd, the aristocracy,
even the King himself, no doubt, were he to meet you. And I
say so. And the other girls are quite similar, don't you think? All
beautiful after a minute or two? Sophie's adorable, is she not? But
hardly a conventional beauty. Have you found a young man yet?'

'They're all dead,' she said, adding, 'I think I might enjoy being
a spinster.'

'Every woman needs a man to torment. She needs someone
to upset her, someone to disapprove of, someone whose pleasures
she can prevent.'

'I'll just disapprove of you, Daddy.'

'Quite right, lassie,' he said. 'I shall approve of you forlornly whilst you disapprove of me.'

Christabel had brought Gaskell home for the first time. Like Christabel, she was tall, but she was much less slender and graceful. Today she affected a monocle, wore tweed plus fours and brogues, with a khaki shirt and tie, like a man dressed for a day's shooting. Her hair was shiny chestnut, cut quite short and plastered into place with brilliantine. She was smoking fragrant Abdullas from a remarkably long cigarette holder with a silver stem and a meer-schaum mouthpiece. Her low drawl as she introduced herself struck Mrs McCosh as alarmingly sensual.

'What an unusual name, for a girl,' said Mrs McCosh, imme-diately suspicious of this extraordinary creature, who was obviously a bohemian of some sort.

'It's not her real name,' said Christabel. 'It's her *nom de plume*.'

'*Nom de brosse*?' suggested Ottilie. 'Daniel, what would it be?'

'Well,' said Daniel, 'by analogy with *plume*, it would have to be *pinceau*. That's an artist's paintbrush. *Une brosse* would be for decor-ating, really.'

'I mostly use a palette knife,' said Gaskell.

'*Nom de couteau*, then.'

'Knife?' enquired Christabel.

'Well, you can say "*couteau de palette*" if you want to go the whole hog.'

'I love whole hogs,' said Sophie brightly. 'It's so satisfying to have the whole thing, and not a mere leg or a sliver of tripe.'

At tea, as Millicent bustled in and out, Gaskell was interviewed by the family, and she explained that she had been a war artist, but was now having to find a new career.

'A war artist!' exclaimed Mrs McCosh. 'You were at the front? Were you allowed there?'

'Mother, there were lots of women at the front. Who do you think the nurses were?' said Ottilie.

'Oh, I wasn't there just as an artist. I was also driving ambu-lances for Lady Munroe. I took a great many photographs, and now I'm working them up.'

'Lady Munroe!' exclaimed Mrs McCosh.

'An ambulance driver! That must have been utterly exhausting and terrifying,' said Ottilie.

'Well, you were at the Pavilion, weren't you,' replied Gaskell. 'You must have seen some equally terrible things, and got just as tired.'

'It really doesn't compare,' said Ottilie admiringly. 'I was never under fire, if you don't count the metaphorical batterings of the matron. And the amorous assaults of the doctors. And the Mahommedans hoping for another wife to add to the collection. The danger you must have been in!'

'I rather enjoyed it, to tell the truth. These days I find myself constantly wondering if I will ever find anything else quite as important to be doing. I don't miss being shelled and sniped at. Or the rats. Or the stench. But I do miss doing important things.'

'She's got a bullet wound,' declared Christabel proudly.

'Tell me, where does your family come from?' asked Mrs McCosh, determined to guide the conversation towards more important topics.

'Northumberland,' replied Gaskell. 'We have a modest estate near Hexham, on the River Allen.'

'An estate!' exclaimed Mrs McCosh.

'Much fallen into decay, I'm afraid. Nearly all the staff left and never came back. All three gamekeepers got killed. How does one start again from scratch? It's difficult. One simply doesn't have the cash any more.'

'The answer is mechanisation,' said Daniel.

'You can't mechanise gamekeeping,' said Gaskell drily.

'I mean the general work on the estate.'

'Well, we had a sawmill, but nobody knows how to repair it and keep it going.'

'I'd know,' said Daniel.

'Daniel has an immense gift for engineering,' said Rosie.

'I'll bear that in mind,' said Gaskell. 'I'll ask Daddy what he thinks.'

'What are you going to do when you've used up all your photographs?' asked Sophie, her mind wandering back to the conversation at its earlier stage.

'I want to paint portraits. Honest portraits. All the wrinkles and malice and vice showing in the face.'

'And blue flesh instead of pink,' said Christabel, 'just like corpses.'

'Gracious,' said Mrs McCosh, 'that will never earn you a living. Can't you paint lovely things like Sargent?'

'They are lovely,' said Gaskell with sincerity. 'I am always astonished that he's mastered so many styles. I do like his Impressionist paintings. And of course the portrait of Lady Agnew is just inexhaustibly wonderful.'

'Impressionist?' queried Mrs McCosh. 'You mean those paintings where the artist has apparently lost his spectacles, and all is somewhat blurred?'

'Gaskell doesn't have his kind of talent,' said Christabel. 'She's got a different kind altogether. She sees the beast within.'

'I have no beast within,' said Mrs McCosh.

'Neither do I,' said Rosie.

'I'm sure I do,' said Fairhead.

'Silly man, no you don't,' chided Sophie, 'you are all kittens and fluffy bits. Fairhead bared his teeth and growled at her. 'I'm horripilated,' she said.

The family warmed to this exotic and entertaining creature and she was invited to stay for supper, which naturally led to her being put up for the night in the old head footman's room, now that there were no footmen. It was neat and comfortable, but it was on the top floor, up a carpetless staircase. Millicent dusted the room and made it up in a hurry, and stole some flowers for it from the vase in the dining room.

After everyone had retired, Mr McCosh remarked to his wife, 'What wonderfully fascinating green eyes she has! I haven't seen such green eyes in all my life! What a lovely melancholy voice! What alabaster skin! What a lovely woman altogether!'

'My dear, she is utterly mannish, neither one thing nor another. Quite the strangest creature. And she has a monocle! Outlandish! Even men don't wear monocles any more. Her eyes are very remarkable, I do concede.'

'She's an artist,' said her husband. 'And she's from the North. And she plays golf. And she shoots. She could help you with your campaign against the pigeons. And those wondrous green eyes! Like emeralds!'

'I can see you are quite in love.'

'I love only you, my dear.'

'Hush, I hear flying pigs,' she said, cupping her hand to her ear.

That night Mr McCosh woke up. He had heard creaking on the stairs, and thought it might be a burglar, but soon he returned to his dream about getting a hole in one on a heavily bunkered 400-yard hole sited inside the oddly attenuated old hall of Eltham Palace whilst Gaskell and Christabel danced a foxtrot on the green.

68

Daniel in the Squadron Leader's Den

Daniel's squadron was back from France, along with all their machines, and based temporarily on the enormous playing fields of a large, architecturally intriguing, but academically undistinguished public school near Brighton. The magnificent but ill-equipped cricket pavilion held the separate offices of the squadron's three flights. The Snipes and the two RE8s were lined up at the eastern edge of the cricket pitch because the prevailing wind came from the west. In the absence of hangars they had been covered with tarpaulins, and roped to stakes, just in case a high wind should flip them. They were awaiting the arrival of some Besonneau hangars, which seemed unlikely ever to come. Small white tents, most of them empty because the personnel had found lodgings locally, were laid out in lines in one corner of a field, where they were sheltered by a row of elms. Six Nissen huts and sheds stood elevated upon railway sleepers, containing the messes of the sergeants and officers of the three flights.

For the schoolboys it was utterly thrilling to have real aeroplanes and real pilots in the grounds, many of them the owners of noisy and wondrous motorcycles, and the 1st 11 had already lost 2–1 at football against the airmen, and won 3–2 against the ground-staff. In the summer it was anticipated that the school cricket 11 would probably triumph because they had two fast bowlers, whereas the squadron could boast solely a leg spinner, and had no wicket keeper. Daniel had high hopes of fielding a good tennis team, and the squadron leader was fully intending to defeat the schoolmasters at golf. He had ordered Daniel to become good at it by Easter, and submit cards for a handicap.

At thirty-two, Squadron Leader Maurice 'Fluke' Beckenham-Gilbert was old by pilots' standards, since most had not managed to survive more than a few months in action. He had started his military life in the Green Howards, and seen enough action on the ground to make him envious of the men circling above. He had risen from second lieutenant to acting major in six months, and calculated that he would be lucky to survive another two. His own father had been something of an aviation pioneer, having had the money and enthusiasm to invest in a Blériot monoplane not long after one such had been the first to cross the English Channel. His father had survived many prangs more or less intact, and had been the kind of father who was quite prepared to allow his heir to take to the skies with minimal instruction. It was therefore easy for Maurice to transfer to the Royal Flying Corps, on the grounds that he already had his ticket and knew how to fly. He had survived service in Rumpties, had got through the Fokker Scourge, had flown Camels and Nieuport 17s, but he maintained that the Sopwith triplane was the sweetest of all. He had actually managed to cadge one from a unit of the RNAS after they had switched to Camels, and now it stood alongside the SE5s like a small lovable terrier at the end of a line of wolf hounds. Fluke had never wearied of each day's improvised adventures, and now wondered somewhat wistfully what possible use the peace might be to him.

When Daniel arrived at the field, he parked his combination amongst those of the other officers, and followed his first impulse to go and check on his machine and have a word with the riggers. He had concerns about the rudder being somewhat creaky and unresponsive. He inhaled deeply. He would never tire of that wonderful smell of aircraft dope, exhaust gas, oil and petrol. It was the smell of his recent life and the months of danger and comradeship that he had managed to come through. All that was missing was the roar of the Viper engines.

Then he went over to the cricket pavilion and knocked on the door of the room where the pads and gloves and stumps were kept. He was immediately called in, and found Maurice Beckenham-Gilbert seated at a small desk amongst the boxes of paraphernalia. Daniel saluted and the Squadron Leader said, 'I am not wearing my cap. If I am not wearing my cap, and I am seated, it is not customary to salute. Not in this outfit, anyway. It may be different in the Guards, for all I know, or one of those god-forsaken Scottish regiments.'

'I am sorry, sir,' said Daniel. 'You get things drummed into you, and then you do them without thinking. And every unit seems to have different rules.'

'You've been with us for years, Daniel. Remove your cap. Then you can call me Maurice. Or "Fluke" if you insist.'

'In the office I think I would rather call you sir, sir, if you don't mind. I like to call you Fluke when we're outdoors.'

'Oh well, Daniel, as you like. What do you want?'

'I've come to ask your permission to get married, sir.'

'Oh dear, I am most terribly sorry,' said the Squadron Leader sympathetically.

Daniel was taken aback. 'Sorry?'

'Yes, indeed.' He paused. 'I think this calls for a snifter, something medicinal. Would you care for a whisky? I have a good single malt from Skye, or my cousin sent me something rather interesting from Ireland.'

'Irish, please, sir. I don't think I've ever tried it before. Did you know that they make quite good whisky in Brittany?'

'French whisky? Gracious me. Do sit down,' said the Squadron Leader. He got up and flipped open the lid of one of the boxes, disinterring a bottle and two glasses from amongst the cricket pads. He poured two large tots, and handed one to Daniel. 'Sniff it first,' he said, 'it's ambrosia.'

Daniel duly sniffed, and felt the rich sharp fumes scrape at the back of his throat.

'Good health,' said Beckenham-Gilbert, taking a sip and sighing appreciatively. He reflected a while, and then said, 'I do hope she's not English.'

'Half Scottish,' offered Daniel.

'Just as bad, for our purposes, old boy,' said Beckenham-Gilbert. 'You're half French, aren't you? Why on earth don't you marry a Frenchwoman?'

'I didn't fall for one, sir.'

'That's too bad,' said the Squadron Leader, 'altogether too bad.'

'Perhaps you could explain, sir.'

'I am married to an Englishwoman. I have two children. And now I might as well not be married at all. Do you catch my meaning?'

'I'm not sure I do, sir.'

'Think about it, Daniel, old boy. I now have enormous expenses and responsibilities, and no pleasures to speak of. An Englishwoman, Daniel, switches off the moment she has the number of children she wants, unless there's something else she happens to want and hasn't got yet. An Englishwoman, at least a respectable one, is, in my opinion, about as much fun as a BE2c. It's like a lifetime of CB, old fellow, believe me. The unrespectable ones, on the other hand, are second to none, especially if they are partial to a drop. I imagine you've found a respectable one, you poor sap.'

'I'm sure they can't be all the same,' said Daniel.

'One listens to one's friends,' said the Squadron Leader. 'Naturally, one hears only hints. One observes. One draws one's own conclusions. For God's sake marry a Frenchwoman. You must have noticed that the French have much larger families than we do. It is not a coincidence.' He sipped his whisky. 'A Belgian would do. The best option would be to marry an Indian, disappear to the subcontinent, somewhere nice like Simla, and live in a large bungalow thronged with servants and children. One can only dream. A dusky maiden! How the heart yearns!'

Daniel looked around at the Sidcot suits that adorned the pegs where cricket whites used to be. He could tell from the way that they hung and their unique patterns of oil stains to which of his comrades they belonged. Each one was accompanied by a canvas bag hanging from the same hook, from which protruded the pilots' fur-lined flying helmets, goggles, or their strange and enormous gauntlets with coarse yellow hair on the back. He thought of all the mess-mates who had gone topsides. Then he recalled himself, and asked, 'Do I have your permission to marry, though, sir?'

'Well, of course you do, old man. One has no right to intervene to prevent private mistakes, except amongst one's own relatives. If you want to be a booby and a BF, you can be one. I have done my duty in warning you. Have you spoken to the sky pilot? It seems to me that he endures a particularly miserable marriage, and may be able to persuade you out of it.'

'My fiancée has a very passionate nature,' said Daniel, almost convincing himself.

'Let's go up in a Harry Tate,' said the Squadron Leader suddenly. 'We'll toss for who's at the joystick and we can take the dogs. Where does she live?'

'Eltham, sir.'

'Eltham? Jolly good, that's very manageable. Chart a course, would you? Let's find the place and buzz it. You telephone and tell her we're coming.'

'We could take two Snipes and loop some loops. A fly-past at eighty miles an hour by a solitary Harry Tate isn't one of the world's great spectacles, is it?'

'You take a Snipe and I'll take the Tripehound – even better!' cried the Squadron Leader, standing up and emptying his glass. 'It's a lovely day to go buzzing a fair maid, even if she's English. Or half Scotch. But how sweet it would be to go and buzz a French one. Alas, those days are gone.'

'You could take leave and go back,' said Daniel. 'It's not far.'

'And buzz her on a bicycle? I'd rather she remembered me in all my glory.'

'Take the Tripehound,' said Daniel, 'everyone knows you don't officially have it.'

'Ah, my lovely Tripehound,' sighed Fluke. 'Who needs a woman if one is blessed with three wings and a lovely warm Le Clerget and a clean pair of Vickers? Remember I can't go as fast as you can.'

'You lead, I'll follow. That means you get to do the navigating. Never my strongest point. When we get to Eltham, waggle your wings and I'll take over.'

Thus it was that Mr and Mrs McCosh, the sisters, the Reverend Captain Fairhead, Millicent and Cookie, a skillet still in her hand, witnessed a most wonderful display of mock combat over their house. Daniel had taken over from the Squadron Leader as soon as the Tarn and Eltham Palace hove into view, and he and Fluke had rolled in unison, side by side, as they roared above the lawns at just one hundred feet. Then Fluke had broken away and climbed almost vertically, spinning once at the top, and then coming down behind Daniel machine. Daniel's flipped his Snipe sideways, with Fluke on his tail, and they seemed to go in ever tighter circles until it was hard to know who was attacker and who defender.

Suddenly Daniel looped and came down behind the triplane, whereupon Fluke dived. This was most unwise in a real combat, unless you could dive faster than your opponent without shedding your wings, because an enemy can simply dive straight after you and fill you with bullets, but this was for show after all, and he and Daniel came down as low as they dared, swooping up into the air just when it seemed they were going to clip the elms at the end of the garden.

Fluke and Daniel flew wingtip to wingtip, and did their celebrated shuffle. When Fluke turned starboard towards Daniel, Daniel dropped beneath him and came up on his port side. That was how you compensated for the inner plane's turning circle being too tight to fit inside the arc of the outer one. They did it going the other way, and then back again, over and over. It was elegant and neat and humorous, and those below clasped their hands together and laughed with delight. They flew side by side, Daniel's two wings tucked inside those of the triplane.

The two planes separated, and the folk below – now most of the neighbourhood – were horrified to see that the two aircraft were hurtling inexorably into a head-on collision. At the very last moment Daniel dived and Fluke went up, almost vertically. At the top the triplane seemed to shudder and stall, and then it started to descend, spinning and rocking slowly, as if the pilot were dead.

Those below gasped, putting their hands to their mouths and clutching each other. Mrs McCosh found herself clinging to Cookie, skillet and all, and got flour on her morning dress.

Daniel's plane circled Fluke's as it descended, stricken and helpless. The two vanished somewhere near the Tarn. 'Oh God,' said Rosie, fully expecting to see a plume of smoke as Fluke's craft smashed into the ground and caught alight. Captain Fairhead muttered a prayer.

There was nothing. It seemed as though the whole town had fallen silent. Then the triplane, waggling its wings jauntily, sped over the house with the Snipe corkscrewing behind it in hot pursuit. The two planes returned, looped the loop together, rolled at the top, and disappeared.

'Oh my goodness, oh my goodness' was all that the women

could say, and Mr McCosh said to Fairhead, 'I had no idea that aircraft could be used to such humorous effect.'

'Two gallant spirits in the prime of life,' observed Fairhead wistfully, knowing that, for all his own bravery and fortitude, he could never hope to match the wondrous natural elan of the pilot of a scout.

A few minutes afterwards the roar of a rotary was heard again, and they all rushed out into the garden to see the Snipe circling the garden with Fluke nonchalantly sitting between the struts of the starboard wing, his legs dangling over the tip, apparently absorbed in a book. Then the plane disappeared, and not twenty minutes later there was a knock at the door, which Millicent answered, to find the two pilots still in their flying gear, their faces and garments dripping with blackened castor oil, grinning at her together.

'We landed on the golf course,' said Fluke.

'Probably a par five,' added Daniel.

'Tucked the babies into the rough,' said Fluke, 'on the left-hand side. More people slice than hook, eh? Hope nobody minds. Did you enjoy the Immelmann turn and the falling leaf?'

'He does an excellent falling leaf,' said Daniel.

Millicent let them in, not understanding a word of what they were saying. They might as well have been speaking French. As they entered the drawing room they received a round of applause, and bowed ironically.

Later on, Ottilie expressed some curiosity about Maurice Beckenham-Gilbert. 'Why is he called Fluke?' she asked Daniel.

'He's had some extraordinary escapades,' replied Daniel. 'He never gets hurt. He attacks whole jastas on his own, head on, and scatters them like chaff. He attacks one plane and one of his stray rounds hits the pilot of another one altogether. His guns jammed once, and he actually brought down a Rumpler with his revolver. He was as reckless as Rhys Davids. Or Albert Ball. He really ought to be dead several times over.'

'A revolver? You still carry revolvers?'

'Or an automatic. You have to. In case of fire. If you can't jump and you don't want to burn. If you can jump, you unbuckle and turn the plane on its back.'

'You commit suicide?' asked Rosie, more horrified by the breaking of God's law than by the thought of the deed itself.

'Obviously,' replied Daniel coolly. 'Oh, and another thing, Fluke was a complete balloonatic.'

'A balloonatic?'

'Nothing he loved more than pipping a sausage. Used to come back with his bus completely sieved, and not a scratch.'

'They're just sitting ducks, aren't they?' said Christabel.

'Oh good Lord no. They have motorised winding gear. The Boches got them downstairs in seconds, and if you tried to follow, you got peppered all the way down. And they ring them with archie because they know a balloonatic like Fluke is going to turn up, and more often than not there's a couple of scouts hiding up in the sun just waiting to pounce. It's about the most dangerous thing you can do.'

'How many did he get?'

'Ten, I think. He'd come back with his fabric in shreds and holes through his struts. He'd be up there looking for balloons every time we got a delivery of Le Prieur rockets or Buckingham rounds. If you crashed in Hunland and the Huns found those on you, they'd shoot you on the spot.' He saw their looks of puzzlement and explained. 'Incendiary ammunition.'

'What does someone like him do in peacetime?' asked Mr McCosh. 'What does someone like you do? You're not the kind of young men who are going to put on slippers, are you?'

'Fluke's staying in,' replied Daniel. 'I'm thinking of getting out.'

'I've got an idea, my boy,' said Mr McCosh, taking Daniel's arm and leading him out into the conservatory.

'Daddy's got another plan,' said Christabel, smiling a little sideways at Fluke, and widening her eyes.

After tea Sophie sidled up to Daniel as he smoked out on the lawn. 'Daniel?' she said

'Yes, old girl?'

'Would it be frightfully imprudent if I asked you a little something about your friend Maurice?'

'Do you mean impudent?'

'Gosh, how would I know? Words are such slippitty-slidey things, don't you think? I am terribly cacoeptical. Anyway, what I want to know is this . . .' and she whispered, 'Is he married?'

'Sophie, what about Fairhead?'

'I'm not asking for myself, silly. It's Ottilie.'

'Ottilie? Well, well. Wife and two children, I'm afraid.'

'Oh,' said Sophie sadly. 'All these years of being hopelessly devoted to Archie . . . I really think she's taken a fancy to this Fluke of yours.'

'She'll be all right,' said Daniel. 'Just you wait and see. One day she's going to surprise us all.'

From inside the house there came the sound of glass shattering, and then Mrs McCosh's voice raised in anger. 'Let's go back in,' said Sophie, 'I think there might be some fun going on.'

In the hallway they found Mrs McCosh berating her husband. 'You're just like Mr Toad!' she cried.

'I have only one craze,' replied Mr McCosh. 'Mr Toad has a great many, one after the other.'

'How many times have I asked you — no told you — not to play golf indoors? Now look what you've done!'

'I will get a new chandelier, my dear, an even nicer one.'

'You've destroyed our best chandelier! How can we possibly afford another one? Look at all these pieces! There's even one on the top of that portrait of your father!'

'I was only taking some practice swings, my dear, as I usually do.'

'And you've frightened the cat! He's up on the pelmet again! And you've worn a patch in the carpet! It is threadbare from your divots! This must stop, my dear, or there will be me to answer to!'

'My dear, I have never had to answer to anyone else quite as much as I answer to you. And I've never hit the chandelier before.'

'That is a driver in your hand! What man of any brain would choose to take practice swings indoors with the longest club in the bag? You should never swing anything longer than a niblick inside the house! Where is your common sense?'

'I had to abandon it, my dear, when I had the good fortune to marry. I was wise before I wed, and now I am otherwise.'

Sophie nudged Daniel with her elbow and whispered, 'Best leave them to it. I'll ring for Millicent and tell her to get her dustpan and brush.'

69

The Telephone (2)

When the telephone rang, Millicent was not in the vicinity to answer it, and as Rosie was at the foot of the stairs on her way to the drawing room, she picked it up herself. It was the kind where the mouthpiece is fixed to the apparatus on the wall, but the earpiece has to be detached and applied to the ear. It was an impractical design because it made no allowance for the height of the speaker, and this one had been mounted at Millicent's height, since it was her job to answer it.

Rosie said, 'Eltham 292,' and a faint and distant voice said, 'Is that you, Rosie? Rosie? . . .' and then the connection was lost. Rosie depressed the hook several times, but it was not restored. She stood quite still for a few moments, and then replaced the earpiece. She felt a cold tremor run up her spine, and the urgent need to sit down and be alone.

She went to the morning room and sat at the window seat, remembering when she had been waiting for the cats' meat man, and Daniel had turned up on his combination instead. Caractacus came by and chirruped as he sprang on to her knee.

She stroked the cat's head absent-mindedly as she questioned herself about the voice on the telephone. It had been a bad line. Did it really have an American accent? Her head began to hurt, as if her brain had turned to lead. She felt hopeless. To whom could she speak about this? Fairhead, perhaps. She had resolved not to go back to Madame Valentine. She certainly could not tell Daniel. She might be able to tell Ottilie and Christabel, but she knew what they would say.

Just then the cats' meat man went by, full of strength and ebullience, with a basket of horseflesh on his head, bawling his latest verse in his loud Irish voice

'Cats' meat, cats' meat,
Make your cats fat meat.'

Everything was unbearably strange. The whole world was out
of kilter. Rosie put Caractacus down and ran to get her coat and
scarf and hat, and hurried down to the Tarn.

Sitting on the bench where she had once sat with Ash, and more
recently with Daniel, she looked out over the water and thought
about that poor old dead dog. She wondered what had become of
the Romany girl. How strange that this small lake should have
played so great a part in all of their lives. It had been everything to
them: a place of recreation, a place for confidences, for being in
love, for grieving, for contemplation. It seemed to have a consciousness of its own, oblivious to those who stood on its banks and
walked its path, as if it knew something that they could not.
Rosie wondered if, in a hundred years' time, the Tarn would still
be the same, with someone just like her beside it, revolving similar
thoughts.

70

Ottilie and Mr McCosh

Hamilton McCosh was sitting motionless at his desk before the window, looking out over Court Road. Caractacus was sitting in the middle of his blotter, bolt upright like a statue of Bast, making work impossible, and he was playing with the cat's ears. Outside it was raining heavily, and the tradesmen were hurrying by wearing shining mackintoshes, and sou'westers. The fingers of his left hand rested limply round a glass tumbler containing a dram of his favourite Bladnoch. He was, as it were, trying to listen to his own body, to attend to its machinery. He had been having pains in his chest fairly frequently, and thought it unlikely to be indigestion. That would not explain the bouts of dizziness that could fall upon him at any time. He was expecting Dr Scott to call in at any minute. There was a tap on the door, and Ottilie put her head round it. 'Daddy, can I come in?' she said.

'Hello, lassie. Is it teatime?'

'No, I just wanted to talk to you about something, now that Fairhead's asked you about Sophie.'

'It's wonderful news, isn't it?' said Mr McCosh. 'Couldn't be better. I'm very glad about it, I'm bound to say.'

'Daddy, I've had an idea and I wanted to see what you thought of it.'

He looked up at her. 'Fire away, lassie.'

'I've been thinking. It's an horrendous expense to have two weddings one after the other.'

'That has also occurred to me. I'd have to sell a lot of shares. It's extremely worrying. Naturally I'd have to do them proud, and one wedding can't be seen to be better than the other. Very worrying indeed.'

'Well, it's hard to say this, but one wedding is bound to be much happier than the other, isn't it? I mean much more joyous. It's going to be terribly obvious to everyone.'

'I fear you're right, Ottie bairn. But what can be done about that? We're stuck with it.'

'That's the thing, Daddy. We're not stuck. We could have a double wedding.'

'A double wedding! Now there's a thought! I believe you might be on to something. It's not as if it's never happened before.'

'Well, if you think about it, it would be largely the same guests coming to both. And the novelty of it would be rather thrilling. And . . . well . . .'

'Yes?'

'Well, the fact is that Rosie will be so happy for Sophie and Fairhead that it will make the day much happier for her too. She'll get caught up in all that happiness, don't you think? And that'll make it happier for Daniel. It'll help to give them a better start.'

'I do wish Daniel and Rosie weren't going ahead with it. It can't come to any good.'

'I think it could work,' said Ottilie, 'but it all depends on Rosie, doesn't it? She's got to cut the cord that drags the ghost of poor Ash along with her wherever she goes. But a double wedding's a good idea, don't you think?'

'We'd have to talk to everyone and see what they think,' said Mr McCosh.

'I've already done it,' said Ottilie. 'Everyone rather likes the idea.'

'Gracious me, Ottie, you could have been a diplomat. Or in business.'

Ottilie smiled and said, 'Actually, I haven't suggested it to Mama yet. I'm sure she'll kick up about it, so I haven't dared. But I do have a plan, if you'd like to hear it.'

Accordingly, Hamilton McCosh approached his wife as she made up her face before dinner, and was peering intently into the mirror. Her reaction to the idea was one of horror. 'Why,' she cried, 'this has certainly never been done in my family before! It can't possibly be! A thousand times no!'

'A thousand times, my dear? That seems an unduly large number, when only a few hundred will do.'

'I will not be mocked!'

'Perhaps not, my dear, but I do have to tell you that two weddings would be unmanageably expensive. It couldn't possibly be done without personal economies.'

'Personal economies?'

'Well, I've been scratching my head about this, and I've realised that we could do two separate weddings if you were to forgo your dress allowance for eighteen months.'

'My dress allowance?! For eighteen months?!'

'The sums work out very neatly, my dear. I'm sure you could bear the sacrifice, for the children's sake.'

'Well!' she huffed. 'I never . . . well, I never did!'

'I'll leave you to think about it,' said her husband. 'Now I must go and change for dinner.'

After dinner, when Mrs McCosh left the room to 'powder her nose', Hamilton McCosh said to the girls, 'I think we might have pulled it off.'

'I told her that the daughters of a Scottish duke had a triple wedding to three Montenegrin princes last year,' said Christabel. 'I think she was impressed.'

'You lied to her?' protested Rosie, amused but scandalised.

'Only a little white lie.' Christabel held up her hand with the forefinger and thumb half an inch apart 'A tiny little white lie only this big.'

Sophie came over to Rosie and put her arms around her, kissing her on the cheek. 'It'll be the best day of our lives,' she said. 'I'm so pleased. I wish we could all be married at the same time. All Eltham would be agog. We'd be the gazingstock of Kent.'

'Has anyone asked Daniel?' said Rosie, over her sister's shoulder, a little horrified. 'We can't possibly decide this without consulting him first.'

Ottilie put her hand up. 'Exchange of telegrams. I said "DOUBLE WEDDING QUESTION MARK HOW ABOUT IT QUESTION MARK" and he sent back "WONDERFUL IDEA STOP SO PLEASED NO QUESTION MARK STOP LOOPING THE LOOP STOP."'

'Honestly, Ottie,' said Rosie, 'what would we do without you?

You're an absolute treasure, and we all really do love you.'

'What on earth did we do in the days before telegrams?' asked Christabel.

71

A Kindness

Hamilton McCosh had invented a new gadget called the Puttperfecto, which was not very different from a carthorse shoe. The idea was to place it on the carpet and use it as a target for putting practice. In its latest incarnation it was like three horseshoes stuck together, so that three people could use it at once, from different directions. He, Mrs McCosh and Christabel had been trying it out in the drawing room, with considerable success despite the disruptive attentions of Caractacus, and Mr McCosh had decided to try to sell it to the Army & Navy stores, who produced their own line of golfing equipment. He had had an idea for another improvement, in the form of a springloaded plate that would send the ball back, in the event of a direct hit.

He was therefore in very good humour when he went upstairs and came across Millicent, in tears, and employing a duster as a handkerchief. When she saw him she got to her feet, exclaimed, 'Sorry, sir,' and ran off down the stairs.

'Dear me,' said Mr McCosh to himself, and he went downstairs to the kitchen, expecting to find Millicent there. Instead he found Cookie, who was making Norfolk dumplings amid much sighing and puffing. 'Good evening, sir,' she said.

'And a very good evening to you, Cookie. I must say, the kitchen smells very nice.'

'As it ought, sir,'

'I perceive you are in a huff.'

'I am vexed, sir.'

'Vexed, Cookie?'

'It's poor Millicent, sir.'

'Poor? Has poverty descended upon her, in one of its many forms?'

'Indeed it has, sir.'

'And in which of its many forms has it descended upon her?'

302

'Far be it from me to question the mistress,' said Cookie righteously.

'It has descended in the form of Mrs McCosh?'

'It has, sir.'

'Manifesting in what manner?'

'She's fined Millicent fifteen shillings, sir, over a matter of woodworm.'

'Woodworm? Gracious me.'

'It's the dressing table in your bedroom, sir, the mahogany one. It's got woodworm.'

'I fail to see how this impacts upon the poor distressed Millicent.'

'The mistress says that it wouldn't have got woodworm if Millicent had been polishing it properly.'

'That is true, is it not, Cookie?'

'Nobody polishes a table on the underneath, sir.'

'And that's where it started?'

'Yes, sir, but it's got into the legs.'

'That's a valuable piece,' reflected Mr McCosh.

'Well,' continued Cookie, 'the mistress got in someone to look at it, and he says it'll cost fifteen shillings to treat, and the mistress is taking fifteen shillings off Millicent's wages, seeing as it's Millicent's fault. In her opinion.'

'And not in yours?'

'It's not my place to question, sir. But nobody polishes a table underneath, sir, like I said.'

Millicent earned twenty pounds per annum, and Hamilton McCosh performed a swift mental calculation. 'That's nearly two weeks' wages,' he said.

'The mistress said that seeing Millicent gets board and lodging, it ain't much of a loss, sir, but it is, sir, 'cause what the mistress don't know is Millicent's got a sick mother what can hardly move any more, and that's where she sends the money, sir, and that's why poor Millicent is inconsolable, sir, on account of her mother what can hardly move.'

'You realise that the master of the house cannot overrule the mistress of it when it comes to domestic matters? It's very bad form, as I'm sure you know. One of the unwritten rules.'

'Maybe it is,' said Cookie sceptically. 'But the master's the master in my opinion. And the mistress isn't quite herself these days, if you don't mind me saying so, sir, ever since she got caught in that raid. I don't believe she'd have dreamed of doing this in the old days. And she wouldn't have got taken in by someone saying it would cost fifteen shillings.'

'I dare say you're right, Cookie, I dare say you're right. We all have a lot to put up with. More than before, at any rate.'

Hamilton McCosh went to his study and took his cash box from the bureau. He removed six half-crowns, and then returned the box to its drawer. As an afterthought, he took it out again, unlocked it, and removed an extra florin.

He found Millicent in the morning room, still sniffling as she cleaned out the grating on her hands and knees. 'Ah, I've found you,' he said, 'looking very like Cinderella.'

The maid got to her feet and wiped her eyes with her sleeve, leaving a streak of ash across her face.

'Something has been troubling me, Millicent,' he said.

'I'm sorry to hear that, sir,' she replied.

'Yes,' continued Mr McCosh. 'I have been fearful for some time that your Christmas bonus, was, shall we say, a little ungenerous?'

'Oh no, sir, it was most generous, sir.'

'Indeed it wasn't. It has been a trouble to my conscience for some months, and I am anxious to rectify it.'

He put his hand into his pocket and removed the small, sealed brown envelope into which he had placed the six half-crowns. He then reached into his waistcoat pocket and brought out the florin, which he put into her hand. She gazed at it in wonderment. 'Very happy Christmas last year, Millicent,' he said, and walked quietly away. Just as he got to the far end of the hall he heard her small cry of joy as she opened the envelope and saw what was inside.

He went into the drawing room and looked out over the garden. As always his eye settled on the mound of Bouncer's grave in the orchard, and he smiled. 'Good evening, you good old boy,' he said softly.

It seemed such a long time ago that one used to give a sick and dying old dog to the head gardener, to be hanged. Nowadays, reflected Mr McCosh, one took them to a vet for a fatal injection. Some things change for the better, he thought, and felt a pang of guilt about Bouncer's undignified death. Still, that used to be normal, like so many other horrible things.

72

My Soul Calls to Yours

As her wedding to Daniel approached, Rosie felt doubt and apprehension weighing her down, but she was committed and could hardly back out. She thought that she probably loved him, or might be able to, but it still did not seem right. In some ways he was too much like Ash. He was not only bold and athletic and amusing, he was even an engineer. How would she ever be able to behold him without seeing the ghost of Ash over his shoulder? Or embrace him and notice how different his body was?

Rosie went to church and prayed. In her room she frequently unwrapped her madonna and looked into that painted face for some hint of advice or direction. She went and sat by the Tarn. She went down into the orchard and looked at Bouncer's grave, as though that might yield a little inspiration. She sat in the conservatory flicking through her autograph book, looking at the loving messages and beautiful drawings, the humorous cartoons of the men she had nursed at Netley. Their faces had faded already, leaving behind an atmosphere in place of an image.

Rosie knew what convention required. Before you married you destroyed all your love letters from everyone else. That's what you had to do, and it made some symbolic sense; it was how you signified that there was now, irrevocably, only one man in your life. It was like the commitment you made when you changed your name.

She had a thick sheaf of Ash's letters, from 1910 to 1915, bound up in a ribbon, and she kept them in her dressing-table drawer, right at the back, behind the powder puffs and compacts, and the cotton wool. They had acquired the feminine smell of cosmetics and scent, and there was no longer any point in sniffing at them. She took them out often and reread them. Their passionate hyperbole never failed to fill her with longing and regret. In those days every month had seemed to be July.

One Sunday after matins she was whiling the time away before lunch when she suddenly found a politician's solution to her dilemma, and accordingly she went out on Monday and bought a small ruled notebook from the stationer's. It was bound in red-and-black leather, and had a ribbon that served as a bookmark. She calculated that it should be exactly the right size if only she edited out the chit-chat and unnecessary detail, and just retained all that was most beautiful and moving. Sitting at the escritoire in her room, with a photograph of Ash propped up at the back of it, she wrote on the first page '*The past is part and parcel of the present*' and then she began to redact.

'*You are now a part of me – I hold and cherish you as a thing sacred.*'

'*Dearest, dearest heart, my soul calls to yours and I feel worn out.*'

'*To me you are holy and I sometimes wonder if Heaven is better than your dear kisses.*'

'*My thoughts are my visionary arms. They cling to you always.*'

'*Last night I dreamed that you came to me and kissed me, and said "I have come to stay with you tonight" – why is Heaven so cruel? Just as I was about to cling to you I was awakened.*'

'*I sit all alone from 8.30 to 10.30 thinking of you – these hours are the most sacred in the day, beloved.*'

'*When you smile on me again the curtains will be drawn from the sun.*'

'*I want to be alone in sunlit fields and feel your dear head against mine until the end of all things.*'

'*I would work and give my life's blood to win you, my beloved. I know I am not worth considering, but I love, want and must have you. I crave for you all day, and sometimes find myself not listening to people, but hearing your voice calling me.*'

'*During the evening will you give yourself to me for just one second? All things earthly and heavenly are outshone by you.*'

'*My prayer tonight is: God, You can take away all that I have, but give me a garden of flowers with my sweet one, for us to live in.*'

'*All I want is a kiss from your lips to fire my blood.*'

'*You know, dearest heart, how an autumn morning can make your blood tingle. Well, that's what happens when I think of those kisses I shall steal from you.*'

'*You will probably never appreciate or understand the gaps you have filled in my life. I was so very lonely before you came. You seemed to understand at once how desolate this country seemed to me, how I struggled with its rigid ways, even as a little boy, and how I couldn't understand its archaic institutions, how I felt so much like a bird forbidden to fly, how I longed to go home to America. It was you who gave me England, made England my home. Thank you for giving me England. Flower of my Eden, goodnight.'*

On the eve of her wedding to Daniel, having copied out all that was most intimate in Ash's letters, when the rest of the house was all afluster with preparations and jollity, Rosie set about doing what she had resolved to do. She arranged balls of newspaper in her grate, adorned them with kindling, and placed lumps of coal strategically. She took the box of matches from the mantelpiece, and found that they were damp. The head of the first match simply came off, and the second broke, but the third one caught, and she tilted it to make the flame climb. Carefully she set light to as many balls of paper as she could. She laid the letters reverently on top.

With horrible detachment she began to watch as Ash's messages burned, the beloved handwriting turning brown and then flaring.

Suddenly she knew that she couldn't bear it. She saw the fire taking, and had the wild thought that if only she acted fast enough her fingers would escape the flames. Her hands darted in, and seized one letter after another, dropping them on the hearth and beating out the flames. She felt the sting and sear of it, but knew that it was too late to stop trying to rescue the letters.

Once all the charred paper was on the hearth, she realised that she had burned the backs of her hands as well as the palms and fingers. As the horrifying pain welled up and the skin blistered, she knew there was nothing she could do but run for the bathroom.

Her hands were too damaged to grip the knob. She kicked furiously at the door and began to wail and moan, waving her hands in the attempt to cool them with currents of air.

It seemed like an age, but it was moments before Millicent opened the door, and Rosie rushed past her, falling headlong on the landing, and unable to use her hands to save herself, she crashed down on her face and elbows. Sobbing, she scrambled to her feet and ran. Millicent ran in her wake. Once in the bathroom, Rosie cried, 'Turn on the tap, turn on the tap! Quick, Millie, quick!'

As Rosie stood there with cold water running over her burns, crying with the agony of it, Millicent hurtled downstairs and, on her own initiative, ran out of the front door without her hat and down Court Road to fetch Dr Scott.

Later that evening the entire family held court in the drawing room whilst the two servants hovered in the hall. Rosie was their favourite of the sisters, and they were overcome with anxiety and confusion. Rosie had resisted being taken to hospital, and had duly succumbed to shock. She had lain on the sofa, pale and with almost no pulse at the wrist, cold sweat pearling on her brow. She neither moved nor seemed to breathe, and the family were appalled by the prospect of her dying the night before her marriage. Hamilton McCosh went up to her room, inspected the charred letters, and immediately understood what had happened. When he returned and informed the others, they all had the same thought. Ottilie said, 'The wedding's got to be called off. Sophie, you and Fairhead will just have to go ahead and get married on your own.'

Dr Scott, a portly middle-aged man of great experience and considerable natural wisdom, arranged Rosie so that her feet were above her head, in order to increase the flow of blood to the brain. 'It's more important to treat the shock than the burns,' he told the family. 'The burns can wait, and they aren't nearly as bad as they look. Kindly ask one of the servants to fetch a large bowl or bucket. The other must fetch blankets, and make as many hot-water bottles as you have in the house. Otherwise I must ask you to remain calm and not to interfere.'

Mrs McCosh bridled, not because she wanted to interfere, but because she felt it was something to which she had the natural right.

Just as Dr Scott had hoped and anticipated, Rosie woke up and was promptly sick into the bowl that he had requested. 'Excellent!' exclaimed the doctor. 'Now we can be certain she'll live. A pot of weak tea please!'

Dr Scott set about preparing the wounds for dressing. The split in her lip he did nothing about. He made sure that no charred paper still adhered to the wounds on her hands, and cleaned them very gently with warm water. Rosie winced and whimpered, and Sophie went behind her and put an arm round her shoulder, placing her head side by side with Rosie's. 'Be most heroical and valorifical and undauntical,' she whispered, and Rosie managed to laugh.

The doctor punctured the blisters and snipped away the pieces of loose skin. He rummaged in his substantial Gladstone bag, and produced a bottle of picric acid, with which he soaked several pieces of gauze. Carefully he arranged Rosie's fingers in a natural position and placed gauze between each one so that scarring would not seal any of them together. Then he placed more soaked gauze over the remaining burns, and gently wrapped the hands in bandages.

In the hall he gave his instructions to Mrs McCosh. 'The dressing can stay on for several days unless there is considerable discharge, in which case I must be sent for. It is possible that shock may return. It sometimes does. If so, send someone for me immediately. The patient will be in great pain for some consider-able time, but in my opinion most of the burns are second degree and should not scar to any great extent. If the picric acid soaks through to the outside of the dressing, I must warn you that any linen she touches will be stained a pleasingly deep shade of yellow.'

'Thank you, Doctor,' said Mrs McCosh, genuinely grateful. 'Please do not omit to send your bill at the end of the month.'

'That is something I never forget to do,' said Dr Scott, 'however great the temptation. And I trust that you will pay it promptly, as is sometimes not your wont. Good day to you.' And with that he donned his top hat and set off briskly for home.

Rosie resolutely refused to cancel or postpone her marriage, repeating, 'I never break promises.' Despite her inability to exorcise Ash, she had an intuition that marrying Daniel was the right thing to do, and in any case she could not spoil the day for Fairhead and Sophie.

73

The Day

It was a splendid morning, to the immense relief of the household, who had set up trestles in the garden, spread with crisp white linen, and laden with food and champagne. A little boy armed with shingle and a catapult had been hired to fend off any birds or squirrels that might take an interest whilst everybody was at church. However, he made more inroads into the spread than the wildlife might have done, and was entirely responsible for the disappearance of a bowl of Brazil nuts and two pies. Caractacus made off with a large cube of Cheddar cheese and ate it in the orchard.

Cookie had been working flat out for days making delicate little items for the reception, and had been adamant that a cake must not be bought in. Accordingly she had created two tremendous confections in three tiers that occupied the centre of the kitchen table, and around which the rest of the preparations had to be conducted. She fussed and perspired and frequently declared that she had never been so busy or so put upon in all her born days.

Ottilie and Christabel had had the idea that it would be very fine if Daniel and Rosie were to be married by Fairhead, prior to his being married to Sophie by the rector, but ultimately it seemed altogether too complicated, and Fairhead himself said that it would be impossible to concentrate on the other wedding when he was preoccupied with his own. Christabel had also had the idea that she should take the wedding photographs, until Rosie had pointed out that if she was taking the photographs, then she herself would not be able to be in them, and that in any case it would seem a bit strange to have one of the bridesmaids take the pictures, all dressed up in frills and furbelows, and partially concealed under a black cloth. Gaskell offered to step in, but in truth Mrs McCosh, for all her egalitarianism when it concerned her own case, was not to be convinced that a lady photographer could be relied upon to do the job properly, so Gaskell curled her lip in quiet disdain and resigned herself to being a mere guest. She arrived on a motorcycle, attired in a manner that would have reminded many people of the flamboyant costumes of Oscar Wilde, were it not for the flying helmet and goggles.

Daniel, in the full dress uniform of the RAF, a sword buckled at his side, strolled down Court Road, past the solid mansions of the new bourgeoisie, to St John's. At his side was Fairhead, dressed in the number ones of the chaplaincy. They had little to say to each other, but enjoyed the quiet reassurance of masculine company. They felt as if they were walking towards the gates of the Garden of Eden, their minds whirling both with nervousness and vague, sweet optimism. They fell into step. They had decided to swap being best man, and carried the other man's ring in their pocket. In Daniel's case Archie had declined the job, quite brusquely – 'Out of the question, old boy, couldn't possibly' – and Fluke had merely said, 'Sorry, old fellow, I've got other plans. I'm afraid I can't even turn up until the reception, much as it pains me to say so.' Strangely enough, the other members of his squadron had told him the same thing. As for Fairhead, it seemed perfectly obvious to him that Daniel should be his best man, since he really had become his best friend in the last few months. Like many clergymen, he really preferred the company of sceptics.

'I've got one more medal than you,' teased Daniel, as they passed the palace.

'No one will notice,' replied Fairhead. 'We both have quite a chestful, and for all anyone knows, mine might be better than yours. Yours might be for peeling potatoes in the face of the enemy. And you don't have a silver crucifix.'

'No, I'm not that kind of sky pilot.'

Ten minutes after the grooms were settled in church, the brides and bridesmaids arrived in an open carriage drawn by a pair of plumed greys. The maids were Ottilie and Christabel, carrying bouquets, and dressed in blue silk that Gaskell and Christabel had designed and made between them, so that they looked like heroines from a medieval legend or a fantasy by

William Morris. About their heads they wore garlands of small white carnations and both wore their hair straight, brushed to a deep shine. They had tossed a coin to decide which was to be bridesmaid to which bride, and Ottilie had been assigned to Rosie, and Christabel to Sophie. Rosie and Sophie were dressed very like the maids, except in white silk, with a simple headdress, also reminiscent of medieval times, and also made by Gaskell and Christabel during many long companionable evenings in the Chelsea atelier. Neither Rosie nor Sophie had wanted to wear a veil, and Mrs McCosh would therefore, very grumpily and resentfully, have to forgo that moment in the ceremony when the bride reveals her face to the groom in time for the kiss.

Sophie had been so well made up that she looked beautiful for the first time in her life. Her stiff frizzy hair had been tamed into a bunch behind, and her dress evened out the lines of her small breasts and wide hips. Rosie's long chestnut hair had been plaited and arranged about her head like a chaplet, exposing the fair skin of her neck and the fine line of her jaw. Both carried a small bouquet of white flowers. They had borrowed a set of pearls from each other, and wore sapphire and topaz earrings inherited from their grandmother. They had each tied a blue ribbon around their leg, just above the knee, where it would not slip.

These young women were handed down by their father, and took up their station at the church door, until such time as the organist would strike up the Wedding March. Sophie stood clutching her bouquet, almost quivering with delight and anticipation, and Rosie stood motionless, feeling that she had been caught up in a strange dream. She looked at the edifice of the church and reflected that this was where she would have married Ash, had he lived. How strange that life was unfolding without him. Her hands were stinging terribly from their burns of the evening before, with agonising flushes of heat coming and going in waves. She now felt ashamed and embarrassed by what she had done, but helpless in its aftermath.

Mr McCosh felt familiar pangs of pain in his chest and left arm, and thought that he really must ask Dr Scott to call round again. Mrs McCosh, conscious of her role, and magnificent in an enormous floral hat that entirely blocked the view of those behind, fretted inwardly about the success of the reception. Now that there were no servants to speak of, one had to rely on people who were hired in, and results were so much more unpredictable.

When the organ struck up and the brides entered on their father's arms, neither Daniel nor Fairhead turned round to look; they wanted to delay the surprise and pleasure.

The service, as it turned out, was slightly muddled, since, although the plans had been carefully laid, the rector became confused under the pressure of the event. He addressed Fairhead as Daniel Pitt, and had to be corrected, and seemed startled when Hamilton McCosh stepped forward to give away each of the brides, and equally startled when each groom presented the other with the ring for his bride.

The greatest difficulty occurred when Daniel had to put the ring on Rosie's finger. It had occurred to no one, not even to Rosie, that the moment would come when she would need an unbandaged ring finger. Daniel took her hand, perceived the problem, was momentarily appalled and perplexed, and then put the ring to the tip of the finger. He held it there for a few seconds, and then palmed it, and was only able to transfer it to his pocket when they all they left to sign the register.

Sophie's infectious joy gave lift to the whole occasion, and when she went up on tiptoe to kiss Fairhead she put her arm round his neck and drew his head down to receive her lips. Rosie surprised herself by kissing Daniel with real tenderness. How strange but delightful it was to be Mrs Pitt.

When the time came to leave, the organist pulled out all the stops, and played Widor, causing the whole church to reverberate. The two couples emerged arm in arm into the sunlight and passed beneath the glittering arch of swords provided by the grooms' military friends, all of them beautifully got up in the bright uniforms of their regiments. The happy crowd of friends and family threw rice over them, clapping and cheering. Some of the women wiped tears from their eyes, and the men necessarily restrained their own.

As the open carriage departed, this time bearing the couples, Sophie threw her bouquet to Ottilie, who skipped a little as she caught it. Rosie's bouquet flew quite accidentally towards Gaskell, who caught it, looked at it with puzzlement, as if it were an inexplicably large and exotic insect, and then tossed it on to Ottilie. 'I can't have two!' she protested, and Gaskell said, 'Of course you can. It'll double your chances!'

At the reception Mr McCosh made a speech in which he declared his regret that he could not have married all his daughters off in one go, and that it would seem terribly dull marrying off the other two in separate ceremonies, but he feared that they might never get married anyway, because there were only two men in the world good enough for his daughters to marry, and they had been snaffled by Sophie and Rosie already. Christabel felt a little peculiar as she listened to this, given that Gaskell was by her side. Ottilie looked over at Archie, who was making a point of standing on his own, grimly enduring the loss to his brother of the woman he had always loved. Ottilie felt very sorry for him, and wished he would notice her, but she knew that he never would, and that one day she would probably find someone else.

Daniel and Fairhead managed to combine their speeches as both grooms and best men, under strict instruction from Hamilton McCosh to keep it brief. Fairhead quoted the Song of Solomon in honour of his bride, looking at her directly, and reciting: ' "Thou hast ravished my heart, my sister, my spouse; thou hast ravished my heart with one of thine eyes, with one chain of thy neck. How fair is thy love, my sister, my spouse! how much better is thy love than wine! and the smell of thine ointments than all spices! Thy lips, O my spouse, drop as the honeycomb: honey and milk are under thy tongue . . ." '

Sophie glowed with pleasure and clapped at the end, jumping up and down like a schoolgirl. Mrs McCosh found herself crying unexpectedly. The speech had caused her to remember her husband's early passion.

Daniel's speech had only just got under way when a droning sound from the south began to get louder and louder. Those who had experienced the Zeppelin and Gotha raids began to feel distinctly uneasy. Daniel was drowned out, as the racket grew suddenly deafening and it grew clear what was happening.

Daniel's entire squadron of Snipes came over at roof level, led by Fluke's diminutive and impertinent Sopwith triplane, with his Squadron Leader's streamers trailing and flapping from the struts. The three flights peeled apart and began to put on a display of synchronised formation flying, looping, banking, flying upside down, missing head-on collisions at the last moment, and diving on the house. At the end they dived together, shot up into the air, hung there for a second, stalled, sideslipped, and fell into a collective falling leaf that had Daniel's heart in his mouth. He was possibly the only one there who knew how dangerous it could be, but it did look wonderful. At the last minute the engines roared back into life, the planes pulled out of their fall, and rose back up into the clouds to perform one more loop with a roll on top. They then set off in the direction of the golf course, whose fairways on this day were to contain an unusual number of fighters. The club's members turned out to watch them coming in to land, asking each other rhetorically whether one really would have to play the ball where it lay, even if an aeroplane happened to be obscuring one's shot.

A few minutes after the squadron had gone, Fluke's little triplane reappeared, trailing behind it a banner that read 'Hallelujah!'

Rosie suddenly remembered the day when they had had their coronation celebration for King Edward VII, and the garden seemed to fill with ghosts. Ash and his brothers, little boys back then, had grown into men and marched away, to vanish into the insatiable stomach of war.

Mme Pitt appeared at her side, dressed in the Parisian style, in a hat with a curved brim trimmed with artificial roses. On her chest she wore a silver-mounted tiger-claw brooch that Rosie had always hated, because she did not think that any animal should be made into jewellery.

'You are remembering, I think,' said Mme Pitt, 'when my boys came over the wall.'

'It was quite a stunt,' said Rosie, a little feebly. Mme Pitt smelled very powerfully of lavender.

She looked Rosie straight in the eye, as if to imply a threat, and said, 'You must look after my son.' Then she kissed her on the cheek, patted her on the shoulder, and left her to herself.

After the traditional reading of the telegrams, just as Rosie was laying her injured right hand lightly on top of Daniel's for the cutting of the cake with his sword, the pilots of his squadron appeared en masse, full of high spirits, to organise leap-frog competitions and wheelbarrow races, and perform treetop fights and handstands. They took Daniel and Fairhead on their shoulders and bore them round the garden in triumph. The level of general happiness and rejoicing seemed to ratchet up several notches, and the level of decorum plummeted. All the champagne and food disappeared. Mrs McCosh became tipsy, and had to totter indoors and lie down.

In her wedding photograph Rosie's bandaged hands are mainly concealed by the long lacy cuffs of her dress, and the monochrome does not reveal the deep yellow stains in it. The split in her lip is discernible but not distracting. The brides' and grooms' friends and relatives look grim, as they always do in pictures where one has had to pose in perfect stillness for too long a time. Sophie and Fairhead are looking at each other. Daniel is smiling, the sole one there who believes that Rosie had an accident with a brazier in the kitchen. He looks handsome, vigorous and happy in his RAF uniform with its double row of medals, and his sword hanging from the Sam Browne. His brother Archie looks magnificent and dignified in the uniform of a major of Rattray's Sikhs. His face reveals nothing of the fact that he is irretrievably in love with the woman who has become his brother's wife. Mme Pitt, his mother, looks as if she is waiting to do something mischievous. Rosie looks subdued and wistful. She is niggled by the promise she once made to Ash, that she would love him and him alone for all eternity. Hamilton McCosh is supporting his wife on his arm, and worrying that Rosie might have done the wrong thing by this young man that he likes and admires. Mrs McCosh is thinking about whether or not there is any cachet in being mother-in-law to someone who is half French. Ottilie and Christabel are wondering what the wedding nights will be like.

That night, having borrowed the AC Six, Daniel took Rosie on honeymoon to a hotel in Henley-on-Thames, and had to feed her himself. She declined champagne, and later on Daniel felt that he could not possibly expect anything of her in her injured condition. Moreover she had, perhaps wilfully, not taken account of certain physiological inevitabilities when planning the date of the wedding. It was very difficult to change the clouts with her damaged hands, as it was to do anything for herself at all.

The couple lay face-to-face, kissing and talking, he in striped pyjamas and she in a copious nightdress. Her kisses were tentative and reluctant, and he construed this as modesty. After she fell asleep at last, he got up, went downstairs, lifted a sash, carefully made a note of which one it was, and went for a long nocturnal walk along the river. As dawn broke he sat on the stump of an oak, took out his cigarette case, removed a cigarette, tapped the end of it on the case, and lit it. He smoked and breathed in the chilly air all at once. In spite of everything, he was brimming with happiness and optimism. He had almost made up his mind to leave the RAF and get a job in civil aviation. Everyone said there were tremendous opportunities just round the corner. If that did not work out, he would go into motorcycles.

Daniel fell into a reverie about a house somewhere nice, such as here in Henley, and he envisaged himself playing cricket in the garden with his children, a pipe stuck in the corner of his mouth even though he did not smoke one, or going fishing on the Thames, when he had never been fishing in his life. In the driveway of the house, on the other side where you can't see it, there would be a beautiful Hispano-Suiza, its engine ticking as it cooled down after a run to Oxford and back. In his mind's eye Rosie was wearing a summer dress and a wide floppy hat. She was smiling at him and the children, and over her arm was a basket of flowers.

74

Nuptials

Sophie lay flat on her back in bed, freshly washed and in a new nightdress with a decorative blue ribbon at the neck, waiting for her husband to come in from the bathroom. They had chosen a small hotel in Dover for the first night of their honeymoon and had come down by train, sending their luggage in advance. It was the kind of hotel where the plumbing groaned and rattled, and light draughts of fresh salty air seeped in through the ill-fitting window frames. They had dined on Dover sole, as seemed only appropriate, and had become very slightly tipsy on white wine that should have been a little bit more chilled, the kind of sour generic wine that the French used to palm off on the British, in the secure knowledge that the British didn't know any better. Because Sophie and Captain Fairhead did not know any better, they had enjoyed it very much.

Captain Fairhead came in at last, and slipped under the sheets. He did not touch her, but turned on his side to face her. She rolled and faced him, so close that they could smell each other's winey hot breath.

'You face looks completely different from so close up,' said Sophie.

'From this close you've got four eyes,' said Captain Fairhead. He planted a small kiss on her lips, and she put her arms around him.

'Do you know what?'

'No. What?'

'Mama asked me if I knew what was going to happen tonight. I said, "We're going to Dover." And she said, "Don't be obtuse, darling." Then she said, "What will happen will be deeply unpleasant, humiliating and degrading, but you must do your duty, and in the end it is worth it for the children that result."'

'What do you think we ought to do?' asked Fairhead. 'I confess,

I do feel quite apprehensive. I haven't been so nervous in a long time. Like the feeling when you know there's going to be a barrage.'

'Didn't you go to borledos in France?'

'Borledos? What on earth do you mean?'

'You know, places for jiggajig and hozirontal recreation?'

'Hozirontal recreation? You mean bordellos?

'Ah, that must be it.'

'There was at least one for officers in Amiens,' he said. 'The queues at the licensed ones for other ranks were quite unbelievable.'

'Didn't you go and brandish your Bible at them?'

'Certainly not. A military chaplain in time of war is solely concerned with consolation, encouragement and death. The men never took us very seriously in any case. They called us "sky pilots". Even the airmen called us sky pilots. Anyway, I never was one for the "borledos". You can call it fastidiousness, or moral principle, or lack of courage. I'm still not sure what it was, and now I'll never know. I'm as pure as the driven snow, I'm afraid.'

'I had some good advice,' said Sophie. 'I got it from someone who married last year.'

'What was it?'

'She said not to try and do it until you both feel comfortable, 'specially not on the first night. That's what someone told her, and it worked out very well, she said.'

'Really?'

'She said just to stick to talking and kissing, and things like that.'

'Are you ticklish?' he asked.

'Don't tickle me, kiss me.'

'Where?'

'Here,' she said, pointing to the tip of her nose. He kissed it. 'Now here,' she said, patting her right cheek, 'and now here,' patting the left. 'Now it's my turn to kiss you.' She placed her mouth fully on his.

Quarter of an hour later, utterly enflamed, he said, 'Do you really need that nightdress on?'

'Do you really need those pyjamas?'

'I'll undress if you undress.'

'You undress me, then I'll undress you.'

He made her sit up, and pulled the nightdress over her head, exposing her small pointed breasts and flat belly. Her cheeks flushed, and she began to fumble with his buttons.

They lay wonderingly, their whole flesh in complete correspondence with another's for the first time in their lives. The warmth, the smell, the textures, were strange, exciting and beautiful. He ran a finger softly down her spine, and she shivered.

Outside the gaslighter doused the street lamps. Their eyes glittered in the dark.

'Shall we go to sleep now?' he suggested mischievously. 'We've got an early start if we want to get to Deauville.'

'Oh drat,' she said.

'Thank God I'm alive,' he said. 'Thank God I made it through.'

'Let's not wait,' she said.

In the morning, when they drew the curtains, a bright shaft of sunlight was thrown into the room, its colour pure and golden. Outside the sky was absolutely clear of cloud, and the whole town and the sea shimmered and wavered in a serene and perfect light. Sophie went to the window, naked as she was, and held out her arms so that the sunlight could bathe her body.

'How beautiful you are,' said Fairhead gratefully.

He went to the bathroom down the corridor, and when he returned quarter of an hour later, freshly shaven and smelling of cologne, he found Sophie in her nightdress and dressing gown, sitting by the window, apparently writing in the air with her forefinger. He stood behind her and saw that she was disturbing the tiny motes that sparkled in the bright shaft of sunlight.

'Look at all the little shiny specks, swirling about,' said Sophie. 'Do you know what they are?'

'Do you? What are they?'

'They're the dust that falls from dreams.'

'The dust that falls from dreams,' repeated Fairhead, his voice full of wonder. He was only just beginning the long journey towards the revelation that he had married a truly original and remarkable woman, and felt again a pang of gratitude and incredulity.

'Yes,' said Sophie. 'This is the dust from last night's dreams. I'm writing our names. I'm writing with my finger in the dust that falls from dreams.'

75

Archie's Letter to Daniel

17 February 1920

Mon frère,

I don't think I've ever been so glad to get back on the boat. It's clear to me that I don't belong in England or even in France any more. I belong in the Hindu Kush, in Waziristan, in wild tribal places where the logic is so simple it doesn't amount to any kind of logic at all, where there's no morality, reason or decency, and there's only custom, honour and religion. You know what it's like, you've served there yourself. Didn't we have a wild and wonderful time? Now I don't suppose you'll ever set foot there again.

I don't honestly care very much about the Great Game. Of course, now that the Russians have gone Bolshevik, anything could happen. We're in Afghanistan so the Russians can't be, it's as simple as that. It's a game of dog in the bloody manger. That's why we're bogged down, dealing with people who aren't like us and don't want to be like us, and don't know the difference between us and the Russians. We're all just faranghi, and all they want is to settle back into their feuds and raids and poppy farming and stoning and tribal war. Killing and dying is all they live for, it seems to me, and we get in the way of their fun. But you know all this.

Well, it is just a great game, isn't it? I'm not going back because I care about it. There's something wrong with me, and I'm out there to get away from myself and the people I love. I don't fit in at home. I'm unsuited. What would I do in Blighty or La Belle F in peacetime? Square-bashing? I'm not bright enough to start a business, and it wouldn't interest me. Can't understand why Hamilton McCosh finds it so fascinating. What else is there? A bloody schoolmaster, teaching French and history, and footling about with the CCF on Wednesday afternoons? I'd be thrashing the boys out of sheer bloody frustration.

No, brother, I'd rather die in Afghanistan for no good reason, and get

323

buried on a hillside where the dogs can dig me up and leave my bones to bleach in the sun for the ants to work on.

I've often thought of writing my memoirs, but I lack the discipline. I have a great deal to pass on, a great many very wonderful stories about everything I've seen and done, but when I sit down with some foolscap and a fountain pen, all that happens is that I light a cigarette and go out for walk.

As you're my brother, I can tell you all the things you already know, and you won't hold it against me. Not very stiff upper lip, I agree, but to hell with it. I've got that Latin part in me that sometimes wants to let go.

I drink too much. Most of my brother officers do. We all do, don't we? You told me about your heroic binges in the RFC. It must have been fun, and you must have drunk more in single evenings than I drink in a month, but the difference is, I need it and you don't. One has to have a clear head to write memoirs. It's no damned use being fuddled. You really ought to write yours one day. Everyone loves an air ace, and you'd be sure to make a few bob from it.

I envy you heading off into marriage and a cleaner life. No more finding comrades mutilated beyond recognition by Pathans, with their balls cut off and their mouth pissed in by the women. God help the faranghi who falls into the hands of the women. I know you used to keep a revolver in the cockpit in case of fire. Out there I never shoot the last round in my revolver before reloading. I count to five.

To think I've been out amongst those people for so long! But I do what soldiers do, I accept what can't be helped. If I had my life again I'd probably do the same. I could have stayed in Blighty after the war. I had a good war, ended up in France just like you, got draped in medals, just like you, and now I'm a Commander of St Michael and St George, but I'm still going back to the North-West Frontier.

A man needs to get away from himself sometimes.

I want to speak to you frankly about Rosie, but it's very difficult. I don't think I can do it. I don't blame you for loving and marrying her. I understand. I also know that she could not possibly have been happy with me, and I do believe most strongly that a man should not even consider marriage unless he can support a wife and children. Even so, one has dreams. It is very hard to endure the sight of them fluttering away like a flock of sparrows. It leaves a taste in the mouth like licking an old penny.

I have been thinking lately about our father. It's such a pity that he was killed when we were still so young. I don't think I will ever get over it. I thought I had, but I hadn't, as I realised when I stood outside the house in Court Road and remembered my childhood.

He looked marvellously handsome in his uniform. I wish that maman *had had a portrait made. He knew* The Hunting of the Snark *off by heart, and used to act it out for me. One doesn't realise until rather too late how important one's father is.*

I remember Rosie when she was a baby. Lovely blue eyes, very innocent, and then she grew up sincere and sober, like a little Presbyterian. You can fall in love with a little girl when you're an adolescent you know. You just wait til she grows up a bit, and there you are, equal at last except that she adored the American boy. A very fine fellow, probably deserved her a lot more than I did. Much nearer her own age too. I didn't begrudge him, but I couldn't switch, if you know what I mean. I never really looked at anyone else. So I joined the Indian Army and got seconded to the Frontier Scouts. I went as far away as I could, and then you came out there too, which made everything so much more fun. And now you're married to her after all, and I'm coming back out on my own.

Well, it doesn't do for Frontier Scouts to have wives, does it? Women drag you down if you're the kind of man who wants to camp in the rocks and hunt antelope and hide in nullahs, and get into firefights with Johnny Mahsud. You can't take women to the frontier, can you? Do you remember that woman who got carried off and went native and didn't even want to be saved? A rum one, that. Then someone bought her for one rifle. That's what a woman's worth. But Rosie is worth a whole world, mon frère, *so do take proper care of her.*

Did I tell you that last year we had a Pashtun recruit who got buggered by every man in his piquet? I told the Colonel that the boy was too damn pretty, and it started a whole six months of fights, and then a blood feud. Do you remember how we used to go out with binoculars, and there'd be Pashtuns buggering sheep and donkeys on every hillside? And the animals not giving a damn. I wanted to tell you about a song I heard called 'The Wounded Heart'. Zakmi Dil. The song says: 'There's a boy across the river with a backside like a peach, but alas I cannot swim.' I wonder what Rosie would think if she knew the world the way we know it. It seems to me that men have to keep the world secret from women, just so that they can go on living in a state of innocence. Come to think of it, being at Westminster was pretty good training for being on the North-West Frontier, wasn't it?

Do you remember poor old Captain Bowring, who got shot by a sentry at Sarwekai because his bare feet were pointed at Mecca? I don't suppose you were there in 1904, though. No, you would have been fifteen, and still at Westminster. The mind gets hazy after Bombay Sapphires. I was just thinking that what happened to him pretty much encapsulates the whole madness of the region. There were tribesmen outside shooting at the tower where the sentry was holed up, and the only choice was to storm the tower or starve the bugger out.

Everybody knew he had to be killed, but who was going to do it? Whoever did it would start a blood feud, and that might last for centuries. Anyway, it turned out that the man's brother was there, and he agreed to do the execution, so he went to see his brother up in the tower, and the brother agreed to be shot fraternally. So he came up on the parapet and threw his rifle down, and he opened his arms wide, and he shouted 'Allah o akbar' because he knew he was sinless and had done the right thing, and then his brother shot him from down below. He stood still for a second and then whirled round and plunged down into the courtyard. That was the end of sepoy Kabul Khan. Another martyr for the Prophet. He was a Mahsud. Talk the hind legs off a donkey, those Mahsuds. Damned treacherous too. Can't trust 'em an inch. Great fun to command, though. Splendid sense of humour. Nothing they like more than plaguing the political agent. Last year, one had the damned cheek to come and demand a campaign medal when he'd been on the other side, and wouldn't give in until he'd got one, either.

Forgive me if I've already told you about Bowring. I'll give your love to the sandflies and mosquitoes, the malaria and dysentery and sandfly fever, the scorpions in my shoes and under the lid of the thunderbox.

It was damn bad luck poor Rosie burning her hands like that, just before the wedding. I do hope she's all right now.

It's a pity I never fell for Ottilie. She's such a sweet girl and I'm very fond of her, but how could I marry her? I'd always be looking over her shoulder at her sister. Every time I saw Rosie I'd get the same lurch.

I'd be a terrible husband. I shouldn't inflict myself on anyone. Sorry about the stain on the right-hand side of the page. It's Angostura bitters.

I'm married to the army and the Afghan hills. I pray to God to let me die there with a bullet through my heart, and I've told my brother officers I only want a cairn of stones.

I've had too many gins to write any more now. I'm in Port Said, and it's as near to Hell as any man gets on earth. I'm going to seal this up and go ashore and post it, before I think any better of it.

I just wanted to tell you that if I die anywhere but in the Afghan hills, I'd like you to take my bones to Peshawar and bury them there.

God knows when I'll be back, mon frère. *If only one of us can be entirely happy, I'm content it should be you. All my love to you and Rosie. I'll write to* maman *when I'm sober.*

Archie, ever yours

76

Consummation

Daniel had become good at golf quite quickly, as ordered by Squadron Leader Maurice Beckenham-Gilbert, and had performed honourably in the match against the masters and senior pupils. He had also triumphed in the tennis tournament, producing some spectacular forehand volleys and backhand slices, whilst keeping the stub of a cigarette clamped firmly at all times between his lips, at dead centre. The squadron had taken more deliveries of some wonderfully jaunty Sopwith Snipes, the very plane in which Major W. G. Barker had won a Victoria Cross for engaging fifteen Fokker DVIIs just two weeks before the end of the war.

Daniel had been married only a month or two, and should have been radiant with happiness, as should Rosie.

Her sisters questioned her doggedly about her obvious sadness, and got nowhere. Mrs McCosh compounded the bad atmosphere by strongly disapproving of Rosie's state of mind, and blaming Daniel for it whenever he was there. The golf club had mowed a special landing strip for him in the rough on a par five, and he would come by in whatever aircraft was available, once even turning up in a Morane-Saulnier parasol that had been all but obsolete even in 1915.

Daniel was sitting on his own on a bench at the edge of the playing field, smoking a cigarette. It was a lovely day with a light breeze, and seagulls were throwing themselves about overhead, apparently just for the fun of it.

Squadron Leader Maurice Beckenham-Smith was walking his two black setters around the pitch, and he stopped and sat next to Daniel.

'Perfect day,' he said.

'Hmm,' said Daniel.

'You mean "Hmm, sir",' said Beckenham-Smith. 'I'm in uniform with my cap on.'

Daniel laughed half-heartedly.

'Down in the dumps?' said Beckenham-Smith. 'Not like you at all.'

'You were right,' said Daniel. 'I should have paid attention. Now I'm scuppered. For life, no doubt.'

'*Tant pis*,' said Beckenham-Smith. 'No joy?'

'None.'

'None whatsoever?'

'None whatsoever.'

'Gracious me! How long has it been?'

'Six weeks, sir.'

'Six weeks. Oh dear, that is too bad.'

'She always has a good reason.'

'Headache, tummy ache, earache, tired, indisposed, that kind of thing?'

'That's about the long and short of it, sir.'

'Should have married a French girl. Or a dusky maiden. Oh for a dusky maiden!'

They sat together in silence, petting the ears of the dogs, and then the Squadron Leader said, 'After a while you can get an annulment for that, you know. Non-consummation.'

'I know, sir. It might be all I have to hope for. It's very depressing.'

'The ancient Greeks believed that the first human woman was created for the punishment of man. Let's go up in a Snipe,' said Beckenham-Gilbert.

The two men went up into the sky and blew their worries away high above the seagulls. They buzzed a courting couple in a field, and did a display of loops over Birchington-on-Sea. Then they landed on wet sand of low tide at Margate and were roundly ticked off by a policeman.

Fluke and Daniel left their aircraft on the strand, and went for a wander in the town. They had tea in the Lyons Corner House, and then noticed a small bookshop, which, in the window, had a copy of Eleanor Farjeon's *Sonnets and Poems*. 'I wonder if Rosie would like that,' said Daniel. 'She's a great one for modern poetry.'

'Don't see the point of poetry,' said Fluke. 'Give me a song to bawl. Doesn't butter any parsnips, poetry, does it?'

'It butters Rosie's parsnips,' said Daniel. 'I've seen a good poem make her cry. I sometimes wonder if she's so religious just because the language of the Bible and the Prayer Book is so beautiful.'

Inside the shop Daniel took a look at the little book. It had a very pretty cover, and the first poem was striking. 'Man cannot be a sophist to his heart . . .' He read the second: 'O spare me from the hand of niggard love . . .'

'I'm going to get this,' said Daniel. 'I'm certain she'll like it.'

'I've found a tome about brook fishing for trout,' said Fluke, brandishing it. 'Don't think I can resist it.'

At the weekend Rosie accepted the little book with surprise. Somehow she had not expected her husband to have regard for what interested her, and she realised guiltily that she had never bought him a spontaneous gift herself.

'Doesn't she mostly write for children?' she asked, wondering if it was going to be at all enjoyable.

'Some of them are for children,' said Daniel. 'The sonnets definitely aren't.'

Rosie settled in the conservatory with Caractacus purring on her lap, and began to read the sonnets. The sun was shining weakly through the glass, and it was deliciously warm. She reached Sonnet XV, and read it over and over again. It spoke directly to her as if the poet were in the room, and she could see her deep, regretful eyes.

> Farewell, you children that I might have borne,
> Now must I put you from me year by year,
> Now year by year the root of life be torn
> Out of this womb to which you were so dear,
> Now year by year the milky springs be dried
> Within the sealed-up fountains of my breast,
> Now year by year be to my arms denied
> The burden they would break with and be blessed.
>
> Sometimes I felt your lips and hands so close
> I almost could have plucked you from the dark,
> But now your very dream more distant grows
> As my still aching body grows more stark.
> I shall not see you laugh or hear you weep,
> Kiss you awake, or cover up your sleep.

Choking with emotion, Rosie put the cat down, and fetched her coat and hat. She hurried down to the Tarn with her new book, needing to be alone with it.

As she sat on a bench, Rosie watched the children. Some were being wheeled about by their nurses, and the poorer ones were walking hand in hand with their mothers. She watched a small girl shrieking with laughter on her father's shoulders as he galloped about, neighing, pretending to be a horse. A little boy and his sister were clumsily throwing crusts into the water for the ducks, and she felt a kind of churning in her stomach that she had never felt before. It was a roiling that she very soon realised was in fact yearning. She realised that she wanted children, that Eleanor Farjeon's sonnet had awakened in her an understanding that nothing else would abolish her deep sadness and loneliness, not even the love of God. She wanted to go to the two children and stroke their heads and talk to them, to pick them up and clasp them to her chest, to smell their hair and their sweet breath.

That night Daniel was utterly astonished and even frightened by the sudden change in Rosie. She knocked at his door, let herself in and silently climbed into bed beside him. He put a railway ticket into *Five Years in the Royal Flying Corps* in order to mark his place, and laid it on the bedside table. Rosie crossed herself, and then turned to him and said, 'I am sorry, you know. I must be a terrible disappointment. And it's all my fault. It's not because there's anything wrong with you.'

He reached out his hand and she took it, lifting it to her lips and kissing it. 'Can we make up for it now?'

'Now?'

'Yes.'

'Shall we turn out the light?'

'Oh yes, I think so.'

In her years as a VAD there had been only one thing that she had not done for the wounded, and the male body held no mysteries. Fired by her longing for a child, she astonished Daniel by the ruthless way in which she took him in and emptied him out. It was a transaction, but a passionate one, and it was to be repeated more often than Daniel had ever dared to hope. Her sheer physical hunger caused him to feel that everything was mended, and that happiness with Rosie was after all his destiny. He began to think that they really were developing a bond.

Rosie's feelings were more ambiguous. Sometimes she wondered if she had merely deepened her bond with the dead, because it was difficult to avoid Ash's image drifting in and out of her mind when making love. It was an Ash embellished and beatified by memory, and she knew it. What she did not know, since it had never been discussed, was that Daniel, too, had a yearning for children. As they made love, they were of the same intent.

Daniel told Fluke 'Finally cracked it', and when, half a year later, Rosie withdrew her favours as soon as she knew she was pregnant, he construed their new celibacy as a sensible precaution against damaging the unborn child. For many months to come he would have to make do with Rosie's sisterly affection, and, against her better judgement, full of sorrow and pity on behalf of her ever-affectionate and disappointed husband, Rosie guiltily procrastinated.

77

Champignonne

Everyone called the new baby 'Babs', except for Daniel. Her real name was Esther, because Rosie had wanted something biblical, and her biblical eponym had been both brave and clever.

According to the custom of the day, Daniel was not allowed to be present at the birth. He was forced to listen to Rosie's cries out in the corridor, and thought he had never heard such agony since he had pulled a German airman with multiple fractures from a crashed Pfalz that had been in imminent danger of catching fire. He had recently been amazed to receive, via the Ministry of War, an Iron Cross First Class with the message, in German, *'This was won by me, but you deserve it more. I will always with gratitude remember you. Dieter Wolff (Staffelführer).*

Daniel endured immense agitation for several hours, and even went out for a while, in the superstitious belief that if he stopped waiting, the baby would arrive. He walked to the Tarn and back, and then to Mottingham, but the child was not born until two in the morning, by which time he was sickened by continuous smoking, and slightly woozy from the prodigious supply of tea that was being sent up from the kitchen.

At last the cries became more frequent and even more horrifying, then there was a silence, and then there was the sound of a baby mewling. He wanted to knock on the door and rush in, but he knew that it was not permitted. He waited for what seemed an extremely long time.

The door opened softly and the midwife emerged. 'Your wife asks me to tell you that she is well and that you have a daughter who seems to be very healthy.'

'Seems?'

'With babies it's better not to speak too soon.'

Daniel looked into the eyes of that stout middle-aged woman, and saw both exhaustion and happiness. 'Thank you so much,' he said, and then he noticed that tears were prickling in her eyes. She sniffed, wiped her eyes with her sleeve, and said, 'I'm sorry. It doesn't matter how often I do this, it always makes me cry. Now do excuse me, but there are still things to do.'

'Can't I come in and see them?' asked Daniel.

'Best wait 'til morning,' said the midwife.

'But I want to see Rosie. Is she all right?'

'She's very well, so far. Just let her sleep.'

'I'm going to put my head round the door.'

The midwife bristled, but did not intervene as he opened the door as lightly as he could. He saw his wife, asleep on her pillows, with her head tilted to one side. She looked flushed and radiant, even in sleep, and his heart seemed to lurch as he saw how beautiful she was.

'I want to go in and give her a kiss,' said Daniel.

'But you can't, sir.'

'Well, I'm going to.'

He tiptoed in, leaned over and kissed her on the forehead, rearranged a lock of hair and then turned to look down at his child. She was so well wrapped up that he could barely see anything beyond an indeterminate bundle. He took the child's tiny pink hand between his thumb and forefinger, and whispered, 'I'll see you in the morning.'

He came out, and whispered to the midwife, 'All's well, it seems.'

'That was very remiss of you, sir. You should follow the advice of those who know better than you.'

Daniel took her right hand, kissed it, and replied, 'Madam, you can court-martial me tomorrow.'

Leaving her confounded on the landing, he went downstairs, and found the whole family in the drawing room, gathered near the fire in their night attire. 'It's a daughter,' he told them, 'and both of them are well.'

After everyone had expressed their delight, congratulated him and drifted away to their beds, he went and helped himself to the Bladnoch from Hamilton McCosh's decanter in the dining room, and drank until he knew that he would sleep.

In the morning, Daniel insisted on bringing Rosie her breakfast, taking the tray from Millicent at the door. Rosie's face brightened as he entered. He set down the tray, and they hugged each other tightly. 'You've done so well,' said Daniel. 'Are you quite all right? Was it hell?'

'It was hell beyond all hell,' replied Rosie, 'and I'm still very sore, but the moment it was over, all the agony just disappeared.'

'You're going to have the whole family going in and out all day. They can't wait. But I insisted on being first. Now I want to hold her.'

Having been instructed to support the baby's head at all times, he gathered it up and looked at it. It smelled very sweet, like warm hay. Babies all look the same, unless you happen to be the parent, so Daniel gazed down rapturously at the tiny, wrinkled, crimson-faced creature and saw nothing but intelligence and beauty. He felt a deep, painful wave of love welling up in his stomach, and started to gabble to the child as he paced up and down the room with her, in a state of elation and triumph.

After several minutes of this, Rosie said, 'Please will you stop speaking French to her? It makes me feel left out.'

Daniel felt briefly cross, but then smiled at her. 'Sometimes, one language just isn't enough, is it?'

Rosie already had an apprehension and an intimation of how her child might become removed from her. It had not previously occurred to her that in that respect Daniel might become her enemy, but now she saw it very clearly. 'Give her back to me,' she said, holding out her arms.

Reluctantly Daniel gave up the baby, kissed Rosie on the forehead, and went downstairs for breakfast. When he looked in half an hour later, his daughter was back in her cot, and Rosie was asleep, so he picked Esther up and took her to the window. He looked into the unfocused blue eyes and said, 'You're just like a little mushroom. *Tu es une petite champignonne. Champi champi champignonne. Mais comme tu es belle et charmante. Et tellement petite. Ma champignonne mignonne.*' He put his forefinger into her palm, and her tiny fingers closed on it. She kicked and bucked in his arms, and he was surprised by her strength.

That was how Daniel arrived at his private pet name for Esther. She became 'Champignonne,' and inevitably he contracted it to 'Shompi'.

335

78

A Lady Maid

M rs McCosh found her husband in the dining room, where he was replenishing his Bladnoch decanter, and sniffing it appreciatively.

'My dear,' she said, 'we need a lady maid. Rosie is quite exhausted, and Millicent is no substitute for the real thing. I always used to have a maid, and now I can't for the life of me remember why I don't any more.'

'She went to work in a munitions factory,' said Mr McCosh shortly, 'and turned yellow. And I used to have a valet, but now my things are collected and taken to a laundry.'

'She was quite a good maid,' said Mrs McCosh, 'very agreeable and amenable, but I would greatly prefer someone a little more *distinguée*.'

'*Distinguée*? In what sense might a maid be *distinguée*?'

'A lady maid, my dear! A lady maid is *distinguée*!'

'A lady maid. What is a lady maid? Is that any different from a lady's maid?'

'A lady maid, my dear, is from a good family that has fallen on hard times. She is a lady, but she finds herself in reduced circumstances and in need of employment. She is finely educated, has a delicate temperament, fine sensibilities, and knows everyone one ought to know. A lady maid, my dear, is quite in vogue at present.'

'How could one possibly not go along with what is in vogue?' said Mr McCosh. 'Fancy that! A fallen aristocrat in the house! How perfectly indispensible!'

'I perceive that you are unconvinced. You are waxing ironical.'

'Well, it is true that Rosie is exhausted – Esther does wail a lot at night. And it is also true that Millicent isn't really up to attending to you and your finery as well as scrubbing things left, right and centre and emptying ash out of the fires. Millicent,

I believe, is grossly overworked, and I have long felt anxious to do something about it. It is also true that a "lady maid" will cost an extra twenty-five pounds a year, or thereabouts. Whence do you propose to derive the money for her wages, my dear? Are you planning to take up painting and sell your masterpieces? Will you play your violin in the Haymarket?'

'The money will come from you, my dear,' answered Mrs McCosh firmly.

'From me? Now, there's a surprise.'

Mr McCosh took another sniff at the whisky, which put him in a better mood quite promptly. He said, 'I will go along with this on condition that your lady maid helps Rosie as a nurse, and then, possibly, as a governess, and if she also helps Millicent and Cookie with their duties as required. If I am to have a fallen aristocrat in the house, she is not to be purely decorative, and if at any time I find that she has become so, I will dismiss her.'

'It is up to me to hire and dismiss servants,' said Mrs McCosh. 'As master of the house, you should not concern yourself with the matter.'

'If I wish to dismiss her, and you wish to retain her,' answered her husband. 'It is easily done. You will pay her from your allowance.' Mrs McCosh huffed at this outrageous suggestion, and Mr McCosh said. 'I will be intrigued to see what you come up with.'

Accordingly Mrs McCosh went by train and omnibus to the nearest registry, and within a month a quiet and dignified young woman was installed in one of the empty rooms at the top of the house.

She was pale-skinned and a little freckled, with tight brown curls, and dressed in very fine clothes that had been skilfully repaired. She spoke the most elegant English with the trace of an Irish lilt, and she had enormous grey eyes that radiated a kind of beautiful sadness. Her name was the Honourable Mary FitzGerald St George.

Mary took to Esther straight away, and had the ability to hush her when she was in one of her periodic fits of infantile hysteria. This made Rosie feel somewhat inadequate, however grateful she was. Mary helped Mrs McCosh to dress for the evenings, and proved to have such exceptionally good taste that Mrs McCosh even took her along when she went shopping. It would be true to say that the Honourable Mary FitzGerald St George considerably lightened the heart of her mistress. Gaskell painted Mary's portrait one day, making her look like a Valkyrie, and Christabel took some photographs of her in the garden that made her look like a dreaming poetess. These representations were admirably juxtaposed at their joint exhibitions.

One evening, after returning from London, Hamilton McCosh encountered the Honourable Mary FitzGerald St George in the morning room, and said to her, 'Miss FitzGerald St George, may I have a word? In the dining room perhaps?'

Mary sat in the carver at one end of the table, and Mr McCosh in the carver at the other.

'Now, Miss FitzGerald, please tell me about yourself, would you? I have only what I know from my wife. I realise that the servants are her business, but I do like to take an interest myself. Now that there are so few of them, it has become very much easier.'

'Indeed, sir, what would you like to know?'

'Well, your father is . . . ?'

'Roderick FitzGerald St George, Earl Edenderry. I'm his fourth daughter, sir.'

'And Edenderry is near Dublin?'

'Not so very far, sir. And not so very far from Tullamore.'

'Anglo-Irish?'

'Oh yes, sir, for centuries, sir. There's an awful lot of us, sir. We don't feel as welcome at home as we used to, though.'

'Quite so. Have you heard of Edmund Burke?'

'Yes, sir, but I can't say I know very much about him.'

'He used to say he was Irish and he used to say he was English, quite interchangeably. It was all one to a lot of people. Sadly, those days are past.'

'Yes, sir.'

'And your mother was Lady Dwyer of Portarlington, my wife says.'

'Yes, sir. May I ask where this is leading, sir?'

'Well, Mary. At the Athenaeum we have a copy of the 1915 *Burke's Peerage*. It is a large volume, most compendious. I sometimes look in it, out of curiosity.'

Mary went pale and began to bite on her lip. Her fingers were working in her lap, and she looked down at them as if they were foreign creatures. 'Am I to be dismissed?' she asked.

'I was at first greatly annoyed,' said Hamilton McCosh, leaning back and stroking his chin. 'No one likes to be taken for an ass. Your references were most persuasive. You clearly have a talent for composition, and indeed for thespianism. And your talk of "the quality" certainly impresses Mrs McCosh. You must have done a great deal of mugging up.'

'I mug up continuously,' said Mary. 'One has to. I have a copy of *Burke's* myself.'

'Hmm,' said Mr McCosh. 'I have given this some thought. I have said nothing to Mrs McCosh, and nor do I intend to. You get on very well with Miss Rosie, and Esther plainly adores you. Millicent and Cookie do not resent you, which is quite contrary to what normally happens when a maid and a cook find that a nurse has arrived in the house. Even the cat likes you, and I find your presence most agreeable, and Mrs McCosh is unstinting in her praise. My feeling, Miss FitzGerald St George, is that when a forgery is as good, if not better, than an original, then the wise man contents himself with the forgery.'

'I am not to be dismissed?'

'No, Miss FitzGerald.'

She gave a little leap in her seat. 'Oh,' she cried, 'I would have been so sad . . . and . . . mortified. And what would I have done?'

'I do think you should apologise for your deception,' said Mr McCosh.

Mary Fitzgerald cast her eyes down and said softly, 'Of course I apologise. I am indeed very sorry. Very sorry. I have hated myself for the deception quite considerably. It was, well . . . thrust upon me, almost.'

'Thrust upon you?'

'I *am* Anglo-Irish,' she said. 'I am the real thing in that respect. It's just so horrible to be there now. One has no prospects. One feels despised and hated and suspected, and even in danger. The Easter Rising spoiled everything. It was quite the wrongest and stupidest thing to kill all those people and make them into martyrs. It turned everyone against us when they weren't even mildly against us before. And now the Fenians are at each other's throats. There's nothing more vile than a civil war, and what a way to celebrate independence! My father won't move, and I worry about him continuously. We have a large farm and a big house, but we have no capital to speak of. To whom could we sell such a place in days like these?'

'I've no doubt that eventually you will make a sound marriage,' said Mr McCosh. 'You are exceedingly personable. I think it quite likely that eventually you will meet just the right man, not least because of being in this situation with us. One of Master Daniel's friends will turn up one day, no doubt, and sweep you off your feet. Of course you would then have to undeceive him about being the Honourable Mary FitzGerald St George.'

'I did have a fiancé, for a while,' said Mary wistfully.

'Killed?'

She nodded. 'At Beersheba. Still, at least we won the battle. It's some consolation. It would have been so much worse if we'd lost.'

'I suppose you added the "St George" yourself,' said Mr McCosh, and she nodded. 'It was a good touch,' he said. 'Jolly good. Well done. Most ingenious.'

79

Kalopsia

Sophie and the Reverend Captain Fairhead bought a house on 1 March 1920, on the day that Charles Garvice died. Neither of them was a fan of his novels, and they were considerably more saddened when Mrs Humphrey Ward died three days later. On the 17th they attended Queen Alexandra's unveiling of the statue of Edith Cavell in London, taking Mrs McCosh with them, who was so thrilled by seeing the Queen that she tripped over the spike of her own umbrella in the general rush to get a better glimpse, and made a rent in her skirts.

On the 30th they moved into their new house in Blackheath, just near the top of the village. It was situated in a tranquil street lined with chestnut trees that attracted all the local children in the autumn, when it would become a battlefield littered with opened shells and smashed conkers. Cries of 'Mine's a thirty-niner!' 'Mine's an eighteener!' floated up amongst the eaves. The clever children drilled holes in their conkers with a skewer when they were fresh, and then left them to shrivel and harden in the airing cupboard until the following year. No doubt they made fortunes in later life thanks to their patient good sense. If one were to defeat an opponent, one would automatically acquire their score and add it to one's own, and so there were exceedingly enterprising children who, when their champion conker was just about to break, would sell the right to the next contest for three farthings. In the summer, residents enjoyed the pink candelabra on the trees, and at night they harkened to the virtuosity and passion of a nightingale which never failed to return. In the autumn it was replaced by a robin, whose voice was just as sweet.

Sophie and Fairhead's house had a pleasant mature garden planted up with azaleas and camellias. Inside it was dark but not gloomy, and Sophie draped everything with paisley-printed cloths that were both cheerful and casual. They bought mahogany furniture at auction, including an imposing but woodwormy four-poster bed that collapsed the first time they made love on it.

Like Daniel, Fairhead was in a quandary about what to do with his future. It seemed altogether likely that one day they would have children. In the meantime Sophie was content to follow the drum, should he be posted abroad or away, but Fairhead himself declared that an itinerant life was no life for little ones, and, furthermore, he was not sure that he wanted to remain in the army chaplaincy, or even remain a clergyman.

'I've painted myself into a corner,' he said to his wife one day. 'I'm unqualified for anything except the Church or a public school. Or, worse, a prep school.'

'Let's go into trade,' suggested Sophie. 'Mama would be so shocked.'

'But your father is in trade,' said Fairhead.

'Well, Mama does find it shocking,' replied Sophie. 'She tries not to think about it. She aspires to inherited wealth.'

'Well, it's thanks to Great-Aunt Arabella that we have this house. Let's not denigrate inherited wealth.'

'I'd only denigrate it if there were no chance of it. Isn't it odd that no one is called Arabella any more?'

'Or Anastasia. Or Rahab. Or Salome. Or Judas. Or Delilah.'

'I'm not surprised about Salome and Judas and Rahab and Delilah.'

'No, neither am I. What do you think I should do?'

'You keep asking, dear, and the only thing I can think of that would really suit would be to be a hospital chaplain, as I keep saying. You are so good with the mortally ill. Simply excelsitudinous.'

'I don't really have the faith any more.'

'Can't you pretend?'

'Honestly, darling! What do you think God would want of me?'

'But you don't seem to believe in Him any more! And God can't want anything, can He? If He's omnipotent He can have whatever He wants whenever He likes, can't He?'

'Gracious me, Sophie!'

'Well, He can, can't He?' She paused whilst she unpicked a bad stitch in her embroidery, then said, 'Why don't we think about what God would want if we were God?'

Fairhead laughed. 'You really are utterly original. I can't imagine where I found you.'

'Court Road, Eltham,' she said. 'The Grampians. And all because of poor Ashbridge, if you remember.'

'I think I must have found you in some exotic place where completely new ways of thinking have resulted from the inter-course of philosophers and angels. What would you want if you were God?'

She bit her lip and thought for a few seconds. 'I would want us to rebuild the Garden of Eden. I'd want us to recreate it.'

'We have a lovely garden,' he said.

'Let's build a wall round it so no one can look in.'

'That would be rather high. And awfully nice. We can't afford it, though.'

'Let's do it ourselves. I'm sure Daniel would help. He loves that kind of thing, and he's at an awful loose end just now, and having to live at The Grampians is driving him quite barmy. He knows everything about stresses and whatnot, doesn't he?'

'Rather like me.'

'You don't know anything about stresses and whatnot,'

'No, I mean the loose end.'

And so it was that over a period of three months, in a desul-tory manner, a red-brick wall rose up and encircled the azaleas and camellias. It was nine-foot high, with occasional buttresses, and was capped by demilunar tiles. At the southern end Fairhead planted passion flower, to remind himself of the religious origin of their idea, and because he enjoyed the fruit, and in the least windy places he planted clematis. Sophie insisted on having climbing roses up one wall, and Virginia creeper up another.

There came the day in late spring when Humorist won the Derby, and the sun broke out of the cloud over Blackheath. The walled garden blocked the wind and trapped the heat, and Sophie and Fairhead put a tartan rug on the lawn and brought a picnic of tea and sandwiches out of the house, in order to celebrate the official opening of their new Garden of Eden.

After they had polished off the food, Sophie flung herself back on the rug and spread her arms wide, saying, 'Bliss, oh bliss, oh bliss!' Suddenly she stood up and pulled Fairhead to his feet. 'Come on.'

'Where are we going?'

'We are walking round the garden two or three times to make sure no one can look in.'

'Are we?'

'Yes we are.'

'As my beloved wills.'

Arm in arm they circled the garden, scrutinising every angle. 'No one can see in,' declared Sophie at last. 'We are invisible and indiscernible.'

'We are indeed invisible and indiscernible and indivisible.'

'We are safe from scopophiles.'

'No scopophilia here.'

'There are no balloonists or aeronauts. Let's take our clothes off,' said Sophie.

'Darling, we can't possibly.'

'We can if we lock the front door.'

'But, darling, it's not done!'

'What is this?' asked Sophie, waving her arm to indicate the whole garden.

'The garden?'

'The Garden of Eden,' she said firmly. 'No clothes, no fig leaves.'

'I'm really not sure I can. I'm a clergyman, for God's sake!'

'Oh fie!' she said, sitting down on the rug and holding her arms up to him. 'Come here, clergyman. It's what God wants if we were God. They were naked and they were not ashamed.'

Afterwards they lay entangled on the rug with the sun on their skin. Sophie rolled aside a little and said, 'Oh, darling one, I've got kalopsia.'

'I'm sure you can cure it with Beecham's,' murmured Fairhead.

'Aren't you going to ask me what it is?'

'No.'

'You old spoilsport. And we forgot to lock the front door. Talking of kalopsia, have I ever told you that you are the apple of my eye, the pineapple of my pineal gland, the melon of my mouth, the nectarine of my knees and the fig of my foot? Have

344

I ever declared before witnesses that you are the most beautiful man in the world? Have I ever informed you that you give me the most truly fearful tentigo, such as will wear me out before I'm thirty?'

'Almost every day. My scepticism remains, however. My teeth are yellow and my moustache is orange down the middle from smoking too much.'

'I know it's only because I love you,' she said.

'No amount of love would turn a moustache orange. I'm sure it's the cigarettes. Do I take it that you're fishing?'

'In what manner might I be piscatorial?'

'You want me to say you're the most beautiful woman in the world.'

'No I don't. I know I am. I have complete confidence. My pulchritudinosityness knows no bounds.'

'It's infinite.'

'Quite. Because you love me. You exist, you love me, therefore I am beautiful. It's a perfect paralogism.'

'I like a nice paralogism,' said Fairhead. 'Let's have one for tea.'

80

The Toasting

It was the custom at Christmas for the McCosh family to do two things. One was for them to wait upon the servants, the day before Christmas Eve, and treat them to a proper Christmas dinner, complete with a goose, roasted parsnips, chestnut stuffing, Christmas pudding, and their own present under the tree, to be opened afterwards. Mr McCosh's father had got the idea from an army friend, who had told him that in the Queen's Bays it was the custom at Christmas for the officers to wait upon the men.

Since this custom had been imported from Mr McCosh's family, rather than from that of his wife, she, needless to say, heartily disapproved of it, even though it originated in the manners of an elite cavalry regiment. Mr McCosh, however, always entered into the spirit of the occasion, and enjoyed it with great gusto even if the servants did not.

He had to concede that it had lately become a somewhat melancholy occasion. Because the male servants had never returned, there were only Cookie and Millicent left, apart from the Honourable Mary FitzGerald St George, who had been given leave to return to her father for Christmas. Whereas before the war the two women had not felt at all self-conscious being served by the family, it was distinctly embarrassing and awkward now that there were only two of them.

This year Mrs McCosh seemed highly confused, and so the sisters ushered her upstairs for a rest, and created chaos as they attempted to conjure a decent supper out of their inexperience. Fortunately Cookie always made two puddings on Stir-Up Sunday, but now she sat in the withdrawing room with Millicent, light-headed from the unpleasantly dry sherry that Mr McCosh insisted on plying them with, in a lather of worry about what appalling mistakes the sisters might be making in the kitchen. Fairhead sat smoking in one armchair, having exempted himself from kitchen duty on the grounds of incapacity, masculinity and general incompetence. Gaskell, monocle in place, her short dark hair slicked back, smoked one Abdulla after another from her immensely attenuated cigarette holder. She was clad, as usual, in such a manner as to suggest that she was just about to go shooting. Her plan was to go to her own family the following day, and she was not helping in the kitchen on the grounds that it was already too crowded down there and she only knew how to cook under the stress of continuous bombardment. Daniel sat next to her, with both Esther and the cat on his knee, peeved at having been excluded from the kitchen, when it was quite clear to himself that the French half of him might have been quite useful. He found it agonising to have to sit still for any length of time anywhere, an agony that always seemed so much worse when it occurred in the McCosh withdrawing room, especially when Mrs McCosh was there. His own mother had gone to stay with her family in France for the Christmas period, and Daniel greatly wished that he could have been there with her. 'Don't worry,' Mme Pitt had said, 'une belle journée we will have a Christmas all ensemble en Normandie.'

Christabel came in, perspiring and flustered, and said, 'Cookie, how long should we rest the goose?'

'About half an hour, miss.'

'Oh dear, I fear that supper will be frightfully late,' said Christabel, hurrying out.

'Would you like me to come and look, miss?' called Cookie after her, in vain.

'I wonder if it will snow,' said Mr McCosh, like the good Scot that he was, who knows only to talk of the weather when no other topic is at hand.

At this point Millicent burst into tears, not merely because she had thought she might spend all her Christmases with Hutchinson, but because an unexpected catastrophe had descended on her family out of the blue, and she was unable to restrain her despair any further.

'Millicent, what is it?' asked Mr McCosh, who had been standing by the fireplace with his left arm on the mantelpiece and a substantial glass of neat whisky in his left hand.

'What's up, dear?' asked Cookie, glad to have something to deal with.

Millicent sobbed into her hands. 'We lost everything,' she cried at last. 'We got nothing left!'

'Nothing left? What on earth do you mean, girl? Lost everything? Farrow's? Do you mean Farrow's?'

'Yes, sir, it's them lot. They've gone and taken everything, and we won't never get it back. How are we going to manage? Every last penny, and now we've got nothing! All our savings! Gone!'

'Oh good Lord,' exclaimed Mr McCosh. 'If I'd known you'd put all your savings into Farrow's, I would have advised you against it. I know Farrow and Crotch, nice enough fellows, and very plausible, but their interest rates were quite mad. I wasn't at all surprised when they crashed.'

'Oh, you poor thing, you should have kept it all under the bed, like sensible folks,' said Cookie.

'Now we know where you keep yours,' observed Fairhead. 'You'll have to put it somewhere else.'

'How much have you lost?' asked Mr McCosh.

'About two hundred pounds, sir. It was everything that me and Mother saved up for years and years, sir.'

'I'll see what I can do,' said Mr McCosh. 'I suppose you know that the government has refused to bail them out? There's no compensation?'

'Yes, sir.'

'I've seen the people outside the branches. The weeping and wailing. It's most distressing. I don't know if you know Mr Hughes at the toy shop in Eltham? He told me he couldn't pay for his Christmas stock, so I lent him the money at 2 per cent for three months. The least I could do. Damned bankers! They're the scum of the earth. I can't tell you how much trouble they've caused me and how many opportunities I've lost because of damn bankers. They only lend to you when they know perfectly well that you don't need it. Damned bankers. Curse the lot of them.'

Millicent sobbed into her handkerchief, and Mr McCosh said again, 'I'll see what I can do.'

'Thank you, sir,' sniffled Millicent.

'Thank God I took my money out of Farrow's to buy a motor-cycle,' said Daniel. 'At least I have something to show for it.'

'I withdraw my remark about the madness of buying it,' said Fairhead.

'Ah, but do you apologise?'

'My dear fellow, that would be to go too far. You will undoubtedly come to grief on it one of these days. Should hospitals ever require spare parts, it will be to motorcyclists that they will turn.'

'In future you should put any spare money into Martin's Bank,' said Mr McCosh to no one in particular. 'They are very solid, very solid. There's a branch in Eltham. Let us propose toasts, as usual. Millicent, to whom would you like to propose a toast?'

'Um, my poor old mother, I think, sir.'

'Well, here's to Millicent's poor old mother!' exclaimed Mr McCosh, raising his glass. 'God bless her!'

Gaskell said, 'I propose a toast to Oxford University!'

'My dear lassie, why?'

'Because on the 14th of October they gave out degrees to women for the very first time.'

'Ah, the monstrous regiment of women gains apace! Here's to Oxford University!'

'And a curse on Cambridge for not,' added Gaskell.

'A curse on Cambridge!' toasted Mr McCosh. 'What about you, Cookie?'

'I'm toastin' Charles Elmé Francatelli, sir.'

'Who?'

'Charles Elmé Francatelli, sir.'

'Gracious me, Cookie. Who's he? Sounds like a wop.'

'Wrote my favourite cookbook, sir. *A Plain Cookery Book for the Working Classes*. That's what it's called. It's a godsend, sir.'

'For the working classes, Cookie? When do you get a chance to use that?'

'All the time, sir. Wouldn't have got through the war without it. You know that giblet pie you like, sir, and that toad-in-the-hole and them Norfolk dumplings and that rabbit pudding? Them's all from that book, sir.'

'Good God, are they? You've been cooking for us from a book

for the working classes? Well, I'm damned. Socialism comes to Court Road! Gracious me.'

'Don't tell the mistress, will you, sir? But he was a cook to Queen Victoria, sir, and I do use the posh book he wrote too.'

'I certainly won't. She would have a thousand fits. And kittens. But she would certainly be swayed by his having been a royal cook.'

'I do use Countess Morphy's book 'n' all, sir.'

'Cookie, you're a dark horse,' said Fairhead.

'Oh well, here's to what's-his-name the gastronomical wop that got us through the war!' Mr McCosh drank, and the company followed suit.

'I propose a toast to Dame Nellie Melba,' said Fairhead, 'the most wondrous warbler of them all.'

'And I to the monstrous regiment of women,' said Mr McCosh, 'and in particular to Cookie and Millicent, without whom we would all grind to an ignominious halt.'

'Dame Nellie Melba and the monstrous regiment of women and Cookie and Millicent!'

At that moment Mrs McCosh entered, having woken from a nightmare and been drawn down by the pleasant aroma of cooked food. 'Ah,' she said as all the menfolk stood, 'drinking the usual toasts, I see. I hope you have not forgotten Their Majesties.'

'We drink the loyal toast after our own Christmas dinner, my dear, as you know.'

'In that case let's drink to King Constantine of the Hellenes.'

'But why, my dear?'

'He's just been restored. One has to stand up for the principal of royalty, my dear, otherwise the whole world falls apart, as we know.'

'I'd quite like to be restored,' said Daniel, resisting the temptation to ask her whether her support of the principle of royalty extended to the Kaiser and the Emperor of Austria. 'I'm exhausted after that drive from Partridge Green. I don't think I have ever been so wet or so cold, not even at fifteen thousand feet. It would have taken minutes in a Snipe.'

Mrs McCosh glared at him, and then, as if having read Daniel's thoughts, Gaskell said, in her languid, rather decadent drawl, 'Well, here's to the Dutch handing over the Kaiser, so we can string him up.'

'I feel sorry for the Kaiser,' said Fairhead.

'What?' cried Daniel. 'Are you mad?'

'Oh, very probably. What I mean is that he seems to have wanted an empire in Europe, when the rest of us have already got one elsewhere. There wasn't anywhere else to get one, really. And now everybody is going to hate and despise him forever, including his own relatives. He must be hiding in Holland, blushing with shame and embarrassment. He must be in Hell, actually, when you consider how omnipotent he was before. He's been well and truly cast out of Paradise, I'd say.'

'The man was a complete and utter fool,' said Gaskell shortly. 'Did he really think he could invade neutral countries and go to war with our Allies, and get away with it?'

'Of course you're quite right,' said Fairhead, 'but one can still feel sorry for a fool. Every paradise has a serpent hiding in it, doesn't it? And he turned out to be his own serpent. A very great fool indeed, I'd say.'

'I find your compassion quite inexplicable and inexcusable,' said Mrs McCosh. 'One simply doesn't declare war on one's relatives, especially in the royal family.'

'Edward IV murdered his own brother,' said Ottilie, 'and I understand that the sultans murdered their brothers as a matter of course. It was fully expected of them.'

'I hardly think one can call a sultan royalty,' declared Mrs McCosh. 'Why, they're not even Christian!'

Rosie said, 'Did he really want an empire? I thought he was just worried about being a sandwich between France and Russia, so he decided to knock out one and then go on and knock out the other.'

'Ah, the Schlieffen Plan,' said Fairhead. 'Yes, you're right about that.'

'He was still an absolute fool,' insisted Gaskell, her green eyes sparking with contempt.

'May I change the subject?' asked Daniel, his eyes aglow with mischief. 'I have a surprise for you. An entertainment. I want everybody here at teatime. Without fail, including Cookie and Millicent, if that's convenient.'

'It's hardly convenient,' said Mrs McCosh, who had been making a vocation of irritating Daniel for some time now.

'Of course it is,' remonstrated her husband. 'Where else would we be at teatime?'

'How exciting,' said Gaskell drily. 'What a shame I shall not be here to see it.'

'Christabel will send you a report,' said Daniel. 'In fact I will ask her to take photographs.'

At that very moment Christabel came in, even hotter and more flustered than before. 'Talking about me?' she said. 'I hope it was nothing uncomplimentary. Dinner is served. Or, to be more precise, charred.'

'Cookie, you will take my arm as always,' said Mr McCosh.

'And Millicent will take mine,' said Daniel. He leapt to his feet and offered it to her.

Millicent blushed and placed her arm softly in his. She felt something like a spark pass between them at the contact, and she knew that he had felt it too. She suddenly wished that she had better clothes to wear, even though she was most grateful for Miss Rosie's cast-offs. After dinner Ottilie would play the piano and she would probably have to take a waltz with Mr Daniel while Cookie took one with Mr McCosh.

Mrs McCosh remembered that it had not, after all, been so unpleasant to take a waltz with the footman, back when they still had one. A scintilla of Christmas spirit sparkled in her eyes, and then quickly faded. It was difficult to enjoy anything these days. She had got halfway through writing a Christmas card to Myrtle, before remembering.

81

The Dancing

Daniel and Fairhead moved all the furniture to the edges of the room, rolled up the carpet and deposited it in the conservatory. Mrs McCosh was displeased, as it was not a man's duty or vocation to decide upon the placing of furniture, particularly hers. She was further put out by Daniel's informing her that there might be two extra people for dinner, and possibly to stay the night, but they would be bringing their own tent, as they were reluctant to cause inconvenience, and he was not going to tell anyone who they were, because that was part of the surprise.

'A tent?' she cried. 'A tent? In this weather? In December? At Christmas?'

'They are both exceedingly tough,' said Daniel. 'They have endured far worse than a night in a tent in Court Road, Eltham, and will think it very luxurious. Really, you shouldn't worry at all. They'll enjoy it.'

'And if we are to feed them, where will they eat? If they are people of quality they should eat with us, but the dining table is already a most frightful squeeze. Of course, if they are of the common sort, they may eat in the kitchen.'

'I have moved a card table into the dining room,' said Daniel. 'All it needs is a nice lacy tablecloth.'

'Christmas is such a trial,' said Mrs McCosh. 'I do most sincerely wish the Lord had been born at some other time.'

Rosie, who had been listening to this conversation as she arranged some sprigs of red-berried holly in a vase at the corner table, said, 'Mama, if He had been born at another time, then that would have been Christmas.'

'We should have called it something else,' replied Mrs McCosh loftily.

Ottilie came in and said, 'When are we opening the presents?'

'At the usual time,' said Mrs McCosh. 'We have "post office" at teatime on Christmas Day.'

'Can't we open them at breakfast? Then we'll have all day to play with them. What about Esther? She'll be desperate.'

'No, my dear, anticipation is half the pleasure. Perhaps we shouldn't tell her it's Christmas until the evening.'

'Mama, that's hardly fair on the poor little thing,' said Ottilie, and went out again.

'Why do we give presents at Christmas?' asked Daniel. 'I've often wondered.'

'Because that is what they do in the royal family,' said Mrs McCosh. 'One tends to emulate one's betters, if one has any sense.'

'It's because God gave us His Son, and the Three Wise Men brought Him gifts,' said Rosie impatiently. 'We celebrate the gifts by giving them ourselves.'

'Oh,' said Mrs McCosh, disillusioned.

An hour before dark, a hammering was heard in the garden, and Daniel could be seen from the windows, erecting a neat military tent. He came back in, the knees of his trousers muddy and wet. 'It would start raining the moment I went out,' he complained. 'It's perishing too. If the clouds clear, I think we'll be in for a frost. By the way, when the bell goes, no one is to answer the door except me, and no one is to go in the morning room. It will become the gentlemen's dressing room.'

'Oh, but it's where the Christmas tree is,' said Ottilie.

'We'll make sure we don't knock it over,' said Daniel, 'and we'll put out the candles and we won't interfere with the presents.'

'You'd better not,' said Ottilie, 'or there will be dire consequences.'

'No presents for peekers!' said Rosie. 'It was our family motto when we were little. Do you remember?'

'Rosie opened all her presents one Christmas,' said Ottilie. 'She came down at dawn. And Mama made her sit in the attic practically all day in the dark.'

'I've never been so cold in my life,' said Rosie. 'I've never been so miserable. Or frightened. Or lonely.'

'Or contrite,' said Mrs McCosh, defensively. 'I'm sure it did you good. I let you out when you started screaming.'

'I was only six! And you gave all my presents to Dr Barnardo's.'

'Well, I wouldn't do it now,' said Mrs McCosh.

'My mother says that the most important thing one can learn from one's parents is how not to be a parent,' said Daniel.

'Quite so,' replied Mrs McCosh, without irony. 'Mine were far too indulgent.'

It darkened outside, and the doorbell rang. Daniel ensured that there were no illicit observers, and ushered his muffled guests into the morning room.

This room was divided from the hallway not by a wall but by a large curtain. It served not simply as a morning room, but also as chapel, reception room and waiting room. Mrs McCosh considered it one of the great assets of the house. From the bench against the window one could observe passers-by, and peep surreptitiously in order to discern the identity of whoever was at the porch.

The house grew heavy with conspiracy, and light with anticipation. 'I wonder what Daniel's going to do,' they repeated to each other, as they sat around the edge of the drawing room and sipped on the tea that Millicent served from the trolley. Sophie ate almost all the langues de chat without anyone noticing until it was too late. 'Who's having the last one?' she cried, taking it herself, and exclaiming, 'A handsome husband and ten thousand a year!'

'Ten thousand,' sighed Fairhead, 'and handsome. One can only dream.'

Just then a roaring and whooping and stamping and drumming was set up outside in the hallway, and Mrs McCosh exclaimed, 'Goodness gracious!'

'Ooh,' said Sophie, 'cacophany and polydindination!'

The door burst open and three Khattak warriors hurled themselves into the room, leaping and whirling. Caractacus hurtled out of the room, between their legs. One was beating on a clay drum with a curved stick, and all were chanting something quite indecipherable in a strange high-pitched yodel. They wore ragged black beards, their equally ragged long hair was tied up in bobs, and their faces were of a golden hue. They wore chappalls on their feet, and, on their bodies, long loose shirts that, on closer inspection, would turn out to be improvised from old sheets. Two warriors held long curved swords, and began to slash at each other ferociously and rhythmically.

Everyone in the drawing room was both appalled and fascinated. It was unclear as to who these prodigiously athletic savages were, and the two showed every semblance of truly desiring to slaughter each other. Their blood-curdling shrieks and the stamping of their feet on the bare floorboards made everything so much more alarming.

One of the combatants raised his sword above his head and slashed downwards. His opponent sidestepped and crouched down, cutting horizontally with a wide sweep that should have taken the other's legs off at the knee, had not the latter skipped lightly into the air. When this manoeuvre was repeated, it began to dawn on the audience that they were watching, not a fight, but a dance.

A blade came down diagonally as if to strike at the base of a neck, but the target ducked and executed exactly the same manoeuvre in return. Then the two circled each other, glaring and snarling, until suddenly they both began to whirl like dervishes, two, three, four times, balanced on one foot and bobbing up and down like shuttles. Finally they faced each other once more, and circled, each with the point of a sword levelled at the tip of his opponent's nose.

Suddenly they broke away from each other and advanced upon their audience, eyes rolling with aggression and insanity, chewing the ends of their beards, and feigning the intention of cutting the poor folk to pieces. Millicent squealed and ran from the room, but Cookie took up a brass candlestick to defend herself. Christabel and Ottilie looked uneasy, aware that this was all a wonderful hoax, but thoroughly disturbed by it nonetheless. Mr McCosh watched with amusement and appreciation, a cigar clamped between his lips, and Mrs McCosh enjoyed it all with a look of immense disapproval on her face. Rosie sat very still, with Esther on her lap, sucking her thumb. Sophie, pretending to be terrified, used the occasion as an excuse to cling more closely to her husband.

The dance ended with a frenzied ratatat-tatting on the clay

drum, and howls of 'Allah o akbar!' from all the protagonists. 'Dadda' said Esther, pointing.

'Gracious me, I do believe it's Archie and Fluke,' said Christabel as the three men linked arms and bowed. 'We haven't seen Archie since the wedding!'

'Feel free to applaud!' said Daniel, and the assembly obediently did so, disconcerted though every member of it was.

'Was that a Pathan dance?' asked Sophie.

'Pathans don't dance,' replied Archie, 'they think it's undignified. Chitralis like to dance. And sing.'

'You had me quite fooled for a moment,' said Sophie. 'How did you do your faces?'

'Wren's polish, of course.'

'Silly me,' said Sophie. 'I presume you got the beards from a goat?'

'Archie, is that you?' asked Christabel.

'Yes, it's me,' replied Archie.

'Introductions and fond reunions later!' cried Daniel.

'We are now going to do the Chitralis' vulture dance,' announced Archie. 'Would anyone like to volunteer to be the corpse?'

'Very much so, I would,' declared Mr McCosh, 'but it may take some time to lower myself to the floor.'

'Do take my arm,' said Archie, and so it was that Mr McCosh was lowered with much aplomb to the floor, where he lay on his back, sportingly puffing his cigar smoke towards the ceiling. Mrs McCosh was thoroughly mortified to witness her husband thus.

'Would anyone like to play the drum?' asked Archie. 'Otherwise Fluke doesn't get a chance to dance.'

'I shall do it,' said Mr McCosh gamely, 'horizontal though I may be. Would someone take my cigar? Fairhead?'

The three dancers got down onto their haunches, and Mr McCosh began to beat the drum. 'Slower!' said Archie, and Mr McCosh obeyed. Fairhead held McCosh's cigar at arm's length. He had always disliked the things quite intensely. Privately, he considered them the turds of the Devil, and went for frequent strolls round the garden when Mr McCosh was smoking one.

The three men performed manoeuvres that can only be

described as macabre and grotesque. They hopped in a curious oblique skipping fashion towards the corpse, leapt back when it showed signs of life, flapped their arms in imitation of wings, pecked at each other and jostled each other out of the way. They gathered around the body and made a brilliant imitation of vultures ripping a hole in the belly and dragging out the intestines with long sideways wrenchings of the neck. The only thing they did not do was stand on the body itself.

At last Daniel fell back and announced, 'I don't think I can do any more of this hopping. My thighs are killing me.'

'Let's eat Daniel!' cried Fluke, and the two remaining dancers switched their attention to him.

'Can I get up now?' asked Mr McCosh. 'I think I need a stiff drink.' Archie helped him to his feet, and he felt a sudden dizziness, from which he quickly recovered.

The three performers sat side by side on the sofa, sipping tea, still sweating and panting, and basking in the admiration of everyone except Mrs McCosh, who disapproved of exuberance, and had been disturbed by the very thought of vultures and corpses.

Hamilton McCosh was standing in the middle of the room with a sword in his hand, waving it speculatively. 'I like the Pathan sword best,' said Archie, noting Mr McCosh's interest. 'It's like a long scalene triangle with a sort of ridge along the top. They're unbelievably sharp.'

'One misses rather a lot from never having been a soldier,' said Mr McCosh.

'One misses a lot of truly horrible things,' replied Archie earnestly, 'and it can make you quite unfit for normal life.'

'Quite so, I'm sure. I bashed the Boche through the power of industry, but it might have been satisfying to spike one in person.'

'I'm still hoping to kill one,' declared Mrs McCosh. 'When I think of poor Myrtle . . . and those dreadful bombers . . . quite beyond the pale.'

'How long is your leave?' Rosie asked Archie.

'I've got three months, and then I'm back to the North-West Frontier.'

'It's most awfully nice to see you again,' said Ottilie, who wondered sadly whether she would ever lose her passion for him. 'I do wish you all still lived next door.'

'I also wish we were still next door. Even so, *maman* is happy at Partridge Green, and it is lovely countryside down there. It's splendid to go up on Chanctonbury Ring. You can see for miles. All the way to Blackdown. *Maman* likes it too. She takes binoculars and tries to look at France.'

'She must have awfully strong legs.'

'Family trait,' said Archie.

'Do you still speak French, *en famille*, the way you used to?'

'Oh, absolutely. French is more intimate than English somehow. And it is far more effective when used on children. They actually obey if you say it in French. Not that I meet many children these days.'

Ottilie pursed her mouth sceptically. 'Are you . . . ?' she began. 'Is there . . . you know, anyone? Are we to expect any, um, good news at all? Is that why you're back? Forgive me if I'm being nosy and impertinent, but we are old friends.'

'What can you mean? Oh! I see! No, I'm not here to get married, or engaged, or whatever. The fact is that I can't possibly get married when I have no income to speak of. I think one has a responsibility to support one's wife properly, and to send one's children to a decent school. Besides, I've spent most of my recent life in one of the most savage places on earth. I'm quite unfit for civilisation.'

'Oh, but you're not,' said Ottilie. 'Archie, you really ought to come back. I'm sure there's lots you can do. You even speak French. You're frightfully noble, and all that, but really you're being a little bit old-fashioned. The war did change everything, you know. People married in droves during the war, without any money or forethought at all.'

'It's sweet of you to say so, but I am a lost cause, I'm sure of it. I'm only fit to instruct grown RAF officers on how to a do a Khattak sword dance and a Chitrali vulture dance, and lead tribesmen in battles against their own kind. And I'm too old. I'm a lot older than Daniel, you know.'

'Oh, Archie, don't. Of course I know how old you are. I always looked up to you most tremendously. You seemed so . . . grown up and out of reach, somehow.'

He looked into her large brown eyes, and realised that she still doted on him even after all this time. It occurred to him once again that it might be very nice to be married to her. She was a good soul, a gentle hard-working girl who had done her bit in the war, and deserved a happy and normal future. She'd be a good mother too, and he would have liked to have children. Then he looked over at Rosie and caught her eye. She held his gaze for a solemn moment, and then dropped her eyes away.

'It's hopeless,' he thought to himself. 'It would have been better not to come. She's my brother's now, and I'm well and truly scuppered. *Entièrement foutu*. The best I can hope for is a grave in Peshawar.'

'I might go back early,' he said to Ottilie. 'We're expecting another uprising. Waziris this time. Wouldn't like to miss it.'

Ottilie looked from him to Fluke. She had been very attracted to the latter when they had first met. She still was, in truth, but it was Archie she had always hankered for, even though he was in India and she hardly ever saw him. Part of her devotion to him was brought about by her natural sympathy for someone who seemed to have been born to melancholy and defeat. He made her feel maternal and sisterly.

Daniel came up and clapped Archie on the back 'Frater meus! Time for the last event. Let's prepare!'

'"*Frater mi*", I think you'll find,' said Archie. 'The vocative of "*meus*" isn't declined like "*bonus*".'

'Well, *frater mi*, it's time to get out on the lawn and arm ourselves.'

'Onward the Pals!' said Archie gloomily. 'Those that are left.'

'Time to turn out the lights!' announced Daniel. 'Not a glimmer from any nook! Nor cranny! All gather in the conservatory! The spectacle is about to begin!'

'Shall I bawl out "The March of the Gladiators"?' suggested Fluke.

'No,' said Daniel, 'everyone will think we're clowns, and not noctambulant prestidigitators.'

'Ooh,' exclaimed Sophie, who, delighted by Daniel's phrase, clapped her hands together and hugged them to her chest.

Fluke, Archie, Daniel and Fairhead went down the steps into the garden, the company assembled in the conservatory, Esther sat on her mother's knee, and Millicent was sent scurrying about the house to dowse the lights. It was quite suddenly very dark indeed.

Down at the far end of the lawn two matches flared, two brilliant fires broke out, and then quite suddenly they flew diagonally across the lawn, passing each other in the middle. Then they hurtled down the sides, and across the ends, only to be sent diagonally past each other once more.

It was wondrously beautiful to see these balls of flame accelerating through the darkness. There was something primeval and exciting about it, something inexplicable. They heard Daniel's voice calling 'Flick!' and the balls of flame were stopped dead, and then, after 'One, two, three!', they arced into the air, stopped, arced again, criss-crossed continuously, until, one after the other, the flames went out, leaving only the smell of smoke and fuel in the air.

'Lights on!' cried Daniel.

The lights were rekindled, and moments later the four men reappeared, pleased with themselves, somewhat sootied about the clothes and hands.

'How did you do that?' asked Ottilie. 'I haven't seen anything so marvellous in all my life!'

'A splendid show,' said Mr McCosh. 'Most ingenious. My congratulations!'

'All you need,' said Fairhead, 'are hockey sticks and some hockey balls wrapped in rags and soaked in petrol. And matches. And people who know how to play hockey.'

'Can we see it again tomorrow?' asked Ottilie eagerly.

'Of course, but we'll have to go and get another can of petrol, or there'll be nothing for the mower. And tomorrow afternoon we're playing cricket, ladies against gentlemen.'

'That's hardly fair,' said Rosie. 'And when are we going to do any dancing?'

'It'll be terribly fair,' replied Archie. 'The ladies will be armed with full-sized men's crickets bats.'

'Is that fair?'

'It is when you consider that the men will be armed with

broomsticks. All bowling will be done left-handed. Unless you are left-handed, of course.'

'It'll be a fiasco,' said Fairhead.

'Well, we certainly hope so,' said Daniel.

'It'll be superhyperfun,' said Sophie.

'Can't stay, I'm afraid,' said Fluke. 'Wife and children, Christmas, unfortunately. Got to get back before curfew.'

The cricket was indeed a fiasco. In the time-honoured tradition of cricket, nobody won. It was generally agreed that Mrs McCosh was by far the most talented player. She had struck a ball into the Pendennises' garden, and broken a window in their greenhouse. Afterwards they played billiards with table-tennis balls, employing the butt ends of golf clubs for cues, and then they danced to Daniel's gramophone. At the end Caractacus came and put on his own show, chasing a golf ball all about the room, and then climbing up the curtain and perching on the pelmet, where he batted at the ostrich feather with which Mr McCosh was teasing him.

82

Millicent and Dusty Miller

Cookie was with Mrs McCosh, going through the next week's menus at the dining-room table, and down in the kitchen Constable Dusty Miller was ladling heaps of sugar into his mug of tea.

'Here, hold on!' exclaimed Millicent. 'That's too much! You and Chalky do us out of sugar every week, and every week Cookie has to make up a reason for where it's all gone. And you're going to have your teeth rotted out.'

'Can't 'elp it. Got a sweet tooth. I like sweet things. That's why I like you.'

'What? What did you say?'

'I said you're sweet,' replied Dusty.

'Give over,' said Millicent, 'or I'll belt you one right round the lughole.'

'Ooh, scary,' said Dusty Miller

He stirred his tea thoughtfully, and asked, 'Why do you think I keep coming 'ere, love?'

''Cause you're a lazy copper who likes to drink a cuppa tea halfway round his beat, that's why. And you like the drop scones.'

'No, it ain't. I can drink tea at the station any time. I come 'ere to see you.'

Millicent sat down at the kitchen table, and said, 'I s'pose you know about Hutch.'

'Course I know about Hutch. I was here when he came in and dropped, wasn't I?'

'I just got this feeling, see?'

'What feeling?'

'I loved him, Dusty, I really did love him. I thought we was going to get hitched. You know, happily ever after and all that.'

'Yeah, well, I know all that.'

363

'Look, Dusty, I like you a lot, but I got something holding me back.'

'Hutch?'

She nodded.

'Where's he buried, then?'

'Walthamstow.'

'Let's go and visit him.'

'Visit him? What are you on about?'

'Let's go and look at his grave. You got Sunday off, haven't you?'

'Afternoon. We have to go to church in the morning. Gives me a chance to snooze a bit at the back.'

'Well, I'll be down at the Tarn with a combination. You make sure you're all togged up, 'cause it does get bloody cold and it ain't even spring yet. Two o'clock all right?'

'Half past one,' said Milllicent. 'I didn't know you had a motorbike.'

'I don't. I'll borrow one off my mate Smiffy. He's a scrap merchant. I know him because every time something metal gets nicked, the idiot what stole it tries to sell it to him, so I just go straight down to Smiffy's.'

'What's in it for Smiffy?'

'Every time a car gets smashed up and I'm on the scene I recommend the owner go to Smiffy for the best price.'

'Is that pukka?'

'What the eye don't see the heart don't grieve,' said Dusty. 'I'll see you on Sunday. Down at the Tarn. Half past one.'

So it was that after an eventful journey, which included stopping to look at the Tower of London and a near miss involving a bolting dray horse, they found themselves standing side by side over Hutch's grave. It was well grassed over and the headstone had already lost the spruce look of newness. Millicent bent down and placed a posy of flowers, then she stood up and said, 'Hello, Hutch darling.'

Dusty put down the single rose that he had brought, and said nothing at all, letting Millicent weep at his side. He resisted the temptation to put an arm around her or to try and console her.

'The thing is,' said Millicent at last, 'it isn't him down there, is it? I mean, it's what's left of what he used be.'

'Well, I don't think he's down there,' said Dusty. 'It's like when you see someone die. What's left isn't them at all, is it? You can tell there ain't nobody in there. Anyway, why don't you ask him?'

'Ask him what?'

'Ask him if Dusty's all right. Go on, ask him. Say "Is Dusty all right?"'

Millicent looked down at the grass, with its sad collection of overblown snowdrops that were waiting to rot back into their roots, and said, 'Hutch darling, is Dusty all right?'

They stood side by side, until Millicent's hand crossed the little space between them, and slid into his.

'I reckon he thinks you're all right,' said Millicent.

As they were leaving, Dusty said, 'Will you wait just a mo? I want to say something to Hutch. On me own, like.'

Millicent waited by the lychgate, and a freezing wind suddenly whipped up her hair and made her eyes water all over again.

Dusty squatted down by the grave and patted the turf. He said, 'Thanks, mate. I owe you one.' Then he straightened up, returned his cap to his head and rejoined Millicent, saying, 'Madam, your carriage awaits.'

'You know what, Dusty?' said Millicent. 'I don't half feel a lot better. And another thing . . .'

'What?'

'You don't half look a bit strange without a uniform on.'

'You'll get used to it, love, you'll get used to it.'

'Quite handsome, really.'

'Give over.'

The following day Millicent was cleaning the morning room whilst Rosie was reading at the window seat, when she suddenly said, 'Please, Miss Rosie, can I ask you something? I mean, I know it's not my place to ask, but . . .'

'What is it, Millicent? I probably won't ask my mother to dismiss you.'

'Well, the thing is, miss . . . have you ever . . . I mean, have you . . . have you thought about visiting Mr Ashbridge's grave?'

'No, Millicent. I really don't think I could bear it.'

'You could, miss, you could. If you don't mind me saying so, miss, I think it would do you a lot of good.'

'Millicent, what on earth has brought this on?'

'Nothing, miss. Sorry, miss. But yesterday I went and visited Hutch.'

'And it did you good?'

'Yes, miss.'

'Well, one day I'll go to France. I'm bound to, aren't I?'

'I think you should, miss.'

'Thanks, Millicent. You're very kind.'

'It's nothing, miss.'

83

The Troglodyte

The family sat at table and bowed their heads. Mr McCosh was on the point of saying grace when his wife said quite unexpectedly, 'I think it would be very nice if Daniel were to say grace.'

'Me?' exclaimed Daniel. 'Really?'

'I am sure the Lord becomes wearied by always hearing the same grace. Perhaps you would like a turn. Do you mind, my dear?'

'Not at all,' said Mr McCosh, who was indeed a little put out by this unwarranted intervention. 'But the poor boy may have nothing prepared.'

'As you know,' said Daniel, 'I have no great association with God. We are nodding acquaintances only, after many years of mutual neglect.'

'More's the pity,' said Mrs McCosh. 'I find it impossible to see how anyone could remain moral unless he believes that the Supreme Being is keeping an eye on him. We do disgraceful things when unsupervised, do we not?'

'I lack the inclination to do disgraceful things,' said Daniel with barely concealed hostility, 'and I think that one should behave properly because it is right, and not because one is commanded.'

'It's an interesting question,' observed Captain Fairhead. 'Does God command something because it is good, or is something good because God commands it? If the answer is the former, which I think it is, then it follows that morality and religion are logically distinct.'

'Gracious me!' exclaimed Mrs McCosh. 'And you a clergyman! I am not sure I follow what you said, but I am certain that you must be a heretic!'

'It's more than likely,' said Fairhead equably.

367

'Do you have a grace that is always said in your family?' asked Ottilie, addressing Daniel.

'We do.'

'It would be awfully agreeable to hear it,' she said.

'Well, certainly, if you like,' said Daniel.

They bowed their heads, folded their hands together and closed their eyes. Daniel said softly:

> '*Pour les bonnes choses sur la table,*
> *Pour les belles choses dans la vie,*
> *Pour l'amour, la paix, la poésie,*
> *Dieu soit béni.*'

They all opened their eyes and looked at him in astonishment, with the exception of Mrs McCosh, whose face betrayed irritation and disapproval.

'That was so beautiful,' said Ottilie.

'My mother made it up,' said Daniel.

'Gracious me,' said Christabel, 'you must ask her to make it longer, so that it's even more like a poem. I'd like that so very much.'

'What does it mean, though?' asked Mr McCosh. 'I am feeling left out.'

'It means: "For the good things on the table, for the beautiful things in life, for love, peace and poetry, God be blessed,"' said Daniel.

'You mean to say that it is not an official grace?' asked Mrs McCosh.

'I am sure it has become hallowed by use in Daniel's family,' offered Rosie, who was aware that her husband was once again suppressing the anger that his mother-in-law continually aroused in him, 'and every grace must have been made up by someone at some time.'

There was a lapse in this conversation as Millicent came in bearing a large silver platter, upon which there was a dish of brawn, compressed whimsically into the shape of a chicken.

They were only a little way into their meal when Mrs McCosh returned to the fray. 'I am convinced', she said, 'that

French is an inappropriate language in which to address Our Lord.'

'Are you proposing that God doesn't understand French?' asked Daniel, knowing that he was being provoked, and, knowing that he should not rise to the bait, rising nonetheless.

'Not at all. That would be most absurd. But French is a light and frivolous language, is it not? One would not expect Him to take it seriously. English has so much more weight and pith.'

'Pith?' repeated Sophie, giggling. 'Pith?'

'Yeth. Pith!' said Mrs McCosh.

Sophie's shoulders heaved and she nearly spat out her mouthful of brawn. She spluttered, got up from her seat and ran out. They could hear her giving way to peals of laughter in the morning room.

'What on earth is wrong with the girl?' asked Mrs McCosh.

'Must have been something you said,' said Mr McCosh, his eyes sparkling with amusement.

'I do apologise on my wife's behalf,' said Fairhead. 'I can't imagine what's come over her.'

'When I was a girl,' said Christabel, 'and I went to stay with that family in Normandy, I was utterly amazed at the cleverness of the dogs.'

'Really?' asked Daniel. 'Why so?'

'Well, they all understood French. If you said "*Assieds-toi*", they sat down.'

'I think you're saying that English is the natural language of dogs as well as of God?'

'That's what I assumed when I was a little girl,' said Christabel. 'Naturally, I am not so naive in my old age.'

Mrs McCosh glared at her. 'I think you are declaring that I am naive. I am hardly naive.'

'Philosophically malnourished, perhaps,' suggested Daniel, under his breath, but not quite quietly enough.

'How dare you! And, furthermore, I must tell you that I most strongly disapprove of your occasional lapses of manners when you are at this table! In this country it is not customary to sit with your elbows on the table. Your arms should be at your side and you should not rest your wrists on the table. And you should

369

not pick up bones to chew the remaining meat from them. That was done in the past but is simply not done any more.'

'But brawn has no bones,' said Christabel, much puzzled.

'I am referring to the lamb chops we had on Thursday last,' said Mrs McCosh. 'I didn't want to say anything at the time, but now I feel I must speak.'

'To leave meat upon the bones is disrespectful of the creature that died so that we might eat it,' replied Daniel icily. 'And, what is more, the sweetest meat is that which is nearest the bone. And as for elbows on the table, in France we have our elbows on the table and we bite the meat from the bones when we are *en famille*. I have made the mistake of thinking that in this house I am *en famille*. I apologise. I also apologise for leaving the table before the meal is finished, and before we have given thanks in God's real language, but I cannot abide it here any longer.'

Mrs McCosh said, 'Whether you are *en famille* or not is a matter of conjecture. However, I should think that there is not one of us here, not even your wife, who thinks you can ever replace our poor lost son, or ever be worthy to step into his place.'

Daniel threw his napkin onto his place setting, bowed to the ladies and Mr McCosh, and strode out of the room.

'Oh, Mama!' exclaimed Rosie. She hesitated, white with dismay, and then went out after Daniel.

'My dear, I think you should apologise to your son-in-law,' said Mr McCosh.

'I will do no such thing,' replied Mrs McCosh. 'I am not in the wrong, and will not be told so. I have taken the trouble to consult several guides to etiquette, including one written by a countess. They are unanimous on the subject of gnawing bones and having elbows on the table! And I will not be told off in front of the children.'

'We will speak afterwards, then,' said Mr McCosh, 'when we are not in the presence of the children. And I happen to know that the late Queen liked to gnaw bones in her fingers. It was often remarked upon. I'm astounded that you don't know of it.'

Rosie came back into the room, saying, 'I don't know where he went. I do hope he hasn't gone home to his mother.'

'What? To Partridge Green? At this time of night?' said Ottilie.

'Daniel is perfectly capable of driving to Partridge Green at this time of the night,' said Rosie. 'His fanaticism for motorcycling is completely inexhaustible, even at night or in the rain. He loves it almost as much as flying.' She ran to the window and tweaked aside the curtain. 'His combination is still there.'

'We would have heard it starting up,' said Ottilie sensibly.

'We have lost both Sophie and Daniel,' said Mr McCosh gloomily. They could still hear Sophie pacing up and down in the morning room, but every now and then they heard a new peal of laughter.

Daniel had gone out of the French windows and into the conservatory. The structure had been rebuilt, and it had lately begun to fill up with plants. During the war, before the glass had been blown out, the family had attempted to grow vegetables in it, without very much success, because they had lacked both assiduity and skill. Somehow the produce had always ended up overwatered, dead from dessication, mildewed, undersized or infested. Now, however, a tiny orange tree was flourishing in one corner, and a lemon in another. A vine was working its way towards the roof, and various pot plants were promising to become worthy of being a centrepiece on the dining table.

Daniel was seeking a refuge where he could calm himself with a couple of cigarettes. In order to get as far from his mother-in-law as he could, he opened the door and took the steps down to the lawn, resolving to go to the far end of the garden where Bouncer was buried. He walked out and looked up at the moon, whose beauty had never ceased to astonish him ever since he had so many times perforce lain out under it *en plein air* when he was serving on the North-West Frontier. Caractacus appeared out of the darkness and wound himself about Daniel's legs. He snapped open his case, drew out a cigarette, and then patted his pockets to locate a matchbox. Finding it, he struck a match and shielded the flame in his hands, as he had also learned to do on the frontier. He remembered advising a fellow officer, freshly arrived from Hindubagh, not to have a cigarette when they were resting on a night patrol, and he laughed in amused recollection of the man's reaction as a Pashtun sniper sent a bullet spinning from the rock next to which the man had been reclining, the moment he lit a match. It was somewhat odd these days, not to be under fire in one place or another, unless one counted the sallies of one's mother-in-law. Not even she was as bad, he thought, as seeing a row of machine-gun bullets stitching their inexorable way towards you through the canvas of an aeroplane. Mrs McCosh was more on a par with flying through archie and flaming onions, except that archie and flaming onions didn't leave you seething with fury. He decided all over again that it was an absolute priority to persuade Rosie to leave this house so they could begin to live more equably elsewhere. Of course, first of all he would have to leave the RAF and find a new job somewhere.

Daniel distinctly heard a cough nearby, and pricked up his ears. He looked around in the darkness, and then heard another cough, very near indeed. He wheeled about and realised that there must be someone in the storeroom below the conservatory.

Steeling himself, he walked to the doorway and peered in, but saw only the absolute darkness. He searched for his matchbox, and struck a match, holding it above eye level. He saw nothing in that orange glow but garden machinery, heaps of sacking, stacks of flowerpots, rakes and hoes. He nonetheless had a very distinct sense that there was someone there.

'Who are you?' he demanded. 'Where are you hiding?' He wondered if electric light had been installed down here yet, and peered about for a switch. 'I know you're here,' he said, as the flame burned down to his fingertips and he was forced to shake the match out. 'If you do not reveal yourself, I shall go back inside and return with a torch and revolver. This is your last warning.'

'Hold hard,' came a rough voice, 'no need going over the top, as the actress said to the bishop. No point wasting a cartridge.'

Daniel lit another match, and a heap of sacking in the corner began to heave. Soon there stood before him a dishevelled man of about thirty-five years of age, holding out a hurricane lamp. 'Light this,' he said, 'and stop wasting yer matches.'

Thinking how strange this all was, Daniel opened the mantle and lit the wick. 'Oh, it's you,' he said.

'That'd be true, whoever you said it to,' replied the man.

'You're the gardener,' said Daniel.

'Lucky you told me. I mightn't have realised. I know who you are. You're married to Miss Rosie,' replied the man.

'What on earth are you doing, camping under the conservatory?'

'Ain't got no home.'

'No home? And the McCoshes took you on?'

'I told 'em I lived in Mottingham. They never asked me more. That Mr McCosh is a decent sort. I asked him for a chance, and he gave me one.'

'The garden has improved enormously. The transformation is wonderful, really.'

'Thank you, sir.'

'You've got no family hereabouts?'

The man shrugged. 'Dr Barnardo boy. Just about managed to keep out of Borstal.'

'No wife either?'

'Sodded off, sir. Went off with a Gordon Highlander. Buggered off to Scotland. Good luck to him, poor sod.' He paused, then added, 'It's all right. She was a ten-pinter, and she was bloody horrible when she had the painters in.'

Daniel briefly tried to decipher this gnomic information, and gave up. 'So you've no home at all?'

'Not any more, sir. Used to, before I went to Kut.'

'You were at Kut? You got through that?'

'2nd Norfolks, sir. The worst thing was the march afterwards, sir. Johnny Turk marched us hundreds a' miles. Johnny Turk thinks everyone else is as tough as he is. No transport, no food, no water sometimes. Sleeping under a conservatory ain't so bad, really, when you come to think of it.'

'All the same, you can't possibly stay here. What if the family finds out?'

'Mr McCosh already knows, sir. He likes coming out in the dark and standing by the dog's grave. He talks to it. Anyway, he caught me. He wanted to throw me out, but in the end he promised not to tell his missus, and he said he'd let me stay here 'til I'd got enough of a wage to take a lodging somewhere. In fact he gave me thirty shillings in advance, and I'm looking already.'

Daniel was impressed. 'He's a decent sort. The longer I know him, the more I think so.'

'Oh, that he is, sir. He's decent in private, like. He just don't flaunt it when anyone's watching. Millicent thinks he's something wonderful for that.'

'And who's feeding you? You must be living off something.'

'Cookie, of course, and Millicent. They're the salt of the earth, they are.'

'In fact, you're at the centre of a huge conspiracy.'

'You could put it like that, sir.'

'Don't you get lonely?'

'The cat comes in and makes a fuss. That's nice, that is. You sleep better with a warm cat purring away in your face.'

'Well, well, well. Is there anything I can do for you?'

'You're about the same size as me,' said the gardener. 'Got any cast-offs?'

'I'll have a look,' said Daniel. 'By the way, I'm not sure I know your name.'

'Wragge, sir. Everyone calls me Oily. You may call me Mr Wragge, if you like, sir, because I was a sergeant major before, sir, and you can call me Oily if ever you know me better. I'll call you sir if you don't mind, sir. You're probably an officer anyways, and it'll save me having to remember.'

'I am Captain Pitt, or at least I was before they turned the Flying Corps into the RAF. Well, Mr Wragge, I'll bid you goodnight. Is there anything I can bring you?'

'Not unless you got a spare floozy somewhere, sir.'

Daniel laughed. 'If I had a spare one, Mr Wragge, I'd be keeping her to myself, and I'd be offering her a bed rather than a heap of sacks.'

'Very wise, sir. I'd be doing the same. Could you spare me a gasper then?'

Daniel took out his case and removed three cigarettes, which he handed over, along with the box of matches. 'I could probably find you a Sidcot suit, and an officer's warm, if you're getting cold at night,' said Daniel.

'That would be very congenial,' said Wragge. 'I'll give 'em back when I find lodgings.'

'Goodnight, Mr Wragge. Time for me to waggle my wings and

venture back into Hunland. I have hail to fly through, an HB to deal with.'

'Hostile battery? That'll be the mistress, then. Goodnight, sir, and thank you, and watch out for archie. Watch out for that Mrs McCosh.'

'I do, Mr Wragge, I do. I always beware of HBs. And the Hun in the sun,' and he set off back up the steps to the conservatory, wondering if he could get to the staircase without encountering any of the family. He would now have to deal with the aftermath of his bad manners, and having left table before grace.

'My shoe is size nine,' called Mr Wragge softly. 'Just in case you was wondering.'

84

Ultimatum

He found Rosie at the foot of the stairs, waiting for him, looking anxious and angry, so he forestalled her with 'I'm going home.'

'Home? To Partridge Green?'

'Yes, Partridge Green.'

'But you can't! It's so late.'

'I have good lights.'

'But what if you break down or get a nail in your tyre?'

'I'll sleep in a ditch. I'd rather sleep in a ditch than spend one more day in the same house as your wretched mother. Then I'll go back to the airfield on Sunday evening.'

'But why do you get so provoked? She does it because it's so easy to get you angry! Why can't you just stay calm, and smile, and shrug it all off like the rest of us?'

'She picks almost exclusively on me. The moment she comes into the room I know I'm going to be attacked, and it gets worse every time I'm here. I'm sick of hearing about how I can't hold a candle to "our lost son", and I'm sick of being insulted and denigrated because of being half French.'

'But you know she's not herself! Don't you remember her, from when we were small? She was so much fun. Don't you remember?'

'Of course I remember. That woman has gone.'

'No, she's still inside, somewhere, she really is.'

'It's immaterial,' said Daniel. 'I can't stand it here and I'm coming back as little as I can.'

'But, Daniel, don't you understand? She found her dearest friend mangled. She saw a child's head on a doorstep, looking at her. She's never been the same. Surely you can see it's not her fault? It's shell shock.'

'Rosie, every one of us has been through their own Hell for

years, you at Netley, where you must have seen the most terrible things day in and day out, and me in France. I've listened to people burning to death and screaming for God in wrecks that I shot down myself. I've come back from patrol and found two, three, four empty chairs in the mess, over and over again, month after month. I could go on. You know perfectly well how long one's list is. Yours is probably longer than mine. Your mother's list has one entry.'

'But we're not all the same! We expected to see what we saw. She wasn't expecting it.'

'In the end we have no choice, do we? We put it behind us, clench our teeth and battle on until the distance becomes sufficiently great. You've been indulging her. The whole family indulges her. No one challenges her, so she just gets worse and worse, until one day she'll be so eccentric and so damned rude that even you won't be able to live with her and you'll have to put her in a loony bin.'

Rosie looked at him desperately, unable to concede.

'Anyway,' continued Daniel, 'there are two ways out. Either you and Esther move with me into married quarters as soon as the squadron gets settled, or I leave the RAF and get a job somewhere quite a long way away, and you and Esther come and join me there.'

'But I can't leave my mother! How will my father cope with her?'

'You have Millicent and Mary. And Ottilie hasn't left home.'

'But one day she'll want to move away and get married! What then? Who'll look after her? What about Daddy?'

'Rosie, you're married.'

Rosie looked at the floor dumbly. She sat on one of the hall chairs and put her face into her hands.

'I've been such a disappointment,' she said. 'I've done everything wrong. I've been a terrible wife, I know it. I'm so sorry. I expect you hardly love me any more, do you?'

'You gave me Esther,' said Daniel. 'That was the best gift anyone could have given me. Whatever happens, I'll always love you for that.'

He went to fetch his Sidcot suit and shuffled it on. He sat on the other hall chair and pulled on his boots, then he stood. 'I'd better be going,' he said. He hesitated, holding his flying gloves in one hand and his helmet and goggles in the other.

Rosie looked up at him, her eyes bloodshot from weeping. 'Don't go, Daniel, please don't go. We've got to keep trying. Please stay.'

85

Conversation in the Pavilion

The Royal flying Corps had been amalgamated with the Royal Naval Air Service a year before, and Daniel had talked it over a great deal with Fluke, in the cricket pavilion of their temporary airfield, and in their local tavern. For old soldiers of the RFC there was far too much navy tommyrot in the RAF these days, and peacetime service was a full-scale bore. The brass hats and chair-warmers were clamping down on all that made aviation joyous. No flying under bridges. No contour-chasing and tree-hopping in case it upset the farmers, the cows and the horses, or made people spill their tea with the shock, or startled drivers into ditches. No more cloud-vaulting, no more split-arsing over the villages. No more binge nights when you smashed up everything in the mess, because now you couldn't send out a vehicle to fetch in the abandoned chairs and tables from the ruins of French houses. Worst of all had been the introduction of endless hours of guards-style square-bashing, the surest sign that the force had lost sight of its purpose and was seeking only to enforce uniformity and keep the men occupied. 'You might as well get us to dig holes and fill them in again,' said Daniel. 'I'm not wasting my mornings stamping around, and I don't see why the men should either. I want my fitter working on my machine, not being yelled at by some numbskull with a head full of drill book.'

'I hate this bloody uniform,' said Fluke. 'The old maternity dress was bad enough, but at least nobody made us wear it. What was wrong with your regimental duds with a pair of wings and your ribbons sewn on? And I'm damned if I like being a squadron leader. I'm a major, damn it. I'm a soldier, not a bloody air sailor.'

'Remember the first uniform they came up with?' said Daniel, and they both laughed. It had been a hideous and ridiculous outfit in vulgar blue, covered with gold. The policy had been that, owing to the shortage of uniforms, only the new boys would have to wear the new outfit. As the old guard were killed off, the replacement of the old by the new had taken place naturally by a process of attrition, but there were plenty of surviving stalwarts who still felt as if they really belonged to their regiments. You don't alter your allegiance by putting on something blue.

'No more WRAFs,' said Fluke gloomily. 'I loved WRAFs. Almost as much as WAACs and dusky maidens. I got driven for miles by one in a combination, getting back to the squadron after a smash. Stout girl, lovely smile, wonder what happened to her.'

'Think of all those empty Wraferies,' said Daniel.

'It's a horrible thought,' agreed Fluke.

'No more airship service either.'

'I don't mind that too much,' said Fluke. 'There aren't any Boche ones to shoot down any more, and you can't pip the ones on your own side anyway. Might as well get rid of them.'

'Good for submarine spotting,' said Daniel.

'No more submarines to spot,' said Fluke. 'I suppose you could sell them off to whalers. And why haven't they issued us with parachutes yet? Don't they give a damn? The Huns had them ages ago.'

'Parachutes are for sissies,' said Daniel. 'True heroes bounce or burn.' They both thought for a while of all those who might have been saved by parachutes.

'Those RNAS types were damn good flyers, and they were all on land anyway, just like us. I feel sorry for them that they didn't get much credit. But I'm damned if I can take all this navy mullarkey they've brought in with them. Why couldn't they just be Royal Flying Corps?'

'They wrote off my Tripe and let me have it,' said Fluke. 'Here's to the naval types and their lovely old Tripes. And here's a curse on all their naval mullarkey. And here's to General Smuts. We forgive him.' He tipped back a neat slug of whisky, and said, 'Do you remember when we got so plastered that we couldn't tell whisky and soda from champagne? Never been so sick in my life.'

'Talking of credit,' said Daniel, continuing on his own line of thought, 'what about the poor bastards in two-seaters? Imagine being in a Harry Tate and getting set on by six Fokkers.'

'And the night-flyers,' said Fluke. 'Got no credit at all.'

'We were the Glory Boys,' said Daniel.

'Actually we can't be, because the Glory Boys are the Norfolk Regiment, and we can't be "Death or Glory" either, because that's the Gloucesters.'

'The Norfolk Regiment are the Holy Boys. You've got in a muddle.'

'Quite right. As you were. Can we be the Glory Boys after all?'

'How about the "Glamour Boys"?'

'That'll do me,' replied Fluke. 'You know we're down from 188 squadrons to thirty-three? From now on it's a tuppenny-ha'penny air force. And God help the navy. We're done for. We are muchly confounded. What's next?'

'Just Empire stuff,' said Daniel. 'There's a squadron of Snipes waiting to pounce on the Huns at Bickendorf if they get frisky, but apart from that it's India or Egypt or Malta or Mesopotamia or Somaliland, for God's sake. Everyone's being sent to Egypt as far as I can see. It's packed full of bombers. God knows why.'

'Don't want to go there,' said Fluke. 'Worst place in the world to catch a dose. That's why we lost in the Dardanelles. We sent the boys to Alexandria first. You can't fight when you're stinging with clap.'

'I wouldn't mind going back to India,' said Daniel. 'There's plenty of action on the North-West Frontier, and my brother's there too. I don't think I can drag Esther and Rosie out there, though. So many disgusting things to die of. Simla's lovely, of course.'

'Never give up, do they, those Pathan wallahs?'

'Indeed they don't. There's no one more stupidly courageous, as far as I know, apart from us. Tell me, Fluke, do you ever have doubts about this Empire business? The White Man's Burden, our civilising mission and all that?'

'After that last bash, there's not much to say for civilisation, is there? We did call it "The War for Civilisation", didn't we, though? It's on our medals. Makes you think.'

'Well, I've been thinking.'

'About what?'

'About the North-West Frontier. Those Pathans.'

'What about them?'

'Well, they're tribal. They don't give a farthing about anyone except their own relations. They're religious fanatics who don't know a damn thing about their own religion because they can't read their own language, let alone Arabic. They think that whatever they do, it was the Prophet who told them to do it, even if it's gelding their prisoners and boiling rice. They're as high as kites on opium and hashish, and can't even make sense of each other. They aren't like us and they don't want to be like us, and the moment we go they'll revert to being exactly as they were before.'

'The moment we go? Are we going? I thought it was all about keeping the Russians at arm's length. I can't see an end to that, can you? Now that they're Bolshies to boot.'

'It doesn't feel like that when you're there,' said Daniel. 'The Russians are the last thing you think of. You pay the chiefs to control their own tribesmen and you burn their villages when they don't. Oddly enough, they often help you do it, because wanton destruction is just about their favourite thing, and anyway they move their pots and pans out first. You hang them for doing things that are perfectly normal for them, like robbing and killing their neighbours, and then you find yourself in the middle of a blood feud that's never going to finish.'

'You don't think it's all worth it, then? East is East and West is West?'

'I'm all in favour of having adventures,' replied Daniel. 'I had a wonderful time when I was a Frontier Scout, and in the Sikhs, but you know, there does come a time when you have to ask yourself, "Well, are you actually doing any good?"'

'Truth to tell, I've had many a furtive doubt myself.'

'I lost two brothers in South Africa,' said Daniel, 'and my best friend at Westminster died of blackwater fever in Kenya. Another old mucker died of typhoid in India, and his wife too, who was a sweetie if ever I met one, and on and on it goes, Britain's finest and best swallowed up by the Empire.' He paused, then added,

'Don't mistake my meaning, old chap, I'm as much of a jingo as anyone, and I've got two countries to be a jingo for, and I enjoy Empire Day and Bastille Day as much as anyone else. The old chest swells with pride, doesn't it? You can hardly help it. Even so, look at the price of it all! You build roads and railways, and set up clinics and schools, and then the subject peoples aren't grateful enough for any of it to be worth it, and when they get awkward about it, we bash them on the head with sticks, and then they get even less grateful. I don't think we should be wasting our lives on them. Look at Macedonia. You set up a League of Nations mandate to guide the liberated but benighted ones towards democracy, whereat they wax exceeding wroth against the infidel, and they simply have a marvellous time taking potshots at us.' He paused, and added, 'In the end, doing something just because the government tells you to isn't enough, is it? That isn't what patriot-ism really means, is it? If you love your country, it shouldn't be at the expense of anyone else, should it?'

'Hmm,' said Fluke, 'I see that ye are one of little faith these days. Bunking off church parades and backing off from the good old imperium. Better not go round telling too many people; they might think you're a socialist and stop inviting you to hunt balls.'

'I generally keep all this to myself. Worry not. And hunt balls are my idea of Hell. But I do suspect that more and more people will start to have the same doubts. I think it's inevitable.'

'Time for us both to resign, methinks, before they catch us at ten thousand feet with idle puttees and without a tie on. Hateful thought. We can always join up again if anything exciting happens. You know what,' said Fluke, 'wouldn't it be wonderful if we could buy up some buses and set up in business split-arsing at county shows?'

'Everyone else has had the same idea; even Rosie's father suggested it. We should have left the RAF the moment the war ended, like Cecil. He got that wonderful job with Vickers and went straight to China. The market is saturated and bursting at the seams. There are thousand of flyers and thousand of machines. The Yanks have got hordes of barnstormers, but here it hasn't caught on. The other thing would be to set up postal services in rather big places like Australia or Tanganyika. Has anyone ever thought of a flying medical service? For civilians?'

'No idea. It does occur to me that if you want to have a passenger service you'd have to buy bombers. Do you suppose there are any Gothas left?'

'Very crudely built. I'd go for a Vickers Vimy,' said Daniel, 'or a Hereford.'

'Let's go upstairs for a flip and throw our buses about,' said Fluke. 'Let us dispel the gloom, and frolic in the empyrean. Rumour hath it that our machines are warmed up even as we speak, and the cumuli are cotton castles on this fine and frivolous day.'

'I'll take that as an order, Squadron Leader,' said Daniel.

'Major to you,' said Fluke.

'And I shall forever be Captain,' said Daniel, 'on the assumption that the prospects of promotion end whenever a war does. If I could take my Snipe with me I'd resign tomorrow.'

What finally caused him to leave was the departure of Fluke himself. Fluke had gone on impulse to the Argentinian Embassy in London in order to offer his services in the setting up of their fledgling air force, and this amazing stroke of initiative had borne fruit almost immediately. There was still plenty of scope for war in South America.

86

Daniel's Last Binge

Daniel forewent the opportunity to go to Argentina with Fluke, because Rosie had bluntly refused to accompany him. The thought of South America filled her with horror, because she had read accounts of missionaries being eaten by cannibals in the Amazon. She could not be persuaded that the Argentines were just like the Italians, but much more prosperous and civilised, even ignoring the firm opinions of her own father, who was still making decent sums from developing the Argentine railways. He had been quite taken with the idea of having his own daughter on the spot, as a kind of ambassador. She was not, in fact, inclined to go anywhere at all, because of worries that she had been keeping close to her chest, for good reasons of her own that she was frightened to divulge.

The night before Fluke and Daniel left the Royal Air Force, there took place the most marvellous binge since the German surrender. Their mess had been removed from the cricket pavilion because of the danger to it brought about by binges, and was now a small complex of Nissen huts and temporary sheds set up on railway sleepers at the furthest corner of the vast playing field, lest the schoolboys fall witness to the antics of the gallant aviators, and be tempted to emulate them. The food was ordered from a nearby hotel, arriving in aluminium vessels resembling enormous mess tins, and the alcohol was brought in from its cellars.

After a comparatively civilised feast of roast beef, followed by bread-and-butter pudding, and after the loyal toast, Fluke made a speech in honour of Daniel, comparing him to Albert Ball, and Daniel made a speech in honour of Fluke, comparing him to Billy Bishop. These were accompanied by jeers and cheers, and the hurling of buns at the speakers. The Wing Commander, who had arrived in his personal Sopwith Pup for the occasion, stood up and made an elaborate speech in honour of them both, describing them as stout fellows and Hun-getters the like of which we will never see again, now that the Huns have all been got, and mighty pippers and balloonatics before the Lord. He proposed a toast to 'Good old Boom and Baring'.

Then the ragging began. Pilot Officer Jenkins played cake-walks on the piano until someone kicked the stool from under him. Daniel stood on the table and sang 'She Was Poor But She Was Honest' in the filthiest and longest version he knew, and then sang it again, accompanied by a banjo player who was playing something else altogether, in a different key. They all sang 'Keep the Home Fires Burning', and Jenkins woke up and played 'Any Time's Kissing Time' and then passed out again. Inspired by this, Fluke took his turn on the table and danced an imaginative Highland fling, like a grasshopper in a frying pan, until the table collapsed, amid great splintering. Not to be undone, the Wing Commander, who was a real Scot, crossed two knives on the rug and demonstrated how to do the Highland fling properly.

Fluke climbed on the piano and tried a Cossack dance, but it was an upright, and the top was hardly wide enough, so his left foot became jammed between it and the wall. Carter and Bressingham cleared everyone to the perimeter of the room and had a duel with chairs, which Bressingham won, to great acclamation.

Then Bressingham proposed a bullfight, and brandished the tablecloth as everyone in turn put their fingers to their foreheads and charged him at a crouch. 'Olé, olé, olé!'

The gramophone was wound up and Wootton demonstrated how to dance whilst performing a handstand. A small group of them played Cardinal Puff, with champagne and whisky, until there was no choice but to go outside and vomit in the fresh air.

> 'Drunk last night, drunk like the night before,
> And we're going to get drunk again tonight
> If we never get drunk no more.'

Daniel shouted for silence and said, 'Brothers, over many months I saw many empty chairs, and nothing gives a sentimental airman like me a greater pain than the sight of empty chairs in the mess. Tomorrow there will be two empty chairs. But grieve not! Fluke and I will return, yea, just like Robin Hood, in the hour of need. We are not dead. We are merely sleeping in the wings.'

'Like King Arthur, you BF,' said Bressingham.

'Like King Arthur,' said Daniel. 'I said King Arthur. Robin Hood? Who said Robin Hood? *Nunc est bibendum!*'

'*Nunc est bibendum!*' they roared, and, at this signal, the rumpus began with high cockalorum, and continued with Harry Kelly's tank game. Fluke emptied out the coal scuttle into a corner, and Daniel went to his hut to fetch another. Then he and Fluke went to one end of the mess and put the empty scuttles on their heads. The sky pilot blew the whistle for the commencement of battle, and Daniel and Fluke charged blindly for the other end of the room whilst their baying and jeering comrades pelted them with coal. It pinged and clanged on the scuttles, and Fluke and Daniel blundered about trying to find the surviving table.

At last the table was found, climbed upon and occupied, and the ammunition had run out and needed to be gathered up. Daniel and Fluke had won, as they always did, once again proving the invincibility of the tank, even when the drivers can't see anything.

There was a wheelbarrow race round the huts clockwise, and then a three-legged race around them anticlockwise. Somebody ripped up the ludo board, and somebody else poured the chess pieces in the piano to see if he could make it jangle.

Boom alert! Take a note, Baring! The Wing Commander will now make shampoo! Orderly! Fetch the whisky and the champagne! Yes, sir! Two bottles, orderly! Yes, sir! Orderly, fetch the sponge and the bucket! Yes, sir!

The Wing Commander emptied the whisky and champagne into the bucket, the sponge was dipped, and the Wing Commander ceremoniously baptised each in turn. The men attempted to catch the drips that ran past their mouths.

We shall each sup in turn from the bucket! Orderly! Time to pass the bucket! Yes, sir! *Dis manibus! Deo invicto Mithrae!* To us!

To the dead Huns! To good old George! To Albert and Mick and Arthur and James and the whole damn lot of 'em! Orderly! Whisky, champagne! Yes, sir! Orderly, arm us with siphons! Yes, sir! Let battle commence! B flight against A and C! Wait . . . wait . . . stand by . . . on my order . . . Open fire! Orderly, the fire extinguisher, the fire extinguisher! Yes, sir, the fire extinguisher, sir!

There was a treetop battle. Men climbed on the shoulders of another, and a general melee ensued, which did not finish until the last pair remained standing. Carter broke his wrist and did not realise until the following morning, when the pain of it surpassed that of his hangover. When it was clear that no more mayhem was conceivable or possible, and that they could not be more sodden, they sang to the melody of 'My Bonnie Lies Over the Ocean' their own squadron's version of the Flying Corps anthem.

> 'A poor aviator lay dying
> At the end of a bright summer's day.
> The weeping ack emmas had gathered
> To carry his fragments away.
>
> The engine was piled on his wishbone
> His Vickers was wrapped round his head,
> A spark plug he wore on each elbow,
> 'Twas plain he would shortly be dead.
>
> He spat out a valve and a gasket,
> And stirred in the sump where he lay,
> And then to his wondering comrades
> These brave parting words he did say.
>
> "Take the magneto out of my stomach,
> And the butterfly valve from my neck,
> Extract from my liver the crankshaft,
> There are lots of good parts in this wreck.
>
> Take the manifold out of my larynx,
> And the cylinders out of my brain,

Take the piston rods out of my kidneys,
And assemble the engine again.

Pull the longeron out of my backbone,
The turnbuckle out of my ear,
From the small of my back take the rudder,
There's all of my aeroplane here."

So hold all your glasses right steady,
And let's drink a toast to the sky,
And here's to the dead already,
And here's to the next man to die.'

'Encore! Encore!' cried Fluke, and they sang it over and over until at last, for the first time in years, it seemed funny again.

Then the Wing Commander ordered a rag, A and B flights against C flight, and Fluke grabbed a cushion. They scrummed down, arms locked about each other, and the Wing Commander tossed the cushion into the middle. Until the cushion burst apart and filled the air with white feathers, they had as good and rowdy a game of indoor rugby as one could possibly hope for inside a large wooden hut. The Wing Commander got a black eye, even though he was non-combatant.

Finally there was no one left standing except Daniel and Fluke, staggering with their arms about each other's shoulders as they surveyed the spillage and the ruin of the furniture and the fallen. Even the gramophone was wrecked.

They collapsed side by side against the wooden wall, sliding down it together, and Fluke put his head back and sighed. 'Ripping binge. The rippingest. Verily, I am by the waters of Babylon.'

'It's the saddest day of our lives,' said Daniel.

'It's all postscript now,' said Fluke. 'Nothing but bloody postscript. We got matched to the hour, thanked God for it, got through it, binged and biffed, cursed God and the politicians and generals, shouted and laughed, lost our friends, hurtled about in the sky, slaughtered and murdered and nearly got killed God knows how many times, got the gust up so we could hardly drink for the shakes, and now it's all gone. Do you remember Albert, lighting a magnesium flare in the dark and walking round it 'til it went out, playing his violin? And Mick playing that "Caprice Viennoise" on his violin and always saying it was too hard? Do you remember the bombing raids with fruit? I got a rigger with an orange, once. What happened to Mick's cat?'

'Piddle the Puss? Don't know, old chap,' said Daniel. 'I always expected to go underground in a wooden kimono. What are we supposed to do with so much life unexpectedly left over?'

'I expected to go down in a flamerino. Sizzle sizzle wonk. Good God! The thought of it! I dream about it every night, and I dream about all the boys roast-pigged and sent west, and now I can't remember which ones are alive and which are dead. The nightmares have got everything muddled up. Sometimes I'm surprised to see you. How many friends did we lose? A hundred and fifty? How many got sent west in a couple of days, and now we can't remember them? Tell me, what now? For what have we been spared?'

'I just asked the same question. Buck up,' said Daniel.

'Nothing to buck up about,' said Fluke.

'We could have ended up as penguins.'

'Fie upon thee. *Quel horreur!*'

'Do you remember Room 613A? Lord Hugh Cecil?'

'Christ, it seems like a lifetime ago. Another life altogether. Have you got a gasper?'

'All gone. Do you remember how we all got worked up over "The Song of the Sword", and thought what a fine piece of work it was? How inspired we were? Look at it now, and it's utter bilge and bunkum,' said Daniel. 'Do you remember "The Abode of Love"? And how utterly ghastly the depot at Candas was?'

'Frolicking in the river in midsummer,' said Fluke.

'The crack of Spandaus. Crickety-crack.'

'Won't miss that much.'

'Needing to piss at twenty thousand feet,' said Daniel. 'What did you do? Funnel and rubber tube?'

'Just pissed on the joystick. Devil of a job buttoning and unbuttoning. No feeling in the fingers at all.'

'Christ, I've never been so cold.'

'You didn't go to Harrow,' said Fluke.

'At Westminster we had frost on the inside of the windows,' said Daniel. 'Wish I'd known about whale grease back then.'

'Par for the course,' replied Fluke. 'At Harrow we had lumps of ice in our tea in place of lumps of sugar.'

'I won't miss the stench of whale grease,' reflected Daniel. 'Did you take chlorodyne, before long flights?'

'Had to. Castor oil plus wind up equals runs, *n'est-ce pas?*'

'I didn't take chlorodyne,' said Daniel. 'I always made a point of going before I went, so to speak.'

'No more *Comic Cuts*,' said Fluke.

'Wish I'd kept them. I've got some *Wipers Times*.'

'No more DOPs, thank God. Or trench-strafing. Or tennis with the padre. Wonderful forehand.'

'Wait for the next war, old fellow.'

'God forbid,' said Fluke. 'Did you know that No. 9's leaving? Going to set up a surgery in Fife, apparently.'

'You know,' said Daniel, 'I never felt so lonely in my life as when we were flying, even in a flight formation.'

'It was the awful distortion of time that got me muddled,' said Fluke. 'All that hanging around from dawn 'til dusk, going on missions at a moment's notice, having two breakfasts and no lunch and sleeping whenever you could. Time stopped. Or it stretched. Like knicker elastic.'

'And then the time had all suddenly gone,' said Daniel. 'Did I tell you about my horrible dream?'

'Lots of times.'

'It's vile. Keeps coming back, just about every night. And now you're going to be split-arsing all over the pampas.'

'So I am. Lucky I'm fond of beef. I think I'm going to be sick.'

'It might be warmer in Argentina. Does one's moustache freeze at twenty thousand feet in Argentina?'

'What happened to the Wing Commander?'

'Tight as a tick. Passed out. By the piano.'

'Let's cut off half his moustache.'

'I've got some nail scissors in my hut. Back in a jiffy.'

Having accomplished the evil deed without opposition, they

settled back against the wall of the hut and set about downing a jug of water. With great pathos Fluke sang:

'Wrap me up in my old yellow jacket,
Give me my joystick to hold, to hold,
Let me fly once again o'er the trenches,
And thus shall my exploits be told, be told.

'Let's drink more water,' he said. 'We shall be peeing all night, but we might get away with not having a hangover.'

'It's me I feel sorry for,' said Daniel. 'I'm dreading saying goodbye to my bus. There's nothing worse than bidding farewell to your bus. I still miss my Pup. What a sweetheart it was.'

'You got over it when you swapped your Camel.'

'I loved my Camels, by God, I loved my Camels, but I did get through three of them, and I had to crash one on purpose because it was such a dud and they wouldn't give me another. Now I love my Snipe. Let's go upstairs in the morning. One last time. Say goodbye to my bus. And you say goodbye to yours.'

'The only answer is to marry a rich woman and buy one.'

'You can buy them for a song these days. But where would I put it? And I'm married already.'

'So you are. Poor bugger. So am I. Poor bugger. Thank God for the children, eh? Only thing that makes it worthwhile.'

'Thank God for the children,' said Daniel, thinking of Esther, tucked up and asleep in Eltham.

'I think I'm going to be sick,' said Fluke.

'You know what, Fluke? We did win an astounding victory.'

'Did we?'

'Against ourselves. We did reckless things, got terrified for months on end 'til we were so FSD'd that we came out the other side in a loop and did it all some more and again and again, and we did it by always winning against our sensible selves. We beat the Huns too. That's something.'

'Did we beat them enough, though? The beaten always come back for another try. It's a matter of honour, isn't it? I come back when I get beaten. That's how I got that bright green Fokker that forced me down at Amiens. And they still think they're better than us. I blame Beethoven.'

'Beethoven?'

'Bound to make you arrogant if you've got the best composer.'

'I expect we'll get the woofits now, *ad aeternitatem*,' said Daniel sadly.

87

Here's to the Boys

Daniel Pitt left the RAF with great misgivings and much heartsickness. He had loved the wild and thrilling times he had recently passed through, but like everyone else who survives in an armed service after the end of a war, he had realised that the last thing anyone wants in such a peacetime service is a warrior with real combat experience. After the fighting, the time arrives for merely keeping things running smoothly. If it moves, salute it; if it doesn't, polish it. People who remember how things were done, what works and what does not, are of no further use to those who are compiling books of regulations, and watching their own backs as they enforce them. Daniel realised that there was no point whatsoever in being a warrior when there was no war to speak of.

In addition he knew that the last two years of the war had taken a terrible toll on him. The stress of fighting is cumulative, and the measures you take to deal with it never quite meet the need. There are a few men who are utterly fearless, but most men have a bank of courage which one can only draw upon until the account is empty. An overdraft on this bank is an impossibility. Like everyone else in the mess he had, almost every night, consumed pints of whisky that should have killed him, and like everyone else he had smashed up the furniture and made a fool of himself every time there was a binge, and you had a binge every time one of your comrades was posted away or survived a crash. He had sung idiotic songs, danced on tables, fallen off tables, woken up in the wrong hut, vomited, gone out and railed at the Hun night bombers, got sentimental and maudlin before passing out, had diarrhoea almost every morning, gone looking for local girls or WAACs from a Waacery because tomorrow we die, cursed the staff officers who stayed behind the lines and awarded themselves medals. He had flown missions blind blotto, stupefied and hilarious, and never been able to get out of his memory's vision the dozens of comrades he had grown to love or had only known for two days who had crashed to earth, leaving behind them fob watches, books, cigarette cases, accordions and violins, and bundles of letters that they had always asked should be destroyed in the event of their deaths.

Daniel had been both lucky and unlucky to have been a Camel pilot. Lucky because for many months the Camel was more split-arse than any other aircraft. It had all the heavy equipment packed into one area. It was built to be unstable, was prone to a sudden right-hand spin, and responded instantaneously to the slightest touch of the controls, which was why it took three months to learn to fly it, and killed many unfortunate beginners. Once you had learned, it became an extension of the body. It could do the most amazing manoeuvres. If it were half rolled onto its back, the nose would drop, and you could loop up behind the very machine that had been chasing you. The pursuer would have no idea what had happened or where you had gone until you came up behind and got him in your Aldiss sights. The Albatri and Pfalz fighters had no chance against it, and the Germans stuck to defensive tactics that did not work, lurking behind the lines in huge formations. The Camels shot them down in droves, and then, months later, the even more split-arse Fokker DVII arrived too late to make enough difference to a lost cause, and in any case they themselves would have been up against the new Sopwith Snipes that also arrived too late.

It had been unlucky because the Camel was useful for strafing. The most nightmarish period had been during the last great German offensive. The Camels had gone out several times a day with their ingenious Cooper bombs, and had been shot down by the dozen by hidden machine guns that had only to execute the simplest of deflection shots. Survival had nothing to do with skill. The pilots suffered the roiling of their intestines and the wrenching fear, and then came home and raged against the horror and danger and sheer strain of it, and yearned to get back up high in the sky to engage in honest jousting with the Hun. When you bombed and machine-gunned the troops, you could see your victims reeling and dying, you saw the horses rearing up and falling over, the lorries catching fire, and if you had any sense you got away as soon as you could, went home, got tight, and tried not to think about what you had just done to other human beings, about what had happened to your friends who never returned, and you tried not to ask too many questions, not about what it was all for, because in reality few people questioned the righteousness of the cause, but rather about whether it was all being done in the most intelligent way. You could tie yourself up in knots. How often Daniel had sat alone, his head in his hands, in a hut with three newly empty beds, and then filled his nights with parades of terrifying dreams and the faces of the looming dead. There was a ground-attack machine being manufactured now, everyone said, called the Salamander, which had 650 pounds of armour-plating, and when it arrived the Camels could go back to the empyrean, where they belonged, but the Salamanders arrived too late, and so the Camels continued to fall to earth, sacrificing the marvellous skill of their pilots for the small reward of spreading terror amongst the enemy.

When the last great German offensive failed and the Allies began to roll the Boche back across the old killing fields of the Somme, the ground attacks eased up, but then you had your memories and your fear to contend with. You blessed the dud days when the cloud was too low, or it was raining, or the wind too strong. You accepted your day off gratefully, except that you felt hard done by if it was raining and you wouldn't have gone up anyway. During the worst times you even hoped to get influenza or a Blighty wound. You spent the rainy days wondering if everybody else had the wind up as badly as you did, and you discussed it only with those to whom you were closest, or you walked out into a field and talked to the cows and horses. You reflected that perhaps it was better to die young and strong, in your prime, as long as it was not, please God, by being burned alive. It might be better if you did die, because, after this, what else could there possibly be? You took your leave and your time on Home Establishment, because it was rightly believed that a pilot could only stand six continuous months at the front, but then you were back, and quite often you were killed on the first day, like McCudden in his SE5, who hit a tree on take-off, perhaps because he had forgotten about the extra weight of bombs, or perhaps because his engine failed whilst he banked steeply away.

Daniel knew that the memories would remain indelibly with him as long as he lived: the little *estaminets* where you could eat good food and drink good wine under the admiring eye of a mother and her daughters; the little propeller that drives the oil pressure on a Camel; the pressure gauge that cuts out in a dive so that you have to pump by hand and switch over to gravity; the days as orderly dog; the pitot, the efell that would one day become the windsock; the conversations through the canvas walls of the latrine, where you would never know who else was there until they spoke; the trigger on the joystick; pushing up goggles to see better; rubbing Vaseline all over your face on freezing days; the use of the thumb to block out the sun so that you could spot the enemy machines coming down on you; the configuration of the instruments in your 'office'; the way that batmen are really better than women, because they don't expect any appreciation; the woofing and clanging and coughing of archie; the crumping of shells; the pleasing novelty of Camel cigarettes when the Yanks arrived; the dud engine signal; the flight leader's streamers; the waggling of wings to warn of a Hun; the horror of your first spin; toasting bread on the fire of the mess; burning out the colonies of earwigs with a candle; turning over and breaking the prop if you have to land in a ploughed field; happy hours with your ack emmas and riggers when they have your machine up on a trestle to simulate the conditions of flight; happy desperate hours talking rot when blotto; the black smudges of archie as the Germans warned their own aircraft of your approach, and the white smudges of Allied archie that warned Allied pilots of Huns; the sharply painful changes of pressure in the ears on a dive; listening to *Chu Chin Chow* on the gramophone a hundred thousand times; bully beef; the terrifying but ineffective blobs of phosphorous that rose into the sky in strings and were known as flaming onions; the superstitions that came out of nowhere; being trapped in a shell hole between the lines when your engine failed; the horrendous mess bills that soaked up all your pay; the pilot who used to do a loop on take-off and could pull off a perfect Gosport landing; the happy hours of rifle practice trying to detonate a Very light from a hundred yards; the roar and clatter and blue exhaust of the Crossley tender; the shows and sallies during leave in London; being hung-over and biffo; the complete absence and preciousness of sugar; the rumours that the Huns were reduced to eating rats because of the naval blockade; beef that was really horsemeat, and why not? with so many horses killed each day; the overwhelming wonderfulness of the Bristol Fighter that was as good as a scout as it was for reconnaissance; Enos and aspirins for days after the nights before; the constant racket of night bombing and the glow like a rising sun on the horizon when an ammunition dump exploded; the unsubstantiated rumours of how the fleeing Portuguese soldiers were shot down by their contemptuous British allies; the blessed stays in hospital where the night nurses clumping around with their lamps turned out to be as inimical to sleep as heavy guns and Gotha bombers and night Camels and Fes and all the other minions of the moon; putting on a split-arsing show for the villagers on Sunday afternoons; chaperoning the Quirks and Harry Tates on reconnaissance; the pale earnest young patriots who could quote Shakespeare and Sophocles, who you took on Cook's tours of the lines to show them the ropes and then died on take-off in their second week; and above all the friends who were better than any friends you would ever have again, who died just when it seemed that they never could, and left a hole in your being like the absence of God. Well my lads, here's to the boys in the Bone Orchard.

88

Henley Motorcycles

So it was that Daniel, through the good offices of his father-in-law, found himself on a train to Birmingham, to visit the Henley premises in Doe Street. Birmingham was a city more filthy than most, on account of its many coal-fired heavy industries that added immeasurably to the smoke of domestic fires. There were days when the yellow smog was so bad that the vulnerable might drop dead in the streets, but on days when the wind blew it was a city as pleasant as any other.

Daniel liked the people at Henley, even though he found that the local accent took a great many months of getting used to, and it was utterly impossible that anyone might ever think it lovely. Henley was an up-and-coming company that produced beautiful machines and was keen on constant innovation. They had been looking for a man who could contribute on a number of fronts. In the first place they needed a safe driver who could deliver machines in pristine condition to the various dealerships around the country. In the second place they needed a man who was both bright and honest, to act as a salesman, and in the third place they needed a man who was an excellent engineer. Having spent so much time with the fitters during the Great War, when the other pilots were in the mess, there was not much that Daniel did not know about machinery. Perhaps what most persuaded Henley to employ him was his deeply respectable middle-class military accent and his astonishing war record. Fluke's enthusiastic letter of recommendation, on the other hand, carried no weight with them at all, since it was so plainly exaggerated.

Daniel's plan was to find a house for his family to live in, but in the meantime to go home at weekends, either by train or on the magnificent 1921 677cc motorcycle that the company had given him on permanent loan. It had a troublesome belt drive that had been superseded by chains in their other models, but

Daniel loved it for its weight and the wondrous power of the JAP V-twin engine. Having dropped it once, and thinking that Rosie and Esther might like to travel with him too, he soon attached a wickerwork Swallow sidecar. He discovered that you could lean in such a way that the combination could be driven with the wheel of the sidecar off the ground, which gave him almost the same sense of reckless satisfaction he had enjoyed when split-arsing about in the air or going on a sausage strafe.

The trouble was that going home was not always a pleasure. Apart from being reunited with Esther, by far the most pleasing aspect of it was seeing Mary FitzGerald St George again. Rosie's behaviour puzzled and exasperated him. Sometimes she treated him as a pal, though sometimes she was genuinely affectionate, and even playful. Her mother continued to provoke him.

He found himself humble lodgings in the home of an elderly Irish woman. There was one cold tap in the kitchen, and the thunderbox was out in the yard, next to the coal-hole, so he very soon acquired a chamber pot and emptied it out when his land-lady was not at home. In his room he had a tiny coal fire, and everything in the house was clean but worn to rags and tatters. He took adequate lunches at a cheap local hotel, and ate nothing in the evenings, until Mrs Burke noticed, and made him eat with her. She subsisted on braised ox liver, colcannon and potatoes cooked in three different ways, all on the same plate.

Daniel's reasoning was that the money he saved could be used to support Rosie, and to save for a house locally. They were cheap, and many of the surrounding villages were sweet and picturesque.

89

Gaskell and Daniel

1

The Grampians

Gaskell Old Thing, Beloved Green-Eyed Monster, etc. etc.,

I have foolishly gone and bought three machines for next to nothing from the Aircraft Disposal Board, which I have to collect eftsoons from Farnborough. They are an Avro 504 trainer, with dual controls, a Snipe and a Pup. I couldn't bear to be without a bus or two.

The trouble is, I have nowhere to put them. Do you have any empty barns on your family estate that are visibly yearning to house some heavier-than-air machines? I would be most rippingly pleased if you did. I could collect them when I have a more certain notion of what the future holds. I trust you have decent fields to land in.

Yours fondly and irresponsibly, and love to the ever-radiant Christabel, Daniel P.

PS Can I come shooting again one day? Not that I want to pot any poor feathered friends myself, because I am a far better shot with an aeroplane than I will ever be with a gun, but because I want to witness once again your extraordinary ruthlessness and proficiency in batting them out of the sky.

2

Our Lamentable and Disgusting Hovel in Chelsea

Dear Daniel, Irresponsible and Feckless,

All is arranged. A barn is cleared out, and the adjacent field will be mown and rolled, given due notice. But when will you ever be able to get up there to look after them and fly them? Don't you have any landed and moneyed friends nearer by? I mean, apart from me? Won't they fall into decay? What about fitters and riggers?

And the condition is that you teach me to fly. I am certain there are many aviation records for women that have not yet been attained. First to fly upside down to Austria? First to loop the loop twelve times with both legs down the same trouser?

No deal otherwise.

Affectionately,

Gaskell the GEM (Green-Eyed Monster)

PS Have just done my enormous painting of a decomposing horse. I am sure you'll adore it. You can positively smell the rot.

PPS Christabel's photographic The War at Home *exhibition has gone frightfully well, and she has made pots of money. Well, one pot.*

PPPS Does Rosie know about your latest folly? What is it worth not to tell her?

90

Daniel at the Gates of Death

Rosie received a telegram which said simply 'MR PITT VERY ILL STOP COME QUICK STOP MARY BURKE STOP'.

During her frequent fits of doubt and guilt, it had occurred to Rosie many times that life would be easier if Daniel were to disappear or die. Whenever these thoughts occurred to her, she was revolted by them and shut them off, knowing that they were unchristian, horrible and wrong, and during the times when she felt that she genuinely loved him, she had thoughts that were quite the opposite. It was then difficult to conceive how she might live without him. She havered between the extremes offered to her by the ambiguity of her feelings. Half of the time she looked forward to moving up to Warwickshire, but the thought of it also induced a kind of panic, because she loved to be in Eltham in the house where she had grown up, and most of all, she loved being with her father, about whom she worried constantly.

Now that Daniel was very ill she felt the same horror as she had experienced when she realised that Ash had been wounded the day after she had failed to pray for him. She flew into a frenzy of activity. She asked her mother to look after Esther until she returned, and told Mr Wragge to prepare the AC so that he could take her directly to Euston Station.

Hamilton McCosh had recently found Mr Wragge with the engine of the motor mower in pieces, decoking it, and had discovered that he was a formidable mechanic, as a result of which he had been bought a smart grey uniform and cap, and, along with a rise in wages, been appointed the family chauffeur. Mr Wragge had erected a wooden garage in the place at the side of the house where people used to tether their horses, and still did if the AC happened to be out. From the iron hooks set into the walls to hold cages of hay, there was now suspended a collection of inner tubes. Mr Wragge was delighted with his extra job, and almost entirely gave up sleeping with the cat on his chest in the wheelbarrow under the conservatory when there was little to do in the garden. Instead, he went and polished the AC.

Rosie was duly dropped at Euston with her suitcase, and Wragge left the AC ticking over outside as they went into the station to buy a ticket and look for a porter. Finding none, Rosie bought Wragge a platform ticket and he carried the case on board the train himself. When he came out, he found that a small crowd had gathered round the AC because it had overheated, and was generating an interesting amount of steam from the radiator. He went to a cafe, ate jellied eels and drank tea, and when he returned he removed the radiator cap gingerly, and topped it up with water from the horse trough.

In Birmingham the weather was cold, damp and still. It smelled of soot and coal dust and wet smuts and sulphur. When she descended from the train it was impossible not to cough. A porter, also coughing, took her case and guided her to the hansom cabs.

She was surprised by the humble terrace in which Daniel had found lodgings. The houses were filthy but well cared for, and the cobbles glistened like dark fish underfoot. The women had been soaping their doorsteps, she noticed. There was no washing hanging across the streets, as one would have expected, because today the air was too full of soot. Urchin and ragamuffin children in hobnailed boots kicked cans in the street, fought and played their clapping games.

After she had paid the cabbie she knocked on the door and waited. She turned to look at the street and noticed to her left that there was a sizeable pack of people of all ages running towards her.

She then realised why. Chasing them along, as high as the houses, was a dense wave of roiling yellow smoke. She saw an old man stumble and fall, and two younger men seize him under the arms and drag him. She turned to the door and hammered on it again, desperate to get out of its way.

The door opened and a small woman in early old age poked her head out. She saw the wave of smog approaching, said, 'Feckin'

Jaysus,' and nipped aside for Rosie to enter. She stuck her head back out and shouted to the smog as it rolled by: 'Missed again, yer feckin' gobshite!'

'Does that happen here often?' asked Rosie.

'Every day,' replied Mary Burke, 'give or take. It's all the factories and coal fires and the bleedin' rain and the cold. It's a brew.'

'It stinks,' said Rosie. 'It's horrible.'

'The stink'll be the brimstone,' said Mrs Burke with some satisfaction. 'It's the one true stench of Hell. It's the twenty-four-carat fart of the Devil.'

'We often get fogs like that in London. You can get completely lost quite suddenly, because you can't see anything at all.' She held out her hand. 'I'm Rosie Pitt,' she said, and Mrs Burke replied, 'I was hopin' yer was. You'd better be coming up the stairs, and mind yer head on the low bit. This house was built for the faeries, so it was.'

'Do you believe in the faeries?' asked Rosie, who had been particularly fond of her Irish wounded at Netley, and had held many conversations with them on the subject of the Little People. Mary Burke replied, 'Course I don't. I'm not stupid.' She paused and added, 'They're still there, though. But you shouldn't be talking about them at all. It's highly unlucky to go in for superstition, so it is.'

Rosie found that Mrs Burke had done her very best for Daniel. The small fire was generously banked up with incandescent orange coals, and the patient would certainly be warm enough. There were other signs of care. An apple, a jug of water. A crucifix with a rosary wrapped around it was on his bedside table, propped upright against the wall. Rosie looked down at the unconscious face, with its mouth open as Daniel's sterterous breath rattled.

'What happened?'

'Well, he got a headache for two days, and that knocked him out. Then he was in and out of his mind for two days, and couldn't do a thing, you know, too weak to talk even. Then he had the collywobbles and the vomits, and then he had the hot and cold shivers, and the hot and cold sweats, and then he was all right, or so I was thinking, and then I was just on my knees with thankfulness, and he goes back to bed and can hardly breathe at all and it hurts too much to cough, and he coughed up brown stuff. And it was then I sent for yer. Poor boy, poor boy.'

'You must let me pay you back for the cost of the telegram,' said Rosie.

'Be gone wid yer!' exclaimed Mrs Burke. 'He's like me own son. If you love that boy like I love that boy, he's a lucky feller!'

'He's had influenza and now I think he's got pneumonia,' said Rosie.

'I knew it, I knew it,' muttered Mrs Burke.

'Did you get in a doctor?' asked Rosie.

'Heavens, no. He was askin' fer yerself. He was saying, "My Rosie's a nurse, my Rosie's a nurse."'

Rosie said to Mrs Burke, 'If you don't mind I'll be the only one in this room, just to keep out the risk of infection, and if you want to come in, could you put a mask across your mouth and nose? A clean tea towel would do.'

'I'll be glad to be handin' 'im over,' replied Mrs Burke. 'The responsibility and the worry was surely killin' me. How long d'you think you'll be stayin'?'

'The crisis comes in seven to nine days,' said Rosie, 'then the temperature drops and I'll take him home if he's still with us. Mind you, I suppose it could be PUO.'

'PUO? What the devil would that be, I'm wondering?'

'Pyrexia of unknown origin. There was a plague of it amongst the soldiers and airmen in the last year of the war. It was thought to be a bacterium and not a virus. It was just as bad as one. It sometimes turns into TB, or so I'm told.'

'Jaysus, Jaysus,' lamented Mrs Burke, and she retired down the stairs to put on the kettle.

Rosie settled happily back into nursing. She loved the sheer purpose of it, and she loved the caring of it. It took her completely out of herself, and it was a pleasure to be watching so eagerly for the signs of deliverance. If she had only one patient, it gave her an immense amount of time for thinking, reading and praying. She looked around the tiny room and memorised every single feature of it. She stood at the window and watched the rain.

She propped Daniel up, knowing that a pneumonia patient

should not be lying down, and she listened to his chest. She was sure that the disease was single rather than double. She ran through all the possible complications and sequelae in her mind: pericarditis, meningitis, abcess, gangrene, colitis, nephritis, jaundice, empyrema, thrombosis – killers, all of them. When she washed him she discovered that he had three bullet wounds, and a burn, and wondered why she had never noticed them before. She thought often of Hutch, and of poor Millicent, rigid with grief and loss, but unable to let it show. She had lost Hutch, but she was certain that she could save Daniel.

Rosie slept in the only easy chair in Daniel's room, and in the morning went out and returned with a bedroll and sleeping bag from the Army & Navy store. She also bought carbolic, a steel dish for the infected sputum, mouthwash and gargle for herself, Friar's Balsam, imperial drink, sodium bicarbonate, calf's foot jelly, Brand's meat essence, Valentine's meat juice, orange juice, cascara and Dover's powder. She very much hoped that she would not need oxygen.

The first time Daniel opened his eyes and saw her, he just said, 'Darling Rosie, I'm a complete WO,' and closed them again.

'Well, I'm not writing you off,' said Rosie.

Rosie went to see Daniel's colleagues at Henley Motorcycles, and was touched by their concern, and their insistence on Daniel taking off as much time as he needed. They told her that they had been making plans to export to France, and that then Daniel would be quite indispensible. They told her what prestige it brought them to have a colleague who was such a well-known fighter ace, with twenty-five victories and the DFC. It was the first time that Rosie had ever given a thought to him being anything other than the boy who used to live next door. It occurred to her that poor Ash, though no less a man, had not really managed to achieve anything at all. They said that when Daniel was ready to go home and convalesce, the boss would drive them both home personally in his Bentley, and he said that on the way he would show them a lovely little house in Wootton Wawen that might suit them very well.

When she was not tending to Daniel, Rosie went downstairs and helped Mrs Burke. She was an irredeemable tittlemouse, and everything needed to be repeatedly scrubbed, dusted and inspected. Mrs Burke showed Rosie how to make colcannon, and they fried up a great many sausages and slices of liver, creating overflowing white jugs of dark gravy with which to drench them.

Quite often they talked about Ireland. Rosie said she had never been, and Mrs Burke observed, 'You'd better be going soon, before we're all long gone.' She told Rosie that the reason she was in England was that she had 'married a feckin' Proddy dog, and the fecker died, and now I can't go feckin' home'. They talked about St Brigid and religion in general, and about the last Pope who was a saint, and many times they set the world to rights. They drank stupendous quantities of thick tea made with condensed milk, and Mrs Burke poured some whiskey in Rosie's tea, just for the craic. Rosie thought how sad it was that her mother would never invite someone like Mrs Burke to stay, and wondered briefly what it would be like to have the nice little house in Wootton Wawen, so that she might see the entertaining and convivial Mrs Burke again.

Rosie had lost her snobbery at Netley, and after tending so many soldiers in agony, had become completely immune to picturesque speech. She loved being with Mrs Burke, and realised that she was going to miss her, when, on the ninth day, Daniel's temperature broke and his fever subsided.

A week later, with Daniel wrapped up in an eiderdown and looking very like the Michelin Man, they were delivered home to Eltham in the Bentley.

Here Daniel, who had been pining for a cigarette, lit one up, inhaled deeply, and doubled over and choked. He was so disgusted that he threw the thing in the fire and ran to wash out his mouth with Listerine. 'Never a-bloody-gain,' he declared. 'That is absolutely bloody vile. Why the hell did I ever take it up, for God's sake?'

Rosie thought, 'Ash didn't smoke, and now Daniel doesn't.'

Daniel was weak for a long time, and felt terribly cold at night, so Rosie climbed in beside him, and spooned him for warmth. They had grown closer on account of the crisis. He bought her a silver necklace with an amethyst in it, for saving his life. She often questioned herself as to why everyone else loved and esteemed him so much better than she did. She was beginning to understand that it is not enough to love someone deeply; you also have to learn to love them well.

91

Millicent's Interview

'A policeman!' exclaimed Mrs McCosh. 'A policeman!'

'Yes, madam,' said Millicent. 'You do know him. I mean, he's been here before. He's the one what arrested that man what killed the little boy with the AC.'

'I think I do remember him,' said Mrs McCosh. 'A big strong fellow.'

'Well, anyway, that's him,' said Millicent.

'You do realise that you will have to move out of this house, don't you? I can't have a policeman here at night. This is a respectable family house. One can't possibly have marital relations going on in it.'

'No, madam. But it's all right, he's a local bobby, and he's got nice lodgings, and his landlady says it's all right with her, until I actually start having kids, madam, and then we'll have to look elsewhere, because the landlady doesn't hold with kids. Nor Irish, neither.'

'You are most unlikely to have Irish children,' observed Mrs McCosh. 'Of course, one would normally expect you to leave upon getting married, but I am prepared to let you stay on until such time as you have children, if you wish. You're a very valuable servant to us, you know, Millicent, and it would certainly be hard to replace you. When you do have children, however, you clearly wouldn't be able to work here any more. You'd have to look after the child, would you not? And no respectable house that I know of has a maid with children.'

'No, madam. Unless there's a granny to palm them off on.'

'Well,' said Mrs McCosh graciously, 'I do wish you and your policeman every possible happiness. You will of course have to endure a great deal of degradation and humiliation, but I always think it worth it for the children that result, and if one holds out long enough, one's husband does eventually give up.'

'Yes, madam, thank you, madam.'

The following day, Christabel announced that she and Gaskell were taking lodgings together in Chelsea.

'But my dear!' Mrs McCosh had exclaimed. 'Two young women on their own? In such a very poor and run-down place? Who will have regard to your virtue?'

'We will watch each other like hawks,' said Christabel, 'and Gaskell does have a pair of Purdeys.'

92

The Incident

Daniel had gone to Cambridge on the train, and had found himself sitting in the same second-class carriage as someone who looked very familiar. They had for some time been sitting, studiously oblivious to each other as the British still are on public transport. The dapper gentleman was reading a book with the intriguing title *Principia Ethica* and Daniel was reading *Every Man his Own Mechanic*. The other occupant was thin and bird-like, but he sported a fairly impressive moustache.

Daniel noticed that the gentleman was struggling to light matches in order to rekindle his pipe, and Daniel reached into his pocket to offer his petrol lighter, which he still carried with him despite having renounced tobacco, because lighting other people's cigarettes was so much an embedded part of modern social ritual. 'Thank you so much,' said the dapper gentleman, in a voice that was exceedingly clipped and aristocratic, and before very long the two had fallen into conversation.

'I see you have most practical reading matter,' said the gentleman. 'It must be very interesting.'

'It is,' replied Daniel. 'It deals with just about everything that one could want to do. I'm learning how to harden blades for different purposes. Yours looks intimidating, if I may say so. Is it in Latin? I wasn't very good at it at Westminster.'

'You shouldn't be deceived by that,' said the stranger. 'It's written in very clear English, as a matter of fact. Do they still teach Latin in a very peculiar accent at Westminster?'

'They certainly did when I was there.'

'You can always tell an old boy from the peculiar accent. I was educated by a tutor, which may or may not have been a good thing. Which house were you in?'

'Rigaud's. It was remarkable solely for the thrashings and its appalling latrines. Worse than anything I saw in France. So . . . your book?'

'Written by a friend, 1903. I've read it hundreds of times, just to make sure, but I still can't approve of it. He's a charming man, however, a very beautiful and innocent spirit, an Apostle, if that means anything to you. I expect to see him when I get to Cambridge.'

'So . . . are you a don? At Cambridge.'

'I am a logician, mathematican and philosopher,' said the gentleman grandly, 'and I used to be a don, but I was turfed out, not least by my own friends. I am, I feel compelled, almost sorry to say, a pacifist. It didn't go down well. In fact you will probably not wish to speak to me.'

'I was in the Royal Flying Corps, and then the Royal Air Force,' said Daniel, somewhat stiffly. 'However, I am aware of the arguments. And I can assure you that just about all of us frequently wondered if it was all worth it. We didn't doubt the cause, I don't mean that for a minute. I mean we doubted whether the cause was worth all that damage. We suffered much exhaustion and despair, and I was often physically sick after I shot someone down, particularly if they went down in flames. In my case it was def- initely worth it because I am half French, and I had a motherland to liberate. If I had been entirely British I think I would have had far greater doubts. Are you, by any chance, Bertrand Russell?'

'I do have that mortification,' said Russell. 'You do not have to converse with me any further, should you find it repugnant, and I shall not find it offensive should you wish to move to another compartment at the next station.'

'I can admire anyone who goes to prison for their beliefs,' said Daniel, 'although not quite as much as those who risk their lives for them.'

Russell bridled. 'If I may say so, my objection was certainly not to dying for my country. I have never had any particular fear of death. I am certainly ready to die in a good cause, but I am not willing to kill for it.

'I had no personal stake in it, in any case,' he continued, 'not until they raised the age of military service to forty-five, and by then I was already in prison, where they forgot they had put me when they got around to trying to recruit me. In other words I was not in prison for anything that could be construed as cowardice, because I was not eligible to serve. I did write an immense amount whilst I was in there, however.'

'Oh, what did you write?'

'*Principia Mathematica.* A great deal of it.'

'In Latin?'

Russell laughed and puffed at his pipe. 'No, but it might as well have been. It concerns the relationship between logic and mathematics. I wrote it with a colleague, Alfred North Whitehead – have you heard of him? No? Well, the book is admittedly vast, and to the taste of very few, but I think it important. Logic is the youth of mathematics, d'you see, and mathematics is the manhood of logic.'

'But does it butter any parsnips?'

'I beg your pardon?'

'This book,' said Daniel, waving his *Every Man his Own Mechanic*, 'butters parsnips. It will tell you how to silver-solder, how to calculate the stresses in girders and how to relieve the stresses in cast iron, and even, at the back, how to make a rabbit hutch and a hen coop. The question is, sir, what difference does it make if logic is derivable from mathematics or vice versa? Does the fact of being derivable imply that that was whence it really was derived? What parsnips are buttered?'

The philosopher was only momentarily flustered. 'For me it simply has its own intrinsic interest and fascination. And, of course, when a theoretical advance is made, it is often an extremely long time before any practical ramifications occur to anybody. There are hundreds of examples, all of which have suddenly escaped my memory just exactly when I need them. Ah! Here's one! In the last century, gentlemen like Gauss and Riemann worked out some of the details of a geometry for spaces that are intrinsically curved. Well, this buttered no parsnips. We did not, after all, apparently live in curved space. And then just very recently Albert Einstein determined that space is in fact curved because of the effects of universal gravity. Suddenly one needed Gauss and Riemann because one needed a geometry of this curved space. Lo and behold! Gauss and Riemann have buttered the parsnips, long after they are both dead!'

'I haven't caught up with all this new relativity stuff yet,' said Daniel. 'I've been meaning to. I have a friend who says you can understand it when you're reading about it, and then when you've finished you no longer have the slightest idea what it was saying. You say it's vast? This book of yours?'

'Well, when it was finished I had to take it into Cambridge in a wheelbarrow. And it's highly technical. It's a pity, really. So few will ever try to take it on.'

'Why don't you write a version for duffers?' suggested Daniel. 'You know, the main ideas, as simply as you can, for the reasonably intelligent man who wants to know?'

'It would still be fearfully specialist,' said Russell, 'but there would be some merit in doing such a thing for other mathematicians and philosophers who just want to grasp the general points. I'm spending the summer in Lulworth. It might be an excellent opportunity to take such a project on. I shall certainly give it some thought.'

'What about a book for duffers about relativity?'

'Well, Einstein's little book of 1916 is perfectly good. It was very recently published in English. Still, it's not a bad idea. I do feel that far too many people are excluded from understanding science through no fault of their own.'

'Am I right in remembering that Rupert Brooke was an Apostle?' asked Daniel.

'Oh, poor old Rupert. Yes, he was. I always said he was the most beautiful man in England. He had a light about him. Almost a nimbus, one might say.'

'My wife adored Rupert Brooke, partly because she once had a fiancé who looked just like him. He was killed, unfortunately.'

'To be as beautiful and well loved as that, and then to die of a mosquito bite . . . well, what can one conclude?'

'I conclude that God doesn't give a damn,' said Daniel, 'or that the Devil is in charge and is masquerading as the Supreme Being, or that the Supreme Being is neither good nor omnipotent, or that the universe is an essentially impersonal and mechanical process and that all values are human.'

Russell gestured with his pipe. 'I see you have the makings of a philosopher.'

'That's very kind of you, sir,' said Daniel, much gratified, 'and with your grasp of mathematics, I dare say you would have made a fine engineer.'

'And buttered plenty of parsnips,' said Russell.

It was the day after his return from Cambridge that Daniel said after dinner, when the family was gathered in the withdrawing room, 'You'll never guess who I ran into on the train to Cambridge.'

'Oh, who? Do tell,' said Ottilie.

'Bertrand Russell!'

'Really? Is he out of prison?' asked Mrs McCosh. 'I hope you gave him a good drubbing!'

'A good drubbing? What on earth for?'

'Such a nasty, drivelling little man. He did absolutely nothing during the war.'

'He did protest against it, Mama,' said Ottilie. 'And he went to prison.'

'I can see why a Christian might refuse to fight in a war,' said Rosie, 'because it does say "Thou shalt do no murder", and Quakers won't go to war, and they are frightfully good people, aren't they? I just don't think that when a soldier kills for a cause it's actually murder. It's something else, horrible, but not actually wrong, unless he knows it's a rotten cause. But Bertrand Russell isn't a Christian, is he?'

'I thought it was "Thou shalt not kill",' said Ottilie.

'It's hard to know the exact translation,' said Fairhead. 'The original is, I think, very ambiguous.'

Daniel had felt his hackles start to rise, not at what Fairhead or Rosie had just said, but at what her mother had. Having lost the art of talking sammy during the war years, and seemingly unable to restrain himself, he turned and said to her, 'I thought you must be a pacifist yourself.'

'What? Me? A pacifist? Why on earth would you think such a dreadful thing?'

'Because, by all accounts, you did virtually nothing yourself during the war.'

A shocked silence took hold of the room. 'I was prepared to die,' said Mrs McCosh at last. 'I went frequently to Charing Cross to welcome in the wounded, and I even learned to shoot. I had many Belgian ladies to tea. I took fruit to the Cottage Hospital. And it is no small thing to run a house. And I kept a niblick by the door in case of invasion. I was quite prepared to brain a German with it.'

'You shot pigeons and rats, and one chicken, I believe,' said Daniel shortly.

There was a long embarrassing silence, and then Mrs McCosh said, 'Our lost son would never have spoken to me like that.'

'Has anyone any idea of what the weather will be like tomorrow?' asked Ottilie brightly.

Later, when they were going to bed, Rosie said, 'You shouldn't have been rude to Mother like that. It was very bad of you, especially in front of Mary. I really think you should apologise tomorrow morning.'

'I will apologise,' said Daniel, 'and all I'll get in return is more provocation about being French and not being her lost son. Rosie, you must move out of this house and bring Esther with you to live with me. I won't take this any longer. I ride for hours every Friday night to get here from Birmingham, often in freezing rain, having to mend punctures on the way because of all the horse nails, and I lose every Sunday afternoon driving back again. I'm too much on my own. I want to be with Esther; I don't want to make do with trying to talk to her on the telephone down a bad line. You don't know how it cuts me up having to leave her. And I've had enough of your mother. You see for yourself how appalling she is, and how badly she behaves towards me. Yes, I know, she's got excuses. I understand all that. We've talked about it a hundred times. But it's not fair on me. You must move out to the house in Wootton Wawen, and we can start to have a proper family and a proper marriage.'

'Esther's very happy here,' replied Rosie. 'She loves Caractacus, and she adores her grandfather.'

'Well, of course she does. We can take the cat with us, can't we? And I love your father too. He couldn't be a better father-in-law. I don't have a father any more, remember? Having him is quite some consolation. That's the problem, though, isn't it? It's your father you don't want to leave.'

Rosie flushed. She felt the anger of someone who has been told an uncomfortable truth, and has to deny it or evade it. Rosie chose evasion. 'Well, I do worry about him. He puts himself under terrible strain with all his speculations and investments. Sometimes we're actually broke for weeks at a time and he's almost at his wits' end. Then the money comes back in. It always does in the end, but it's killing him, I know it is.'

'I'm not giving you much longer.'

'Don't try to bully me. I won't have it. If I'd known you were a bully I wouldn't have married you.'

Daniel looked at her balefully, and she cast her eyes down. 'A bully, eh? And there's me thinking I'm a man who loves his daughter and his wife and wants to live with them.'

'I think I'd better sleep in my own room tonight,' said Rosie quietly.

'I won't sleep at all,' said Daniel, 'so I might as well be sleepless on my own. Goodnight. Close the door when you leave, would you?'

Rosie turned and left, closing the door softly behind her. She stood there for a while, stock-still in the corridor, wanting to go back, but then she went to her own room with a leaden heart.

93

Mr Hamilton McCosh Learns a Lesson

One morning Mr McCosh stood on the top doorstep of the house, berating the grocer, Mr Ives, who stood before him at the bottom of the steps with his brown shop coat and apron on and his cap in his hands. Mr McCosh was in an uncharacteristically bad temper because both the Malay Rubber Company and the Argentine Railway Company had failed to pay dividends on time, and consequently he was temporarily in a state of deep financial embarrassment. Mr Ives was a solid fellow with a glossy chestnut-brown moustache, and one of his ears flopped over where it had been creased by a bullet.

'Ives, how dare you?' bellowed Mr McCosh. 'How dare you come here demanding money in broad daylight? Have you no respect, man?'

'I have respect for those who pay their account when it's due, sir. Those who don't, sir, I consider to be thieves and scoundrels.'

Mr McCosh was astonished. 'You are calling me a thief and a scoundrel, man?'

'You owe me for six months' provisions,' replied Mr Ives. 'I have four employees, a wife and four children. You are not doing your duty by them, sir, when you force me to put them off work, or when my children get no meat and can't have shoes. You either pay me, sir, or you will oblige me to instruct a bailiff.'

'A bailiff? A bailiff?!'

'The bailiff, sir, will enter your property, by force if necessary, and remove goods to the value that you owe, sir.'

'I know what a bailiff is, Ives. You are threatening me with a bailiff? Do you know who I am, my man? Do you know what I do? I am an investor, a speculator! I build ships and railways and invest in rubber and gas masks and gadgets! Sometimes I have no money at all and sometimes I have an absurd amount. I move it

419

around the world. For six months I have had nothing, and next Monday I will have an absurd amount.'

'Next Monday, sir?'

'Yes, next Monday. Now get out of my sight, before I call the police.'

'You are welcome to call the police,' said Mr Ives.

'Away with you, man, away with you!'

Mr Ives turned and walked away, with considerable dignity.

When he returned the following Monday, Millicent fetched Mr McCosh, who emerged moments later carrying an envelope. Instead of touching his cap and leaving, as expected, Mr Ives tore open the envelope and inspected its contents.

'You have overpaid, sir,' said Mr Ives.

'No, I haven't,' retorted Mr McCosh impatiently, 'I've paid not only the account but the outstanding interest on the money owed.'

'That's very good of you, sir,' said Mr Ives, 'but I would rather have the debts paid on time. In my business cash flow is every-thing. Without the flow, everything seizes up, sir.'

'Quite, quite.'

Mr Ives withdrew an unsealed envelope from his pocket and handed it to Mr McCosh. 'Be so kind as to deal with this now,' he said.

Mr McCosh opened it and unfolded the paper within. He read: '"I Hamilton McCosh promise henceforth to pay Mr Ives for his provisions promptly on the due date at the end of each month." A contract?'

'Yes, sir, it's a contract. You sign and date it immediately, sir, or you will kindly take your business elsewhere.'

'This is outrageous! It's unheard of!'

'You have the choice, sir. If you do not pay on time, the following week your kitchen will receive my third-quality box, and the week after it will receive nothing.'

'Third quality, man?'

'Third quality. It's a box with the bruised apples and broken biscuits. Things a bit old and dried out, sir. Dented tins. Bread that's about to turn or got some mildew you can scrape off. It's what I do for those that's down on their luck, sir, and that way nothing gets wasted and the poor folk get something to eat.'

'Good God!' exclaimed Hamilton McCosh. He could envisage Cookie's reaction upon receipt of such a box, and the prospect was not one to be relished.

'I will take my trade elsewhere!' threatened Mr McCosh.

'You won't, sir, although you may attempt it. All of us round here, we have a blacklist, and we let each other know who not to do business with. You may find yourself, sir, going to market with a basket on your arm and buying third-quality stuff from duckers and divers.'

'Wait here,' said Mr McCosh, and he went into the morning room and signed and dated the contract.

'I appreciate it, sir,' said Mr Ives, tucking the sheet back into its envelope, and installing it in the pocket of his apron. 'And another thing I'd appreciate, sir.'

'Yes, man?'

'You will no longer address me as "man" or "Ives". I will address you as "sir", and you will address me as "Mr Ives". I was a company sergeant major by the end of the war and I got used to the officers calling me "mister", so I am sticking with it.'

'Good God! Whatever next?! Whatever happened to deference?'

'Died of wounds at Wipers,' replied Mr Ives. 'When you've been lumped together with people from all walks of life, deference ends up going to those who've earned it.' He touched his cap, turned on his heel and fetched his bicycle from where it had been leaning against the gate pillar. He mounted it and rode back to Mottingham with a light heart.

94

The Spring Clean

M rs McCosh had ordered the annual spring clean, once again failing to recall that there was no longer the staff to perform it. Before the war, all the servants had banded together to take down the curtains, shift the furniture away from the walls, clear up after the sweeps, and, above all, gather the rugs and carpets and take them out for beating. In a large house the whole business could easily take a fortnight.

Millicent found herself expected to do all of it on her own, and she was at her wits' end. Cookie was, naturally, cooking, and was disinclined to help, since she had never been required to do so before. Mary, since a lady maid was considered to be more than a mere servant, was unaskable. Mr Wragge had wrenched his back pulling up the last of the parsnips, and was groaning at home in bed, wondering if he would ever be mobile again.

Daniel arrived on his Henley late one Saturday morning in April, and, as he always did in April and May, reflected upon how extremely lucky he had been to be on Home Establishment and instructing at Upavon during Bloody April in 1917. He knew that otherwise he would not have survived the war. When he had returned to his squadron in July, he had found almost no one left that he recognised, and that most of his comrades had been shot down in ground attacks.

He met Sophie in the hallway, and she said, 'I think you've got a loose tappet. Your Henley sounds egregiously valetudinarian.'

'Gracious me,' said Daniel. 'You're right of course. I did notice, but –'

'You mean, it is stupendously teratitistic and inordinate that a mere handmaid of Adam should have noticed such a thing?'

'Honestly, Sophie! Teratitistic? Where do you find all these funny words?'

'If I need a new word, I make it up,' said Sophie, pertly. 'That one means "monstrous" I hope. The metilogomy is Greek.'

'Metilogomy?'

'Etymology, silly.'

'Well, anyway,' said Daniel, 'I do know that you know everything about engines these days. It just takes some getting used to, the way that everything's changed. Would you be offering to correct the fault yourself? I'm certain you know how to adjust a tappet.'

'Piece of cake,' said Sophie. 'But it's so bad for the hands, and trying to get the oil stains off afterwards dries the skin most terribly. Now that the war's over I am most sublimely content to be a non-practising expert. I am prepared to stand over you and offer advice, encouragement, expostulation and verba sapienti. Yea, verily, I am prepared to be thy Nestor, but –' and she raised her hands to show him – 'I've only just done my nails.'

'Hmm,' said Daniel, 'what a good egg you are. Is Fairhead here?'

'He is imminent, and shortly to be manent. In time for lunch I do hope.'

'And Esther?'

'Out for a walk at the Tarn with Rosie. Mama is cleaning her air rifle, preparatory to further columbal slaughter, and Papa is due back from the Athenaeum incontinently.'

At that point Millicent reversed by, dragging a large roll of carpet towards the withdrawing room. She was making virtually no progress, and was in a sweat and a fluster.

'Millicent! Let me help,' said Daniel, taking up the carpet under one arm. 'Where are we going?'

'The garden, sir. Oh thank you, sir.'

'What are we going to do with it? It's damnably heavy.'

'Beat it, sir. Get the dust out.'

Daniel found that a stout rope had been stretched across the lawn from a pear tree to a large hook set into the masonry of the garden wall.

'It's best if you put the carpet over at one end of the line, sir,' said Millicent, 'otherwise it droops something rotten.'

'What shall we whack it with? May I join in? I can imagine it's the Kaiser. Or my old housemaster. I can take vicarious revenge.'

'There's a carpet beater, but I like a broom handle. There's nothing like a broom handle for beating carpets with, sir. And laundry bats work pretty nicely.'

'I'll use the beater and you can use your favourite weapon.'

Daniel took up the beater and swung it at the carpet. He was immediately enveloped in a cloud of choking and foul-tasting dust. 'Oh good God!' he exclaimed, leaping out of the way of the cloud.

Millicent put her hand to her mouth, and laughed. 'Oh, sir! Excuse me, but you do want to make sure which way the wind is.'

'Just like take-off and landing,' said Daniel, spluttering. 'I'm afraid I am a most ignorant amateur.'

'It's not often a gentleman gets to beat a carpet,' said Millicent.

'I'm a quick learner,' said Daniel.

'We'll take turns,' said Millicent. 'You go that side, and I'll go this side, and I'll beat first and then you beat, and we don't stop 'til there ain't no more dust, hardly.'

'Righto,' said Daniel.

Ten minutes later, they carried the carpet up the steps of the conservatory, through the withdrawing room, and into the dining room. Daniel started to unroll it, but Millicent said, 'I've got to give the floor a good sweep and a polish first, if you don't mind, sir. The mistress has mixed up some beeswax and turpentine, and it's to get used up, sir, or there'll be what for.'

'It's all damned hard work, isn't it, Millicent?'

'It is, sir.'

'Didn't you ever think of leaving?'

'Leaving, sir?'

'Well, you could have worked at Woolwich or something. The wages were extraordinary, weren't they? They went up by five and six once, didn't they?'

'It was fondness, sir. I didn't leave because of the fondness.'

'Fondness?'

'I like it here, sir. I like Mr McCosh, and I like the sisters, and I like Cookie, and I even like the mistress. I like the cat and Mr Wragge, and I even liked the dog when there was one.'

'Bouncer. He was a good old boy.'

'And I didn't want to be a canary anyway,' said Millicent.

'A canary?'

'Those women at the arsenal, sir, they turned yellow, they did, 'cause of all the explosives they were packing in them shells, sir. We called 'em canaries.'

'Good Lord, I had no idea!'

'And I didn't want to be a dilutee, neither, sir.'

'Hmm, I never thought I'd hear that word again. It's suddenly gone out of use, hasn't it? You say you even like the mistress?'

Millicent nodded. 'She wasn't always, you know . . .'

'Impossible?'

'No, sir, she wasn't. It was the Folkestone raid, sir, she was never the same after.'

'I know. Miss Rosie told me. She says the same as you.'

'Well, she had a friend called Mrs Cowburn, sir, and she had her head blown right off, and Mrs McCosh was there and found the bits of body, sir, and then there was the head of a little golden girl just sitting on the doorstep of a shop, and since then she ain't been what she was at all, sir.'

'Oh,' said Daniel. 'Thank you for reminding me.'

'It'll make a difference if you bear it in mind, sir,' said Millicent.

'You're right, Millicent.' Daniel paused, and then said, 'Is there anything else I should know?'

'There is, sir, but it's not my place.'

'I absolutely promise not to tell anyone anything that you tell me. Word of honour. Hope to die.'

Millicent hesitated. 'Well, sir, she plays the violin, like an angel she does.'

'We thought she'd given up. When does she do it?'

'When everyone's out, sir, 'cept me and Cookie, 'cause we don't count. She takes that big Bible off the lectern thing in the morning room, and she puts her music there, and she plays like nobody's business. It's like nightingales, sir, all sad and lovely. And if she sees anyone coming in the drive, she packs it all up straight away, and the Bible goes back on the stand, like she's ashamed or something.'

'Well, gracious me. I never would have guessed.'

'She's as good as anyone could be,' said Millicent. She looked up at him and bit her lip. 'Not that I know about it much, sir.'

'There's something else, isn't there?'

'Well, sir, she's as good at golf as Mr McCosh is, and it was 'er when she was ladies' captain who got the rules changed at the club, so the ladies could play on the men's.'

'And could the men play on the ladies'?'

'Dunno, sir.'

'There's something else, isn't there?'

'Well, sir, please don't, like, pass it on, sir.'

He held up two fingers. 'Scout's honour.'

'Well, sir, when she was young she was led on something rotten by that Lord Denmore. Right up the garden path, sir, and it nearly did for her altogether, sir. That's why she married so late in life, sir. She's older than the master, by a long chalk.'

'How long is a long chalk?'

''Bout five years, sir. And another thing, sir, the mistress was a suffragette. Caused quite a stir.'

'I seem to remember Miss Rosie telling me that once. A suffragette? Not a suffragist?'

'No, sir, a proper "ette". She was out and about with them Pankhursts. Going to them WSPC meetings at the Queen's Head, and them suffragette teas.'

'Good Lord – was she throwing bricks at windows and jumping out in front of horses, and getting force-fed?'

'Don't know, sir. The coppers didn't get her, far as I know. She was on the Conservative Association too, sir. Still is.'

'And what did Mr McCosh think of her being out and about with the Pankhursts?'

'Mr McCosh has always been a bit ahead, hasn't he? He said as far as he was concerned she damned well ought to have the vote. And me too, come to that. Excusing the language, sir.'

'How do you know all this, Millicent?'

'Gets passed down the servants, sir. We know more about that lot than they do.'

'Millicent, do you like compliments?'

'My mum said never trust a gentleman with compliments.'

'Your mother was right, but nonetheless, I want to say that I think you're a delightful girl. I hope everything works out for you.'

'Can I tell you something what's been bothering me, sir?'

'Yes, Millicent, of course.'

'You won't take it wrong of me?'

'I very much doubt it.'

'Well, sir, if you don't mind me saying, sir, I think you should take Miss Rosie to France and go and visit Mr Ashbridge's grave.'

'Do you? Good Lord, I never –'

'I did something like that, sir. I went to see my Hutch. I went with Dusty, and now me and Dusty's married, and everything's all right.'

'It worked for you, eh?'

'Yes, sir.' She looked around, as if suspicious of being watched. 'The mistress will tell you off for helping me, you know, sir. Improper and all that, she'll call it.'

'I rather fear that she will.'

That evening Daniel was in the conservatory enjoying the light pattering of rain on the glass, when Fairhead came in.

'Ah, there you are. Avoiding the lady of the house again, I take it? Not on deep patrol today?'

'No, I'm not avoiding her. I'm beginning to think I should make more allowance, in fact. I've received some sobering revelations. People have a far greater hinterland than you can possibly imagine, don't you think? Besides, as you know, she's recovering in bed.'

'From having her finger severely bitten by a parrot when she called on Mrs Smart,' said Fairhead. 'You'd think that a woman of her age and experience would know better than to offer her finger to a parrot.'

'You would. Anyway, to get back to your question – they're all playing cards, and I really don't enjoy cards any more. We played a vast amount in the Flying Corps, when the weather was dud. If you got hold of a book, it was like finding the Holy Grail. Thank God I could read books in French. Obviously they were easier to find. I used to like chess, but my opponent got a Blighty wound, and when he came back he was shot down the day after. It's surprising how quickly one lost the knack. Have you noticed that there aren't any gasbag cars any more?'

'I have now that you've mentioned it. You don't seem very cheerful. Got a fit of the glums?'

'Feeling a bit useless. What exactly am I for, Fairhead?'

'I think you're for giving Esther and Rosie the best possible life.'

'I'm really not useful unless there's a war on,' said Daniel.

'Twitchy, eh?' said Fairhead. 'Don't blame you actually. Comes to me often enough. When you've been biting on red meat for years, you've got no patience for fairy cake and meringue, have you?'

'Everything I learned will be lost,' said Daniel. 'I am an encyclopedia of redundant information.'

'Example?'

'Well, a tank trail looks exactly like a snail trail, except with a tank on the end of it. And if you want to hear what shells sound like when they're passing by, you can just switch off the engine. And, if you want to go out and shoot down a balloon, you should load the belt in groups of three. First a Sparklet, so you can see where the bullets are going, then a Brock to blow the fabric open, and then a Pomeroy or a Buckingham to set the gas on fire.'

Fairhead absorbed this information, got out his pipe, packed it thoughtfully and lit it.

'I see what you mean,' he said at last. 'That's pretty damned useless.'

95

The Interview with Mr McCosh

'Daniel, dear boy, how do you feel about being my partner in a four ball against the One-Armed Golfers Association team? You're reasonably good, aren't you?'

'I'm down to fourteen, sir.'

'Perfectly acceptable. You can't make any allowances for these one-armed fellows, you know. It's going to be tough. One of them's almost scratch. And how is it going at Henley's?'

'Very well, sir. The turnover is good, and all the new ideas are working out. The oil-cooled Bradshaw engine's a big success, and we've got a supersport version with Blackburne engines and a sidecar. We win a great many races, and that's how you sell.'

'Still driving everywhere in a truck? Delivering?'

'Yes, sir, but I do a lot more than that. We're setting up in France.'

'Um, well, my boy, I have cornered you in this manner because I am well aware that the situation cannot go on as it is.'

'The situation, sir?'

'Yes, the situation. The antagonism between you and Mrs McCosh is painful to all of us, including yourselves. Let me put this all in order, eh? Firstly, you have to keep coming here to be with your wife and daughter, and secondly, Rosie havers and dithers about leaving this house and going to live with you in Birmingham, even though you've got a lovely house in a pretty village.'

'Yes, sir.'

'And thirdly, you and Mrs McCosh have become mortal enemies, and fourthly, the occupation you currently have is some-what below your natural level of ability.'

'I wouldn't say that, sir. It's very interesting, and not at all easy. As you know, I'm very set on engineering. Engineering is the whole future of the world. And naturally one often has to start at the bottom and work up, and, as I said, I expect to be going to France quite a lot.'

'Quite so, quite so, but how would you feel about the prospect of a job where the machinery is magnificent and enormous, and made in Birmingham to boot, and the climate exquisite, and where you can live like a king?'

'Is one able to fly there?'

'I've no idea. I'm talking about Ceylon, old boy. Ceylon!'

'Ceylon, sir?'

'Ceylon, Daniel! The Pearl of the East!'

'I loved it in India.'

'Well, I have a friend who is looking for a manager. It's a long shot, but they lost an assistant manager who ran off with another planter's wife, and there's been no sight nor sound of him for months. I told him all about you, and he recognised the name. My dear boy, I knew you were distinguished, but I had no idea until now how famous an ace you actually were. Why on earth didn't you tell us? How did that pass us by?'

'Didn't seem worth mentioning, sir. As far as aces go, I'd say I was in the first rank of the second-raters.'

'You are altogether too modest. I asked him what he wanted exactly, and he said he would show you the ropes, and then expect you to manage mostly on your own. You'd have to be good with the natives, learn Tamil, and keep your hands off the wives. You also have to be good at sport, or you won't have much fun.'

'I *am* good at sport. There's nothing I like better.'

'I understand they even have a wonderful golf course and some trout streams, and plenty of tennis. Well, dear boy, it would be a huge adventure and a tremendous opportunity. Are you prepared to take the gamble?'

'I'd be very sorry to leave Henley's. But yes. I think so. I'd do it. The question is, would Rosie? I couldn't possibly leave Esther for any length of time. It's bad enough having to be away in the week.'

'If Rosie is difficult, I will have to steel myself to order her out of the house. We are in a knot, Daniel, and someone has to cut it. First of all we have to see if you and Colonel Bassett get on, of course. I've invited him to Sunday lunch.'

'Colonel? He was a soldier?'

'Indian Army. One of the Sikh regiments, I believe.'

'We'll certainly get on then.'

And they did. No one else at lunch got a word in, because all the talk was of Sikh regiments and sepoys.

Because Daniel was thirty years old, much older than the average 'creeper' who came out to learn the ropes, and because he was bringing a wife and child, he was to be treated less harshly than the youngsters. He would have servants, and his bungalow would be a mere mile from the factory, but he would still have to muster at dawn, and he would have to spend six months in the company of a young assistant manager at his division. Colonel Bassett told him he would have to learn twenty new Tamil words every day, and be tested on them, and his pay would at first be a pittance.

The one thing that he would not tolerate, said the Colonel, was Daniel ever thinking that he had become an expert on anything to do with Ceylon and its people until he had been there for twenty years. Until that time, only honest bafflement would do.

96

Tea at the Fairheads'

'Gracious me, it's you,' said Fairhead, as he stood at the door and looked at his visitor. 'How on earth did you know where we live?'

'Well, I am psychic,' returned Madame Valentine. 'I have powers, exceptional ones, such as the power to read what you wrote in my visitors' book! And you have the only house in the street with an unpronounceable name.'

'Sophie's idea. It was called The Laurels, even though there aren't any.'

'What on earth does it mean? Paleo something or other.'

'Paleo Periboli? It's Greek. The Old Garden. Sophie has a notion that we should recreate the Garden of Eden in our own domain, energy and weather permitting. Ah, forgive me, do come in. My wife will be glad to see you, I'm sure. I think she's in the conservatory mangling some pelargoniums. Darling!' he called. 'Madame Valentine is here!'

Sophie emerged shortly, wearing wellington boots, and bearing a pair of scissors and a ball of green gardening twine. 'Madame Valentine!' she cried. 'How positively miradibulous to see you.'

'Miradibulous?'

'One of her neologisms,' offered Fairhead. 'Darling, should you be wearing wellies indoors?'

'These are my indoor wellies,' she replied. 'They leak, so I can't wear them outdoors. They are ideal for gardening in the conservatory.'

'The ultimate fate of all wellington boots is to spring a leak,' said Fairhead. 'That is the habitual manner of their demise. In the trenches a leaky wellington boot did more than anything else to make one doubt the love of God.'

'They make wonderfully eccentric flowerpots,' said Madame Valentine. 'Put them by the door with a geranium in each, or a little clump of marigolds. The leak acts as drainage. One can make use of one's misfortune.'

'I shall do it immediately,' said Sophie, kicking them off so that they flew across the hallway and crashed into the walking-stick stand, causing the canes and shooting sticks to rattle.

'Do be careful, darling,' said Fairhead.

'Henceforth I shall horticult barefoot in the conservatory, and leaky wellies shall be herbiferous.'

When they were seated in the drawing room, with their cups of tea on their laps, and Victoria sponge cake waiting on the trolley, Fairhead asked, 'And how is Spedegue?'

'Oh, grumpy and disapproving and truculent, as always,' responded Madame Valentine.

'If there were prizes for truculosity she would scoop all of them,' said the barefoot Sophie.

There was a pause, and Madame Valentine noticed the book that lay upon the small table by Fairhead's armchair. It was *The Historical Jesus and the Theological Christ*. 'Is that any good?' she said. 'I've been thinking of reading it.'

'It's excellent,' replied Fairhead. 'It describes what we can work out about Jesus the man from the synoptic gospels, and then talks about how he got theologised, if there is such a word. I should probably say "Christologised". The author assures us that there will be no Second Coming, which, I must say, is something I've already been suspecting for some considerable time. It's a marvellously clear read, but I suppose I ought to be resisting anything that might exacerbate my scepticism.'

'We strongly disapprove of exacerbation,' said Sophie brightly. 'It's so draining. And of course one should definitely eschew egregious obscurantism.'

Madame Valentine laughed, then composed herself, and said, 'I have come to ask you about something that is very close to my heart, and is causing me a great deal of unease.'

'Oh yes?' said Fairhead.

'Yes. Well, the long and short of it is, do you think I'm a fraud?'

'A fraud? Good God, no. Why would you think that?'

'I worry that I might be. I mean, sometimes I don't know the answers to things, and I just make something up. And then

433

sometimes the things I made up do come true. Sometimes I'm certain of something and it never happens. I can't tell you how worrying it is. And sometimes I think that perhaps I am, after all, just another madwoman of a certain age with delusions.'

'You're dressed very respectably in tweeds,' said Sophie, 'you can't possibly be mad.'

'Do try to be serious, darling,' said Fairhead.

'Oh, but I am being! Mad people nearly always dress up in odd ways, don't they?'

'If you were mad,' said Fairhead, 'it wouldn't explain the noises and the music and the strange apports at your séances, and it wouldn't explain why you get so many things right. How would it explain the photograph of my sister in Christabel's camera?'

'The best explanation,' said Sophie, 'is that you have an unusual but unreliable gift.'

'One clergyman told me it was a gift from the Devil, and he was using me to spread false belief and delusion. That kind of accusation is very unsettling. I lose faith in myself. I wonder if I should give up and simply teach music. I could scratch by on that.'

'Being a clergyman is no licence to infallibility,' observed Fairhead. 'The world is far stranger than I used to think it was. I have considerable doubts myself. When it comes down to it, I am probably more sceptical than Bertrand Russell himself.'

'Are you?'

'Oh yes. I question the truth of almost everything I used to believe.'

'Really? I suppose it was the war.'

'Of course. The men used to have a prayer which went "Dear God, if there is a God, save my soul, if I have a soul." I know exactly how they felt, as I felt the same myself. The way I see it now is that I am a clergyman because it seems like exactly the right thing for me to be, as if I had little choice in the matter. It is a vocation. I can console a dying person even if I do not believe in the virgin birth or the supremacy of the King, or even if I think the doctrine of the Trinity is an incomprehensible muddle, just to take some examples. I grew up Anglican, so this is where I fit and the place from where I inevitably start. I still see how beautiful my version of Christianity is. I still love it, as one can still adore an unsuitable lover or a cruel mother. I will work from where I am, in order to do what I am called to do. My advice to you is to see your gift as a vocation, and follow it through even if it troubles you.'

'As yours troubles you?'

'Indeed. As mine troubles me.'

'I have no vocation,' sighed Sophie.

'Of course you do,' said Fairhead.

'Oh, I think you do,' said Madame Valentine, 'you just haven't perceived it yet.' She sipped her tea. 'And there's another thing. I am concerned about your sister.'

'Which one?'

'The one who only came once.'

'That'll be Rosie,' said Fairhead. 'She stopped coming on the advice of a curate.'

'She would have stopped anyway,' said Sophie, 'you can't just blame the curate. She does what she thinks the Bible tells her to do, and that's that.'

'Oddly enough, a young curate did come and see me for a while. He wanted to know about his brothers. Anyway, that young man who was trying to get through to her when she came is still agitated and still wants to tell her something.'

'Does he? How do you know?'

'He tries to come through even when I'm not sitting.'

'What does he say?'

'Well, I don't know. All I know is that he's got something urgent to say. When I feel his presence I suffer terrible disturbance. It's hard to take.'

'Oh dear,' said Sophie, 'your gift is a bit of a curse, isn't it?'

'We're all worried about Rosie,' said Fairhead. 'It's clear that at times she makes Daniel extremely unhappy, and then they're all right again for a while. There's talk of them going to Ceylon. Daniel might have landed a plum job, it seems. Let's hope it comes to something. By the way,' added Fairhead, changing the subject, 'do you think it's possible that one can, so to speak, project one's spirit to another place when one is still alive?'

'Witches used to call it "sending their fetch",' replied Madame

Valentine. 'As a matter of fact, somebody published a book about it a few years ago. Um, it was called *Phantasms of the Living*, I believe. I can't remember the name of the author, but he was a psychical researcher, and he collected hundreds of stories. It was a frightfully big book.'

Fairhead found a pencil and pad of paper and scribbled the information down.

'Why do you ask?' said Madame Valentine.

'You know that I went to see a great many families of men under my pastoral care who were killed in the war?'

'No, but now I do. How very good of you.'

'It was remarkable how many people told me that they'd had inexplicable visits from their loved ones either when they were dying or when they were still perfectly all right in the days just before their death. And Daniel, you know, Rosie's husband, said that many of his comrades knew exactly when they were about to die, and gave him instructions about what to do, often with some urgency, it seems.'

'How wonderfully strange the world is!' exclaimed Sophie. 'Do you think that anyone will ever really understand it? I mean get to the bottom of it? I don't think they ever will. I'm sure that I won't.'

Fairhead reflected, and replied, 'Even if you did, how would know for sure that you had finally arrived? What is the criterion for arrival? Wouldn't you go on looking anyway?'

'I think you'd have to,' said Madame Valentine, 'even when you were dead. As far as I can tell, even dying makes us none the wiser.'

'It's wretchedly frustrating,' said Fairhead. 'I'm a minister of religion, and I don't think I really know a damned thing. Did I tell you about Caroline Rhys Davids, the mother of the ace? She wrote all those books about Buddhism. No? Well, she told me that after he was killed she had long sessions of automatic writing with a planchette, and that he came through very clearly. She said it was comforting, but when she began to feel a bit better she stopped doing it.'

Madame Valentine said, 'Did you know that fictional characters sometimes come through? What could be stranger than that?'

Fairhead stubbed his cigarette out, and said, 'Madame Valentine, what do you think of the idea of collaborating on some books on these subjects?'

'Collaborating?'

'Well, it's a fascinating subject, isn't it? I mean the afterlife, if there is one. Your experience is vastly greater than mine, but even so, I think I have enough for several volumes of my own.'

'I have no talent whatsoever for writing,' said Madame Valentine, 'I'm a musician.'

'Well, I do have some facility. I'll do the writing, and anything you do write, I can smarten up. Shall we? Shall we give it a bash? Think what a success *Raymond* was.'

'Yes, do let's. I have so much to get off my mind. I think it might help.'

After she had left, Fairhead said to Sophie, 'Do you mind, my dear? It was very spur of the moment.'

'Mind? Why should I mind?'

'Well, you know, working with another woman. On a project.'

Sophie laughed. 'Darling, I couldn't possibly be jealous of Madame Valentine. She is very obviously Uranian.'

'Uranian?'

'She bats for the other side. A tribadist. A fricatrice. The other Love That Dares Not Speak Its Name Because It Is Still Unsuspected.'

'What? What on earth are you talking about?'

Sophie sighed and shook her head. 'Do I have to speak . . . darling, she is very obviously Sapphic.'

'Sapphic?'

'Yes, an invert. Like Christabel and Gaskell.'

'Are they? Gaskell and Christabel? Sapphic?'

'You can't possibly have imagined otherwise.'

'I just thought that all the young men got killed, so a lot of girls are left out.'

'Darling, Gaskell is viraginous. You must have noticed, surely?' 'What?'

'Androgynous. Darling, she's practically a man.'

'Yes, but Christabel is really quite . . . feminine, is she not? I know she's fearsomely lithe and athletic, but even so, she's an English rose if ever there was one.'

'Well, I dare say she might have been attracted to a man if the right sort of man had turned up. But he didn't.' She paused. 'I've always wondered if Christabel might be a bit of both.'

'Ambidextrous, so to speak?'

'I expect there's a proper word,' said Sophie.

'Ambisexual perhaps?'

'I believe that "ambisextrous" is just catching on.'

Fairhead leaned back and put his hands behind his head. 'I really am very sorry that you've enlightened me. How am I supposed to feel comfortable with Christabel and Gaskell any more? And write books with a Sapphic medium?'

'*Amor vincit omnia!* You adore them and they adore you, and you firmly believe that Gaskell has the most fascinating eyes that anyone ever saw, and your pen name will be Valentine Fairhead, or Fairhead Valentine.'

'Better toss for it,' said Fairhead, 'or it might lead to bitterness. And for some reason I've just remembered that I think it's high time we got a cat. Caractacus is such a character, isn't he? It would be nice to have a quirky cat like that, with amber eyes and a lopsided moustache.'

'Hmm,' said Sophie, 'you might have been reminded because "ambisextrous" rhymes with "puss". Anyway, I couldn't possibly be jealous of Madame Valentine. She's not your sort at all.'

'Yes,' said Fairhead, 'I like little waifs like you, but Madame Valentine is "luggage in advance and heavy goods to follow", without a doubt.'

'She is macromastic and steatopygous.'

'Yea, verily.'

Thus it was that Fairhead failed to feel uncomfortable working with Madame Valentine, and the first of their books, *Intimations of Immortality*, was published the following year, in time for Armistice Day.

97

A Letter from Willy and Fritzl

19 *March 1922*

Very Honoured Captain Pitt,

We are writing with the help of a dictionary. Naturally when we prisoners were in Scotland we English learned.

We are aye much hoping that you survived and this letter to your mother's address are sending. We are ever thankful for your mercy and knightliness and we wish always that you with God's blessing go.

We have often asked ourselves what happened to our Walfisch. Did she live, and where lies she now? According to our opinion the Snipe a frigging excellent even more than the Camel was. We like to fly again one day, but now we for jobs are long time searching. We small hope. We want motorcycle shop to attempt. You know that our fatherland Germany buggered and scunnered is, but getting better.

If you still live, please dear Captain Pitt, to us reply. We should meet us somewhere and talk of aeroplanes. Come to Germany!

Fritz Hoffman and Wilhelm Spatz

PS While we prisoners were we have learned from the Jock guards mostly the bad words. Ecrivez en Français si vous préférez.

98

The Letter to Mme Pitt

23 March 1922

My dear Mme Pitt,

I write to you in some haste, but hoping that you are well, as I am.

My dear Mme Pitt, we have a sticky situation that I believe a visit from you may be able to resolve. I have no doubt that Daniel will already have spoken to you about it.

In short, Daniel has landed a most wonderful position in Ceylon which will suit him perfectly and, I believe, set him up for life. The problems are these, however.

Firstly, Rosie is extremely reluctant to leave the family home. Hitherto she has evaded going to Birmingham, which is perhaps more understandable, and also to Argentina, where there was an opportunity in aviation, but in this case she is flailing around for reasons that one knows are simply spurious, such as that Esther might get ill on the ship or get leprosy once she has arrived. I have told her repeatedly that the climate in the highlands of Ceylon is most salubrious, but she will not listen.

Secondly, Mrs McCosh has in recent years grown more and more arbitrary and unpredictable (and, one might say, eccentric) in her behaviour, and at present her greatest joy is to provoke Daniel into a rage by taunting him about France and the French. He may have spoken to you about this, and if he has not, it may be well to ask him. This would possibly not matter very much if Daniel did not have to come here to be with his wife and daughter, but at present he does, simply because Rosie is finding reasons not to go elsewhere.

Thirdly, I have every reason to believe that Daniel and Rosie do not enjoy proper marital relations. This is very hard for a father to talk to a daughter about, and Mrs McCosh's advice would almost certainly be detrimental to the case, so I would not think of asking her to intervene. You are a forthright person (I am sure you will take this as a compliment) and I suspect would not suffer from inhibitions such as mine.

It is my opinion that Rosie has never recovered from the loss of a much adored fiancé in 1915, and that this explains all that is otherwise inexplicable in her behaviour.

I have failed completely in the exercise of paternal or marital authority, through no want of cajoling, ordering and even shouting. Rosie's sisters have also failed in their many interventions. The situation is quite beyond us. I am certain, however, that the situation is not beyond you, and that a visit from you, carried out with the inexorability of purpose for which you are rightly renowned, is the one thing that might do the trick.

I will telephone you from the Athenaeum on the afternoon of Thursday next, by which time you will have had some time to absorb this infor-mation. When you see her, please do tell the operator at Partridge Green post office not to listen into the conversation after she has connected us. There is no excuse for it, and I find it most aggravating, as I am sure do you.

I look forward very much to seeing you. My dear Mme Pitt, you are my great hope.

Affectionately yours ever,
Hamilton McCosh

99

Daniel and Mme Pitt

Daniel Pitt turned his combination into the small gravelled yard in front of his mother's house in Partridge Green. Behind him the South Downs rose sheep-cropped, breasted and majestic into the air, and before him nestled the small detached house in which his mother was passing the remaining years of her passionate life in relative tranquillity. There was wisteria growing up the walls and prying into the cracks and corners of the window frames, and a climbing rose all but obliterating any glimpse of the porch. It was exactly the kind of house that Helen Allingham liked to paint.

All it lacked was a winsome dairy maid with a pail of milk in each hand. Instead there was Mme Pitt, with a tattered bonnet on her head, galoshes on her feet, a trug basket over her left arm and a pair of secateurs in her right hand. Daniel adored her. '*Ah, te voilà!*' she cried, dropping her impediments and advancing towards him with her arms spread wide. '*Une bise! Une bise!*' she exclaimed, kissing him on both cheeks before he could even remove his flying helmet.

'But how dirty your face is!' she said. 'And you have white rings round your eyes! *Comme c'est marrant!*'

'You should have seen me in the war, *maman*,' said Daniel. 'I was covered in black blobs of castor oil just about all the time. Got sick of the stuff. Had to put whale grease on my face.'

'*Ah, la guerre, la guerre*,' sighed Mme Pitt. '*Quel horreur, quel grand dommage. Ça me rend triste d'y penser. Viens, viens, je te ferai un* nice cup of tea.'

'*On parle franglais aujourd'hui?*'

'*Comme d'habitude! Comme d'habitude!* Why are you so *en retard*? I had almost given in to *désespoir*, and then *apathie*.'

'Damned nails from horseshoes,' said Daniel. 'Had two punctures. It's always nails from damned horseshoes. Every time I go out. The sooner we get the horses off the roads, the happier I shall be.'

'*Ça n'arrivera jamais,*' said his mother. 'How would we get along without the horses?'

'With motors, *maman.* You must have noticed. We've had them for about twenty years.'

'And *les chevaux* we have had for *des milliers,*' replied Mme Pitt, 'and they don't need gasoline.'

'*Ils ont besoin de foin. Une énorme quantité de foin.*'

'But the hay is in the fields! *C'est partout!* You don't have to make holes in hot places to find it, *n'est-ce pas?*

'*Vous avez raison, maman. Comme toujours.*'

'*Ne me moque pas! Viens.* I have made a cassoulet. *Lave-toi, et viens t'asseoir. J'ai du bon vin, et du vrai pain.*'

As they mopped up what sauce remained by scouring the dish with bread, Daniel said, 'I'm not allowed to do this in Eltham.'

'The English don't trust the pleasure,' said his mother. '*Autre pays, autre mœurs.*'

'I think I'm in the wrong country,' said Daniel gloomily.

'You would be just as *énervé* at home in France, because they are not English enough. And *ici* you are irritated because they are not sufficiently French.'

'*C'est vrai.*'

'Now, I have to speak to you.'

'*Je m'en doutais, maman.*'

'Rosie.'

'Yes? What about her?'

'I have a letter from dear Mr McCosh. Everything is not good. *Tais-toi!* I know everything. I am going to speak to Rosie and to her mother, but I am going to speak to you first.'

Daniel was thoroughly used to being told off and lectured by his mother, and, as he had grown more mature, he had learned to appreciate her advice. She was always humorous, never malicious, and was incapable of annoying him. In this she made a sharp contrast to Mrs McCosh.

'Rosie is a sweet girl. She is *vraiment sympathique.* You must make more effort.'

'More effort? *Maman*, I have had to exercise more patience than you can possibly imagine!'

'Rosie is clever and interesting, and she worked so hard all through the war that she is worn out completely. *Je crois qu'elle est encore épuisée*. Especially in the heart.'

'*Maman*, she is still in love with a dead man. She can't relinquish him. I have no idea why she married me. Sometimes she seems to love me a great deal, and sometimes she's an absolute stranger that I can't get through to.'

'*Et pourquoi tu t'es marié avec elle?*'

'I was in love with her. Or I thought I was.'

'Of course. And, naturally, you still are.'

'Strange to say, I also thought it was a question of destiny.'

'*Pas de choix?*'

'*Pas de choix. Exactement.* And I love Esther. I go back to be with Esther. I feel I will never really have Rosie. I've stopped hoping for a happy marriage, or any kind of marriage at all. Sometimes she's wonderful, and I think everything is going to be all right, but then sometimes I think that she did me terrible damage by agreeing to marry me and that I'll never forgive her.'

'I say that you still love Rosie, and the love is hiding under all the rage, *n'est-ce pas?*'

Daniel looked at her and said nothing, unwilling to agree. Finally he said, '*Je ne sais pas.*'

'*Tu sais! Tu sais bien! Tu l'aimes encore! Je suis ta mère!* Believe me!'

'*Maman*, being my mother doesn't make you omniscient.'

She reached across the small wooden table and the remains of their meal, and patted his hand. 'But I am! When it comes to my boys there is nothing I cannot know.'

Mme Pitt took a sip of wine and held it in her mouth for a moment before swallowing it.

'Marriage is like a wine,' she said. 'Sometimes it can only be drunk very young, and then it goes bad and gets worse and worse. Sometimes when it is young it's horrible, *affreux*! And then the years pass and it becomes wonderful, and perhaps you don't even notice, and then you realise that at last the wine has become beautiful and you are happy. Sometimes a wine must be left alone and sometimes it must be blended and tasted and changed a little. And sometimes someone must come along and turn every bottle over, many times. I am going to turn the bottles over, *tu sais*? I am going to go and see Rosie and your *belle-mère*, and I am going to be very blunt with them, I will say things that are cruel, and they will have to excuse me because I am only a mad old Frenchwoman. But I am going to turn your bottles first, *tu comprends*?'

'*Maman*, I see you're not going to let me do otherwise.'

'*Oui! Mon fils*, I know that you still love her. I think she loves you and doesn't know it. She has her dead man standing between, and he is blocking the view. I will tell her to look at the view.'

'*Maman*, have you ever talked to Archie? You must know . . . how he feels about Rosie. I did a horrible thing to him when I married her. I think I might have brought about his destruction. In the end, that is.'

'Archie *m'écrit*, and I write to him, of course. He adores his life in India, with his wild tribes and his ambushing, and his soldiers with their blood feuds. Yes, I have thought that it was very bad of you to marry Rosie when he has always loved her, and when poor sweet Ottilie has always loved him too, *mais je te confie quelque chose quand même*.' Mme Pitt leaned forward and patted his hand again. 'I am certain that Rosie could never have loved him, she would have dragged him down into the misery. But I am certain that she loves you.'

'*Vous en êtes sûr?*' Daniel felt a small wave of hope pass through him.

'Yes, but you must understand that Rosie is not a man. You have been with other men too much. A woman is not a man, *d'accord*? It is no good stating facts and reasons and good arguments and making accusations. *Il faut faire la cour. Il faut courtiser. Il faut de la patience, de la générosité, de la liberalité. Il faut montrer que pour toi elle tient sa juste valeur*.'

'*Maman, il est trop tard*. I only have my daughter. I doubt if I will have any more children. I hate to say it, but there it is. I'd like lots of them. Esther is the only good thing to come out of this fiasco.'

'It is not too late. I am going to go and turn over the bottles.'

'Good luck, *maman*. But what are we going to do about Archie?'

Mme Pitt stood up and looked out of the window, as if she could see through the Downs all the way to the North-West Frontier.

'I grieve for him,' she said. 'What can we do? *Je suis en deuil.* I lost your father over some *affaire d'honneur ridicule*, I lost your poor dear brothers in South Africa. *Archie s'enivre, et se cache dans les déserts et les montagnes avec les sauvages.* You are the only son left that gives me hope.' She turned round and said, 'You have so much charm, so much energy. Of course I hope.'

100

The Intervention of Mme Pitt

Mme Pitt arrived at the house like a man-o'-war in full sail, billowing with chiffon and taffeta. Her clothes were scrupulously matched and were of that lovely shade of soft blue grey that one sees on the back of a wood pigeon. Her hat bore a brim splendidly wide, and its band was trimmed with a single dark red rose, very cunningly made. It was most effective, being the only red item against the field of smoky grey.

Her arrival, although fully expected, had the same effect as an unexpected visit from royalty. The driver of the hansom, having carried her boxes indoors, bowed so low upon being paid, that she quite thought he would topple forward onto his nose. 'How perfectly charming you are,' she said to him, patting his arm, and he blushed to the roots of his hair.

Mme Pitt ascended the steps and entered the house in a blaze of invincible French elegance. '*Bonjour, tout le monde, bonjour, bonjour!*' she cried, and, ignoring protocol bent down first to hug Esther so tightly that the child stuck her tongue out in mock strangulation. '*Une bise pour ta gran'mère,*' she cried, pointing to her cheek. '*Encore une bise!*' she cried, pointing to the other. '*Encore une bise! Encore une bise!* Oh, but my! How you've grown! *Mais comme tu es devenue belle! J'espère que tu es encore sage! Tu es sage? Mon ange! Ma petite champignonne!*'

Mme Pitt seized the stupefied Mrs McCosh by the shoulders and planted four kisses upon her cheeks in rapid succession. Rosie received the same fusillade, as did Mr McCosh, who was so delighted by such a display of affection that the smile did not leave his face for several minutes. She held out her hand to Millicent, and Millicent curtsied. '*Mademoiselle* Millicent! How lovely that you are still here.'

'Thank you, madam, you are very kind, madam,' said Millicent, curtsying again.

'Cookie's in an awful flap,' said Mr McCosh. 'She says she's prepared to cook for the Queen, but cooking for a Frenchwoman is altogether beyond her!'

'*Ça se comprend!*' exclaimed Mme Pitt. 'I shall go down to the kitchen and help. But first, to business! *En avant!* I have come to say certain things, and when I have said them, we can all relax, and I can give Esther her little *cadeau.*'

'A present?' said Esther. '*Cadeau*' had been almost the first French word she had learned.

'No, I will change the plan! I will give it to you straight away, because life is short, *non*?

She reached into her capacious bag and brought out a large brown bear. She held it out to Esther and said, 'This bear is made in France, and its name is French Bear.'

'French Bear,' repeated Esther, taking it and holding it to her cheek.

'What do you say?' asked Rosie.

'*Merci, Gran'mère*,' said Esther shyly.

'*De rien, de rien!*' said Mme Pitt, leaning down and patting her face.

'*Gran'mère* smell nice,' said Esther.

'Is Daniel not here yet?' asked Mme Pitt. '*Bon!*'

She turned to Mrs McCosh, saying, 'To you I will speak first.' To Millicent she said, 'A cup of tea, my dear, but without milk or sugar, and very weak, *à la française.*'

'Oh, just like Master Daniel,' said Millicent, hurrying away.

Mrs McCosh, feeling for the first time in years that she had no control whatsoever over events, meekly followed her into the dining room. Mme Pitt took a seat at the head of the table, obliging Mrs McCosh to sit at one side. Mme Pitt said nothing at all until her tea arrived, by which time Mrs McCosh was in a state of considerable anxiety.

'I hope you have not come here to hector me,' said Mrs McCosh unconvincingly. 'I will not be hectored.'

'Well,' said Mme Pitt, 'I am very disappointed, I will not hide it. How can I hide it? My son is extremely unhappy, and you do nothing about it. In fact you make him more unhappy. You provoke him! He tells me that you provoke him beyond all possible endurance, and that your provocations are always about him being French, even though he is as English as you are, as well as French. His father was in the Royal Navy! The Royal Navy, not the French Navy. His father was an officer on the Royal Yacht. Is that French? Is that a French yacht? And furthermore, you provoke him so much that he can hardly bear to come here any more, and if it were not for Esther he would not come here at all. And furthermore again, he has won a job in Ceylon which is the opportunity of a lifetime, and Rosie is refusing to go, and you are supporting her in this, even though Mr McCosh has told her to go. Now, tell me, are you crazy? What kind of mama are you that you hold on to a full-grown woman and keep her tied to the apron, when she has a husband and a daughter, eh? Tell me, tell me.'

Mrs McCosh sat with her mouth open, quite unable to respond to such obvious truths.

Mme Pitt looked at her imperiously, and continued. 'Well, I for one will not stand for it. You will cease your provocations, immediately. You will tell Rosie that she has to go to Ceylon! You will tell Rosie that she has to be a proper wife, not switching on and off like a lamp! You will tell Rosie to find some love in here,' she said as she thumped her chest, 'and give it to my son. Now you will go and tell Rosie that it is her turn for me to be speaking to her.'

Mme Pitt was considerably older than Mrs McCosh, and the latter felt quite unable and unentitled to argue with her. She rose to her feet and found that she was trembling too much to walk. Supporting herself by leaning partially on the dining table, she managed to reach the door. She turned to say something, but found herself, once again, utterly wordless. She went to the morning room to recover her composure. She resolved to write a letter to His Majesty, and then go out with the airgun and see if there were any pigeons in the garden.

When Rosie came in she felt like a schoolgirl who has been hauled before a headmistress.

'You will sit down,' said Mme Pitt, patting the chair beside her.

Rosie sat down and folded her hands together, looking at them as they lay in her lap. Mme Pitt chucked her under the chin very lovingly, and said, 'Rosie, Rosie, Rosie.'

'*Gran'mère?*'

'You know this can't go on, you know it, don't you?'

Rosie nodded her head miserably.

'I will be telling you exactly what cannot be going on,' said Mme Pitt. 'In the first place, now you have married a living man you cannot be married in your heart to a man who is dead. There is no good dead man who has ever wished for this! Think how much you are hurting this dead man if he looks down and he sees that you are making unhappiness! If he sees your husband so unhappy that he would not come home at all if he did not love his daughter! If he sees your mother provoking, provoking, all about being French, and you do nothing to stop it! That you never say, "*Maman*, this is enough! Leave my husband alone!" Do you think this dead man is happy on high, looking down and seeing that you make a *grande pagaille* all in his memory? Do you think this dead man is pleased about your husband who is alive and is not being with his daughter that he loves because you want to stay at home with *maman* and you won't go where he works even to a beautiful place? What selfishness is this? You think this dead man is proud of a woman who is like this? Rosie, you are a saint, a veritable saint, everybody says it, but you also have the cruelty of saints. The cruelty that has no eyes. Have your eyes not seen that in this life there is one thing sacred? And this one thing sacred is the little children? And you have one of these sacred little things, and she is called Esther, and she must have a nest with a mother and a father in it? How does the bird fly with one wing only?

'And another thing. You are a bad wife in another way. Daniel has admitted it and I believe him.'

Rosie was by now sobbing, quite unable to cope with this barrage that was forcing her to see herself from the outside.

'Are you telling me to do my duty?' she asked.

'Duty! Paf! I am not talking about lying on your back and thinking of something else! I am talking about generosity, and *plaisir*! Are you a woman?

'I will tell you a secret. This is a Frenchwoman's secret, you understand, no? First of all, what did your mother tell you about, you know, making babies?'

Rosie wiped her eyes on the back of her sleeve, and said, 'Mama said I would have to go through great humiliation, but it's worth it for the children. She says that relations with a husband are the price you pay for marriage, and marriage is the price that a man pays for relations.'

Mme Pitt was visibly shocked. She shook her head slowly from side to side. '*Oh, mon Dieu, mon Dieu!* Your poor father. This is terrible! *Oh là là!* I will tell you what my mother told to me. She said, "*Chèrie*, a good wife is a lady in the drawing room and a slut in the bedroom."'

'A slut?' repeated Rosie incredulously.

'A slut, my dear. *Une salope!* She said, "God Himself does not see what those who are married do when they are alone He minds His own business when people love." And this is the most important of all: "If a woman does not bother with her husband she gives up her right to his fidelity. And if a man does not concern himself with his wife, he gives up his right to her fidelity." *Ça, c'est entendu partout. Tu comprends?*'

Rosie nodded her head.

'I am talking about *pratique*,' said Mme Pitt, 'I am not talking about any theories or what it says in any Bibles.'

'But women and men are so different, aren't they?' said Rosie.

'It seems to me that this is the excuse only. I ask you a question, OK? What do you call a woman who only gives herself to a man when she wants something from him?'

Rosie thought for a second, and ventured, 'A prostitute?' The word tasted vile in her mouth; it was difficult even to say it.

'*Exactement.* I believe that you have been interested only when you wanted the baby, and when you had the baby, paf! No more interest.'

Rosie flushed deeply and began to shake. She felt a most terrible shame and embarrassment, but also a rebellious sense of having been misjudged, and the sweat began to pearl on her head. She could hardly breathe. 'Are you calling me a prostitute?' she said at last.

'I call you nothing. I was, you know, asking like Socrates. You know what a prostitute is. You told me yourself. You work it out. You use your brain.'

Rosie bridled. 'Are you going to let me speak?'

'Well, of course my dear. Speak.'

'Isn't a . . . prostitute . . . a woman who does things with people she has no feelings for? I do have feelings. I realise more and more that I do love Daniel, and it pains me that I'm no good for him. I cry about it sometimes, and I don't know what to do. I was very fond of him when he was a little boy, and now I know him properly and I admire and respect him, and I do love him. When I accepted his proposal, I knew it was right. But I have always felt as if . . . as if I was being unfaithful.'

Mme Pitt leaned back and put her hands in her lap, looking at Rosie gravely. '*Chérie*, you are quite right, that is what a prostitute does, and I see after all that it was a *mauvaise comparaison*. *Je te demande pardon*. But, *ma chère*, you overcame your problem when you wanted to make Esther, *non*? And remember, you are talking about my son. He is not any man, he is my son, and I love him, and I am determined he should be happy.'

'I've been sick with guilt. And worry. I think about it all the time.'

'*Chérie*, I am certain that your dead man would not want you to be faithful to him. He would want you to be happy. He was a friend of Daniel, remember? And I remember him too. What a handsome and nice young boy! How we all loved him! To think he's dead, *ça me fait pleurer*. But he would want you and Daniel to be happy because he loved you both, I am sure of it.'

'What about . . . what about when we die?'

'When we die?'

'Afterwards. When I get to Heaven, who is my husband?'

'Can't you leave that to God? And I think the good Lord said that in Heaven there is no husband and no wife. I remember, because when I heard it I didn't like it! When I die I will go straight away to find my husband, whatever it says in the big book!'

Mme Pitt dipped a hand into her reticule and brought out a tiny lace handkerchief. She dabbed her eyes.

'Once I had four sons and now I have only two. They are the most precious things I have on this earth. If Daniel is going to be miserable . . . Rosie, I can't bear it!'

'You are telling me to do my duty, aren't you?'

'*Non, non, non!* That is what your mother would say. I am not at all like her. It is not a question of duty. It is a question of generosity, of *savoir vivre, savoir aimer.* So, Rosie, *ma chère,* you will go to Ceylon. You will be a proper wife. You will open your heart. You will please your dead man by making a living one happy! You will remember that your dead man was once a very good friend of the living one, and the dead one would not want you to make his friend unhappy. You will make little brothers and sisters for your daughter! And one day, a long time from now, you will look back, and you will say, "*Mon Dieu,* I have been happy for years and I didn't know." This is what happened to me, Rosie. This is what happened to *Gran'mère* Pitt.'

'I can't go to Ceylon.'

'*Mais pourquoi pas?* You must go. *C'est evident.*'

'I can't go. Esther would be broken-hearted to leave the cat.'

'What? Are you serious? Come on, Rosie, this is not believable! What is the reason? Tell me! *J'insiste!* Your father has already told me your excuses, and I don't believe them!'

Rosie looked down at her hands. After some time she lifted her head and managed to say, 'Daddy is going to die of a heart attack quite soon. I want to be here when it happens. I want to be with Daddy when he dies.'

'*Mon Dieu!* Die of a heart attack! How can you possibly know this?'

'He feels dizzy when he stands up. He gets pains in his chest and his left arm. Sometimes he's very tired. He spent all last Sunday in bed. He said he was "having a browse" but he was feeling weak.'

'What about the doctor? Surely you called in the doctor?'

'Dr Scott says his blood pressure is very variable, too high or too low, and he has a heart murmur. He told Daddy not to run for trains, and not to play thirty-six holes in one day any more.'

'But does this doctor think there is danger?'

'He says that we don't have the proper skills yet, to know what is really happening, or what we should do. But I was a nurse. I know what I think, and I think that Daddy is going to have a heart attack. Ottilie isn't as sure as I am, but she's worried too.'

'And does your father know what you think, *chérie*?'

'No, *Gran'mère*.'

Mme Pitt said, 'Well, now I understand a little bit more. *Comprendre c'est pardoner, n'est-ce pas?* But you know what your father would say, don't you?'

'He would tell me to go to Ceylon. He already has. Lots of times. He shouted at me, and he's never done that before, even when we were little. It was horrible.'

'Have you spoken to Daniel? What does he say?'

'I've only told him I'm worried about Daddy.'

'You said nothing about the heart?'

'Only to Ottilie. I have a superstition.'

'A superstition?'

'If I talk about it, I'm afraid I'll bring it about. It's like worrying about falling in a ditch if you want to leap it. If you worry too much about it, you always fall in, don't you?'

'*Je ne sais pais,*' replied Mme Pitt. 'I have never in my life jumped over a ditch. But I know what you mean. Talking will often make things happen. But I do not think it will make heart attacks. Shall we agree something? Shall we say that if your papa falls ill, we will send a telegram, and you will come home immediately? I shall speak to my son, and he will not resist, *je te jure.*'

Rosie nodded. 'Even so, it takes two weeks to get back from Ceylon.'

Mme Pitt reached down into her bag and brought out a book, wrapped in blue-grey tissue that matched her dress. 'Here,' she said, 'for you. *Un petit cadeau.*'

Rosie took the book and clutched it to her chest. She stood up and faced the old lady, kissing her on each cheek. 'I know I haven't been the kind of wife that Daniel deserves.'

'Hush, hush!' said Mme Pitt, waving her hand dismissively. 'I love you. It's enough. One forgives if one loves. And now I know what has been going on in your heart, *ma chère*. And, Rosie, I know I am asking for what is not possible. It is my duty to my son to ask for what is not possible, *tu comprends? Il faut que tu m'excuses.*'

Rosie stood up and began to go, but then she turned and confessed, 'I just want to say that I've been telling myself the same things as you have. For ages. All you've done is make me hear them out loud. I know you're right. Daniel . . . how could I ever forget him vaulting over the wall?' Rosie bit her lip, clutched her parcel to her chest, and looked at her mother-in-law. 'The thing is, I've always loved him, without really knowing it. And now I have to make a new start. But leaving Daddy . . . it'll be the most difficult thing I've ever had to do. I just don't know how I'll manage to do it.'

'*Chérie*, I'm so happy to hear you say this. But there's been so much damage. How will you mend it?'

'I think he still loves me. It mightn't be too late.'

Rosie went straight upstairs to her room and unwrapped her present. It was a book about Ceylon, and was mainly pictorial. Rosie looked at its religious monuments. There was a photograph of an elephant at the Temple of the Tooth, very smartly caparisoned. There were photographs of mountains curtained with mist, of water buffalo wallowing in paddy fields, of the elegant bungalows of the planters, of smiling tea-pickers who were plainly gleeful that anyone might want to take a picture of them. She read the opening lines, in which it said that Ceylon was originally known as Serendip, and that Muslims believed it was where Adam and Eve had reconvened after having been expelled from Paradise. She closed it and laid it on the bed, planning to read through all the text later.

She picked up the Bible by her bedside, intending to look for the passage about husbands and wives in the afterlife, but instead came across St Paul talking about celibacy and marriage. 'Let the husband render unto the wife due benevolence: and likewise also the wife unto the husband. The wife hath not power of her own body, but the husband: and likewise also the husband hath not power of his own body, but the wife. Defraud ye not one the other, except it be with consent for a time, that ye may give yourselves to fasting and prayer; and come together again, that Satan tempt you not for your incontinency.'

Further down she found the solution to something that had troubled her for many months, which was the issue of Daniel's frank unbelief. 'If any brother hath a wife that believeth not, and she be pleased to dwell with him, let him not put her away.

And the woman which hath an husband that believeth not, and if he be pleased to dwell with her, let her not leave him. For the unbelieving husband is sanctified by the wife, and the unbelieving wife is sanctified by the husband: else were your children unclean; but now they are holy.'

Excitedly, she leafed through the pages until she found the passage for which she had originally been looking.

She knelt by the side of her bed and tried to talk to Ash, but had no sense of a response apart from a growing feeling of optimism and serenity. There had been catharsis in talking to Mme Pitt. Sometimes one discovers what one really thinks because of having to say it aloud. Now that she had talked openly about her father's health, the problem seemed to have got smaller. She found herself looking forward to Daniel's return, and went to the window, just in time to see him come into the driveway in a cloud of aromatic blue smoke, and park next to the AC.

She watched him fiddling with the levers, and then ran downstairs and out into the drive to greet him, almost being beaten to it by Esther, who was desperate to introduce him to her new French bear.

'Gracious me,' said Daniel, 'what a welcome! Shompi, what a lovely bear! Is *Gran'mère* here yet?'

Esther seemed to spring vertically in the air, landing neatly in the crook of his arm and puckering up her lips to kiss him on the mouth. Rosie put her arms around his neck and laid her face next to his. 'My darling,' said Daniel, astonished by her unwonted display of affection, 'how nice it is to be back.'

101

Ottilie

Ottilie was the quietest of the sisters, and on that account the most mysterious. She had the gift of serenity, and was capable of sitting quite still for an hour with her hands folded in her lap, which is to say that she had a rich interior life. She had survived her time as a VAD in Brighton without apparently having become too traumatised. It had instead given her an intense interest in the subcontinent. If she did not suffer nightmares, she did, however, retain very vivid memories of the heartbreaking suffering that she had witnessed, and of the utter exhaustion that had once been her normality. In the peaceful aftermath of such an implacable welter of death she had become someone who was surprised to be yet alive, her amazement constituting a kind of deep and placid pleasure.

Ottilie was fortunate in possessing a tranquil faith in her own destiny, knowing that something good and satisfying was going to happen, but without having any idea what it might be. It was simply a case of waiting, with patient curiosity. Her mission in this life was simply to make sure that those she loved were as happy as it was possible to be, and to go to as many lectures and talks as possible, in the hope that one day she would meet somebody at one of them who would sweep her off her feet and console her for the absence of Archie.

She had witnessed Christabel's unconventional attachment to Gaskell mostly with anxiety on the former's part. Like almost all her contemporaries, she had no clear idea of what such a relationship involved, either emotionally or physically, and so was protected from being shocked by it. She assumed quite naturally that Christabel would eventually meet the right man, marry him, and have children, and that Gaskell would be a dear friend to both. Fortunately, she liked Gaskell immensely, and found her inexhaustibly fascinating.

Sophie and Fairhead had so obviously and irrevocably created each other's paradise that she had no worry for them at all, other than to be niggled by the thought that every paradise carries within it its own tragedy, when it inevitably comes to an end. What on earth would Sophie and Fairhead do if something happened to the other? She had recently written a letter to them, ostensibly to congratulate Fairhead upon being appointed chaplain in a hospital, but really for the sake of the envoi: 'My dears, be extra sure to enjoy every single minute, won't you?'

Of her mother, Ottilie thought very little. She was increasingly eccentric and difficult, but her father was adept at jollying her along, putting his foot down when neccessary, and repairing any damage behind the scenes. Of his mistresses, who were the principle reason why he was able to continue to live with his wife, she knew and suspected absolutely nothing. His dizziness and occasional chest pain she mainly ascribed to his cigar smoking, and so was not as troubled as Rosie about the state of his heart.

As for Daniel and Rosie, the case was altogether different. They had not dived into natural bliss like Sophie and Fairhead, and they had not glided down into the mutual tolerance and respect that occurs as a marriage transmogrifies passion into friendship. From early on it had been clear that Daniel had been angry and confused, and that Rosie had often closed herself up, finding her consolation and satisfaction in Esther. Daniel, too, had only been coming home to be with Esther, pointedly embracing the child rather than his wife whenever he returned.

Lately, however, things seemed to have changed very much for the better. Rosie had at last become openly affectionate with her husband, and had apparently changed her mind about never wanting to leave the parental home. Ottilie knew that Rosie was obstinate enough to resist the pressure that she had been receiving from everyone except her mother, and now she could clearly see that Rosie was not behaving like someone who has been browbeaten or defeated. She was behaving like someone who has had a small revelation perhaps, or someone who has at last made the right decision and is proud of herself on that account. Her step was light, and she sometimes laughed as she once did before Ash was killed. A few days before Rosie's departure, Ottilie knocked on the door of her room and came in.

'It's goodbye soon,' said Ottilie. 'I'm going to miss you most awfully.'

'I expect we'll be coming back once a year,' said Rosie. 'A lot of people do.'

'Oh, but I might have absconded,' replied Ottilie. 'Who knows? I might meet an American millionaire and go to live in Guernsey.' She sat on the bed. 'Dearest, I want to say a few things to you.'

'Do you? Should I be worried?'

'Silly! Of course not.'

'Well, what do you want to say?'

'I just wanted to say that Daniel is a very fine man.'

'I know he is. Of course I know he is.'

'I want you to know it properly.'

'Properly?'

'Yes, really and truly properly with brass knobs on, and pink ribbons and silver bells.' Rosie laughed and Ottilie continued. 'I know . . . we all know . . . that . . . there are things . . . I mean, we all know that you can't get over Ash. I think . . . even all your religiousness is to do with Ash.'

Rosie bridled. 'No, it isn't. Without my faith I'd die of loneliness. And despair. And fright.'

'Well, it doesn't matter,' said Ottilie quickly. 'What matters is that Daniel is a very fine man, and that now you've got the chance to make a new start.'

'I know. That's why I'm going. To make a new start.'

'You've got to throw yourself into it,' said Ottilie, 'you really have. No half-measures.'

'It isn't so easy,' said Rosie. 'I have . . . you know . . . because of Ash . . . How shall I put it? I've been suffering from a disengaged heart. I've often thought that I shouldn't have married poor Daniel.'

'Am I right in thinking that, when you married Daniel, you were only . . . how shall I put it? . . . *demi-vierge*?'

'Ottilie! Why do you say that?'

'I'm not condemning you or criticising. I know you were

459

promised to each other absolutely. In your minds, in everybody's minds, you were married already, weren't you?'

'We didn't . . . you know we didn't . . .'

'Go all the way? Well, I'm sure you were sensible.'

'And obedient. It was obedience, that's all.'

'Obedient?'

'God's law.'

'Oh, I see.' Ottilie paused. 'But that didn't stop you knowing . . . many pleasures, did it? You did manage to be alone together an awful lot.'

'What's this got to do with anything, Ottie? Why are you questioning me?'

'Well, I've heard it said, and I expect it's true, that a woman gets terribly attached to the first man who, well, you know . . . and I'm sure that must have made it most awfully difficult with Daniel. Does he know about you . . . being a *demi-vierge*?'

'He hasn't said anything.'

'Let me tell you something,' said Ottilie, putting her hand on her sister's arm. 'When I was at Brighton, at the Pavilion, with all those Mahommedans and Hindus and Sikhs, well, just about all of them have arranged marriages. You know, Mummy and daddy arrange for someone suitable. None of them marries for love, Rosie, but do you know what? You know how wounded men talk, late at night, when they are in too much pain to sleep, and someone is having a nightmare and yelling? And all you can do is hold a man's hand and listen?'

Rosie nodded. She knew it as if it were engraved upon her psyche.

'Well,' said Ottilie, 'those men, who didn't marry for love, it's obvious that when they talk about their wives, they do love them, they really do. Rosie dearest, you don't have to love the man you marry. You can marry and the love comes later. It truly can. It does. I know it. I learned it from those poor wounded Indians.'

'I know what you're saying,' said Rosie, 'but it's not as bad as you think.'

'I know it's specially difficult for you,' said Ottilie, 'I really do know that it is. We all do. Even Daniel knows. All I'm asking is, do try properly.'

'Properly with brass knobs on, and pink ribbons?'

'And silver bells.'

The sisters laughed, and Ottilie said, 'I wouldn't ask, but Daniel really is a good catch. I wouldn't ask you if he was a bounder. And I think he probably still loves you.'

'I'm sure he does,' replied Rosie, 'and things have already begun to get better. They really have. You didn't have to talk to me about this at all. What about you, Ottie? What's going to happen with you?'

'*Moi?* I shall be deliriously happy, you wait and see.'

'What about Archie?'

'Not to be, I don't think. He's not here any more, is he? And when he is here, he's just desperate to get back to the North-West Frontier. And it's you he loves, not me. That's why he's such a sad man who can't wait to go. Not a hope for me, I'm afraid. I've just got to bear up and see what's round the corner. I did take a little fancy to Fluke, between you and me, but he's already spoken for. Two children, I believe. And gone to South America. And let's face it, he's an aviator. They don't last much longer than a meteorite, do they? That's what they are, meteorites waiting to hit the ground. Aviators are born to become a beautiful memory, like a poppy whose petals are ripped away in a storm.'

'Daniel's an aviator,' said Rosie. She looked at Ottilie, taking her in now that it was almost time to part. Ottilie was quite short, and even dumpy if one were to be uncharitable. She wore her black shiny hair in a simple bob, and her large oval face seemed little more than a neutral setting for her enormous dark brown eyes. Rosie thought, 'How many ways there are of being beautiful!'

Ottilie said, 'I want to give you a hug, like when we were little.'

After a while, Rosie said, 'Ottie, I'm so sad. I feel I hardly know you.'

'It's not your fault,' murmured Ottilie. 'I'm the quiet one. Anyway, it doesn't matter. I know you right down to the last drop.'

'Dear Ottie,' said Rosie. 'Please look after Daddy, won't you? If anything happens send me a telegram and I'll come straight back. I know you don't entirely agree with me, but I really do think there's something wrong with his heart.'

'I'll keep Daddy wrapped up in cotton wool,' said Ottilie.

102

The Clonking

One Sunday after church (which he endured patiently for the sake of the family's respectability) Daniel came down the front steps of the house and found Mr Wragge in his Sunday best, gazing at the AC with a worried look on his face.

'Good morning, Mr Wragge. Not taking your day off?' said Daniel.

'I am, sir, but this car's giving me a right headache. Can't stop thinking about it. Just thought I'd call by and take another look.'

'I see that Caractacus has been walking all over it,' said Daniel.

'I only have to polish it and the bleedin' cat walks all over it with muddy feet,' said Wragge. 'I've had to resign myself. The family don't seem to mind. And when you go anywhere you have to check he isn't sitting in the back like a bloody gentleman off to the races.'

'What's the matter with it, then?'

'Noises, sir. Horrible noises.'

'What sort of noises, Mr Wragge?'

'Clonking, sir. Specially when you start off, stop or go round corners.'

'It sounds like the perfect excuse for a drive,' said Daniel. 'I've got an hour before lunch. Get her started and we'll go for a spin. Can I drive?'

Mr Wragge looked doubtful. 'Just so's you remember it ain't a Sopwith, sir. Long as you don't throw her about, sir.'

'I'll drive very sedately, Mr Wragge. Start her up!'

Daniel heard the clonking the moment they pulled out of the drive. They set off down Court Road, he applied the brakes and there it was. They turned into North Park, and it was even worse. When Daniel braked at Footscray Road and turned right to go round behind the golf course, it was horrendous. Daniel stopped the car and it clonked again.

'Do you think it's safe to drive?' he asked.

'Well, that's the odd thing, sir. It drives perfectly sweet, and you can't feel nothing strange at the wheel. It's not like she's juddering, or wandering about the road or anything.'

They started off again and completed the circuit back past the Tarn. In the driveway of The Grampians, Daniel switched off the engine and said, 'I think we'd better jack her up at the back and take a look. You get the jack out and I'll go and get some overalls.'

Ten minutes later Sophie came out of the house on her way to post a letter, and saw Mr Wragge crouched down at the side of the car next to Daniel's feet. She heard Daniel's voice drifting out, as if he were talking to himself. 'Nothing wrong with the propshaft. I mean, it feels perfectly solid. It couldn't be the diff, could it?'

'Don't think so, sir. Diffs grind. They don't clonk.'

'The suspension looks absolutely fine. I see you greased the springs recently.'

'I did, sir. I take care of her as best I know.'

Sophie interrupted. 'Do we have a little local difficulty, oh comrades stout and true? May a mere slip of a sliver of a very slight female be of any assistance?'

Daniel emerged from beneath the car, with a long streak of heavy grease across the bridge of his nose and down one cheek.

'Gracious,' said Sophie, 'your *maquillage* is all lopsided. You must go to the agency and get yourself a better maid.'

'There's a hideous clonking when you brake,' said Daniel.

'And when you go round corners,' added Wragge. 'It's a right mystery.'

'Whence cometh it? What is its provenance, where its domicile, where and what its dwelling?'

'Somewhere in the back, sort of behind and below the driver and passenger.'

Sophie put her forefinger to her lip and adopted a theatrically thoughtful expression. 'Well, *enfant de la patrie*, would you con-descend to lift up the back seat?'

'The back seat?'

'Yea, verily, the back seat.'

'As her ladyship wishes,' said Daniel. 'But you must know there's no machinery under there.'

''Tis true,' said Sophie. 'Beneath a back seat dwell no cogs, gudgeon pins or big ends. The latter repose upon the seat but do not occupy the space beneath.'

Daniel reached in and pulled up the leather tabs at the back of the seat. Sophie leaned over and looked. Her hand darted down and she plucked something up.

'Just as I ratiocinated,' she said, holding up the golf ball, and tossing it to Daniel. 'Toodle-oo, gentlemen of England. Must go and post an epistle. *Vivat floreatque* gynocracy!'

Daniel and Mr Wragge watched her go. Even from behind they could see her triumphant amusement.

'Bloody hell,' said Mr Wragge, drawing the syllables out.

'I bet she put it there herself, the little minx,' said Daniel. 'I'll ask Fairhead.'

'I'll fetch us a cup of tea from the kitchen,' said Mr Wragge.

They drank it side by side on the step outside the boiler room. 'Mr Wragge,' said Daniel, 'have you ever thought of setting up a business?'

'Wouldn't know how, sir. What kind of business?'

'Well,' said Daniel, 'something mechanical. Cars or motorcycles. Or both. Aeroplanes if possible.'

'I dunno, sir. Why do you ask?'

'I have two friends in Germany. Willy and Fritzl. I captured them in 1918. They've started a motorcycle business in Germany. They've written and asked me if I'd like to go over and pitch in. It occurred to me that you would make up the numbers perfectly.'

'You'd go to Germany, sir? After all that?'

'It wasn't the Germans, Mr Wragge, it was the bloody Kaiser. If His Majesty went mad and told the young men of this country to go out and conquer France, you can bet that half of us would go.'

'Well, maybe so, sir, but you're a gentleman. Gentlemen aren't mechanics.'

'I am beginning to think that I have no future as a gentleman,' said Daniel. 'And in any case, in business it helps if you've got a gentleman on board. And the sad truth is that I love machinery.

If I can't spend my life tinkering, I shall live unhappy, I know it. I was born to make things work.'

'Well, I'm not a gentleman. We'd have to rub along, wouldn't we?'

'You're a bloody good mechanic, Mr Wragge. That's why I asked you. You're damned useful with a spanner and you understand how everything works.'

'Anyway, I thought you was going to Ceylon, sir.'

'I am. I'm just making a plan B. In case it doesn't work out. My wife . . .' Daniel stood up without completing the sentence. 'Give me your cup and saucer, Mr Wragge. I'll take them back to the kitchen.'

'Gentleman don't take washing-up to the kitchen.'

'I'm getting in practice for when I have to give it up,' said Daniel.

As he left, Mr Wragge said, 'Thanks for helping me find that there golf ball.'

103

A Letter to Gaskell

Thursday

Gaskell Old Thing, Green-Eyed and Monstrous to Boot,

Your exhibition was a delight. I particularly liked the portraits of rotting horses. I'd say you've got it down to a T.

I don't know about you, but I think there are two ways to have come through the war. You can either let it haunt you and torment you, like the poor Bs who hide under the table because of the snipers, and tremble so much that they can't hold a cup of tea steady, and wake up terrified the moment they go to sleep; or you can be thankful for what beauty and honour came through it intact, and are steadily growing now that the fighting's over. I am not sure whether one can choose which one to be, and sometimes I wonder if I am somewhat both, but I am inclined to think that I have come out of it mainly with the more positive attitude. I was walking up by Chanctonbury Ring some weeks ago, with Esther on my shoulders, and Rosie was there with a big wide hat on, trailing behind looking at the flowers, and my mother somewhere far below making bread, and I was so filled with the pleasure of how perfect it is up there that I felt a kind of gratitude, at the same time as I felt sorrow that so many of my friends will never see it. I had a sense of wonder that I was still here to experience all that loveliness. We have come through, old thing.

So let's remember the rotting horses and shattered houses, and let that memory make us thankful for the lives we lead now. That is how I want to look at your war work, as something to make me grateful for what's left, and for what is still to come. I have been thinking that when this vein is exhausted, you will need to start mining a new one, and it has occurred to me that it would be marvellous if you were to do a portrait of Christabel, in one of her blue dresses, perhaps in profile, by a window.

466

I can vividly imagine how well you would do it. Do ask her to write and tell us how her photographic exhibition goes next month. We are very sorry not to be seeing it.

As you know, Rosie and I are going to Ceylon, in the hope of making a new start. Why that is necessary, I think it is plain for all to see. You and Christabel will, I know, be pleased to learn that Rosie has been perking up considerably in recent days, and I am catching frequent glimpses of her as I remember her when she was a girl. That great cloud of unhappiness seems to be dispersing very gradually, and I live in the greatest hope that one day before too long she may be free of it entirely. Going to Ceylon does, however, leave me with the problem of what to do with my three aeroplanes.

I know you quite well enough to know that you will probably try and fly them without even one minute's instruction, and so I am strictly enjoining you not to. If you start one up on your own, it will be inclined to trundle away without you in the cockpit. You should join an aero club, use the club's riggers and fitters, and learn from an instructor like everyone else, and get your ticket properly. The one crucial thing I must tell you, and any instructor will tell you the same, is never never never try to turn back if your engine fails on take-off. Turning back is an almost irresistible impulse, and it is invariably fatal. Even crashing head-on into a tree or a house is better than what happens when you try to turn back on take-off. Promise me faithfully. I am worried for you. I fear that you are like a French cavalry officer, more brave than sensible.

Of course, if you lose power in flight, you pick a distant field and just go for it. Be very careful to watch out for power lines. Those planes can land on a sixpence, and you will be simply amazed at the hospitality and assistance that will be given to you by all the locals. I'd say it's worth the inconvenience almost every time! Watch out for bulls, as well. I was charged by one in France, and it stove in the side of my Camel. It got its head and horns entangled in the interior bracing wires, and it was the Devil's own job trying to disengage it. In the end the farmer fetched a hacksaw and we cut one of its horns off. It was probably the most frightening thing I had to do in the whole of the war, and the d----d thing kept standing on my foot and bellowing. After that the plane was unflyable and had to be collected by the tender. In retrospect it would have been more sensible simply to cut the wires, but in the heat of the moment the old man and I can't have been thinking straight. I remember thinking that if we cut the wires, well, I never would get off the ground, and then I didn't anyway. Somewhere near Arles there is a one-horned bull called Pierre. I wonder how he is. Do horns regrow?

And do please take out insurance.

I am sincerely hoping that there might eventually be opportunities in aviation in Ceylon, but in the meantime it's tea for me. It's lucky I like it, and of course one can do the most marvellous things there. When we are settled in, it would be a delight if you and Christabel were to come out and see us. You can bring your golf clubs, and do bring your Purdeys and keep us satiated with duck.

The gong has rung for supper. The house reverberates. Time to sign off. We shall miss you!

Chin-chin, and love to the ever-glorious Christabel,

Daniel P. (ex RAF, soon to be tea planter)

PS And for God's sake don't fly blotto. We sometimes used to do that, and now the thought of it fills me with horror.

PPS I came across my father-in-law in the dining room recently. He was trying out a cast-iron contraption with a golf ball suspended on it from a rod. There is a dial with a needle on it. It is called the McCosh Patent Driveometer, and the idea is that you whack the captive golf ball and the dial shows how far it would have gone. In his own way, the man is a genius, n'est-ce pas? He is now working on a version that tells you if have sliced or hooked it. This will be the McCosh Patent Stratedrive.

104

Young Edward

Mr Hamilton McCosh was practising his putting on the drawing-room carpet with his new McCosh Patent Flagsure Stainless Putter when Millicent came in to tell him that someone was at the tradesmen's door, hoping to speak to him. Putter in hand, he went out of the front door, and round the side of the house, where he found a woman of about thirty, accompanied by a boy of twelve. They were respectably dressed, but in clothes that had been greatly patched up. 'Poor people who take pride in themselves,' thought Mr McCosh approvingly. The woman was brown-haired, with early silver streaks, and her pale face was thin and pinched. She had once been very pretty.

'Good morning,' said Mr McCosh. 'I am Hamilton McCosh, master of this house. How may I be of assistance?'

'We've come to thank you, sir,' said the woman.

'Me? What have I done?'

'I mean, thank all of you, for what you did. I mean, taking care of my Edward here, and calling the ambulance, and going to hospital with him, and visiting him an' that, and bringing him food.'

'That was my daughters,' said Mr McCosh.

'We think you paid the hospital bill,' said the woman.

'What makes you think it was me?'

'Who else would it be, sir? It was quite a lot. It was more than we could've managed in a month of Sundays. They wouldn't tell us, but we think it was you.'

'The point is, is the bairn all right?'

'He's all right, sir. Edward, speak to the gentleman, would you?'

Mr McCosh held out his hand, and the boy shook it. 'I like a laddie who looks you in the eye when he shakes hands,' said McCosh, looking into the boy's large, intelligent, sensitive brown eyes. 'I suppose you're called Edward after the late King. A good name to have.'

'I like it, sir,' replied the boy. 'I don't want any other.'

'So, young fellow, are you all right now? Completely cured? Your legs seem very straight.'

'I'm not fully strong yet, sir, but I expect to be. I'm off the crutches. It still hurts. They ache like billy-o at night, sir. And I'm limping rather a lot.'

'You're still growing. That's lucky for you. Growing will get rid of that.'

'I've got to do lots of walking to get them strong again, sir.'

'Lots of walking?'

'Yes, sir.'

'Are you at school?'

'Well, he was, sir,' said his mother. 'He was bright too. They said he'd go far. But we can't afford it, so now he's out and he's just doing errands 'til something comes along.'

'And his father?'

'Killed, sir. He was a wheelwright. In the Horse Artillery. I take in washing, sir. I do what I can. All the widows are taking in washing, and patching and mending. The competition is something terrible.'

'Other children?'

'Only a dead one, sir. It was the influenza.'

Mr McCosh looked at Edward and said, 'Do you see this big house? Well, my grandfather lived in a little croft made of turf and lived off practically nothing. Are you really very bright?'

'Ask him anything you like, sir. He's like a sponge, he is.'

Mr McCosh thought for a second, then asked, 'What are the smallest bones in your body?'

'The ones in your ears, sir.'

'Capital of Egypt?'

'Cairo, sir.'

'How many halves are there in thirty?'

'Sixty, sir.'

'And if you add three thousand, four hundred and twelve drops of water to forty-two thousand, three hundred and forty-four drops of water, what have you got?'

'A puddle, sir.'

'Aha! Very canny! And how far do you think it is from where we are standing to that lime tree over there?'

'Fifty yards, sir.'

'Wait here,' said Mr McCosh. He went round the back of the house and fetched the tape measure from the room under the conservatory. It was the one used for measuring out the tennis markings on the lawn. He handed the reel to the boy, and said, 'Off you go, laddie.'

Edward walked off towards the lime tree, carrying the end of the tape with him. He touched it to the tree and looked expect-antly back at Mr McCosh, who said, 'Forty-eight and a half. Well done, Edward.'

Mr McCosh looked at Edward's mother and said, 'Madam, your boy is going back to school. You will kindly bring me the bills and I will pay them.'

'Really, sir? Why, sir?'

'That's between me and the gatepost,' replied Mr McCosh. 'You don't have to agree, of course, but it would be a waste of a fine young man if you don't.'

'It *was* you who paid the hospital, wasn't it, sir?'

'I've nae idea. Edward!'

'Yes, sir?'

'How would you like to learn to be a caddy? Just when you're not at school?'

'I don't know nothing at all about golf,' replied Edward.

'Do you know what you have to do? You carry the bag of clubs and you give advice to the player. You say, "This shot is one hundred and twenty-five yards with the wind against, so I think you should use a mashie." Or, "Aim this putt six inches to the left of the hole." Do you think you could do that kind of thing?'

'I'll do my best,' said Edward.

'I'll tell you what I'm thinking,' said Mr McCosh. 'You get a good long walk carrying a light weight. That'll strengthen your legs. You get fresh air – good for your health. You get to know many of the ladies and gentlemen around here. Always useful! And caddies often grow wonderfully good at the game. Just about all our club professionals started out as caddies. That's how Harry

Vardon started, caddying for Major Spofforth. Have you heard of Vardon? Six times Open Champion! What a lovely job, being a club professional, eh? Whacking balls, giving lessons, mending and selling clubs, flirting with the ladies. What do you think? You can start off with me. Two and six a round! I'll teach you everything I know and then you can go solo. How about it?'

Edward was dumbfounded. Two and six a round! You could buy books for that, and marbles, and gobstoppers, and elastic for catapults.

Mr McCosh leaned down and whispered, 'But you must promise to give two shillings of it to your mother. Understood?'

After Edward and his mother had gone, Hamilton McCosh went into the hallway and looked up at the portrait of his father. The painting was somewhat flat, but the likeness was sufficient. It showed Alexander McCosh in the dignified prime of prosperous middle age, in Scottish evening dress, posing improbably against a backdrop of the St Andrews Clubhouse, leaning on a brassie, and gazing directly at the artist.

'Well, Father,' said Hamilton McCosh, 'I just did for someone else what someone did for Grandpa. What do you think of that, eh?' He seemed to hear his father's voice: 'Well, laddie, always gie back as much you're gi'en, and ye'll nae go far aglee.'

He went down to the bottom of the garden and stood in the orchard by Bouncer's grave, looking back at his magnificent house. What a long way it was from a turf croft.

105

A New Beginning

D aniel and Rosie went to Foyles and came back with several
books about Ceylon, taped up in brown paper. In the
evenings they sat by the fire and read passages to each other,
working themselves up into a state of eager anticipation. It did
indeed seem to be an exotic and interesting place, and it was
clear that many who went to live there never really wanted to
come home again. Daniel and Rosie were struck by how socio-
logically and religiously complicated the island was, and began to
worry that they would never understand it, just as Colonel Bassett
had warned.

Rosie and her mother went to Selfridge's and came back with
all sorts of things that eventually turned out to be of no use, or
easily available at Rosie's destination, and Daniel went up to
Birmingham to visit Ruston Hornby, the company that had made
all the machinery on the estate where they were to live. The
company sent out engineers every year, and also on request, and
they showed Daniel the detailed plans of everything they had
supplied. Obviously, it could be a disaster if any of the machinery
failed, but the fact was that it very seldom did. The machines
were so vast that they were intrinsically robust, and the Singhalese
engineers were, in any case, masters at their vocation. Daniel also
called in at Tangye's, because it was conceivable that one day he
might find himself on a plantation which had their machinery.

There was then notification by telegram that the voyage was to
be delayed owing to a coal miners' strike, and so it was that, two
weeks later, on the eve of departure, Daniel encountered the
Honourable Mary FitzGerald St George in the corridor of
the second floor, in the servants' quarters. Since there were so few
servants these days, Daniel had commandeered one of the empty
rooms to use as a study when he was *en famille*, and now he was
clearing out all those things that he was either taking with him, or

473

of which he was disposing. He met Mary as she was coming out of her room. Mary cast her eyes down immediately, and Daniel observed her awkwardness. Then she looked up and said, 'So, Master Daniel, it's goodbye, is it?'

'It's goodbye tomorrow,' he replied.

'I shall be very forlorn when you're gone,' said Mary.

'Will you? How sweet of you to say so. I shall certainly miss you. I do hope we meet again.'

'You have no idea when you'll be coming back?'

'None at all, I'm afraid.'

'I expect I'll be gone.'

'I do hope not.' He looked into her large grey eyes and saw that she was tearful. Her lower lip was working, and she was restraining it with her teeth.

'I shouldn't be sad, should I?' she said. 'For you it's a new start.'

'I'm sorry you're not coming with us. You're so good with Esther. I'm sorry that Mrs McCosh won't let you go.'

'It's probably just as well,' said Mary, looking at him with extraordinary directness and honesty.

'I think you're probably right. May I kiss you on the cheek? Not very English, I know, but I think I would feel painfully deprived if we merely shook hands.'

'You may.' She offered her right cheek for him to kiss, and he lingered about the business as much as he dared. She smelled of something fresh and subtle, and her cheek was wondrously soft. He kissed the other one.

She held out her hand and took his. 'We will meet again, you know,' she said, 'I am absolutely sure of it. One day there'll be more time.'

Shortly after this, he encountered Millicent on the way down the stairs, and Daniel made his farewells to her too, giving her a five-pound note 'just to say thank you'.

'Thanking *you*, sir,' said Millicent. 'That's very kind of you, it is. That's an awful lot, sir.'

'Well, shrouds have no pockets. And you'll be needing it. If you don't mind me asking, when is the happy day approximately?' asked Daniel.

'Happy day? How did you know?' asked Millicent, quite shocked.

'There are signs, you know,' observed Daniel. 'I wasn't born yesterday.'

'Don't tell the mistress, sir,' pleaded Millicent. 'She'll make me leave as soon as she notices. I need to work as long as I can. I'm dead lucky she let me stay on after I was married. You're expected to go, aren't you?'

'Well, not these days. People are desperate to hang on to a good servant, children or not. I do understand, though. Mum's the word. Even so, times are changing, aren't they? I expect she would keep you on, you know.'

'Mr Miller and me are thinking of going to Canada,' said Millicent. 'It's a lovely place to be a copper, and I could have a little shop. It's not so cold out west, they say. He wants to be a Mountie, and he can't even ride yet!'

'Hmm,' said Daniel, 'that's the kind of life that would appeal to me too. But I rather like the idea of being a bush pilot. I do hope it works out for you. I don't suppose you want to be a tweeny all your life, do you? And I can't see you becoming a pug, can you?'

Millicent laughed. 'No, sir, I'd make a very poor pug. I'm not bossy and disapproving, and I'm much too cheerful.'

'Well, I wish you and Mr Miller the best of luck. I wish you a very happy life, the happiest possible.'

'You too, sir,' said Millicent, and she watched him wistfully until he reached the bottom of the stairs, on his way to leave a thank-you present for Cookie. Still, she could always boast about having known an aviation ace, and say what a gentleman he was.

Rosie and Daniel left in spring, from Southampton, in the company of a variety of other folk on commercial or colonial business. Daniel had his combination crated up on the docks and loaded into the hold. Having given up aeroplanes, his loyalty had altogether been transferred to his Henley, and he would not have wished to go anywhere without it. The sensation of speed would never reach the incomparable pleasure of flying a scout two feet above the ground, but it was sometimes enough to be reminded of it. During the voyage he liked to go below and check that his combination was still content, running his fingers along the packing case as if he were caressing a horse.

Rosie and Daniel had already made their farewells to Mme Pitt, having spent the previous weekend at Partridge Green. Both of them had received another lecture, which they took in good part. Back at The Grampians, Rosie had deliberated for a long time in her room, and had eventually decided to pack neither Ash's letters nor her madonna and child. She did, however, decide to take with her the notebook in which she had copied out the most tender parts of his letters, but then she forgot to put it in her trunk.

Rosie went through the blue door to say goodbye to Mr and Mrs Pendennis. She found them in their drawing room, reading quietly. Rosie saw how they had aged, how pale and thin they had both become, and had a small revelation. She suddenly realised that many thousands of others had suffered far worse grief than she had. It occurred to her that there had been a kind of selfishness in her own mourning. 'I should have come round to see them more often,' she thought.

'I've come to say goodbye,' she said, as they stood to welcome her.

Wordlessly, Mrs Pendennis came and put her arms around her. 'Oh, Mamma, don't cry,' said Rosie, trying to suppress her own tears.

'Well,' said Mrs Pendennis, 'all these years . . . you've been our daughter too, you know. We'll miss you so much. You will write?'

'Of course, Mamma. Every week at the very least.'

'It'll be very exciting for you,' said Mr Pendennis. 'I do hope it's a great success. May I hug you too? I am American, after all.'

Mrs Pendennis took her hand. 'Come, I've something to show you.'

She led Rosie out into the hall and gestured to the wall that faced the stairway. There hung a life-size portrait of their sons. Ashbridge was standing on the left, leaning, as it were, against the frame. His pose was casual and his smile ironical, and his right hand was on Sidney's shoulder. He looked directly back at Rosie as she gazed on him. Sidney sat on a reversed chair, with his chin resting on his arms. He was looking into the distance, as if into eternity.

Albert was standing on his right, his left hand on his brother's shoulder, but glancing towards Ashbridge. All of them were in the service dress of the Royal Horse Artillery, with their forage caps at slightly irreverent angles. In the background was a landscape, showing a steep hill in the distance, with three tiny crosses at its summit.

Rosie was stunned by it. She gazed, unable to speak. It was almost too perfect, easily as good as a Sargent.

'The artist did it from photographs,' said Mrs Pendennis. 'John and I come out here and stand for hours and hours. You can almost imagine we have the boys back in the house.'

'It's the first thing we see when we come downstairs in the morning,' said Mr Pendennis.

'Why isn't it finished?' asked Rosie, pointing to the bottom right-hand corner, where the confident detail of the rest of the picture seemed to break down into a thin, messy wash of broad dark green strokes.

'It was the artist's idea,' said Mr Pendennis. 'She thought the picture should be uncompleted because the boys' lives weren't completed. We didn't like it at first —'

'— But we gave in,' said his wife. 'She wasn't the kind of artist you can argue with. And now we think it's just right, and we're glad we gave in.'

'She?' said Rosie, moving forward to look at the signature. 'Gaskell!' she exclaimed. 'She certainly kept quiet about this! But of course I haven't seen her for ages.'

'We've never met anyone quite like her,' said Mrs Pendennis. 'In fact we can't make her out at all. What extraordinary green eyes! But doesn't she paint like an angel? She collected photographs from us, and then six months later she arrived with this. She's got them all down to a T.'

Mr Pendennis said, 'We've no one to leave it to. Would you like to have it? After we've gone?'

'I'd love it,' said Rosie, 'but I think it wouldn't be very kind to Daniel. I know we were all Pals, but I think, you know, it might come between us. I will ask him, and see what he thinks, but it might be better to leave it to one of the other Pals, then I can just go and look at it sometimes. Why don't you leave it to Christabel?'

'I think you're quite right to ask Daniel,' said Mrs Pendennis. 'You know, John and I very much want to see you and Daniel happy together. Making a success of it.' She gestured up at Ashbridge. 'It's what he would have wanted. Ashbridge wasn't selfish. He didn't have a selfish bone in his body.'

Rosie said nothing, but gazed at the face of Ash in the portrait. He looked back with quizzicality and steady sympathy.

Now they all stood in the driveway of The Grampians as Wragge warmed up the AC, and Rosie clung to her father and wept, saying, 'Please take care, Daddy, please look after yourself, won't you?'

'Rosie bairn,' he said, ironically donning his strongest Scottish accent, 'I've nae plans to die afore ye come back. Dinnae fret. Go forth and have some fun wi' yoursel'.'

Mrs McCosh gave Daniel a brown paper bag. 'I've decided that from now on I am going to cook the bread. This is my first loaf. I would very much like you to have it.'

Daniel took it and looked inside. It was presentable and appetising. 'How very kind,' he said, touched by the gift, despite its eccentricity.

Mrs McCosh inclined her face to him. 'You may kiss me on the cheek,' she said.

He kissed her on the right cheek, felt suddenly sorry for all the bad blood between them and kissed her on the left.

She blushed and said, 'I do really think of you as a son, you know. I do hope . . . well . . . I'm sorry . . . you know.'

'We'll come back every year,' said Daniel.

'I do so look forward to seeing you again.' She looked away. 'It was such a pleasure to meet you at last.'

Esther, who had been cuddling Caractacus, kissed the cat on the top of his head and handed him to her grandfather, saying, 'Grandpa play with him now.'

After they had gone, Mrs McCosh asked her husband if they would be back in time for tea, and added, 'My dear, do remind me, was it Daniel or Ashbridge who died in the war?'

Christabel and Gaskell were in Snowdonia, walking the Horseshoe and climbing Cadair Idris from both sides, but they had sent Esther a photograph of Caractacus, staring down from

478

the top of the pelmet, and a little painting copied from it, admirably portraying him with his lopsided ginger moustache, yellow eyes, and humorous, slightly insane expression. Esther had been delighted, and everyone elsed laughed when they saw it.

Only Ottilie was there at Southampton Harbour to wave the couple goodbye, having travelled down with Wragge in the AC, bringing with them the luggage that had not been sent in advance by train. As the ship hooted, and began to move away, it occurred to Rosie once again how little she really knew this particular sister of hers. Ottilie's main interest was still going to lectures. She attended everything that was available locally, whether it was about Fabian Socialism, or eugenics, or psychoanalysis. She was engaged in an intellectual quest, but never talked about it. All Rosie really knew about Ottilie was that she had a heart brimming with love, and was waiting for someone to whom she could give it. She resolved that, when she returned, she would contrive to get to know Ottilie better.

To this mysterious sister, Rosie, Daniel and Esther waved goodbye on that spring morning, her large brown eyes vivid in the white face beneath a dark blue cloche hat. Rosie then had the experience of sailing past the vast facade of Netley, where she had spent the war years, mostly on her knees, she now seemed to recall, hopelessly expiating the sin of having forgotten to pray for Ash the day before he was struck down. The great green dome flanked by its endless turrets and towers and innumerable windows was peaceful in the sunshine, and through Daniel's binoculars, Rosie saw that there were very few patients out in their blue 'hospital undress', strolling away their injuries. She guessed that much of the hospital must by now have been mothballed.

'There goes Spikey,' she said to Daniel.

'It must be a funny feeling,' he said.

'It's all a blur now, just a sea of faces, fading away.'

'You've never told me much about it. What was it like?'

'I wouldn't know where to start. It was the hardest work you can imagine, and absolutely piteous. The TB ward, and the syphilis ward, and the gas ward, oh dear. It's hard . . . The gas victims gave off gas for ages, did you know that? They stank of it. And did you know there's an elephant skeleton set up in the entrance?

And huge sets of antlers, and a school of fish set into the plaster under the stairs? And dozens and dozens of pickled snakes in glass jars?'

'Gracious! Really?'

'And there's a huge collection of skulls and mummified heads, called "Skull Alley", skulls from all over the world, labelled. You know, "Hottentot", "Bushman", "Maori". They looked the same really. And there's a collection of deformed foetuses.'

'I'd love to see all that.'

'Oh, Daniel, really! Look, you can see the Seaweed Hut!'

'One of my friends sent me a postcard of that once,' said Daniel. 'It doesn't look as though it's going to be there for much longer.'

'No. It's hopelessly rotten. There's even an observatory. And we had ghats in the woods for burning Hindus, and the ashes got thrown into the Solent. The idea was that one day they'd float far enough to meet up with some water from the Ganges. The wards got so full that we filled the corridors with beds, and the poor men froze in the winter and got baked in the summer. You can imagine how long those corridors were. And the grounds were all full of Doecker huts and tents and Fairley fieldhouses, and a Welsh hospital and an Irish one that Lord Iveagh paid for. It was all in the land behind, so you wouldn't have seen it from here. It was like a city, but all neat and set out in rows. Did you know that a hundred and fifty-one trains of wounded came in after the Somme?'

'A hundred and fifty-one? How many men is that?'

'God knows. We didn't even have time to think about questions like that! You wouldn't believe what I saw.' She hung her head.

He put his arm around her shoulder. 'I know, I saw it all too, remember?'

'Not so many all at once,' said Rosie. 'It wasn't your job to mend them when they couldn't be mended.'

'I've pulled broken friends from burning aeroplanes,' said Daniel softly. 'But obviously it was far worse for you. It must have been.'

But Rosie was off with her own thoughts. 'There was a soldier who was haunted at night by a German that he'd bayoneted in the stomach. The German would turn up and say, "Now I've got you" and shoot him, and he'd wake up screaming.'

'Did you have any Boche patients? Did they get treated here as well?'

'Oh yes. But in the end they were taken away because of a riot by the local shipyard workers. They invaded because they said the Germans were getting better treatment than our own boys.'

'Were they?'

'Well, of course not. The reason they were kept in the wards and not the tents was so they couldn't escape. They were padlocked in. It was just stupid. After that I'll always despise a mob, I think. Baying like hounds. Oh, and there was a scrap shop.'

'A scrap shop?'

'They did experiments on animals. I went in and I couldn't believe my eyes. That's why I'm an antivivisectionist.'

Daniel had not known any such thing. In fact he was increasingly realising that he barely knew his wife at all. 'Funnily enough, I am too,' he said. 'Archie always used to say that they should conduct the experiments on criminals.'

'Oh, I didn't know you were an antivivisectionist too,' said Rosie. 'It's nice that we agree. Did I tell you about the Grey Lady? Your Madame Valentine would have loved to know about her.'

'I didn't go to Madame Valentine. It was the others. It didn't seem quite right to me somehow. I baulked. But I don't think you've ever mentioned the Grey Lady.'

'She was a nurse who accidentally killed a patient, so she committed suicide by jumping off a tower. An amazing number of people saw her ghost, including the switchboard operator, and the Catholic chaplain, and if one of the men saw her, you knew he'd die the next day. You could smell her perfume, so they said, and her silk dress rustled.'

'A nurse in silk? Did you ever see her?'

'No, not me. All the ones I see are in here,' and she tapped the side of her head.

He put his arm around her again, and squeezed her shoulder. 'Think how lucky we've been,' he said. 'How lucky we are, to have a future.'

'No more wars,' said Rosie. 'Not big ones, anyway.'

'Just little ones, to keep Archie amused,' said Daniel. 'Just side-shows for the lost souls. I do miss flying, though.'

'We ought to do more talking like this,' said Rosie.

Rosie quickly found that she was not a natural sailor, and that she felt nauseous if she did much walking about. Whenever possible, she sat or lay down, especially whilst passing through the Bay of Biscay. The result of this was that Daniel began for the first time to get to know his daughter properly.

Since Esther's birth, he had been, as it seemed to him, the victim of a determined and coordinated female conspiracy to keep him out of the picture. If Esther cried, and he picked her up, she was immediately dragged from his arms by a woman who knew how to comfort a child properly. It might be Rosie, or Ottilie, or Mrs McCosh, or even a visitor. If he wanted to shovel food into her mouth, the spoon was wrested from him.

He had found this very irritating, but the fact was that this is how everything was done, and this was how women saw the world. Bits of it belonged to them, and bits of it to the men, and that was that.

Working in Birmingham at Henley's had not made it any easier to forge a bond with Esther, and neither had the hiring of Mary FitzGerald St George, something which, although she was a lovely woman, Daniel had found inexplicable and pointless in a house-hold where there were at least three women with very little to do, and where there were two other women who were somewhat busier but adored the child just as much. He had all but missed the periods when Esther had been a babe-in-arms, and when she had been crawling about at random, pulling books off shelves and chewing the tassels off the rugs.

Mrs McCosh had flatly declined to allow Mary FitzGerald St George to go with her charge to Ceylon, because 'she is quite indispensible to me', and so it was that Daniel and Rosie had hired a 'travelling nurse' to accompany them as far as Ceylon, where they would hire a resident one. Daniel reflected again that it was just as well that Mary was not coming. There was some-thing dispiriting about having to face temptation, and an inevitable sense of impending catastrophe if one gave way to it.

The travelling nurse, it transpired, had travelled a great deal in trains, even going to Constantinople on the *Orient Express*, but had never gone very far by sea. The ship was a small one, about twenty-five years old, with three exiguous masts and one funnel, set back at a jaunty angle. It sat low in the water, and earned its keep on the run to India and back, through Suez. Thanks to its constant rolling and yawing, the travelling nurse was prostrate with sickness almost from the moment of departure, and Rosie and Daniel saw very little of her during the whole voyage, even forgetting her name within a few months of arrival. She was the kind of person whose photograph would turn up in a family album, and nobody would be able to remember who she was or why she was there.

Rosie's lack of sea legs meant that Daniel had to look after Esther whether he wanted to or not, and he found that for the most part it came very naturally, especially as she was such a sweet-natured child. She was by now two years old, frolicsome and skipping, and very pretty, her hair still in golden yellow curls, and her eyes as periwinkle blue as her mother's. Fortunately she was extremely fond of Robinson's Patent Groats, which Mme Pitt had donated in enormous quantities, and loved boiled eggs with soldiers, so he had no trouble persuading her to eat. She was very attached to her father, and would gaze at him adoringly with one thumb in her mouth, and French Bear clamped under her arm.

The SS *Derbyshire* was a fantastically hazardous place for a child, with its steel staircases and gangways, and sudden lurches, and so he found himself spending almost all of Esther's waking hours either holding her hand, carrying her, or with her on his knee as he struggled to read one of his books about Ceylon. Esther liked to fall asleep on her father, thumb in mouth despite Rosie's fear that she would end up with crooked teeth, and he found himself pinned down for much longer periods than he would have liked. Many hours were devoted to looking for French Bear, which she abandoned in all sorts of strange places, only to panic about it later.

During that time he came to love the sweet scent of her hair and the milky scent of her flesh, the patch of heat she created against his chest and stomach. He liked to point things out to her – ship! – seagull! – aeroplane! – and she would say the words after him. He taught her nonsense rhymes:

> Yesterday upon the stair I saw a man who wasn't there.
> He wasn't there again today. Oh, how I wish he'd go away.

He taught her some Royal Flying Corps songs, since he had never had any time for nursery rhymes, and neither did he know any. In her quavering, tuneless little voice, she sang:

> 'Take the pistons out of my kidley,
> And the gugjon pins out of my brain,
> From the smallamabak take the clankshaft,
> An assemmel the engines gain.'

Daniel crooned:

> 'Mademoiselle from Armentières, parlez-vous?
> Mademoiselle from Armentières, parlez-vous?
> Mademoiselle from Armentières, hasn't been kissed for many
>   a year,
> With an inky-pinky parlez-vous.'

He taught her 'Frère Jacques', of course, and 'Chevaliers de la Table Ronde', and 'Sous le Pont d'Avignon'.

They made paper aeroplanes and launched them off the stern, and played a clapping game that Daniel remembered his father teaching him when he was about Esther's age, which went:

> A sailor went to sea sea sea
> To see what he could see see see,
> But all that he did see see see
> Was the bottom of the deep blue sea sea sea.

They did it faster and faster until their hands were a blur, and finally Esther was laughing too much and the game collapsed, whereupon Esther would throw herself into his arms, giggling with delight. Then she would cry, 'Again! Again!' and off they would go, very slowly at first. Then Esther taught it to Ali Bey, a solemn and dignified Egyptian gentleman whom Daniel had befriended on board. She made him learn to do 'This is the way the gentleman rides' and he assisted in the games of 'One two three whee' upon which Esther insisted as they promenaded about the decks. They tossed the little girl to each other and pretended that they were going to throw her over the side, which of course she did not believe for a second. Ali Bey was not only very taken with Esther, but was interested in the politics and culture of France. He presented Daniel with a fez, and they sat together on deck after Esther and Rosie were in bed, talking nostalgically about the Loire Valley, the novels of Zola or the effects of the Franco–Prussian war.

Daniel was at first wary of the intimacies of caring for an infant. He felt dubious and nervous about having to wash her at bedtime, and clean her up after going to the lavatory, as if he were worried that she might share in the abashment of a mature woman, or as if he might accidentally damage what his mother always referred to as 'sa belle chose'. It was as good a euphemism as any, so he began to use it himself. Esther was quite frank and unembarrassed, however, and would simply announce, 'My bottom's ready, Daddy,' when she needed cleaning up. When the travelling nurse was indisposed, which was most of the time, he fretted about how to dress her properly. He watched the nurse or Rosie doing it, and quickly realised that it could not have been simpler. Esther had distinct preferences that changed every day, and she would rummage through her own small suitcase throwing unwanted garments onto the floor of the cabin. She had exceedingly fine hair, and Daniel found it difficult to brush it or comb it without causing shrieks of protest.

When Esther was asleep Daniel and Rosie played *vingt-et-un*, which Rosie won, or chess, which was always won by Daniel. Rosie taught him how to play draughts, and racing demon, a furious game which inevitably ended up in the destruction of the cards. For the first time in their acquaintance they had long hours to fill with reminiscence and conversation, and began to know each other ever better. Rosie had mostly avoided being alone with him for any length of time, but now she beqan to perceive that he was not only handsome, a fact obvious to all, but also amusing and interesting. In this sense, the long journey had the reverse effect to that had on most couples by such voyages. The other passengers were becoming more and more wild with the racheting up of the temperature, and relationships and infidelities were being created and destroyed on a daily basis. Daniel found it entertaining, but Rosie was shocked.

He had the good fortune to befriend the captain of the ship. Captain Franklin had a naval beard, and very much resembled the King, causing Daniel to reflect how much he would have been admired by his mother-in-law. Franklin had served on HMS *Hood* during the war, and the two men felt comfortable with each other, as those who have seen action commonly do. Captain Franklin also took a liking to Esther, who therefore spent time up on the bridge gazing out of the windows at the sea whilst the former explained all the workings of the ship to her father, let him take the wheel, and pull on the lever that signalled engine speed to those below.

Daniel had guided tours of the machinery from the engineers and stokers, and was repeatedly amazed by the size of the cranks and pistons, rods and shafts. The boiler room was as hot as Hell, manned by sweating men, wild-eyed sailors who worked like devils. The engines of aeroplanes seemed such bijou contraptions by comparison that Daniel felt obscurely ashamed of having been so fascinated by them.

Rosie only sprang to life during those hours when the ship was in port. Even so, she felt quite nauseous when she got onto land and found that it was not moving. She staggered as if to allow for movement that was no longer occurring. In Gibraltar they went to see the apes, and Rosie had a handkerchief snatched out of her hand when she was just about to blow her nose. Daniel tried to retrieve it, but was no match for the ribald, scampering thief, which skipped away and bared its teeth at him. There was a left-handed ape that liked to pick up its excrement and hurl it at people, causing gratifying screams and panics.

In Valetta, having learned their lesson in Gibraltar, they left the impractically huge perambulator on the ship, and Daniel hoisted Esther onto his shoulders. They strolled around the small walled town in a very short time, and then made another circuit. The place was full of British sailors in sparkling white uniforms, and vast grey warships lay at anchor in the harbour. Daniel insisted on going down there to look at the seaplanes. The heat radiated from the stones, and the light cut precise black shadows. Rosie felt the heat entering the bones and muscles of her body, freeing both her limbs and her spirit. After her eyes had adjusted to the light, she began to feel her mood lift with every step. The distance from home, and all that home implied, was releasing her from the loops that had been going round in her thoughts for so many months. She thought of Ash's letters and uniform, wrapped up in tissues in the small suitcase, and she thought of her madonna and child, and the image of them in her memory no longer had any great reality.

They ordered tea at a cafe, and Rosie said to Daniel, 'Isn't this wonderful? I haven't felt as happy as this since I don't know when.'

'I've never seen you so happy,' replied Daniel, wondering at the new vivacity that made her look younger and more beautiful. The bright light made her blue eyes seem especially luminous.

'I wish we could stay here,' said Rosie. 'It's paradise.'

'Ceylon's even more of a paradise,' said Daniel, 'once you're up in the highlands. Malta's terribly dry and baking hot in the summer. I think we must be here at the best time of year.'

In Port Said, at precisely the moment that they were passing the statue of de Lesseps, Esther, Rosie and the travelling nurse picked up gippy tummy before even leaving the ship, and so Daniel transferred them for two nights to the Marina Palace Hotel, where they sat on the veranda of their room watching the liners arriving and departing. Because Ali Bey had relatives to visit, Daniel went about town on his own, before realising quite quickly that the level of harassment and aggression from both beggars and merchants was more than one man should have to cope with, so he went back to the ship and waited for Captain Franklin to finish filling in the port authority's documents. Then the two men ventured out and made a fair fist of standing up for themselves, fending off those who wanted to know whether they wanted to meet their sisters or buy 'feelthy pictures', or hashish. Captain Franklin assured Daniel that meeting a sister in Egypt was the one infallible way of picking up syphilis, and the feelthy pictures were never quite as feelthy as one might have hoped. The streets were crawling with tiny Arab boys and girls who would do anything whatsoever for money, and Daniel found it altogether depressing and vile. He and the Captain drank prodigious quantities of sweet mint tea out of small glass cups, and talked about the war, which already seemed a peculiar dream. They devoted much ingenuity to avoiding the small *boyagis* who would dart out, put a blob of polish on your shoe, and then offer to polish it off. There was many an obstinate and irritated European walking about with such a blob drying and congealing on his toecap.

Daniel bought another fez for himself, and for Rosie a small enamelled silver camel whose hump opened to reveal a hiding place for a ring or a brooch. For Esther he bought embroidered slippers with turned-up toes, and a tiny scarlet jacket with a high collar.

The Suez Canal by day was a hell of flies and heat for all of them, but at night it was wondrous and magical to stand at the prow and watch the waters and the banks by the beam of the immense searchlight. Once they were out through the Gulf of Aden, and steaming at first for Bombay and then for Colombo, the excitement and pleasure grew in all of them. They slept on deck to escape the insufferable heat below, and suffered very little from sickness, since the waters were unusually placid off the coast of Socotra. They had been warned to expect it to be worse than the Bay of Biscay, especially as the south-west monsoon was due within weeks. In the evenings, as the small ship's orchestra played popular waltzes and polkas, Daniel played deck quoits with Ali Bey who, by his own account, worked in the court of King Fouad, and had been educated in Ceylon whilst his parents had been there in exile. It turned out that not only was he a Francophile, but he also had an astonishing knowledge of the novels of Sir Walter Scott, and an insatiable need to discuss them. He and

Daniel walked the promenade deck with Esther, doing 'One two three whee' until their arms ached. Rosie began to find her sea legs at last, and liked to lean over the ship's rail with the wind whipping her hair about her face. She felt well enough now to sit in a deckchair in the shade of a canopy and reread the books on Ceylon that they had brought with them. One of the passengers lent her a novel by Mrs Oliphant, and she read that too. She played bucket quoits and bullboard with Esther to keep her amused.

Esther forced her father to make up stories day in and day out, until he thought his brain was going to rattle in its bearings from the wear and tear of continual invention. One day he told Esther to tell him a story for once, and she astonished him by coming up with a narrative that was both interminable and senseless, brimful of the natural surrealism of the child. When he fell asleep, she merely continued to sit in his lap and tell it to him while he snored, until she too nodded off.

By the time they reached Colombo, Daniel had found a new harmony with his wife, and a deeper mutual love with his daughter. The evening before their arrival, after the ship's last formal dance, when Esther was in bed and her parents were leaning over the rail on the promenade deck, looking at the southern stars, Rosie said to Daniel, 'Don't you think it's time that Esther had a little brother or sister?' and his heart had jumped in his chest.

He looked at her sideways and said, 'It would help us make a proper new start.' Her eyes were glowing in the half-dark.

They arrived in Colombo at dawn, two weeks before the onset of the south-west monsoon. While Esther and her nurse still slept below, Rosie and Daniel watched the port appear. The palm trees waved gently along the shores, at the back of the narrow sands. It was cool, but the steaming heat of the day was already impending. Daniel said, 'Ah, the smell of the East! How I love it!'

'It smells a lot nicer than Bombay,' said Rosie, breathing in the scent of coriander, cumin and fenugreek, garlic, woodsmoke and tumeric, ajowan, blossom and sweat. 'It smells all friendly and inviting.'

'It is going to be terribly hot and humid,' Daniel warned her for the hundredth time, 'but don't worry, it'll be lovely in the highlands.'

'I don't think I'd mind it anyway,' said Rosie. 'Nothing could be hotter than the corridors of Netley in the summer.'

'The tropics drive white men quite mad, you know,' said Daniel. 'They cope by drinking vast quantities of alcohol, and then after a few years that stops working, and they go downhill like an avalanche. They come home with malaria and can't get used to being back, and they keep drinking and then they die. Half of them accidentally set their armchairs alight with their pipes and cigarettes, whilst they're in a coma, and the whisky makes them quite extraordinarily combustible. And the women –'

'Oh, do say something cheerful,' said Rosie.

'I *am* cheerful,' said Daniel. 'We aren't going to be in the lowlands. And of course, there's Esther, so we probably can't stay here forever.'

'Esther? What do you mean?'

'What are we going to do when she's old enough to go to school? I'm not sure there are any where we're going.'

'We could send her home to live with Granny? Or Gran'mère? She could go to one of those nice little schools in Sussex, and frolic on the South Downs in her spare time.'

'Not sure I could bear that. I'm not sure that you could. I'm told that colonial wives usually have to choose between their husbands and their children. I know there are at least two boys' schools in Kandy. Ali Bey told me about them, because he'd been to one, and terribly proud he is of it too. But we'll have to find out if there's one for girls.'

They heard the shouts of the sailors, and the clank and the booming bass rattle of the anchor chain. 'Look,' said Daniel, 'there's the steam launch coming to get us.'

'I think I'll go and get Esther up and dressed,' said Rosie. 'And I'll see that nurse is awake. We'll be docking any minute, won't we?'

'I'll miss this ship. I don't have to say goodbye to Ali Bey yet, though. With any luck he'll be in the same hotel. I've invited him to come and stay sometime. We've had such a lot of fun.'

'Yes,' she said, 'we have. After I got over the seasickness, anyway. I'll miss it too. We must remember to thank the Captain and the purser.'

106

Et in Arcadia Nos (1)

T he square on the inner harbour was lined on three sides by about thirty motor cars, four rickshaws and one bullock cart. Daniel had expected it to be teeming and chaotic, like an Indian port, but it was quiet and orderly. He and Rosie were merely lucky, however. On future visits, it would always be teeming with touts and idlers, beggars, sharks and opportunists, with much anarchy and hubbub.

On the quayside to meet them was Hugh Bassett, son of the Colonel. Like Daniel, he was dressed in tropical whites, and wore a topee. He was a tall man with a rubicund face, an exiguous ginger moustache and rheumy blue eyes that betrayed considerable good humour.

'*Ayubowa!* Welcome to Colombo, welcome to Ceylon!' he cried, as he pumped their hands, and then he bent down and offered Esther his hand too. 'You have brought a little princess with you! Your Royal Highness, how d'you do?'

'I do do well,' replied Esther, shaking his proferred hand. 'Mostly. I'm a bit hot. I know some poems.'

'I understand you were in the Flying Corps,' said Hugh to Daniel.

'And previously in the Frontier Scouts and Rattray's Sikhs. I suppose I'm an RAF man now.'

'Once RFC, always RFC,' said Hugh. 'I was in the RNAS.'

'Gracious, really? We'll have masses to talk about. We can have pistols at dawn about whether to stand or sit during the loyal toast. You didn't know Collishaw, did you?'

'Just met him at a do. Not in my squadron, I'm afraid.'

'Anyone who has met Collishaw automatically has my greatest admiration,' said Daniel, 'Did you know A. K. Smithells? Son of the scientist? Crashed a Sopwith?'

'Everyone's crashed a Sopwith,' said Hugh. 'I have myself.'

'Did you fly Tripehounds?'

'Certainly did. Loved them.'

Rosie took Esther's hand, and said, 'Come on, darling, I can see that you and I aren't going to get a word in edgeways with these two.'

'I'm so sorry,' said Hugh. 'Anyway, I'm sure you'll get on terribly well with my wife. She was a FANY. You were a VAD, weren't you? You can talk to your hearts' content about gangrene and aneurysms and sebaceous cysts. We have some lovely diseases here that you will find quite novel.'

Rosie laughed. 'I'm hoping to be helpful in the estate clinic. I've been told you have one.'

'We certainly do. Now, the plan is that we will spend today in Colombo. If there's time and you like the idea, we can go to Mount Lavinia for the afternoon. It's very pleasant by the sea. Tonight we will all stay in the GOH, and tomorrow morning we will set off reasonably early, and wend our way in a somewhat leisurely fashion, seeing all the sights.'

'I'll look forward to that,' said Daniel.

'What's the GOH?' asked Rosie.

'This,' said Hugh, waving his arm towards an impressive and highly Romanesque building right in front of them, with canopies over the windows, 'is the Grand Oriental Hotel. That's why it has "GOH" at the top. And you'll never guess what that is.' He pointed to a smaller but prettier building on the left. It had 'VICTORIA ARCADE' written along it, at the level of the first floor.

'I'm only guessing,' said Daniel, 'but I think it's probably the Victoria Arcade.'

'Oh my,' said Rosie, 'I think the GOH is much too grand for the likes of us.'

'Nonsense!' replied Hugh. 'Even the most banal and vulgar of monarchs have stayed there. It has electroliers and electric punkahs, and a wondrous billiards room. Anyone play billiards? There are six tables, and the hotel will even provide you with a marker to play with, should you need an opponent. Watch out for Perera – you can't possibly win if it's him you're up against, so don't lay any wagers. I've got you a room overlooking the harbour. There's a charming little dwarf on the staff, called Chandan, and I've briefed him to be very attentive to you at all times and keep away the tip cadgers. You'll find him most appealing and comical. And,' he added, turning to Daniel, 'the reason we are going to be tourists for a few days is that we are going to work you absolutely flat out for at least six months. This is your brief respite before the apocalypse.'

'I shall enjoy it as the condemned man relishes his last meal,' said Daniel.

'Your baggage will be brought straight to your rooms by the porters.'

'And what about my Henley?'

'You've brought an entire town?'

'My motorcycle. It'll have to be unloaded and uncrated, and I'll have to check it's all working. Unless you're taking us in a lorry, I'll need to come in convoy with you.'

'And leave me alone in the car with your lovely wife? Foolish man. You may live to regret it. I do hope you brought plenty of spares. You'll find that the engineers at the station are extremely able, but it might take months to get new parts. A motorcycle is really not the most practical way of getting around here, I'm afraid.'

'I've brought three of everything that most commonly lets me down,' replied Daniel. 'Every time something fails I'll order another one, and it should turn up before the two spare ones conk out.'

'That's most ferociously sensible of you. How well off for books are you? You'll get through an extraordinary number of them, unless you hit the bottle instead. Or you can play tennis. There's a marvellous bookshop here in Colombo. H. W. Cave & Co. It's got all the very latest things, a month late, and some tremendous relics that no one's read since 1850.'

'We've got lots,' said Rosie, 'but I love bookshops. Can we go to it anyway? They might have a good poetry section, with any luck.'

'Your command is my wish,' said Hugh, 'and vice versa. Now, I expect you'd like to rest a little in your hotel. Shall I come for you at ten? You're probably dying to try out a rickshaw, and you'll need me there to keep the prices reasonable.' Bending down to

Esther he said, 'Is your bear very tired? Does he want a rest?' and Esther replied scornfully, 'No. He's only a toy. And what's a rick-shaw? And why is everybody brown and wearing funny clothes? And what's that funny smell? And why's that man got red teeth and dribble?'

'Lots of people are brown,' said Daniel. 'In fact most people in the world are brown, probably. And the funny smell is spices and a few other things, and the funny clothes are normal in Ceylon, and they think our European clothes are funny. So we're all a bit funny, aren't we?'

'What's European? And why's it getting so hot? And who's that man over there who's looking at us?'

'Oh gosh,' said Rosie, 'she's off on one of her exhausting quests for knowledge.'

'Let's get you settled in,' said Hugh Bassett.

At ten o'clock, Hugh Bassett returned with a motor car, and, leaving the travelling nurse to her upset stomach, they motored together to Mount Lavinia, to sample the famous 'Fish Tiffin'. Rosie thought that the rocks in the sea looked like semi-submerged elephants, with little boys fishing from their backs. The waters were quite crowded by fishermen, with their outrigger canoes. Then, when the day began to cool, Hugh brought them back to stroll along the Galle Face Promenade. 'This is the best place to be in the evenings,' said Hugh. 'The gossip is unsurpassed anywhere. And it's all thanks to Sir Henry Ward. There's a little plaque over there, recommending the place to ladies and children.'

'What did he have against men?'

'Oh, nothing probably. I expect he was a wife-beater and sweet-snatcher and ear-tweaker who wanted to conceal the truth.'

'Was he the one who was married to the novelist and anti-suffragist?' asked Daniel.

'That was Humphrey Ward, not Sir Henry,' said Rosie.

'Contemporary literature not my strong point,' said Daniel. They walked along the seaward edge of the green, and watched the waves crashing in. A schooner in the distance sailed past, all its sails bellied out, and a Dutch flag flying at the mast.

'Further round the coast you can watch the whales going past at migration time,' said Hugh.

'This is simply wondrous,' said Rosie, as they loitered amid a throng which seemed to consist of people of every race in the world. There were Malays, Chinese, Arabs, Afghans, Parsees in conical hats, Muslim men in their embroidered skullcaps, their children flying kites and robed in white. There were bourgeois Sinhalese, the men in suits and their wives dressed as European ladies, with enormous hats like fruit bowls. There were genuine European ladies with lacy parasols pausing under trees in blossom, or looking at the flower beds, on the arms of gentlemen, tagged along and protected by their dark servants in their white uniforms and yellow sashes. There were throngs of the improvising poor, with their exotic-looking snacks for sale, or hawking little gimmicks and gewgaws both to the richer folk and to each other, with cries of 'Cheap! Cheap! Made in England! Better than Harrod's!' At the roadside, carriages, landaus, turnouts, rickshaws, dog carts, gharries and automobiles arrived in increasing numbers, and deposited their occupants.

'The whole point of this,' observed Hugh, 'and the only way to appreciate it, is to realise that this is where the beautiful women come to be admired, and everyone else comes to admire them. So, my dear Mrs Pitt, you must put your best foot forward and be as determinedly beautiful as your rivals.'

'That may be difficult,' said Rosie, fanning her face with her hat. 'I am not feeling at all beautiful at present. I'm very much overheated.'

'Then you are disguising your feelings very well, if I may say so.'

Rosie and Esther had come out dressed identically, in white muslin dresses, and broad-brimmed straw sun hats trimmed with artificial cornflowers, and they did look very pretty. Rosie knew that she could never match these other ladies, though, who had about them a kind of happy and secure sensuality that left her feeling gauche and undesirable.

'It's a pity we haven't much time in Colombo,' said Hugh, 'but you can always come back. We've got an excellent railway. You should take the chance to have a tram ride through Pettah. It's an epitome of the Orient, all in one small trip. And Victoria Park is lovely. Our little Princess Esther would be very happy there.'

'Oh well, another time,' said Daniel.

'By the way, I've been meaning to tell you, when you're given mutton, it's really goat. It's rather delicious, actually, if you've got strong jaws. And you must come back for the races. And the State Ball, if you can wangle an invitation. Shall I take you back to the GOH? Let's all meet up for supper, shall we? I'll be there at seven and we can have a sundowner first.'

That evening, after supper, Rosie went upstairs to see that Esther was happily asleep, and Hugh Bassett had the opportunity to tell Daniel something that he felt was important. 'If you don't mind, old boy, just between you and me, there's something you really do have to know straight away. It's somewhat ticklish.'

'Ticklish? Don't worry, I'm not at all squeamish or refined, I do assure you.'

'It's the native women. You've probably already noticed how delightfully pretty a lot of them are.'

'How could I not?'

'Well, they're also very sweet-natured and, shall we say . . . accommodating? Quite adorable, really. A dream come true.'

'But? Do they carry fearful diseases?'

'No, it's not that. Sometimes a father arrives with all his daughters and offers to let you choose one. Or you fall for one of your servants. Of course, it's much more likely if you're a bachelor, but none of us is immune.'

'And?'

'Well, there's a catch – rather an awkward one.'

'I see.'

'You don't. What happens is that the moment the girl has a child, she leaves you, and takes you to court. For some reason the judges and magistrates here are a fantastically puritanical lot, and you end up paying for the girl's housing and maintenance for the rest of her life, and most of the money actually goes to her relatives. So do bear in mind that the sweet little thing you fall for is very probably on the make. They're perfectly capable of adoring you until the crunch comes, and then the crunch turns out to be damnably big.'

'Hmm,' said Daniel. 'Thanks for telling me all this, but I scarcely think –'

'It happens to plenty of married men, too,' said Hugh. 'Believe me, it really does. And I would just like to tell you again what my father no doubt has told you already.'

'Don't think I know anything about Ceylon until I've been here for twenty years?'

'Exactly. Exactly that. We don't understand the natives and they don't understand us. We only get on because we become fond of each other and make a great many allowances. And the Sinhalese are quite different from the Tamils. You'd be absolutely amazed at the things they believe in.'

'I'm very often amazed at the things *we* believe in,' replied Daniel. 'But here comes Rosie. Is Shompi all right, darling?'

'The room's a bit steamy,' said Rosie, settling herself down in her seat.

'It's the price you pay for the view,' said Hugh.

'The harbour's twinkling with lights,' she said.

107

Et in Arcadia Nos (2)

The following morning at seven, seen off by a lachrymose Ali Bey who waved forlornly after them, they departed for Kandy along the road originally built by the British for the purpose of conquering that inaccessible kingdom, at the request of the Kandians themselves, it appeared. Rosie sat in the front of Hugh's car, with Esther on the back seat. She spent most of the time waving to her father, who was trailing behind on his Henley, trying to avoid the cloud of road dust being thrown up by the vehicle in front.

They stopped in Belummahara to buy pineapples, and in Kajugama, where they bought cashews to snack on during the journey. Near the beginning of the hill country Esther suddenly started shrieking with delight, and when Rosie turned round, she saw that her daughter was pointing to a troupe of monkeys that was hurtling through the roadside trees. She alerted Hugh, and Hugh slowed down to look, whereupon the monkeys slowed too.

'They're racing us,' said Hugh. 'You often see that. I like to slow down to make it more sporting. Give them more of a chance. Of course, the moment there's a break in the trees, they have to give up.'

'Are there lots of monkeys here?'

'Millions. Sometimes you get a big male setting up house in your garden. They're extremely aggressive. You have to hire a monkey man with an even bigger male, and it lives in your garden for a few days until it's driven off the other one, and then the monkey man comes and fetches the giant one away again. You'll notice in all the hotel rooms there's a sign saying "Please don't feed the monkeys".'

'Gracious,' said Rosie. 'It makes a change from "Don't feed the seagulls", doesn't it?'

'Look,' said Esther, 'there's a black cow asleep with a bird on it.'

'It's an egret,' said Hugh over his shoulder. 'The birdlife here is a wonder.'

'I like all the smart little dogs,' said Rosie.

'Chipper little fellows, aren't they? We'll stop by a paddy field later and see if we can spot some water buffalo. And there's a place where the elephants go down to bathe at the same times every day.'

In Kandy they strolled around the lake, looking at the water-fowl, and then they entered the Temple of the Tooth, and got as near to the Buddha's tooth as they could. Hugh said, 'You really must try to see the Perahera. It's something like sixty elephants, all gorgeously got up. It starts here at the Dalada Maligawa. There's a great ding-donging as the elephants come in from the villages. Anyway, the biggest elephant of all carries the tooth in a golden dome. He's well worth seeing, a real giant, and they've silver-plated his tusks. They put swathes of white cloth in front of him wher-ever he goes, so that he doesn't have to be demeaned by touching the earth. You see all the Kandian chiefs in their costumes, and there are dancers and whip-crackers and gong-bashers and God knows what else, for two weeks solid. I'm always amazed by the elephants. They know exactly what to do, somehow. You get tens of thousands of pilgrims and hawkers, and then on the last day they have a huge fancy-dress party at the Queen's Hotel. You have to book a room months ahead. By the way, all the jaded old sceptics who have seen the tooth think it isn't human. The original one disappeared because of a conquest, or something, and reappeared miraculously, so they say. Anyway, what does it matter, really? As long as everyone has fun.'

Hugh took them round the botanical gardens at Peradeniya, with its avenues of wondrously tall trees. Daniel was impressed by the thundering, cascading river that surrounded it. He wondered whether the fish in such a furious torrent had a chance of not being swept out to sea. They settled on a bench, and Hugh told them, 'These gardens were originally built by a Kandian king in the eighteenth century, and I don't suppose you'll find nicer ones anywhere in the world. I've certainly never found a nicer place to have a picnic. I like to come here and remind myself that civilisations other than ours have achieved things just as great.'

'That's something we all know,' observed Daniel, 'but somehow we never seem to digest it.'

'There's never been an empire as big as ours,' said Rosie. 'I think we're a good thing. Don't you?'

'Well, I would say so,' said Hugh. 'I'd rather be under the British than the Belgians, that's certain, but of course I'm biased. It seems to me that in the end all empires just die of fatigue. I'm not sure that we're tired yet, but I do think that one day we will be, and we'll be gone, and all the tea plantations will revert to jungle. We'll be just be a memory, like the pharaohs, or the Aztecs or the Romans.'

'Gracious me, do you think so?' said Rosie.

'Well, I've never heard of a civilisation that's lasted forever. Have you?'

'No, I haven't but . . . all the same.'

'There used to be an extraordinary civilisation here,' said Hugh, 'and the population must have been hugely bigger. They irrigated an entire region. A lot of the lakes and channels are still there and still working. For some reason we call the lakes "tanks". Anyway, it's worth coming here just to see the giant bamboos and rubber trees. And these cabbage palms. Let's go to the golf club at Nuwara Eliya. Do you play golf?'

'My Squadron Leader forced me to learn,' said Daniel. 'I quite enjoy it, actually. Rosie plays, but I wouldn't say that she finds it all-consuming.'

'My father's a fanatic,' said Rosie, 'and my mother's very good too, without even practising. It's become our family game, all because Daddy's Scottish. I like golf, but it does seem to cause a sort of madness in some people, doesn't it? My father's a hopeless case. He even practises indoors.'

'Well, I'll introduce you to the secretary. And tonight we'll stay in the Grand Hotel. You'll think it's straight out of Sussex, apart from the staff, who are all natives, and all frightful snobs. Very quaint and amusing, really.'

'It's starting to rain,' said Rosie.

'Rains all the time round here,' said Hugh cheerfully. 'It's like Ireland. And when you're at your bungalow and it rains, you'll think you're in the Highlands of Scotland.'

The next day, towards the end of the afternoon, after three hours travel from Nuwara Eliya, Rosie, Daniel and Esther found themselves at their bungalow at last. Daniel was exhausted by all the motorcycling on difficult switchbacked roads, full of intricate curves and sudden inclines, but was both amazed and grateful that he had suffered no punctures, or major breakdowns, other than having to remove and clean the magneto. Rosie and Esther were still surprised by all the sights they had seen in the villages and little towns through which they had passed. People seemed to live their lives with complete openness, in buildings that had no frontage. They had looked into those impassive dark faces with their darker eyes, and the locals had looked back at their red faces and blue eyes, neither understanding what they were seeing, until Esther waved to them from the back of the car, and they waved shyly back. The little settlements were teeming with hommos sellers, pingo bearers, and roadside vendors sitting with heaps of enormous fruit of which Rosie did not even know the names. Tiny brown children frolicked everywhere.

Hugh stopped the car in the road outside the bungalow, and announced that he would have to come in and introduce them to the servants, and fetch water for his radiator, which was beginning to boil.

As they opened the garden gate, there was a sudden rush and patter of feet, and four servants appeared to empty the vehicles of their luggage, disappearing back into the house with it just as suddenly.

'They're all Tamils,' said Hugh, 'just as you'd expect. Hindus. I think you'll find them very conscientious and eager to please.'

'We haven't really had many servants since before the war,' said Rosie. 'This is going to be a bit strange. We all got used to doing things for ourselves. My father says he wished he'd known before what fun it was cleaning your own clubs and decanting wine, and working out whether it needed cinnamon or not. I don't really need anyone any more.'

'Well, I think you'll like them. They're charming people, and of course one has a duty to find work for people and spread a little prosperity. That's how I see it, anyway.'

'You're quite right,' said Daniel. 'Without work, life is completely meaningless.'

'I'll line them up and introduce you. You'll soon learn their names, and very shortly afterwards you'll find out all their foibles.'

'Am I going to have any friends?' asked Esther.

Having been introduced to the servants (three young men in immaculate tunics, and one extraordinarily pretty maid) they sat on the veranda in the declining sun, and were served tea and biscuits by one of the young men, who was both excited and nervous.

'I think Kandy is one of the most beautiful places I've ever seen,' said Rosie. 'Not the town itself, I mean the views, and the lake, and the fireflies at night, and the jungle. Luxuriant is hardly the word, is it?'

'Wait 'til you've been found by a leech,' said Hugh.

'I like all the monkeys,' said Esther. 'Can we have a pet monkey?'

'They have very horrible habits,' said Hugh, 'and very strong opinions.'

'I have a feeling that this island is going to be inexhaustible,' said Daniel. 'It couldn't be less like the North-West Frontier. I don't know why, but I was half expecting it to be similar for some reason.'

'That's like expecting Norway to be like Spain,' said Hugh. 'Oh, and you'll find that your cook thinks that we eat only mutton chops, by the way. Goat, in other words. If you want anything else you'll have to educate him into it very gently. Servants here are easily shocked. They're horrified if you want to try any of the local dishes. They strongly disapprove of us going native. And they won't cook beef, obviously.'

'Perhaps I'll teach him our cookery if he teaches me his,' said Rosie. 'But I suppose I'd have to learn ours first.'

'I'm not sure that spotted dick with custard and bubble and squeak would appeal very much to the natives,' said Hugh.

After they had eaten their supper, which had indeed consisted of 'mutton' chops, Hugh proposed a long and gracious toast of welcome, and Daniel replied with a short speech thanking him for his time and hospitality. Hugh rose to leave, saying, 'My bungalow's the next one along, five hundred yards. Do call by if you need anything or have any questions.' He turned to Daniel. 'Work starts tomorrow. I'll be calling for you at half past eight, but more often than not we'll be out at dawn.'

'I look forward to it,' said Daniel, shaking his hand warmly, 'and thank you so much again for your time, and all you've done for us.'

'I needed the little holiday, to tell the truth,' said Hugh. 'And I was desperate to meet another flying man.'

'Do you think there's a future in aviation here?' asked Daniel eagerly. 'I noticed there weren't any seaplanes in the harbour.'

'I knew you were going to ask that! It's something I've thought about a great deal. It's actually a question of the enormous expense of setting up an infrastructure. But let's talk about it tomorrow. It's late, and you've got to get your little princess tucked up in bed. You must be tired too, if you're as tired as I am. Come and eat with us tomorrow; I'll introduce you to my wife.'

That night, as Daniel and Rosie lay in each other's arms, wide awake as the owls called outside, Rosie said, 'I'm so glad we came.'

'It couldn't be further from Eltham or Birmingham, could it?' said Daniel. 'But Argentina would have been nice.'

'I am sorry about that. I know how disappointed you were.'

'Well, now I understand the reason. You really should have told me, instead of bottling it all up.'

'I know. I'm sorry about that too. Anyway, I hope the climate's as nice as you promised. Esther and I did get terribly sticky and clammy down in Colombo. Any more, and we would have got grumpy.'

'Well, Kandy was perfect, wasn't it? This will be even more perfect.'

'You can't be more perfect than perfect,' said Rosie.

'Pedant.'

The next day, Rosie had a chance to take proper stock of her new domain. There was a wonderful bathroom with a large cast-iron bath on lion's feet, and black-and-white tiles up the walls and on the floor. In her bedroom she admired all over again the enormous carved four-poster bed draped in white muslin to keep out the mosquitoes, where only last night she and Daniel had set about the creation of their next child. Everywhere there were gleaming teak floors and clean white walls. She thought of her mother in Eltham, mixing up beeswax and turpentine once a year, just in case Their Majesties should call in and expect to see a polished floor. How she would have loved to have seen the ones here in this bungalow.

Best of all was the roofed veranda, with its tiled floor and wicker chairs. Here she wrote letters home to tell everyone that her new address was a house called Taprobane Bungalow, near the Wanarajah Tea Factory, near Dickoya Village, Central Highlands. As an afterthought she wrote to Mrs Burke in Birmingham, and to Dr Scott, to remind him to keep a close eye on her father.

Daniel returned just before sunset, exhausted, aching and happy. He sat on the veranda with Esther on his lap, thumb in mouth as ever, and French Bear under her arm. He said, 'You wouldn't believe what hard work this is going to be. I have a staggering amount to learn in no time at all, and you need legs like a sherpa. It seems that manufacturing tea is 50 per cent science and 50 per cent intuition. It's a bit worrying, really. I had been hoping it was all science, and then I could get a grip on it straight away. Still, you should see the machinery! It's perfectly marvellous . . . quite massive, but beautifully made, a real joy.' He reached into his pocket and produced a folded piece of paper. 'Here are my first twenty Tamil words to learn. Would you test me? We should do it before we go to dinner with Hugh.'

'Ooh, I can learn them too then,' said Rosie. 'The cook does know plenty of English, and so do the others, but you can tell they're never quite sure what you really mean. They're devastated if they think they've disappointed you. I've already learned to say "arre".'

'I see you've been reading Rupert Brooke again,' said Daniel, nodding towards the collected verse that lay on the coffee table beside Rosie's seat.

Rosie pulled a wry face. 'I'm rather afraid I might be going off him. All that breathless flinging and so on. And that wisdom in women one is really beginning to pall. It's so condescending, don't you think? As if women don't have any nouse of their own.'

'I've always thought that. I mean that it's condescending, not that women don't have any nouse. I still love the one about the fish, though, and the one about the funeral of God. I expect you need a break from Rupert B. You'll probably get your enjoyment back if you leave it for a while. I see you've taken the cover off, or did you lose it?'

'I put it in a drawer. It was getting awfully tatty, and that photograph of Brooke in his huge poetic cravat was beginning to irritate me.' She reached over and brushed a small ball of fluff from his jacket. 'You know,' she said, settling back into her seat, 'now that we're here I'd like to start writing poetry again. I think I'm going to be inspired.'

'Again?' he said, raising an eyebrow, in quest of an explanation.

'I used to win the poetry prize every year at school. But it was always old-fashioned stuff. You know, I loved Elizabeth Barrett Browning and Christina Rossetti, and people like that, and I still love them really, but I don't think we can go on writing all that thee and thou stuff any more, do you? And striking poses? And coming up with strange word orders just to accommodate a bad rhyme? I think it's got to be more up to date somehow.'

'At Westminster we memorised reams of heroic narrative verse,' said Daniel. '"Horatius at the Bridge", and so on. I can still recite them perfectly. "Lars Porsena of Clusium, / By the nine gods he swore, / That the great house of Tarquin / Should suffer wrong no more . . ." If you recited them faultlessly, you got plus marks, and if you failed badly enough, you got beaten.'

They both laughed. 'I want to be a proper Georgian poet,' said Rosie, 'but how will I keep up to date? I can't rely on lucky accidents, like yours, when you found Eleanor Farjeon in Margate. You know, be aware of where the tide is flowing, and know what to be inspired by? Who to read for useful tips?'

'Just drop a line to Cave's in Colombo and tell them what you want. That way you'll only be two months out of date at most, and a heavy little parcel in brown paper and tied with string will arrive every few weeks or so.'

'Can we afford it?'

'Well, if it gets too much we can cut back. I'd have thought that books would be the last thing to give up. Why don't we take it in turns to read a book, so we can talk about it afterwards?'

'That would be fun. As long as I don't have to read too many things about aeroplanes.'

'It's a pity you don't read much French,' said Daniel. 'My more intellectual French friends tell me that we're writing the most interesting modern poetry in the world. Claudel, Jules Laforgue, and so on.'

'When we get the books you can go over them with me,' said Rosie. 'I want to learn to speak better French anyway.'

'The best thing is to pay attention when I'm chattering to Esther,' said Daniel. 'It's always best to learn the same way as a child.'

'There's a newish poet called T. S. Eliot,' said Rosie. 'He's considered a bit shocking, so I'm going to try and find out more about him. I saw something called "Prufrock" and it really is quite different from anything else. The metre is terribly loose, but it's still obviously poetry. I'd love to be able to write like that.'

They looked out over the garden, which was terraced in three stages down the mountainside below. A wizened gardener was on his hands and knees, apparently doing intricate things with individual blades of grass. On the right there stood a fantastically tall red turpentine tree, straight as a guardsman, and on the second terrace, next to a croquet lawn, there stood a round white gazebo. The beds were planted with busy Lizzies and red salvia. A tiny squirrel with a black stripe along its spine approached the place where they sat, went up on its haunches, and sniffed the air to discover what they were. Rosie threw it a cashew. It suddenly occurred to her that 'Gilbert the Filbert' had stopped going round and round in her head. What a relief it was. She seemed to have so much more space for other thoughts.

'We're an ill-assorted pair, aren't we?' said Daniel.

Her heart seemed to stop for a moment, and she looked up at him with a kind of horror. 'What do you mean?' she asked, knowing perfectly well what all the possible answers might be, except for the one that he came up with.

'I've just spent several years killing hundreds of people,' he said, 'and you've just spent years saving the lives of hundreds of people.'

'Hundreds? You've killed hundreds?'

'Yes. If you include the ground attacks through 1918. I must have killed hundreds. I saw it with my own eyes. Either bombed or machine-gunned. Mostly machine-gunned.'

'But you had to, didn't you?'

'Yes, on the face of it. Even so, one can't help but wonder. How much sorrow and mourning must have come out of it.' He paused '. . . and how much waste. I must have killed people who were going to be musicians, or poets, or doctors, or scientists. People who loved their children. I might have killed the German Rupert Brooke.'

'Don't forget they were trying to kill you too. You probably killed a lot of petty criminals and murderers and wife-beaters and dog-kickers as well.'

Daniel laughed. 'No doubt.'

'And they were doing the same to us. Think of poor Fairhead's little sister. She might have got married and had six beautiful little children, and one of them might have grown up to be a genius.'

'Or a lunatic.'

'Well, we cannot possibly ever know, can we?'

'What if Ash had survived and you'd married him instead of me?'

'We wouldn't have had Esther. Would you want to live in a world without Esther?'

'No, but I'd rather live in a world that still had Ash. I expect you would too, if you were honest.'

'You can drive yourself mad with what ifs, can't you? If ifs and ans were pots and pans –'

'– There'd be no need for tinkers' hands.'

Rosie looked down over the valley. 'Just think, if Esther has children, there will be a whole new line of people who only existed because Ash was killed. Thousands and thousands, as time goes on. Ash would have made one future if he'd lived, but instead he made another one by dying.' She fell silent for a few moments, then said quietly, 'Before Ash died he told me that he would be the keeper of my soul.'

'Perhaps he is,' said Daniel. 'I'd like to think he's keeping an eye on both of us. We were all in the Pals, weren't we?'

On the mountain slope opposite rose rank upon rank of tea plantations, topped by wispy cloud. Thousands of feet below them, from a valley floor that would one day, long after they had gone, become the serene and majestic Lake Castlereagh, a mist began to rise and swell.

'You were right about the climate,' said Rosie. 'It's been like a lovely morning in May all day.' She looked up at him and he saw that her eyes were softening with emotion. 'Thank you. You really have brought us to paradise, I think. All I need now is to find something useful to do. I don't want to spend all my time on Esther, or just sitting around reading. Is that awful of me? We are going to get an ayah, aren't we? And the estate has its own clinic.' She looked down at her hands. They were ready for work, and you'd never know they'd been burned. She thought of Dr Scott, of his essential goodness, his efficient compassion.

'You won't be singing "Take Me Back to Dear Old Blighty" then?' said Daniel.

'Not for quite a while. Wouldn't it be wonderful if the story could end here?'

'End here? What on earth do you mean? We're only just starting.'

'I mean wouldn't it be wonderful if it could all end with us being perfectly happy in a wonderful place, with all our troubles behind us, and nothing having gone wrong yet. Wouldn't this be a good moment for the whole world to come to an end? Everything going dark, quite suddenly, like a candle blown out?'

Daniel bent down and kissed the top of her head. 'I do know what you mean, but it wouldn't really be wonderful at all, would it? You'd miss out on the best parts of the future. What about Esther being the first of thousands? As far as I can see, one gets happiness in periodic bursts. You slog through the rest of the time, making the most of the better moments, and just hanging on until the next burst comes. Let's do our best to enjoy this one, shall we? Later on there'll be other moments just as good, wouldn't you think? As for tomorrow, sufficient unto the day is the evil thereof, as far as I'm concerned. And anyway, it's Esther that matters now.'

'And any more that might turn up,' said Rosie. 'Did I tell you that I started to write a poem about you?'

'About me? Gracious!'

'I've only got the title and one line so far, though.'

509

'What's the one line?'

'"I'd have you take me further on this journey to my heart."'

Daniel was momentarily confounded. Then he said, 'Is that the first line?'

'Probably. But you never know with poems. They have a mind of their own. It might be better as a last line, or the last line of every verse.'

Daniel repeated the line to himself, and counted on his fingers. 'That's perfectly iambic. It's an iambic heptameter.'

'You know about metre?'

'Don't be so surprised! I have hidden depths. And a terrific aversion to being beaten by the English master. And what's the title?'

'"For Daniel" of course. And by the way, I've been thinking, I don't know why, but for some reason I've decided that I'd like everyone to call me Rosemary rather than Rosie. Apart from you. You can still call me Rosie, if you like.'

'I normally call you darling, don't I? I'll call you Rosie if I'm angry, perhaps, and Rosemary when I'm being reproachful. I've noticed that you don't call me anything. Not darling or dear, anyway.'

'Something will come spontaneously, I expect. One of these days. We'll have to wait and see what it is.'

'I've always wanted someone to call me sweetheart,' said Daniel, 'but definitely not *chou-chou*. Or *nou-nou*.'

His eye was caught by a scuffling movement near at hand, and he stood up to look. Not far from where he had been sitting he saw, huddled in a corner beneath a vine, a small bird in a strangely contorted position. He picked it up gently, bringing it over for Rosie and Esther to see. It had a claw of its left leg caught on the topside of its wing. 'Must have been scratching its head,' said Daniel. 'I've never seen anything like it.'

'Daddy, don't kill it, Daddy,' said Esther.

'Honestly, sweetie! Of course I won't.'

'It looks like a very tiny magpie,' said Rosie. 'Do you think you can untangle it?'

Daniel sat down, and carefully bent the left wing down as he lifted the claw from its trap of pinions. The bird remained perfectly calm. Then her father let Esther stroke the top of its head, and he carried it to the edge of the veranda. He opened his hands, and they watched as it hesitated, hastily straightened a feather on its chest, and flew out over the valley, banked, dived and disappeared.

Acknowledgements

With thanks to those who read early drafts and gave me good advice which I did not always like; and to my grandfather's Canadian friends, whose contributions will, I hope, bear fruit in future volumes; and to Ralph McTell, for his friendship, and his peerless guitar playing, and for reassuring me that if you know how many guitars you have, then you don't have enough, and for letting me have 'I'm writing with my finger in the dust that falls from dreams' in return for a simple bribe of a pint in a Great Yarmouth pub.